Winds OF FORTUNE

What Reviewers Say About Radclyffe's Books

A Matter of Trust is a "...sexy, powerful love story filled with angst, discovery and passion that captures the uncertainty of first love and its discovery." – *Just About Write*

Shield of Justice is a "...well-plotted…lovely romance...I couldn't turn the pages fast enough!" – Ann Bannon, author of *The Beebo Brinker Chronicles*

"The author's brisk mix of political intrigue, fast-paced action, and frequent interludes of lesbian sex and love…in *Honor Reclaimed*…sure does make for great escapist reading." – *Q Syndicate*

Change of Pace is "...contemporary, yet timeless, not only about sex, but also about love, longing, lust, surprises, chance meetings, planned meetings, fulfilling wild fantasies, and trust." – *Midwest Book Review*

"Radclyffe has once again pulled together all the ingredients of a genuine page-turner, this time adding some new spices into the mix. *shadowland* is sure to please—in part because Radclyffe never loses sight of the fact that she is telling a love story, and a compelling one at that." – Cameron Abbott, author of *To The Edge* and *An Inexpressible State of Grace*

Lammy winner "...*Stolen Moments* is a collection of steamy stories about women who just couldn't wait. It's sex when desire overrides reason, and it's incredibly hot!" – *On Our Backs*

"With ample angst, realistic and exciting medical emergencies, winsome secondary characters, and a sprinkling of humor, *Fated Love* turns out to be a terrific romance. It's one of the best I have read in the last three years." – *Midwest Book Review*

"*Innocent Hearts*...illustrates that our struggles for acceptance of women loving women is as old as time—only the setting changes. The romance is sweet, sensual, and touching." – *Just About Write*

Lammy winner "...*Distant Shores, Silent Thunder* weaves an intricate tapestry about passion and commitment between lovers. The story explores the fragile nature of trust and the sanctuary provided by loving relationships." – *Sapphic Reader*

In *When Dreams Tremble* the "…focus on character development is meticulous and comprehensive, filled with angst, regret, and longing, building to the ultimate climax." – *Just About Write*

Winds of Fortune

by

RADCLY*f*FE

2007

WINDS OF FORTUNE

ISBN10: 1-933110-93-7
ISBN13: 978-1-933110-93-6

THIS TRADE PAPERBACK IS PUBLISHED BY
BOLD STROKES BOOKS, INC.
NEW YORK, USA

FIRST EDITION, OCTOBER 2007

CREDITS
EDITORS: RUTH STERNGLANTZ AND J. B. GREYSTONE
PRODUCTION DESIGN: J. B. GREYSTONE
COVER GRAPHIC: SHERI (graphicartist2020@hotmail.com)

By the Author

Romances

Innocent Hearts
Love's Melody Lost
Love's Tender Warriors
Tomorrow's Promise
Passion's Bright Fury
Love's Masquerade
shadowland
Fated Love
Turn Back Time
Promising Hearts
When Dreams Tremble

The Provincetown Tales

Safe Harbor
Beyond the Breakwater
Distant Shores, Silent Thunder
Storms of Change
Winds of Fortune

Honor Series

Above All, Honor
Honor Bound
Love & Honor
Honor Guards
Honor Reclaimed
Honor Under Siege

Justice Series

A Matter of Trust (prequel)
Shield of Justice
In Pursuit of Justice
Justice in the Shadows
Justice Served

Erotic Interludes: *Change Of Pace*
(A Short Story Collection)
Erotic Interludes 2: *Stolen Moments*
Stacia Seaman and Radclyffe, eds.
Erotic Interludes 3: *Lessons in Love*
Stacia Seaman and Radclyffe, eds.
Erotic Interludes 4: *Extreme Passions*
Stacia Seaman and Radclyffe, eds.
Erotic Interludes 5: *Road Games*
Stacia Seaman and Radclyffe, eds.

Acknowledgments

As I complete the final edits of this work, I am fortunate to be staying in the seaside village that is as much a character in these stories as the people who populate the novels. The harbor at sunrise, the sounds of the ocean, and the spirit of those adventurers and artists who have come before never fail to inspire me. I'm sure I have not yet captured more than a glimpse of the beauty, grace, and history that is Provincetown, but it continues to be my very great pleasure to try.

My thanks go to my first readers Diane, Eva, Jane, Paula, and RB, as well as to my editors, Ruth Sternglantz and J.B. Greystone, and the generous proofreaders at Bold Strokes Books for making this a better book. All the credit goes to these dedicated individuals and the responsibility for any shortcomings to me.

Thanks also to Sheri for yet another standout cover.

To Lee, for sharing the adventure. *Amo te.*

DEDICATION

For Lee
For weathering every storm

Chapter One

Dr. Victoria King dropped a chart on top of the eight inch stack on her desk and checked her watch. Ten minutes to two. God, she was going to be late for her own daughter's first birthday party.

"Why don't you get out of here," a voice said from behind her.

Spinning around, Tory smiled at the trim African-American woman in a white lab coat who stood in her office doorway. Like Tory, her new associate, Dr. Nita Burgoyne, was dressed casually, but in contrast to Tory's pressed jeans and boatneck navy cotton tee, Nita's stylish emerald green blouse, sand colored slacks, and tan sling-back, low-heeled shoes hinted at designer labels. She hadn't quite made the transition from big city ER doctor to small town doc just yet.

"You've been here, what—five weeks," Tory said, "and already you're reading my mind?"

"Didn't take telepathy." When Nita shook her head, the gold clasp she used to restrain her shoulder-length, wavy black hair at her nape glinted in the overhead lights, echoing the amusement that shimmered in her deep brown eyes. "I could hear your thoughts out in the hallway."

"Well, I'm glad I didn't finish what I was thinking, then." Tory grimaced. "How many more do we have?"

"Not enough for you to worry about." Nita lifted a shoulder in the direction of the hallway behind her. "Now go while the coast is relatively clear."

Tory hesitated, torn between wanting to be with her family and knowing she was needed at the clinic. During tourist season, the East End Health Clinic was open seven days a week, and patient hours often stretched well beyond the scheduled times. Here emergencies were the norm, rather than the exception. Minor accidents, fender benders, forgotten medication, common colds, and more serious events ranging from heart attacks to strokes were daily fare. It might be quiet right this minute, but chances were it wouldn't be for long—not on Sunday afternoon of Fourth of July weekend in Provincetown—and Nita hadn't worked a holiday alone yet.

"I'm not some green intern," Nita chided good-naturedly, obviously continuing to read Tory's mind despite her earlier denial. "Sally is the best nurse I've ever worked with and better than a lot of the doctors I've known. We'll be fine."

Tory considered arguing, but she could tell by the set of Nita's slender shoulders that her mind was made up. She had learned very quickly that in Nita's case, looks were very definitely deceiving. Although Nita's dark almond eyes, sculpted features, and smooth coffee-and-cream complexion gave her a look of exotic, nearly delicate beauty, she was neither delicate nor insubstantial in any way. Ten years Tory's junior, she was a self-assured, highly capable professional, and wonderful with the patients. Even though she was personally reserved and rarely talked about her private life, her genuine warmth and compassion were obvious, and Tory liked her.

"You'll call me if things get busy?" Tory asked.

Nita folded her arms beneath her breasts and pursed her lips.

"Okay. Okay." Tory held up both hands in surrender. "Will you at least stop by the party later? We'll have plenty of food and the adults will out-number the kids, I promise."

When Nita looked uncertain, Tory felt a surge of guilt. As far as she knew, Nita had yet to really meet anyone in the community outside of patients and the office staff. Part of that was Tory's fault. She should have had a welcoming reception for her when she joined the practice, and what she'd greeted her with instead was a crisis. Nita had only been with her a few days before Reese had been reported missing in action in Iraq. With her lover probably wounded or possibly dead, Tory had barely managed to keep her sanity and had foisted all but the major responsibilities of the clinic onto Nita. Everything else had fallen by the wayside. Even now, though she tried not to let it show, Tory still felt as if her life was on shaky ground.

"It'll just be some good friends and family," Tory urged.

Finally, Nita nodded, hiding her reluctance behind a smile. A child's birthday would be harmless, and she only needed to make a brief appearance. "Thank you. That would be nice."

"Good. Then I'll just finish up these chart—"

"Tory! Get!"

Laughing, Tory shrugged out of her lab coat and tossed it onto the high backed leather chair behind her overflowing desk. "I'm gone."

Just as Tory stepped out into the hall, their receptionist rushed in from the waiting area and skidded to a halt beside her. Lithe and handsome, Randy's blond hair was uncharacteristically mussed and his big blue eyes were overly bright.

"Sorry," he said breathlessly, looking from Tory to Nita and back again, "but Deo Camara just brought Joey Torres in, and he's bleeding all over the waiting room. Sally's putting them in the procedure room."

"What happened?" Tory inquired sharply, turning back into her office for her lab coat. If Randy was ruffled it must be serious, because he could simultaneously handle five emergency calls, three hysterical mothers, and a recalcitrant insurance rep without breaking a sweat.

"Deo said something about a saw."

"Thanks, Randy," Nita said calmly. "Why don't you get the waiting room cleaned up and let the other patients know there might be a little bit of a wait."

"Okay, right." As quickly as he had appeared, Randy was gone.

"I've got this, Tory," Nita said.

Tory drew up short, one arm in and one out of her lab coat. Nita was a board-certified emergency room physician. She was trained to handle anything that might come through the door. Rationally, Tory knew that. Still, it was hard to leave. She had hired on temporary help before, but Nita was the first physician she had contracted for a possible long-term association. The only partner she had ever considered had been KT O'Bannon, the woman she had once considered the love of her life. But KT had left her with a broken heart and broken dreams. Then Reese Conlon had come along and mended her heart, but until now she'd never really considered sharing her professional life with anyone else.

"You might need an assistant," Tory pointed out.

"If it's that bad, the repair will need to be done in the OR and we'll transport him to Hyannis. Otherwise, Sally can help me. Now I'd better get in there—and you have a party to go to."

Nita disappeared down the hallway. Tory could either follow her, making a clear statement that she didn't trust her to handle the problem alone, or she could go home where the people who loved her were waiting.

She hung her lab coat on a hook behind her door, and with one last glance down the hall toward the patient rooms, she left.

❖

Nita pushed through the door into the procedure room and stopped short at the incongruous sound of laughter. Their clinic nurse, Sally, stood at the counter on the far side of the room setting up an instrument tray. Two young men in khaki work clothes and dusty boots, one seated on the stretcher and the other leaning against it, faced away from the door toward the petite blond nurse. Apparently no one heard her enter because the revelry continued.

"We need to make sure this gets fixed up right," remarked the deeply tanned, curly haired Adonis who nudged the shoulder of a similarly handsome man whose right hand was wrapped in a bloody towel. "Otherwise, Joey's sex life is going straight down the toi—"

"Oh I don't know," Sally laughed as she laid out gloves and irrigation solution, "it doesn't look like any of Joey's critical equipment is in danger."

"That's just the problem, he needs that hand to take care of his *main* business," the Adonis smirked.

"Come on, Deo," Joey said, "I'm in pain here." He glanced over his buddy's shoulder and, spying Nita, instantly looked chagrined. "Besides, there's a lady present."

"Oh, well, excuse me," Sally said archly, rolling the metal instrument stand up to the table. "*Now* you two decide to get some manners?" She waved to Nita. "We're all ready for you."

"Thanks." Nita crossed the room briskly. "I'm Dr. Burgoyne. What happened?"

"Joey here picked a fight with a table saw and lost," the uninjured member of the pair replied, turning in Nita's direction. Deep-set eyes so dark they verged on black did a slow survey of Nita's face, flickered lower for an instant, then returned to lock on Nita's. "Well, hello."

Nita blinked, bombarded by a series of quicksilver images—wide, sensuous mouth; midnight curls tumbling onto a broad forehead; thick, almost straight black brows; and skin, she realized—not tanned—but a rich natural bronze. An Adonis, no doubt. But very much not a man. For one second Nita completely lost focus and everything else in the room receded from her consciousness except her awareness of this woman. How she hadn't realized immediately that Adonis was a woman, despite the nondescript work clothes, she couldn't imagine. Even partially turned away, her sharply-carved profile was just a little bit too exquisite to be male, despite its strength. And not even the well-developed shoulders and thighs could diminish the undeniably feminine nature of her body. The subtle swell of her breasts, the narrow waist, the slight curve of hip all screamed woman. Beautiful woman.

Nita felt her skin warming as the woman continued to stare at her with a mixture of amusement and frank appreciation. Nita knew the look. Not just beautiful, beautiful and arrogant. This one knew she was gorgeous and no doubt knew the effect she had on women. Women and men, probably. She was looking at Nita as if she expected Nita to melt. Nita mentally shook herself—that wasn't going to happen. Not now, not ever again.

"Perhaps the *patient* would like to fill me in," Nita said, dragging her gaze away from the dark hypnotic eyes. She knew she sounded irritated. She *was* irritated. And disturbed. Irritated at herself for even *noticing* how striking the woman was, and definitely disturbed for being intrigued—if only for an instant—by the admiring look in the woman's eyes. Being stirred by *any* woman's attraction was something she had thought she'd expunged from her mind and body, but apparently she'd been wrong.

"If you could step back, please," Nita said, "I need to see to your friend."

"By all means," Deo said with a slightly mocking tone and a sweep of her arm, "be my guest."

Deo Camara wasn't surprised by the doctor's initial consternation. She was used to that. Strangers often took her for a guy, especially in her work clothes, or confused her with one of her many cousins. The anger that had quickly surged in the piercing, raw umber eyes was unexpected, though. What was even more unanticipated was that the doctor's antagonism bothered her. She didn't know the woman, so why should it matter what she thought? Annoyed at being off-balance, she shrugged and shifted a few inches, folding her arms across her chest and rocking back on her heels.

"Thank you," Nita said dryly, edging around the stranger when she failed to make room. Apparently she was as rude as she was good-looking. She smiled at the patient. "Hi. Joey is it?"

"Yeah. Uh, yes ma'am." He dropped his eyes and blushed.

"I'm going to need to examine your hand. Why don't you lie down." She looked to Sally. "Gloves?"

"Here you go." Sally handed Nita a package of sterile gloves and then pulled on her own pair. "I've got a basin and sterile saline when you're ready."

Nita glanced over her shoulder at Deo, who still stood so close Nita could smell a faint mixture of salt air and sawdust clinging to her. For some reason that struck her as more alluring than a fine perfume. Nonplussed at the thought, she said edgily, "This will probably take awhile. You might want to have a seat out front."

"I'm staying."

"As you wish."

Once Joey was settled comfortably with his arm extended on a narrow arm board canted out from the table, Nita removed the bloody towel from his right hand. As she worked, she was disconcertingly aware of Deo's presence just behind her. She could almost feel the heat coming off her body.

"Would you step back just a little," Nita said without turning, frustrated that her concentration was affected by a stranger this way.

"Sure thing."

Nita didn't hear her move, and she could *still* sense her nearness. *This is ridiculous*. Determined to banish the exasperating distraction from her consciousness, Nita focused on Joey and immediately her discomfort abated.

"This might be just a bit uncomfortable," she said, gently supporting his wrist in her palm.

"It's okay, Doc," Joey said, his eyes fixed trustingly on her face.

The bleeding had slowed to a trickle, but his small finger drooped and angled unnaturally. Nita noted an irregular laceration through the layer of caked-on blood. *Saw blade*. Another laceration slashed across the mid-portion of his ring finger. She carefully repositioned his hand on a sterile towel.

"Sally, go ahead and soak his whole hand in quarter strength Betadiene for ten minutes and then irrigate the lacerations. In the meantime, give him a tetanus shot, a gram of Zinacef, and set up for an X-ray." She patted Joey's shoulder. "You've cut a tendon or two and nicked a nerve. Nothing we can't fix. I'll be back in a few minutes and we'll get started."

Pushing back from the table, Nita stripped off her gloves. She tossed them aside and quickly left the room, still strangely disquieted by her reaction to her patient's friend. She didn't get derailed by the attention of a beautiful woman. Not anymore.

"Hey!"

Nita turned and saw that the woman was following her down the hall. Her long strides were forceful, more power than grace, and her physical presence combined with her natural beauty made an eye-catching package. Despite her appreciation, Nita carefully kept her expression flat. "Can I help you?"

"He's got insurance. Workman's comp. Whatever he needs—"

"You can give all that information to our receptionist out front." Nita hoped the woman wasn't suggesting Nita might not do everything necessary for the patient. "My only concern is taking care of his injury."

"Look. If he needs to go to a hospital or something—"

"My decisions regarding his course of treatment are not based upon his ability to pay." Nita regarded Deo with annoyance. "I didn't get your name."

"Deo Camara. I'm his boss. And his cousin." Deo thought about extending her hand, but for some reason she didn't. She had the uneasy feeling she was acting like an ass chasing after the doctor, but she couldn't seem to stop herself. This woman was so cool and detached and *dismissive*. Maybe that was it. She wasn't used to women just brushing her off. Usually she was the one that had to do the kissing off.

Nita took a breath and struggled to regain her professional composure. Deo could hardly help the way she looked. Her manners could stand some polish, but she was probably worried. "As soon as I complete my evaluation I'll let you both know what needs to be done."

"He works with his hands."

"I understand." Nita glanced at Deo's hands, curled at her sides. They were the same dark bronze as her face, broad and strong, capable looking hands. An irregular white ribbon of damaged tissue slashed across the top of her left hand from the base of her thumb to the opposite side of her wrist. An old scar from what must have been a painful injury.

Sympathetically, she said, "I can see you've had some experience with this kind of thing."

Following her gaze, Deo stiffened and tightened her fist until the skin turned pale and the scar disappeared. "No."

Nita's immediate impulse was to apologize, because she heard not anger, but pain in Deo's voice. Then a sudden realization turned her cold inside. She knew nothing of this woman except that she was beautiful and at the moment, in pain. A dangerous combination that she found all too compelling, and exactly the kind of woman she wanted nothing to do with.

"I'll be in to see your cousin in just a few moments," Nita said, then pulled a chart off the nearest door and quickly stepped inside.

Deo stared at the closed door, feeling the sudden silence in the hall like a weight on her chest. She had let a stranger stir her up, and worse, rouse banished memories. No one did that. She never let anyone close enough to risk awakening those unforgiven sins.

❖

"Is Reese home yet?" Tory asked breathlessly as she hurried through the door into the sunny living room. She petted the concrete block-sized head of the Mastiff that ambled to greet her. "Hi Jedi."

"Not yet." Kate, a blond version of her dark-haired, blue-eyed daughter Reese, held out a squirming toddler to Tory. "And the birthday girl has been asking."

"Hey, honey," Tory said, taking her daughter. Reggie replied with a string of excited words, the bulk of which sounded like *ma ma ma ma ma*. Tory laughed. "That's me. Well, one of them anyways."

When she kissed Reggie's forehead, the wind coming in from the open door to the deck off the living area blew her hair into Reggie's face. Reggie promptly grabbed a handful and held it to her mouth. Reggie's red gold locks were lighter than Tory's own auburn hair and her eyes more blue than green, but everyone said they could see Tory in Reggie. Sometimes when Tory looked at her daughter, she was struck with helpless wonder at what a miracle she was. At the sound of the screen door closing, Tory lifted her eyes from her daughter to the other miracle in her life.

When she returned from Iraq, Reese had been thinner than Tory had ever seen her, as if the desert winds and searing heat and senseless, relentless death had carved away everything except what she needed to survive. But she had survived. And she had come home. Wounded, disillusioned, weary in body and soul. But alive. She had come home where she was loved and needed.

With her coal black hair trimmed neatly at her collar, her intense deep-blue eyes, and her imposing body in a crisp khaki uniform, Sheriff Reese Conlon radiated strength. But Tory saw what others didn't. Though Reese insisted she was recovered, she was still too thin, and there were still too many shadows under her eyes and *in* her eyes. Tory knew Reese tried to hide them, just as she knew that she tried to hide the fact that she rarely slept an entire night—or even more than an hour at a time. She didn't know if Reese would ever talk about what haunted her. Not all pain could be purged. Until the time came, if it ever came, when Reese asked her to share that pain, Tory would give her the only thing she had to give—herself, in every way she could.

Tory smiled at her lover. "Hello, darling."

"Hi, baby. I'm sorry I'm late." Reese tossed her uniform hat and car keys onto the counter that separated the kitchen from the living area, smiled at her mother, and strode across the room to Tory. She put her arms around her and the baby, kissed Tory gently, and nuzzled Reggie's neck, making her laugh. "Hi, Champ."

"You're not late. I just got here myself." Handing the baby off to Kate, Tory rested her head on Reese's shoulder, still unable to forget what it had been like being without her. She had gotten up in the morning, had cared for Reggie, and had gone to the clinic and looked after her patients while all the time sensing that some essential part of herself was missing. She had never experienced anything as frightening as the hollow ache inside that she had known without doubt would never be filled if Reese did not come home. "I love you."

"Me too," Reese whispered. Reluctantly, she let Tory go and glanced around the house. "So where's the party?"

"Jean is picking up some last minute things at the store," Kate said, referring to her lover. "Pia called a little while ago and said she and KT were on their way. I assume you know where Bri and Nelson are?"

"Oh hell," Tory muttered. "I wonder if anyone called Pia and told her Joey was hurt."

"What's the matter with Joey?" Reese asked, stopping near the closet where she stored her gun belt.

"I'm not sure, exactly. Deo brought him into the clinic just as I was leaving." Tory unclipped her cell phone from her waistband. "I'd better track Pia down and let her know."

"Let me know what?" Pia Torres said as she came through the door holding hands with her lover, Dr. KT O'Bannon. She hefted the bottle of wine she carried in her other hand. "Let me dump this in the kitchen."

KT, tall, dark-haired, and roguishly good-looking, kissed Tory on the cheek. "Hi, Vic."

Tory smiled at the old nickname and felt KT studying her. KT could read her face better than anyone in the world except Reese. There had been a time when KT had *been* her world, before the wild and wildly attractive surgeon had strayed one too many times and finally crushed Tory's innocence. Now, KT had found Pia, a woman who gave her the freedom she needed never to leave. Pia embraced the dangerous parts of KT that Tory hadn't been able to, and in recognizing that, Tory had finally been able to accept how much goodness there was in her ex-lover and how much love they still shared.

"Deo brought Joey into the clinic just as I was leaving," Tory said as Pia walked over. "He had some kind of accident with a saw at work. Nita's evaluating him."

"Oh my God." Pia grabbed KT's arm. "I have to go over there. I don't want my mother to hear anything until I know what's going on."

"It's okay, babe. Nita's good." KT slid an arm around Pia's waist, "Come on, we'll go right now. I'll drive."

"I've got the cruiser," Reese said. "I'll take you, Pia."

"You'll take us both," KT corrected.

"Actually, you'll take all of us," Tory said, hurrying to join the group. She called over her shoulder to Kate, "I'll update you as soon as I can. Keep the ice cream cold."

Chapter Two

"Nita," Tory said quietly from the door. "Can you talk?"

Surprised, Nita looked up from examining Joey's hand and swiveled on the short metal stool to face Tory. "Back already? What's up?"

"Joey's sister is here. Do you mind if she comes in to see him?" Tory nodded to Deo. "Hi, Deo."

"Crap," Joey muttered. "I *told* you we should call her."

"Jesus, Joey," Deo scoffed. "Did you want me to call your mommy too?"

Ignoring the back-and-forth behind her, Nita gestured to Joey's hand draped in sterile towels on the table. She had yet to repair the damage and it didn't look pretty. "She might want to wait until we get him cleaned up a little bit more."

"Pia is a hand therapist. She'll be fine with it," Tory explained.

Nita raised her eyebrows. She didn't mind family in the room when she was working. Medical personnel, however, sometimes took special handling, because they usually wanted to direct the treatment. This sounded like one of those situations.

"KT's here too." Tory looked mildly chagrined.

"Ah," Nita said, the pieces suddenly falling into place. She'd worked with KT a few times right after Reese had been captured in Iraq and Tory had needed extra help in the clinic. She recalled now Randy mentioning over lunch one day that KT's lover was an occupational therapist in town. "Well, you might as well all come on in."

After covering Joey's hand with moist gauze, Nita rose and stripped off her gloves. Then she went to intercept the group just inside the door to the treatment room. The woman with KT and Tory looked like an elegant version of Deo and Joey. She had the same glossy, wavy black hair and dark expressive eyes. Her skin was a slightly lighter shade than theirs, closer to her own, and her features a little more finely detailed. Whereas Deo's compelling beauty verged on androgyny, Pia was the archetype of female loveliness. *God, can this family get any more attractive?*

"Hi," Pia said, holding out her hand. "I'm Pia, Joey's sister. Sorry to barge in."

Nita took her hand. "That's quite all right. Hi, KT."

"Nita. What have you got?"

"The X-rays are over here." Nita led the three to the light box. "He's got a fracture of the middle phalanx of his small finger. Fortunately, it's favorably angled and once we reduce it, he should do well with a splint."

Nita waited while KT leaned forward and perused all the films. Then she went on. "He's completely transected his extensor tendon in that finger and nicked the one in the ring finger."

"Looks like he's bought himself a couple of months out of work," KT commented.

"No way," Deo said, having moved closer while everyone was talking. "He's still got one good hand and two legs. He's not laying off for half the summer. He can have until Tuesday, then he needs to get his candy ass back to work."

Nita was about to remind Deo that *she* was making the decisions when Pia wrapped her arm around Deo's waist and kissed her cheek. Struck by the obvious affection in Pia's gesture and the fleeting look of tenderness that passed over Deo's face, she hesitated.

Pia said, "You okay, tough girl?"

"I'm fine." Deo's voice sounded surprisingly husky. "I'm sorry about this, Pia."

"We'll talk later," Pia murmured. "It'll be okay."

"Yeah. Right."

Once again, Nita caught a glimpse of something raw and vulnerable in Deo's eyes, and against her will, she was drawn to it. Heart pounding, she turned her back to the cousins. She needed to get Joey taken care of and get them all out of the clinic. Especially Deo Camara. The woman was dangerous.

"I was just about to do the tendon repair. If you want to do it, KT, it's fine with me." Even though it was a straightforward procedure, Nita wasn't about to stand on ceremony when one of the best trauma surgeons on the East Coast was available to do the job. Especially not when a family member was involved.

"Why don't we do it together." KT grinned. "Then we can all get back to the party."

"I'll see the rest of the patients while you two take care of Joey," Tory offered.

Nita nodded in surrender. "Well, I guess it's decided."

❖

"Look," Deo said, trying to extricate herself from Pia's grasp as they crossed the parking lot outside the clinic. "I don't want to crash this party."

"It's a baby's birthday party!" Pia gave Deo a playful shove before she opened the passenger door of Deo's camo green Defender and climbed in. Waving goodbye through the open top to KT, who was headed back to the party in Reese's cruiser, she said, "It's just a bunch of people you already know—and Tory invited you, so you can't be crashing. Come on. I know you've been working fifteen hours a day since April without a day off. Why pass up free food and beer and good company?"

"I can manage to get food and beer and plenty of company on my own," Deo grumbled. "Jesus. I don't need a social director."

"Yeah? Well I didn't see you at the Memorial Day picnic or the Fourth of July barbecue yesterday."

"You know why." Deo gunned the truck out of the parking lot, spewing gravel. "No point spoiling everyone's day."

Pia rested her hand on Deo's thigh. "You don't know it would have been like that."

"Don't I?" Deo said darkly. "It was a family gathering, wasn't it? When was the last time I came to one where my father didn't get drunk and practically call me out and my mother didn't cry?"

"Honey, it's been ten years. Everyone needs to let it go."

Deo clenched her jaw. "Then someone should tell them that."

"I know, you're right."

"And Christ almighty, wait until everyone hears about Joey. It'll be Gabe all over again."

"My mother is not going to get hysterical and blame you," Pia said. "And it isn't your fault. Joey had an accident."

Deo shook her head as she turned onto 6A and headed west toward Reese and Tory's home. "He got hurt working for me. I'm supposed to be looking out for my crew. It *was* my fault."

"Joey is a carpenter. These things happen."

"Let it go, Pia."

Pia sighed and patted Deo's leg. "So, who are you dating now?"

"What, now you want to find me a girlfriend?" Deo grinned. "I don't think our tastes run in quite the same direction."

"You don't think KT's hot?"

"Jesus, Pia, don't put me on the spot here."

"Come on, admit it," Pia teased. "She's got a gorgeous body, a face to die for, and a mouth that can make a girl's cli—"

"Whoa. Whoa whoa whoa!" Laughing, Deo stuck out one arm as if to cover Pia's mouth. "None of that. Jesus, I don't want to look at her and have those pictures in my head."

"Well we used to share things about our girlfriends."

"Yeah, maybe when we were sixteen! Besides, you never did anything except kiss, as I recall, so there wasn't much to tell."

Pia blushed. "You were doing enough of everything else for both of us."

Deo shot her a glance. "You really didn't…you know, get it on with anyone before KT?"

"Well I wasn't living in a convent, but, no. Not entirely."

"It's nothing to be ashamed of, you know," Deo said gently. "KT is a lucky woman. She knows that, right?"

"Yes, cousin, she knows, so you don't have to defend my honor." Pia stroked the top of Deo's hand where it rested on the gear shift between them. "Do any of your girlfriends know what a big softie you are?"

"Don't spread nasty rumors about me," Deo said, pulling into Reese and Tory's drive. "They've got enough reason to be pissed off at me when I don't marry them."

"Someday someone's going to see through that tough girl act of yours," Pia warned playfully. "Then you'll be in trouble."

Deo didn't bother to argue. She definitely didn't feel like explaining that what had once been an act had long since become second nature. Life was simpler that way.

❖

"I take it that's your sister," Nita said to Tory, indicating a fair-haired, blue-eyed woman in a sun dress and sandals who bounced a laughing Reggie on her knee. "She looks a lot like you."

"That's Cath," Tory said. "My brother-in-law just took their two kids down to the beach. And that guy over there," she pointed to a husky, middle-aged man with dark hair shot-through with gray ensconced in a wooden Adirondack rocker and deep in conversation with Reese, "is Chief Nelson Parker, Reese's boss."

"Wait a minute. Parker. Isn't that the name of that skinny, black-haired walking hormone with the adorable little blond girlfriend?"

Tory laughed. "You mean Bri? The one leaning against the railing in the corner over there while her girlfriend tries to climb inside her skin?"

"Oh my," Nita said, after sneaking a peek. Sure enough, Bri, in tight black jeans and a sleeveless black T-shirt that accentuated her wiry frame, had her arms around her girlfriend, who wore nothing but itty-bitty white shorts and a pink halter top. The little blonde was wedged between Bri's thighs with her arms around Bri's neck and the two of them looked like they might need to be hosed down any second. She shook her head. "I'm not *all* that much older than them but they make me feel ancient."

"Believe it or not, Bri and Caroline have been together almost six years and as far as I can tell, they've still got the non-stop hungries for each other. Bri's an officer in town, too. Caroline's an artist, studying in New York City."

"Well I'll say one thing for this place," Nita said. "You've got drop-dead gorgeous cops of all species."

"Mmm," Tory said, watching Reese. "We do." She glanced at Nita. "You've got cops in your family, right?"

"Everywhere you look," Nita said flatly.

Tory regarded her curiously. "Did they pressure you to carry on the family tradition?"

"You couldn't exactly call it pressure. I don't think anyone ever considered that I *wouldn't*. It was pretty much a given. My grandfather, my uncles and aunts, my older siblings—they're all cops. One renegade sister is a firefighter, but close enough." She wrapped her arms around her middle and stared down toward the harbor, remembering the astonishment on her father's face when she had announced at seventeen that she wanted to go to medical school. She had thought he would be proud. Looking back, she didn't know why she'd expected that. She had never been as tough as her brothers and sisters, not in the obvious ways, at least. Knowing that she couldn't measure up to her physically competitive brothers and sisters, she had worked tirelessly to excel in the only way she could. She had been first in her class year after year, but it never seemed to be enough. No matter how good she was academically, she didn't measure up. "One of my brothers went to a two-year college before entering the academy, but all my other siblings went straight on the job after high school. I was the odd one out."

"Breaking with tradition that deep is hard." Tory couldn't help but think about Reese, raised by her father to follow in his footsteps in the marines. Reese had done everything her father expected. She had been willing to sacrifice anything, including her life, for her duty, but all that paled in his eyes when he learned she was a lesbian. Tory shook her head. "Sometimes the people who love us are our toughest critics."

"I've gotten used to the fact that I'm a disappointment to them." Nita wished it were only her choice of careers that set her apart from her family and wondered why she was thinking about those mistakes now. She'd been very careful in the last year not to repeat them. As she glanced around, she realized it was probably just the family atmosphere of the gathering that had her thinking of the past. Even when she went home for obligatory visits, she never felt as welcome as she did here, among strangers. Surprised that the realization could still hurt, she scanned the crowd for a diversion to take her mind off her unwelcome reminiscences. The distraction she found was the last one she wanted.

Deo Camara sat on the deck railing opposite her, arms braced on either side of her splayed legs, head thrown back as she laughed at something a pretty young blonde in a cropped T-shirt and hip-hugger shorts whispered in her ear. The sight of the blonde's hand curled around Deo's thigh and the seductive way she leaned into Deo aggravated Nita, and that awareness didn't help her mood. She turned away and refocused on Tory. "I admire you for being brave enough to have children. I'm not sure I am."

"I hope when Regina gets older that I have the strength to let her live her life however she needs to." Tory sighed. "Even if I don't always understand her choices."

"I think the fact that you even think about it means that you will."

"Well, I'll have lots of help." Tory pointed across the deck to where Reggie slumped sleepily in Cath's lap. "I think the birthday girl needs a nap. I should go collect her."

"Thanks for the invitation," Nita said as Tory moved away.

"Consider it a standing *order*," Tory called over her shoulder.

Nita watched the partygoers for a while longer, fixing faces to names, relieved that Deo had disappeared. When she felt she had stayed long enough to be polite, she gathered her half-empty bottle of beer and paper plate to take inside. As she turned toward the house, she nearly bumped into Deo.

"Sorry," Nita said, instantly noting that Deo had removed her work shirt. Her tight, sleeveless white undershirt left nothing to the imagination. Her shoulders were muscular, as were her arms, and her breasts were just full enough to tent the shirt in a very enticing manner. Nita felt an involuntary tug of appreciation in the depths of her belly and immediately squashed it.

"You look ready for a fresh beer. That one's got to be warm." Deo held out a bottle of the brand Nita was drinking.

Observant. And smooth. Nita recognized the confident, almost cocky look in Deo's eyes. *And a player.* It stood to reason that someone as gorgeous as this one would be used to having women fall at her feet. Well, not this time.

"Thanks, but I'm on call. One's my limit."

Deo cocked her head and narrowed her eyes appraisingly while regarding Nita's beer bottle. "Looks like you've only had half. Might as well enjoy something fresh."

"I'm fine, but I'm sure someone else would appreciate what you have to offer." Nita barely managed not to add, *Like the sexy little blonde who was hanging on you earlier.* God why did she care? But she knew why and had been avoiding the knowledge all afternoon. Deo had the same breathtaking good looks, the same edgy sensuality—God, even the same way of looking at a woman that said *You're so special*—as Sylvia had had. Angry that she could still be susceptible to such empty charms, and disgusted with herself for allowing thoughts of Sylvia to surface after she'd worked so hard to obliterate them, Nita snapped, "Don't waste it. There will be plenty of takers around."

"That's okay, I brought it for you." Deo had no idea why she was having this conversation. She'd been watching Nita for the last hour. The woman stood out in a crowd without even trying. She was beautiful, sure, but it was more than that. She was alone and obviously preferred it that way. She smiled warmly when people spoke to her, but she never touched anyone and she rarely laughed. And when people moved away, she closed in on herself again. She was beautiful and untouchable and Deo wondered what it would take to penetrate that isolation. Why she even gave it a thought, she didn't know, other than she knew something about being alone. Still, she persisted in trying to charm the aloof doctor into responding. "I'm not interested in offering it to someone else."

"You should be," Nita said, sidestepping to make her way around the obstacle Deo presented. "Because I'm not interested."

"You might change your mind."

Nita stopped and squared off with Deo. "No. I won't."

"You don't know me."

"I think I do."

"You're wrong," Deo bit out, unable to curb her temper. What the hell was it about this woman? She never cared what anyone thought of her, hadn't cared for years. She certainly never wanted the women she indifferently dated and casually bedded to know anything more than the careless façade she showed them.

"If I am mistaken, then I guess that will just be my loss. Excuse me." Nita skirted around Deo and disappeared into the house.

For the second time that day, Deo was left staring after a stranger she wanted to know.

Chapter Three

"Strike out?" Allie Tremont's soft Southern accent was as slow and languid as her movements as she sidled up to Deo.

"Never even made it to the plate," Deo muttered, watching Nita disappear into the house.

"That's got to be rare." Allie plucked the beer from Deo's hand. "You mind?"

"Go ahead. It's not spoken for."

"Well, it is now." Allie circled her lips around the mouth of the bottle and pulled on the beer, her eyes fixed on Deo's. She licked a bit of froth from her lips, her eyes closing slowly for an instant. "Nice."

Grinning, Deo regarded the young dark-eyed brunette, enjoying the flirtation and appreciating a game that she understood. She knew Allie, she knew all the cops in Provincetown, although she and Allie had never really crossed paths socially before. She remembered seeing Allie with a hot looking older redhead right after Allie had moved to town the year before, but she couldn't recall seeing her with anyone in particular recently. Not on a regular basis, at any rate. Deo figured Allie was six or seven years younger than her, but plenty old enough to know the rules. "Not working today, Officer?"

"Off shift." Allie settled her hip against Deo's. "I'm free and clear until tomorrow at seven a.m. How about yourself?"

"I'm always free and clear."

Allie laughed. "I heard that about you. At least you don't pretend otherwise."

Deo shrugged. "Why should I? All that does is make for trouble."

"Was there an invitation that went along with that beer?"

"Not exactly," Deo said, surprising herself when she thought about approaching Nita. Ordinarily, when she hit on a woman at a party it was because she was looking for company. For an afternoon, or an evening. That hadn't been what was in her mind with Nita. Sure, she wanted to kiss her. In fact, she could imagine kissing her until the sun went down and came up again, but she hadn't planned on taking her to bed. And not just because Nita just didn't seem the type for a fast hook-up. The automatic way Nita discounted her, as if she already knew all there was to know about her, made Deo want to prove her wrong. Mentally, Deo laughed at her own premature plans. Christ, she couldn't even get the woman to give her the time of day. Forget about kisses or anything else. With a start, she realized that Allie was staring at her curiously, obviously waiting for her to say more. Time to get in the game. "Are *you* looking for an invitation?"

Allie's wide, luscious lips slid into a sensuous smile. "I wouldn't say no."

Deo glanced over her shoulder to the harbor. The sun was going down, and the angled shafts of sunlight fractured across the water in an impossible array of orange and pink and purple. Why waste the chance to spend time with a woman who *was* interested. She caught Allie's hand and grabbed her work shirt off the railing. "Walk on the beach?"

"Mmm. For starters." Allie stroked Deo's arm. "Just hang on one minute—I caught a ride over with Bri. Let me tell her not to wait for me."

"Anyone I need to worry about coming after me tomorrow?" Deo asked when Allie returned. She didn't poach in anyone else's waters. She didn't have to, and besides that, the town was too small to risk inciting that kind of bad blood.

"Nope. Not a one." Allie forced a note of nonchalance into her voice as she threaded her arm around Deo's waist and slipped her fingers beneath the waistband of Deo's khakis just above her hip bone. Deo's body felt exactly as she expected it to, lean and hard. She had a fleeting image of those tight hips moving between her thighs, and she welcomed the rush of heat that settled in her belly and trickled down her legs. There hadn't been anyone serious, in bed or out, for a long time. After Ashley had left her ten months before, claiming that Allie wasn't old enough or experienced enough to make a commitment, she had burnt out her anger at her older lover by sleeping with enough women to prove that Ashley was probably right. Then, one day she woke up and didn't want to do it anymore. What had started out feeling really good, even great, for a few moments, made her sad in the morning.

"Broken heart?" Deo asked quietly.

"What?" Quickly, Allie laughed, covering her shock that Deo had almost read her mind. That wasn't what she expected from someone with Deo Camara's reputation. A great looking, love 'em and leave 'em playgirl like Camara wasn't usually interested in what a woman thought, only what line was needed to get her into bed.

"There are only two reasons I can think of for you being single," Deo said. "Either you haven't met her yet, or you have—and she did something stupid."

"What makes you think *I* didn't do something stupid?" Allie grabbed both Deo's hands in hers and started walking backwards down the sandy path to the beach, swinging their joined arms between them. She rounded a bend and the house disappeared. "Or maybe I'm single because I want to be."

"Maybe." Deo shrugged. "I am." She stopped abruptly and pulled Allie toward her, causing Allie to stumble slightly and fall into her arms. Grasping her around the waist to steady her, she kissed her lightly. "But you were thinking of someone back there, and it made you sad."

"And there's nobody you ever think about who makes you sad?" Allie teased, settling her body into the curve of Deo's. She curled her arms around Deo's shoulders and enjoyed the heat kindled by the press of Deo's breasts against hers. She didn't want to talk about Ashley, and for the first time in a long time, she wanted to be touched.

"No," Deo said quickly, covering Allie's mouth with hers, searching for the passion that obliterated everything else. *Not the way you mean, anyhow.*

❖

Nita sat on the steps leading from the deck to the path that snaked through the scrub and dunes to the beach. She had grown up by the ocean, but she never tired of watching the sun set over the water. Even the brief glimpse she had of Deo and a sultry young woman disappearing hand-in-hand couldn't obliterate her pleasure. In fact, she was happy that she had seen the last of Deo Camara and refused to analyze the brief flicker of disappointment she'd felt upon seeing her leave the party with an attractive woman.

"I didn't get a chance to thank you properly for taking care of Joey," Pia said, settling next to Nita on the wooden stairs.

"You're welcome," Nita said, "although it's not necessary. I'm just glad his injury wasn't worse."

"God, so am I." Pia sipped red wine from a plastic cup. "Sometimes I'm amazed that one of them doesn't get hurt more often, but most of the time I try not to think about it."

"I take it that Joey isn't your only sibling in construction?"

"You figure right." Pia smiled. "All of my family started out as fishermen or shipbuilders, a few generations back. My father and one of my brothers still fish, but over the years, shipbuilding dwindled away. The rest of the family naturally gravitated into construction."

"Family businesses," Nita said almost to herself.

"Yep. I'm the oddball, I guess."

Nita wrapped her arms around one bent leg and rested her chin on her knee. Pensively, she asked, "How do they handle that?"

"Things were a bit tense when I lived in Boston, but now that I've moved home—well, not *home* home—but back in town…I'm a little too old to live with my parents," Pia laughed, "we've pretty much fallen back into our old dynamic. It's good."

"Everyone else stayed? Your siblings?"

Pia nodded. "Amazingly enough, yes. Even the ones that went away to college came back. I guess this place is in our blood."

"I can certainly see why. It's beautiful. In fact, I'm buying a house myself." Nita paused. "Torres. I don't suppose you're related to the real estate—"

"My mother." Pia grinned at Nita's surprised expression. "She's not Portuguese, obviously. She came here on vacation one summer when she was just eighteen, met my father, and fell in love. Six kids later, the rest is history."

"Do your siblings all resemble you?"

"Every one."

"Amazing genes. I couldn't believe how much you and your brother look like your cousin when I saw you all together this afternoon."

"My father and Deo's mother are twins." Pia studied her wine. "I was sort of a gangly teenager, but Deo has always been gorgeous."

Nita laughed, consciously not thinking about Pia's gorgeous cousin. "Well you certainly caught up."

"Thanks." Pia grinned. "So, a house, huh? Where?"

"I bought a sea captain's house in the West End."

"The big old rambling place with the widow's walk? That's a great place, although it's been empty for quite a while."

"I know it needs some work, but I fell in love with it."

"When do you settle?"

"Just a couple of days. No one has lived in it for so long we had a quick closing." Nita smiled self-consciously. "I can't wait to get started renovating the place."

"Well, be sure to ask my mother about construction regulations. The township is very strict about what you can do to those historic places. You should probably start getting bids now."

"Thanks. I will." Nita stood and stretched. "Joey is going to need a wound check tomorrow. If things are looking good, you can start some gentle rehab with him in a day or two."

"I'll come by when he has his appointment with you. Okay?"

"That's great. I think I'm ready to call it a night. We've still got another day left of the holiday weekend, and if it's anything like today was, the clinic's going to be busy tomorrow." Nita glanced down toward the beach. The entire time they had been talking, she'd half expected to see Deo return. She was glad she hadn't. "Well, good night."

"See you tomorrow," Pia called.

❖

"Everything okay?" Reese inquired, leaning against the door in Reggie's bedroom. The last bit of the fading sunset filtered through the white curtains, and as Tory bent over the crib, she looked timelessly beautiful framed in the golden glow. So beautiful that Reese ached. She had imagined this scene a thousand times in the weeks that she'd been away. When everything around her had been senseless chaos, when the sky turned to fire and death rained down from the heavens and exploded from the earth, she had clung to the only thing that kept her sane. She had been shocked when her determination to fulfill the mission she had trained for all her life failed to sustain her and when only the memory of her wife and child kept her going. Leading her marines into battle and in some cases to their deaths while secretly questioning her purpose had shaken the foundation of her world. She had built her life on her belief in her duty and responsibility, and she had come home doubting both. She had come home no longer certain of who she was.

Smiling, Tory turned from the crib, her finger to her lips. After switching on the nightlight on the bright blue dresser by the door, she joined Reese. Once outside in the hall, she said, "She might not have known what the party was for, but she definitely had a good time. I think she sat on everyone's lap at least once."

"She didn't have dinner."

"We'll feed her later when she wakes up." Tory grasped Reese's hand. "How about you? Did you eat something?"

"Yeah, I'm fine."

"That's not exactly what I asked," Tory said quietly.

Reese stopped at the top of the stairs and pulled Tory close. She nuzzled her hair, then kissed her neck. Some of the doubts that plagued her receded. Tory was real. Tory was alive. "I'm *fine.* Stop worrying."

"Comes with the territory, Sheriff." Tory stroked Reese's cheek. "Besides, I enjoy looking after you."

"You'll get no argument from me." Reese wasn't hungry for food, but she still felt empty. Nothing filled her up except Tory. In the recesses of her mind she heard the thunder and felt death coming. She hesitated, uncertain for the first time in her life of how to face it. She gasped, "Tory."

"What, sweetheart?"

In her mind, Reese saw Tory silhouetted in the moonlight, saw her shimmering in the bright light of day. Tory knew her. Tory touched her inside, beyond the fear and doubt. Tory was all that kept her from the dark. Reese pressed Tory into the shadows, maneuvering her back against the wall. Gripping her shoulders, she kissed her neck again, then her mouth. Pinning her with the weight of her body, she slid one hand under the lower edge of Tory's T-shirt. Tory's breasts weren't as full as they had been when she was breast-feeding, but they were still firm and hot under her thin satin bra. Reese cupped her, squeezing until Tory's nipple tightened in her grasp. Groaning, she kissed her way down Tory's neck and fumbled to push Tory's shirt up with her free hand.

"Reese, honey, we have people in the house," Tory warned.

Aching, echoing with emptiness, Reese worked her hand into Tory's bra and lifted her breast free. She bunched Tory's cotton T in her fist and caught a nipple in her mouth.

"*Reese.*" Tory sank her fingers into Reese's hair and pulled her mouth from her breast. She cradled Reese's face against her throat, not wanting to push her away. Reese had only been home a few weeks, but it had only taken a few days for Tory to realize that something was wrong. Something had changed. Reese had always been passionate—sometimes gentle, sometimes urgent—but always *always* exquisitely present. Now, her need rose with the fury of an unexpected storm that broke over the horizon and lashed everything in its wake. Sometimes Tory wasn't certain Reese was even aware of what she was doing. "Sweetheart. We can't."

"Sorry. Jesus. I'm sorry." Drenched with sweat, Reese broke Tory's hold and jerked her head away. "Tory, I'm sorry."

Reese was trembling, and that nearly broke Tory's heart. "It's all right, darling. It's all right."

"No it isn't," Reese said sharply, backing away another step. She held up her hands to ward Tory off when Tory reached for her. "My need. Not yours. I'm sorry."

"No," Tory whispered fervently. "Your need is mine. It always has been."

Reese shook her head. "Not this way. Not this way."

Before Tory could protest again, Reese turned and disappeared down the stairs. A minute later Tory heard the door slam. When an engine revved in the driveway outside and tires kicked up stones that cracked like rifle shots, she knew it was Reese in the patrol car. Leaving. Reese had never, ever walked away from her before and the pain was so acute she was nearly ill.

❖

"Hell of a party," Cath said, dropping into a chair next to Tory on the deck. "Wait'll next year when she actually knows what's going on."

"Thanks for helping out." Tory sipped her wine, then set it aside when she realized she couldn't taste it. "Where are Marcus and the kids?"

"I sent them back to the B&B. Where's Reese?"

"Working, I think."

"You think." Cath reached across Tory and grabbed her wine glass.

Then she settled back and took a swallow. "I noticed she disappeared earlier."

"She's not quite herself."

"Is she having a hard time with what happened over there?"

"Yes. At least I'm sure that's part of it."

"How are you doing?"

"I'm not sure." Tory regarded her sister. "No, that's not true. I'm scared to death. I don't know what to do for her."

"What's wrong, exactly?"

Tory laughed humorlessly. "I don't know and I feel like I should. I'm her partner and I should know."

"Uh, I don't think just because you love her you're supposed to be a mind-reader." Cath took Tory's hand. "Give yourself a break, honey. You've both been through a lot. Is it post-traumatic stress?"

"At first I thought so. I'd pretty much expected it. Even troops who haven't been captured or wounded suffer some form of reentry shock." Tory watched the stars overhead, thinking of the nights she had sat out here alone wondering if Reese could see the same stars from where she was. "She certainly has reason to show those kinds of symptoms, but now I'm not so sure. She's not eating or sleeping, and that's typical enough—but there's something more. Sometimes she seems so lost. I *hate* not being able to help her."

"It hasn't been that long. You both probably just need some time."

"I know. I've been telling myself the same thing, but tonight..." Tory swallowed back tears. "She left tonight. She left the house, she left *me*, because she was upset. She's never done that before."

"Does she... God, this is really hard to say. Does she drink or abuse drugs or anything like that?"

Tory laughed incredulously. "Reese? God, no. She has always been so solid, so certain. She's unshakable."

"Until now."

"Yes, until now." Tory said softly, wondering where she was. If it had been KT leaving after being rebuffed, Tory knew where she would go. KT would have sought respite with another woman, at least when she and Tory had been lovers. But Reese was not KT—she had never... would never... "God, I want her to come home. She's the strongest woman I've ever known and seeing her like this just about kills me."

"You're no pushover yourself, honey," Cath said. "You can be strong for both of you until Reese heals."

"What if I can't? What if I can't give her what she's always given me?"

Cath squeezed Tory's hand again. "You will."

Tory held her sister's hand and ached for the touch of her lover.

Chapter Four

How about some pizza?" Deo clasped Allie's hand as they strolled along a sandy walkway between two buildings that led up from the beach to Commercial Street. When the party at Reese and Tory's had broken up, Deo offered to drive Allie home, but instead of saying good night, Allie suggested they head into town. Even more so than most weekend nights during the season, tourists and summer residents packed every available B&B and condo for the Fourth of July. For another hour or so, the streets would be filled with mostly same-sex couples celebrating the freedom to be visible and among community. Deo hadn't been anxious to return alone to her condo at the end of Bradford Street, and Allie was fun—easy to talk to and easy on the eyes. And she seemed okay with a relationship that was just as easy. A little mutual company, a few hours of shared pleasure, an encounter with no expectations. In Deo's experience, a lot of girls *said* they were okay with that, but after a couple of dates, things changed. Now, she was careful not to see anyone more than a time or two, and she didn't sleep with half the women everyone gave her credit for. It didn't seem worth disavowing everyone of their notion that she scored more than most guys, and her reputation kept the women she saw from expecting much more than a casual night out.

"Pizza. Hmm. I sort of thought you had an appetite for something else," Allie said suggestively.

"Oh, I do." Deo laughed. "But certain activities burn a lot of calories, so it's always good to stock up when you can."

"Is that right?" Allie slowed within the slanting shadows of the overhanging eaves and kissed Deo, squeezing her ass with both hands while rolling her pelvis against Deo's crotch. "Then I suggest you have two slices."

"Much more of that and it won't be pizza I need," Deo muttered breathlessly, surprised not only by Allie's aggression but by her own swift response. Her stomach tightened with urgency, and she felt herself grow hard and tense. She skimmed her fingertips over the outer curve of Allie's breast and smiled to herself when Allie moaned. Good to know she wasn't the only one with a hair trigger tonight. "I'm a little past groping girls in dark alleys, but Jesus, you feel good."

"Baby, you have my permission to grope." Allie hooked her calf around Deo's thigh and rocked into her crotch again, digging her fingers into the firm muscles of Deo's backside for balance. She ran her tongue around the edge of Deo's ear and nibbled on her earlobe. "I can't believe how hot I am. I'm ready for you to fuck me right here."

"You've really got me stoked too," Deo gasped, tilting her head back as Allie sucked on her neck. When she pinched Allie's nipple and Allie whimpered, her vision went hazy and all she could think about was being inside her and making her scream. "Time out. Oh man… Allie, time out." She grabbed Allie's hips and put some air between them. "I'm about two seconds from forgetting where we are, and I'm not going to do this up against a building."

"I know, I know." Allie shivered. "But I want you to."

"You're making me a little bit crazy."

"Bad crazy?"

Allie sounded genuinely worried, and Deo experienced an unexpected rush of gratitude. Usually her companions figured she didn't care about anything except the sex, and it was nice to have someone actually ask what she felt. Deo circled Allie's waist and started walking again. "Feels pretty good to me. You?"

"Better than good." Allie stroked Deo's stomach before sliding her fingers an inch or two underneath the waistband of her pants. She purred when Deo groaned. "You tripped all my switches and there's no off button. I'm so wired my whole body's buzzing."

"Still want pizza?"

"Sure. Just don't fill up on it."

Laughing, Deo led her through a horde of men spilling out onto Commercial in front of Spiritus Pizza. "Grab us a seat and I'll get the food. What's your pleasure?"

Allie grinned. "For now, cheese. I'll tell you the rest later."

Deo kissed her. "Coming up."

"Hurry." Allie staked out a spot on the low brick wall edging the sidewalk in front of the restaurant.

Deo grinned. "Count on it."

❖

"Hey," Carre shouted above the din, tugging on Bri's arm as they edged through the crowd. "There's Allie."

"Huh? Where?" Bri slowed and followed Carre's gaze. She stiffened when she saw Deo Camara settle down behind Allie and slide a leg on either side of Allie's smaller frame. Allie snugged her ass back into Deo's crotch while Deo dangled a piece of pizza in front of Allie's mouth. Bri grunted when Allie chased it with her tongue. "Cute."

Carre gave Bri a look. "What's with you? Jealous?"

Bri stared. "Jeez, babe. No. Come on." She saw the fire in Carre's eyes and knew better than to blow her off. Allie had always been a sore spot between them, ever since Bri had been a jerk the year before and almost slept with her. *Almost.* Well, she'd been in bed with her, and she'd been naked, and she'd let Allie touch…

"Fuck," Bri breathed, not blaming Carre for being sensitive about it. And just what *was* she feeling right now anyhow that made her want to punch Deo for licking the sauce off the corner of Allie's mouth like she was doing at the moment? "I like Allie. She's my friend, and besides, she's my partner."

"I know that," Carre said, pulling Bri closer to the building across the narrow twisty street from where Allie sat wrapped up in Deo's arms. "What I don't know is why you're getting twitchy about her and Deo." She stuck her hand under the bottom of Bri's T-shirt and rubbed her back. "What's that about?"

"Allie has a crazy streak, you know?" Bri said, working it out in her head while she watched Allie run her fingernails up and down the inside of Deo's leg. "Sometimes I think she does stuff so she doesn't have to think about how she's feeling."

"Baby," Carre said reasonably. "Maybe she just wants to get laid."

Bri grinned and kissed Carre nice and slow and deep. "Could be. I'd say she's gonna get her wish."

"And you're okay with that?"

"Not my department." Bri turned Carre until her back was against the building and kissed her again, teasing her with her tongue until Carre rubbed against her and moaned. "*That's* my department."

"Yeah," Carre said breathlessly. "And you should maybe take care of it. Soon."

"Top of my list." Bri grabbed Carre's hand and pulled her into the street in the direction of their apartment. She didn't glance over at Allie. Not her department.

❖

Deo fumbled her key into the lock while Allie practically climbed up her back, rubbing against her ass and licking the back of her neck. "One more minute. Just hold on one more minute, and I'll take care of that charge you've got running through your circuits."

"You've had me wound up all night," Allie murmured, wrapping her arms around Deo's middle from behind and cleaving to her as they stumbled inside Deo's condo. "You have your work cut out for you."

"That's okay." Deo tossed her keys onto a small table by the door and threw her shirt after them. Her skin tingled and even the T-shirt chaffed her sensitive nipples. "I love my work." She twisted enough to free herself from Allie's grasp and grabbed her arm. "Come on. The bedroom's upstairs. Let's see what I can do about taking care of you."

"What time is it—one?"

"About," Deo muttered, hurriedly twisting the rheostat on the switch inside her bedroom door until the light was barely a glow. "Gotta be somewhere?"

"Nope." Allie gave Deo a playful shove and then another, until Deo hit the bed and fell onto it. Allie dropped on top of her and writhed against her. "You might have enough time to take the edge off by morning, at least."

Deo grabbed Allie's ass, thrust up her hips, and flipped Allie over. She circled her crotch against Allie's while holding Allie's arms against the bed with her fingers clamped around each of Allie's wrists. "Is that some kind of challenge?"

"Uh-uh. Just a warning to let you know what you're in for." Allie raised her head and clamped her teeth onto the side of Deo's neck, sucking until Deo groaned. "I'd really really like it if you fucked me."

"That could be arranged." Deo rubbed her cheek over Allie's breast until the nipple stood up beneath Allie's stretchy top. She grasped it in her teeth and shook her head while she pumped her crotch into Allie. She kept up the rhythm with her mouth and her hips, harder and faster until Allie twisted and shook beneath her.

"Oh God I'm hot," Allie gasped. "You have *got* to fuck me. I'm not kidding."

"Would you like a little something extra when I do?"

Allie scraped her nails down the back of Deo's thin T-shirt. "Will it be good for you too?"

Surprised again, Deo kissed her softly. "Yeah. I'd like it."

"Then fill me up," Allie whispered, her mouth against Deo's ear, "with something nice and thick."

Deo's stomach rolled, and for a fleeting second she was afraid she might come just thinking about pushing inside her. She was breathing so fast she could hardly talk. By the time she struggled upright to get ready, Allie was already pulling off her clothes. "I need a minute."

"I've waited this long." Naked, Allie rubbed her own breasts, arching her back and moaning. "I'm so wet."

"Take it easy," Deo said as she shucked her pants and underwear and opened the bedside table. "Don't get too far ahead of me."

"I can come more than once."

The words went through Deo like a shot. Her hands were shaking so badly she fumbled while sliding the thin leather straps of the harness over her legs. "There's a condom in the top drawer there. Get it for me." While Allie leaned over to retrieve the safe, Deo swung around and propped her back against the pillows, half-sitting with her legs stretched out on the bed.

"Mmm, that's nice," Allie murmured, tearing the foil open as she knelt on the bed. She smiled up at Deo. "Nice and big."

"Too big?" Deo steadied the cock with one hand as Allie rolled the condom down on it. The pressure made her clit ache. "Because I've got a smaller—"

Allie laughed. "Oh no. This is perfect." As if to prove it, she swung one leg over Deo's hips and lowered herself until just the broad, round tip disappeared. Her head snapped back and she whimpered quietly. "Oh my God, that feels so good."

Deo struggled not to move when every instinct cried out for her to pump her hips. She clasped Allie's waist with both hands, helping to support her as she slowly took more and more of Deo inside her. "You look beautiful like this."

Lids half closed, Allie smiled unsteadily. "I need to come and I'm really really trying not to."

"You do whatever you need to do," Deo groaned. "If you have to come, do it."

"Oh I will." Allie shivered. "Once I get you inside of me and start to move, I won't be able to stop it."

"I want you to feel so good." Deo lifted her hips slowly, pushing inside just a little bit at a time. When Allie's eyes closed and she sagged forward, catching herself with both hands on Deo's shoulders, Deo stilled. "Okay? You okay?"

Mutely, Allie nodded, her hips gliding back and forth in Deo's lap.

Deo cupped both of Allie's breasts and squeezed. "You go ahead now. You ride me any way you want to. Ride me until you come."

"Uh-huh." Allie's belly undulated as she forced Deo deeper. "Uh-huh. Uh-huh. I will. I will." She pumped hard twice and her eyes opened wide. "Touch my clit. Can you touch my clit?"

"Good?" Deo said, watching Allie's face twist with pleasure as she massaged her with her thumb.

"I'm coming already. Uh, I'm coming."

"You're beautiful. You're so beautiful." Deo thrust her hips in time to Allie's cries, feeling the push and pull between her legs as Allie climaxed hard on her. Slowing when Allie finally slumped forward into her arms, she kissed her hair and her face. Allie trembled, making small broken sounds of pleasure. "It's okay, baby. It's okay. You're so beautiful."

"Don't move," Allie murmured, rocking her hips slowly with Deo still inside her. "I'll come again in just a second."

Deo caught her breath. Allie was so raw and sensual and vulnerable she wanted to cry. She stroked her back and her shoulders and kissed her gently until Allie released a soft cry and shuddered with another orgasm. Deo groaned. "Oh yeah."

"I'll say." Allie lifted her hips and let Deo slip out, then curled on her side with her cheek on Deo's chest. She caressed Deo's breasts and stomach. "You're very patient. That's nice."

"I could watch you like that all night." Deo drew a deep breath and let it out, feeling strangely content. She hadn't come, but the pent up urgency that had plagued her for hours had dwindled away effortlessly as Allie had climaxed. It happened that way fairly often for her. Satisfying a woman satisfied *her* in some deep way that she'd never really bothered to analyze. It just was. She was lucky that was so, because there were plenty of times when the woman she was with showed no particular interest in her pleasure. Their lack of reciprocation never really bothered her. But Allie had not been selfish. She had given her a gift. She'd given her trust and allowed Deo to witness her need. Deo was more than satisfied. She was honored. "You are mind-blowingly sexy."

"Oh yeah?" Allie propped herself up on an elbow and kissed the tip of Deo's chin. "Well, I wasn't doing it all by myself. Believe me, the way you look at me, the way you touch me, sets me on fire."

"Then let's feed the flames because…" Deo kissed Allie's neck, then her breasts, then her nipple, "I want to hear you come again."

Allie laughed. "Maybe. I need a little bit more time to catch my breath." She pushed herself down on the bed and started to unbuckle the leather strap around Deo's hips. "And while I'm recovering, I know just how to occupy myself."

Deo lifted up so Allie could free her and then spread her legs as Allie settled between them. She closed her eyes and stroked Allie's hair, her mind clear and mercifully free of memory or regret. She whispered a silent *thank you* as Allie took her into her mouth.

❖

"What are you doing to me," Bri moaned.

Carre kissed her as she languorously stroked between Bri's trembling thighs. "I'm making you feel as good as you just made me feel."

"I'm going to explode, babe." Bri twisted in Carre's arms, her mouth against Carre's neck as every fiber in her body tightened. "Feels so good. I'm gonna…oh yeah I'm gonna—"

"Mmm. *You* feel so good." Carre relaxed her grip on Bri's turgid clit and vibrated her fingers lightly. "Too good to let it end now."

"I gotta, babe," Bri pleaded desperately. "Really, I'm hurtin'. I gotta."

Carre sucked on Bri's lower lip and teased her tongue in and out of Bri's mouth. "I love when you get like this. So hard. So freakin' wet." She grasped Bri's hair and tilted her head back so she could nip down the center of her throat. "I love to make you come."

Bri choked trying to catch her breath. "Please I'm right there, babe. If you just, oh God… oh God…"

"I know, baby," Carre whispered, stroking again, too slowly and too lightly to make Bri come. "I know what you need."

Bri tried to keep her eyes open but the terrible wanting in her belly was too much to hold. "I love you so much."

"I love you."

"No one else," Bri gasped, her body shaking with a series of bone wracking shudders.

"I know baby," Carre whispered, milking her in long firm strokes. "You come now, baby. You come."

Bri's eyes rolled back in her head and she clutched Carre as if she were drowning and Carre was all that stood between her and oblivion. "*Fuck!*"

Laughing, Carre wrapped her legs around Bri and held her sweat-streaked face to her breast. "God, you are so sexy."

"Trying to kill me," Bri muttered, still quaking. "Think maybe you *did* kill me."

"You know I have to go back to school in six weeks." Carre caressed Bri's shoulders. "I don't want you to forget who you belong to."

Bri opened her eyes and struggled to focus. Her vision was still blurry but clear enough for her to make out the scared look on Carre's face. Bri's heart plummeted when she realized that she was the cause of that fear. "I've only ever loved you. The only thing I'm gonna do while you're gone is count the minutes until you come back." She pushed herself up on both arms and waited until Carre looked into her face. "I'm only ever going to love you."

"Me too." Carre wrapped her arms around Bri's shoulders and pulled her down until Bri's body covered hers. She pressed her face to Bri's neck. "Only ever you."

❖

"I'm awake," Tory said as the bedroom door opened and a sliver of light slanted in from the hall. "You can turn the light on."

"That's okay," Reese replied. "I'll just...should I come to bed?"

Tory closed her eyes for an instant, the swift pain of the unthinkable question making her breathless. She pushed the sheets aside, making room. "Of course."

Reese undressed in the dark and a moment later, settled onto the bed. She lay on her back, her arms by her side. When she spoke, her voice was hollow and flat. "I'm sorry."

"For what, darling?" Tory inched closer and lay on her side facing Reese. She lightly placed her hand in the center of Reese's abdomen. Reese's skin was cool, and her muscles felt stretched tight over bones that were far too prominent. "You need to tell me, because I can't help you if you don't."

Reese gripped the sheets, her body rigid. "I shouldn't have left like I did tonight."

Tory waited until the silence stretched so thin she feared the air would shatter like glass. "Why did you?"

"I was ashamed. Ashamed of forcing myself on you."

"Oh no," Tory murmured, grasping Reese's shoulders in both hands and pulling her into her arms. She cradled the back of Reese's head and pressed Reese's face to her breasts. She rocked her, bleeding inside with the need to ease her pain. "You could never ever do anything to me that I didn't want." She kissed Reese's forehead. "I love you. I've wanted you since the first instant I saw you. I will want you until the moment I die, and if there's anything beyond that, I'll want you forever."

"I don't know what I'm doing sometimes, Tor. I feel like I'm lost and you're all I have to hold on to."

"It's okay. You hold on to me, darling. You hold on just as tight and just as long as you need to." If Tory could have pulled Reese inside her body and sheltered her with her very breath and the last drop of her blood, she would have. Instead, she was left with inadequate words and what she feared was an all too fragile strength to fight off whatever monsters shadowed Reese's soul. She tightened her grip and steeled herself for whatever might come. Reese was her life, and she had nearly lost her half a world away in a godforsaken desert in the midst of a war that no one understood. Now Reese was home again, and she would not lose her to whatever demon had followed her back.

"If I'm ever going to be any good to you again, maybe I need to go back," Reese whispered in the dark. "Maybe I need to go back and find whatever parts of myself I left over there."

Tory's world teetered on the verge of collapse. She wanted to scream *no*, but she stopped herself even though holding back made her feel as if she were dying. She didn't say no, because what if Reese was right? She didn't say no, because she didn't want Reese to know the truth. *I'm not strong enough to let you go. I'm not strong enough to be without you again.*

"Promise me you won't do anything without talking to me first," Tory said shakily.

"I promise," Reese whispered. "I'm sorry, baby. I'm so sorry."

Tory pressed her fingers to Reese's lips. "Shh. Go to sleep, darling. It's all right."

Tory held Reese, wondering if either of them would sleep. As she listened to the lie echo in the stillness, Tory felt her heart breaking.

Chapter Five

When Tory awoke, the bed beside her was empty. Heart racing, she threw back the covers, grabbed her robe, and hurried into the hall. Reggie's crib was empty, and the smell of coffee drifted up the stairs. Immediately, she felt calmer. Reese was downstairs with the baby. She was home, she hadn't gone anywhere. Taking a deep breath, Tory went to greet her family.

"Hey," Tory said casually as she bent to kiss Reggie, who was sitting in her high chair in front of the breakfast bar. Her hair smelled like baby shampoo and apples. The apples, she noted, were part of breakfast. Reese still had her desert tan, and her arms and legs in her faded green T-shirt and boxers looked sinewy and lean. Muscle and bone. A fighting machine, but she wasn't a machine. She was a woman. "Good morning, darling. How did you two get up without me?"

"You were sleeping pretty soundly, so when Reggie started making hungry noises, I got up." Reese's eyes held an apology. "You must have been really tired."

Tory wrapped her arms around Reese's waist and kissed her. "I slept fine." She could tell by the circles under Reese's eyes that she hadn't. She rubbed her hand over the center of Reese's chest and kissed her again. "Nita is working today. I'm backup. Any chance you could switch your shifts around and stay home with us?"

"I don't think so," Reese said, stroking Tory's hair. "You know, what with me only being back a few weeks, I think I should be there."

"Okay. I'll probably take the baby to the beach with Cath and the kids." Tory sidled around Reese to the counter and poured coffee. "Dinner then?"

"I'll try."

Tory put the pot down and left her cup on the counter beside it. She slid a slice of toast off a plateful and handed it to Reggie, who promptly tore it in half. With the baby occupied, she focused on Reese. "We need you here, Reese. I know how busy things are during the season, but you can't work twenty-four hours a day. Even if it makes you feel better somehow, it's not the answer."

Reese braced both hands against the counter and lowered her head. She was quiet a long moment before meeting Tory's eyes. "I'm screwing everything up pretty good, aren't I?"

"No, you're not." Tory traced the pink three inch scar that slanted across Reese's forehead. It was healing well, and before long it would be only a faint reminder of the rifle butt some madman had swung into her face. That shattered collar bone, the burns on her arm, the shrapnel tear in her leg—they would all fade into the background. The real damage was on the inside, and she had no way of judging how deep it went or how permanent it might be. "I'm not going to make any excuses for you, because you're not doing anything wrong. Just remember that we're both dealing with something we've never had to face before. It might take us a while to figure it out."

"I was trained to face it," Reese said angrily. "That's who I am."

"And if you hadn't been so well trained, God only knows what would've happened to you and the people who relied on you." Tory struggled to keep her voice even because she didn't want to upset Reggie, who thankfully was happily piling stewed apples onto her toast. "You kept them alive. You kept yourself alive. You did your duty."

"Maybe I missed something. Maybe we ended up separated, cut off, because I wasn't as sharp as I needed to be. Because I *questioned* why I was there."

Reese spoke softly, almost to herself, her expression distant. Tory had seen the look before, but this was the first time she realized that Reese was replaying the events surrounding her capture. She had never once imagined that Reese blamed herself for what had happened, because it was so obvious to her that it was Reese's skill and absolute dedication to her troops that had gotten them all through it. How could she not have realized that Reese would accept all the responsibility, even when she couldn't have prevented what had transpired? Gently, she grasped Reese's hand. "Darling, you couldn't have foreseen that firefight. And from everything you've told me, you did exactly what needed to be done."

"I should get ready for work while the baby finishes breakfast with you," Reese said, evading Tory's gaze. "Then I'll get her dressed if you want to take a shower." She kissed Tory's cheek and started to turn away.

Tory clasped Reese's forearms, holding her in place, forcing Reese to look at her. "I love you with all my heart. Don't ever walk out on me again. It hurts us both too much."

Reese pulled Tory into her arms, gripping her so tightly it nearly hurt. "I need you so much, it doesn't seem fair."

"I need you every bit as much, I always have." Tory stroked Reese's face. "We'll get through this, darling, I promise."

Reese kissed her again and Tory felt a tremor go through her. When Reese abruptly let her go, she knew Reese was struggling to contain her desire.

"Don't. Don't try not to want me." Tory framed Reese's face. "I need you to want me. My need. Not yours. Don't take that from me."

Reese covered Tory's hand and kissed her palm. "I have to go to work."

"I know. Be careful."

"Thank you for believing in me."

"Always."

Tory watched her walk upstairs, knowing that it didn't matter what she believed. It only mattered what Reese believed. All she could do was be there for her, which at moments like this didn't seem like enough.

❖

"Oh shit!" Allie jumped out of bed and nearly tripped in the tangle of shoes and clothes next to the bed. "Ow. God damn it."

Deo bolted upright. "What's the matter?" She rolled over, yanked open the dresser drawer, and pulled out a .38 Smith & Wesson. Then she leapt upright and threw herself between Allie and the bedroom door. "Did you hear something?"

"Ho! Take it easy!" Allie held her hands out, palms forward. "Deo, baby. Easy. I'm just late for work."

"Late for work?" Deo looked at her like she was crazy. "Jesus. What do they do, flog you?" She shook her head, breathing hard, and put the gun away. Then she grabbed Allie and kissed her. "Good morning."

"I'm not going to ask if you have a license—"

"I do, Officer Tremont." Grinning, Deo kissed her again. "I carry a fair amount of cash for the payroll and other things. I got jumped once in the parking lot on the wharf."

Allie didn't mention that Deo had reacted as if she'd expected someone to break in and accost them. She'd slept with her—well, they hadn't actually done much sleeping. She'd spent the night letting Deo explore just about every part of her body and had revealed a good deal of herself to Deo in the process, but four outstanding orgasms still didn't give her the right to get personal.

"I've got first shift," Alley said, hastily picking through the clothes on the floor, "and Reese will kick my ass if I'm not on time." She dropped her panties back into the pile. She couldn't wear those again. "Shit. I don't have time to pick up my car at the station, go home, shower, change, and get back to work on time."

"Is there a plan B?" Deo grabbed her khakis off the floor and pulled them on, not bothering with a shirt.

"I've got a spare uniform in my locker, and I can shower here." Allie grimaced. "'Course I'm still going to have to walk in there with the same clothes on as I was wearing last night. Nothing like announcing I've been out all night fucking." She scanned Deo's body. Her biceps swelled even when she was relaxed and her chest and abdominal muscles rippled beneath the smooth burnished skin. Despite the hard body, her breasts were just large enough to soften her image. That—in addition to the fact that she opened so beautifully when Allie was inside her—made Deo a spectacularly delicious butch treat. Allie got a flash of how Deo's stomach tightened when she was about to come and her clit pulsed. "Jesus, you're sexy. I feel like a cat with a big ball of catnip. I just want to roll around in you."

"If we weren't on the clock, I'd drag you back under the sheets. I woke up with an urge."

"Sorry," Allie said, patting Deo's crotch. "I can't."

"I know. That's why I'm going to make you coffee instead of getting into the shower with you. Go."

"You could give me a break and put a shirt on too."

Deo laughed and stretched. "Sure."

On her way to the bathroom, Allie called back, "I don't suppose you have any underwear that aren't boxers, do you?"

Deo laughed. "Jockeys?"

"Nevermind."

Five minutes and a quick shower later, Allie returned to the bedroom with a bath towel wrapped around her to find a steaming cup of coffee on the dresser next to a pair of plain black silk panties. Deo slouched in a scuffed brown leather reading chair by the window with her own cup of coffee balanced on her knee. She'd added a sleeveless grey T-shirt which was an improvement, but Allie still got a rush just looking at her. She scooped up the panties and dangled them on her finger. "Let me guess. You're a collector."

"You wound me."

When Deo absently pulled her T-shirt up and rubbed her bare stomach, Allie felt a sharp twinge of arousal and forced herself to look away. What she really wanted to do was drop the towel and climb onto that chair and rub herself all over Deo's amazing mouth. She slid on the panties. "Ex-girlfriend?"

"A present from one who liked her packages wrapped a little differently than what I was offering."

With a shake of her head, Allie walked over and pushed her hand into Deo's crotch. "Any girl who'd want to change a thing about you doesn't deserve you."

"You better quit that," Deo said, not moving a single muscle. "You're getting me hard again."

"That makes two of us." Allie squeezed Deo for another second and then let go with a groan. "Really really sorry."

"Get your clothes on so we can get out of here. I'm weakening."

Allie laughed and pulled on her jeans and top. "Just in case you weren't sure, last night was great."

Deo shrugged and collected her keys. Straight faced, she said, "After the third time I figured we were doing okay."

"More than okay." Allie kissed her quickly and hurried from the room. Fortunately, they were only a few minutes from the sheriff's department and there was a chance she might make it *almost* on time.

"Is there anything we need to get clear on?" Deo said as she gunned her truck down Bradford. At seven twenty-five in the morning, vehicular traffic was scarce but the runners and cyclists were already out. She scanned both sides of the road, on the lookout for unwary tourists and frolicking dogs.

Allie turned sideways in her seat. "About last night?"

"Yeah."

"We've got some kind of heavy-duty chemistry thing going on, because I can't even look at you without getting wet." Allie smiled with satisfaction when Deo tensed. She liked turning her on. "So I wouldn't mind a repeat. But if it doesn't happen, I'm okay with it."

Deo looked over at her. "I'm working twelve, fourteen hours a day. Most of the time I have a beer or two after work and fall into bed."

"I've been working a lot of doubles myself. If you're awake some night and want company, call me."

"Same here." Deo swung into the parking lot next to the rambling, one story white building that looked like a cross between a Cape Cod cottage and a ranch house. Two cruisers and a van marked Provincetown Sheriff's Department were parked in the lot, along with a few civilian cars and a Harley.

Allie released her seatbelt and slid across the seat toward Deo. She skimmed her hand under Deo's shirt and caressed her stomach while nuzzling her ear. "All those nights I'm sleeping alone, I'm going to be making myself come thinking about you inside me."

Deo kissed her hard. "You're such a fucking tease."

Laughing, Allie pulled away and jumped out of the truck. Leaning on the door, she said, "Are you complaining?"

"Do I look crazy?" Deo tilted her chin toward the building. "Better go to work. Take it easy, sexy."

"I'll see you around, hot stuff."

Allie slammed the door and stepped back so Deo could back out. Waving, she sprinted up the steps to the side entrance to the station. With luck she wouldn't run into anyone in the short hall that connected the squad room in the front with the small locker room in the rear. She banged through the door into the unisex locker room and nearly flattened Bri.

"Sorry," Allie said breathlessly, sidling around Bri. She grabbed the combination lock on her locker and hastily dialed in the numbers. It didn't open. She muttered a curse and started over again. So much for her luck holding.

"Reese is waiting to start shift change," Bri said. "I just came back to look for you."

"I'll be there as soon as I get dressed."

"It looks bad when you show up like this, Al."

Allie shot Bri a look. Like she didn't feel stupid enough already for forgetting to tell Deo to set an alarm. "Well thank you so much. What are you, my babysitter now?"

"I don't know," Bri snapped. "Seems like you need one."

"Oh, fuck you, Parker." Allie whipped her top off, then remembered that she hadn't put her bra on. Well, it wasn't as if Bri had never seen her tits before. She could just close her eyes if it bothered her. She toed off her shoes, pushed down her jeans, and kicked everything into the bottom of her locker. Then she yanked her uniform shirt off the hanger. "Just because *you* think being married is the answer to everything doesn't make it so."

"This isn't about me. This is about you not thinking about what—or who—you're doing half the time."

Allie jerked her pants up, jammed the tail of her shirt in, and zipped up. Then she grabbed her equipment belt and realized her weapon was locked in the trunk of her car in the parking lot where she'd left it last night when she'd hitched a ride with Bri to the party. "Crap."

"Give me your keys. I'll go get it."

"Forget it." Allie dug her keys out of the pocket of her jeans and shouldered past Bri. "Don't do me any favors."

Bri caught up to her in the hall and yanked on her arm. "Don't be stupid. Finish dressing. It will only take me—"

"Would you two officers care to attend the morning briefing?" Reese said from the far end of the hall. She stood with her hands behind her back, her legs slightly spread, her gaze unflinching. "The chief is waiting."

"Yes ma'am." Bri snapped to attention. "We'll be right there."

"Now," Reese said quietly.

"Go ahead," Allie murmured, slinging her belt around her hips. "Go."

"Both of you."

Silently, Allie finished buckling up and walked beside Bri into the squad room. Tony Smith and Jim Winters from the graveyard shift sprawled in chairs around a conference table in the corner of the room opposite the small communications center, waiting to make their reports and go home. Chief Nelson Parker leaned against the counter next to the table, munching on what Allie figured was a Tums. He seemed to eat them like candy lately, and at the moment his expression suggested he had indigestion. When he saw her, his scowl deepened. "Your uniform needs some work, Officer Tremont."

When Tony and Jimmy smirked, Allie checked her shirt and realized she'd missed a button. It was a good thing her tits weren't any bigger, because they would have been sticking out. Hastily, she turned her back and straightened her shirt. "Sorry, Chief."

"Since you and Officer Parker don't seem to be in any hurry to start your shift, you can both take the desks this morning."

Desk duty was the worst. Filling out forms, answering phones, dying of boredom. Allie was pissed at Bri for being such a tightass all of a sudden, but she couldn't let Bri take the blame for her screw up.

"It's my fault Bri…that Officer Parker is late, sir—"

"No it isn't," Bri said firmly.

"Shut up, Bri," Allie muttered.

"I don't really care whose fault it is," Nelson grumbled. "It's 0740 and neither one of you…" He winced and rubbed his stomach. "Who the hell made the coffee this…" He caught his breath and his face lost all color. "Christ."

"Chief?" Reese just managed to catch him as Nelson slumped to the floor.

"Dad?" Bri blurted. "Dad!"

"Call fire rescue," Reese ordered, feeling Nelson's neck for a pulse. She couldn't find one. "Tell them to get here code four."

Then she started CPR.

Chapter Six

Bri's hands were shaking so badly she couldn't push the right numbers on the phone pad. The last time she'd been this scared was when she saw Reese take a round in the chest when they had been trying to apprehend an arsonist. When she'd thought Reese was dying, she'd felt just like she did now—like she was crumbling inside, collapsing in on herself, the way the towers had in New York City when the steel had superheated and simply disintegrated. She fumbled with the phone. "I can't…Jesus, I can't—"

"Here, I've got it," Allie said in a calm, unruffled voice, plucking the receiver from Bri's nerveless fingers. She kicked the desk chair out with her foot as she punched in the number to fire rescue. "Sit down here."

"No, I've got to—"

"*Sit.* Reese will handle things." Allie dropped her hand to Bri's shoulder and guided her into the chair. She kept her hand there, softly stroking, as she spoke. "Geri? This is Allie Tremont at the station—we need a unit over here code four. Yeah…at the station. I don't know, a heart attack I think."

Allie disconnected and shouted to the room in general. "Everyone's out on calls. Ten minutes, they said. Should I call Tory or someone?"

"Take too long," Reese grunted as she knelt astride the Chief's body. She compressed his chest with the steady rhythm of a metronome and intermittently directed Tony to administer a breath.

Allie hesitated, then made another call and spoke softly into the phone.

Bri stared past Allie to where Reese worked. She couldn't see her dad's face, but he wasn't moving at all. When she'd only had twenty-four hours' notice that Reese was leaving for Iraq, she hadn't slept at all. Instead, she'd lain awake trying to think of how to thank Reese for everything she had done, starting with the day Reese had picked her up by the side of the road after she had screwed up her knee. For training her in the martial arts—teaching her to be strong, not just tough. For telling her it was okay to be with Carre and for making her see what a big deal it was to love someone. She hadn't been able to figure out a way to thank Reese for all that. And to tell her that she loved her.

Now twenty-four hours seemed like a lifetime. She hadn't even had one minute to thank her father for always being there, even when he was pissed at her. To tell him she tried to make him proud. To tell him that she loved him. Lurching to her feet, she catapulted herself to Reese's side and dropped to her knees.

"Don't let him die." She grabbed Reese's arm. "Reese. Please—"

"Allie," Reese said sharply without looking up. Sweat dripped from her forehead onto Nelson's face. "Take her outside."

"Come on, honey," Allie said gently, grasping Bri's shoulder. "You gotta give Reese some room."

"I won't get in the way," Bri said desperately, releasing Reese's arm. "I won't."

Allie squatted down next to Bri, curved her arm around her shoulders, and put her mouth close to Bri's ear. "Come outside and call Carre. You don't want her to hear about this from anybody except you, do you?"

Bri glanced from her father's gray face to Allie and nodded. "Just for a minute."

"You can come back in when fire rescue gets him squared away. They'll be here in a second."

Mutely, Bri rose and followed Allie as far as the front door, but she could not make herself go outside. Instead, she leaned in the open doorway with the bright sunlight illuminating half of her face while the other half remained in the otherworldly shadow of the squad room. Maybe it wasn't happening at all. Maybe it was just a bad dream. She fumbled her phone from her belt and couldn't remember her own number.

"I'll do it." Allie took the phone from Bri. "She's still at home, right?"

"I think so. What time is it?" Bri felt like she'd been clobbered with a pipe.

"Never mind, honey," Allie murmured, brushing her fingers through Bri's hair. "I'll find her." She continued to stroke Bri's arm while she watched what was going on inside the station. "Caroline? It's Allie. No...she's fine. She's right here, but Chief Parker...he's had a heart attack or something." Allie turned her back slightly and lowered her voice. "At the station. Not so good. Could you get over here like right now? I think I hear sirens...that must be fire rescue. Hurry, okay?"

❖

Tory parked her Jeep on the side of the road where she wouldn't block the Sheriff's Department parking lot. An emergency vehicle idled with its doors open near the front entrance. As quickly as her damaged ankle would allow, she hurried up the sidewalk. A small group of people congregated just inside the reception area—Gladys Martin, the middle-aged dispatcher who'd been with the department longer than Tory had lived in Provincetown, and several uniformed officers, one of whom was Allie Tremont.

"Excuse me. Excuse me, let me through please. It's Dr. King."

Miraculously, the crowd parted, and she pushed through the waist-high gate into the main section of the station house. Bri, her face bloodless, rocked on her heels a few feet from the epicenter of activity. Caroline pressed close against her side with one arm encircling Bri's waist. Closer now, Tory could make out Nelson on the floor between the conference table and a desk, being administered to by two paramedics. Reese squatted nearby amidst torn IV tubing packages, discarded syringe caps, and empty IV bags. Her face was still and hard as stone, but her eyes blazed with what looked like fury. Tory wanted to go to her, but she couldn't. Not yet.

"Hi Luther," Tory said, bending down close to the paramedic's shoulder. She knew all of the medical personnel for fifty miles. Hers was the only major clinic between Provincetown and the hospital at Hyannis. All the units brought their non-life-threatening, and sometimes even their dire, emergencies to her. "It's Tory King. What do you have?"

"Hey Doc," the gruff, ex-army medic said without looking up. "MI—his anterior ST segments are flipped. He was friggin' flatlined when we got here but we jumpstarted him with intracardiac epi. His blood pressure's for shit still. Amy is talking to the ER at Hyannis."

Tory nodded briefly to the small redhead who sorted drugs from the emergency box as she talked on the phone, presumably getting instructions from someone at the hospital. "Amy, tell them I'll take over until we get him there."

With a grateful look, the redhead relayed the message and disconnected. "Sure rather have you running the show, Tor."

"Thanks. How's his rhythm?"

"Jumping around—a lot of PVCs," Luther said.

"Lidocaine drip going?"

"Just started it," Amy replied.

Tory nodded with satisfaction. "Okay then, then let's run MI protocol and get him ready to transport. Morphine, O2, Nitro."

"You want us to start tPA?"

"How much time are we down?" Tory asked, faced with a critical decision and not nearly enough information. The ideal treatment for someone with a heart attack was to open the blocked vessels as quickly as possible and insert thin plastic stents to keep the arteries open. However, irreversible cardiac damage would occur quickly if this treatment was delayed for even an hour or two. If they lost too much more time on the trip to Hyannis, Nelson might have a better chance if she started intravenous drugs that would dissolve any clots blocking his coronary arteries and hopefully allow more blood to flow to his heart. But tPA, as it was called, was a less reliable treatment than stenting and could have significant side effects.

Everyone looked at Reese.

"Eighteen minutes."

"Amy," Tory snapped, "call Hyannis and tell them to get the cath lab ready—we're bringing in an emergency angioplasty. Let's get him loaded guys, and make sure he's strapped in tight. I'll ride with you."

"I'll take point," Reese said, "and clear the way."

"Good," Tory said softly and squeezed Reese's hand before hurrying after the paramedics.

Reese watched Tory leave, then pivoted to Bri. "You'll ride with me." Her eyes flickered from Bri's pale, stunned face to Caroline. From the looks of Caroline, she wasn't about to let Bri out of her sight. "Both of you."

"I'll call in the evening shift to cover, okay, Sheriff?" Allie asked.

"Yes. And Tremont," Reese said as she grabbed her hat and keys, "run the shift change and get these other guys home as soon as back-up arrives."

"Yes ma'am." Allie glanced at Bri. "Uh, do you think when you get a break someone could call—"

"I'll contact you with an update." Reese clapped Bri's shoulder briskly. "Let's go, Officer. We've got work to do."

Bri twitched as if she were awakening from a dream and took a long shuddering breath. Clasping Caroline's hand tightly, she said, "Yes ma'am. I'm ready."

❖

"Tory's on the phone," Randy said as Nita stepped out of a patient exam room. "She says it's urgent."

"I'll take it in the office. Thanks."

Nita scribbled a note into the chart and tossed it onto the dictation pile. Then she grabbed the phone.

"Tory? It's Nita." Frowning, she held the phone in one hand and flipped through the next patient chart on her desk with the other. "Don't even think about leaving until the situation is stabilized." She sighed. "Tory, I don't *mind* working another shift. That's why I'm here...How do things look?...Damn, Okay...call me later, then. Thanks."

Aware that Randy hovered in the doorway, Nita traded the phone for the file folder marked Joey Torres and joined him. After checking that the hallway was clear, she said quietly, "Tory's fine." She lowered her voice. "Nelson Parker has had an MI. Keep it quiet for now, okay?"

"Oh hell," Randy replied. "Let me know if you hear anything?"

"I will." Nita indicated the chart. "I'll be in doing a wound check on Joey."

When she entered the procedure room, it looked like an instant replay of the day before, except this time Pia had joined the party. Sally, still laughing at something, laid out clean dressings and splint material on an instrument tray. Joey sat sideways on the procedure table, his injured right hand cradled against his chest in a sling. Pia stood next to him, her hip propped against the edge of the table. The person who held Nita's attention, however, was Deo Camara.

Today Deo wore faded blue jeans that hugged her narrow hips and a faded grey T-shirt with the sleeves torn off. The neckline was ripped down the center, and Nita thought she glimpsed the soft swell of a smooth, creamy breast. She quickly averted her gaze, but she saw that Deo was smiling in a way that said she knew exactly where Nita had been looking. Annoyance at having given Deo more than a glance and, worse, having Deo catch her at it, set her on edge. She hated that Deo could throw her off stride with just a look. Deliberately, she turned away from Deo and smiled at Joey.

"How are you feeling?"

"Terrible." Joey feigned a pained expression. "I think I might need three or four months off."

Deo laughed. "Like hell. You're not spending the summer on the beach."

"Let's have a look." Nita kept her back to Deo, whose deep rich voice reminded Nita of hot summer air on a lazy August afternoon. That wasn't all Deo reminded her of, and that was the real problem. Deo actually looked nothing like Sylvia, who had been the epitome of blue-eyed, blond beauty, but they shared the same seething sensuality. And apparently, if her racing pulse were any indication, she was still susceptible to such empty charms.

With effort, Nita put Deo out of her mind and, after donning sterile gloves, carefully removed the bandages from Joey's hand. Pia watched from nearby.

"Incisions look good," Nita reported. "There's anticipated swelling, but nothing out of the ordinary. Finger position indicates the tendon repairs are intact."

"What do you think about a functional splint?" Pia asked. "I'll keep the affected fingers blocked for now so there won't be any motion, but we'll be ready for a little bit of gentle ranging in a few days."

"All right. Sally can get you what you need if you want to fashion the splint yourself."

While Pia worked on the splint, Nita re-bandaged the injured fingers and quickly recorded a chart note. On her way out into the hall, she said, "Two weeks for suture removal."

She was almost to her office door when she felt a hand on her arm. She slowed, knowing who it was and silently chastising herself for the sudden swell of anticipation. Slowly she turned and met Deo's eyes, knowing what she would see. Deep set eyes, liquid and dark. So dark.

She could imagine how they would look when Deo was aroused, when that sultry shimmer turned to fire. When Sylvia orgasmed, her glacial blue eyes sharpened until Nita feared she'd bleed on their edges. Deo's eyes…Deo's eyes would be molten, hot enough to scorch the flesh from her bones.

"What is it?" Nita asked, her voice sounding breathy to her own ears. *It's only chemistry. Mindless attraction. Ignore it. Haven't you learned?*

Deo was entranced by the rapid flurry of expression on Nita's face. Annoyance, appreciation, intensity…desire. Even though the break in Nita's careful façade had been fleeting, she hadn't been wrong. She knew what desire looked like in another woman's eyes. What she hadn't expected was the quick surge of heat in the pit of her stomach. Taken off guard, she fumbled for words.

"I…uh…I wanted to thank you for taking care of Joey."

"That's not necessary." Nita backed up a step, aware of her open office door just a few feet away. Sanctuary awaited. Being near Deo made her feel as if she were Daniel cast into the lion's den. Her common sense told her to flee, but what she really wanted to do was reach out and sink her fingers into the thick black hair and thrill to the power of feline muscles rippling under her fingertips. *Lions kill,* she reminded herself. "It's my job."

"I know." Deo took a step closer, wondering what it would take to stir that fire in Nita's warily shuttered gaze again. Unused to women hiding their desire, she found the situation challenging. "How late are you working?"

Confused, almost certain she could feel heat pouring off Deo's body, Nita said, "What? Why?"

"I'd like to take you out to dinner tonight."

"No."

"Why not?" Deo grinned, but she didn't feel her usual confident self. Nita confused her. She couldn't get a read on her—one second Nita looked at her as if she wanted to put her hands all over her, and in the next instant, her expression vacillated between fear and fury. Deo never chased after women, because she didn't want to spend time with anyone who wasn't interested in exactly what she was interested in—pleasant company and shared pleasure. Women came to *her* for that and that was the way she liked it. So why the hell had she just asked Nita out for a…date?

Nita considered making an excuse, but then realized that she wasn't the one pushing the issue. She had already told Deo the night before that she wasn't interested, regardless of how her traitorous body might respond, and she didn't appreciate being forced to do it again. "You're not my type."

"You don't know that."

"Yes, I do."

"Why?" Deo snapped. "Because I'm a construction worker? Or because I don't have a college education?"

"No," Nita said, trying unsuccessfully to curb her anger. She pressed her fingertip to the side of Deo's neck. "Because you've got a lovely bite from whoever you took home last night. If you happen to remember."

"I just asked you to dinner, not to go to bed with me."

"When's the last time you had dinner with a woman you didn't take to bed?"

Deo hesitated.

"That's what I thought. Like I said, I'm not interested."

Deo caught Nita's hand as she started to turn away. "That's not what your eyes tell me."

"You're mistaken."

"No I'm not," Deo whispered, rubbing her thumb over the top of Nita's hand. Reluctantly, she loosened her grip and Nita snatched her hand away. "Sooner or later, you're going to admit that."

"That is never going to happen."

"I'm going to change your mi—"

Nita stepped into her office and closed the door, cutting off the last of Deo's sentence. She leaned her back against the solid oak, grateful for the barrier between them. Deo's hand had been hot, her thumb a delicate tease as it swept back and forth over her skin. That brief caress had touched off an unwanted but undeniably pleasant spark within her. Apparently she was helpless to resist not just Deo's beauty, but her touch. That was a terribly dangerous combination, and she had no intention of tempting herself any further. Not when she wanted very much to give in.

Chapter Seven

"Thanks, Nita," Pia said, lingering in the hall outside the procedure room.

"No problem." Nita smiled at Pia, but her gaze followed Deo and Joey as they disappeared through the door into the reception area. "He's really a sweetie."

"He's the baby and everyone spoiled him. Sometimes he still thinks all it takes is a smile, and most of the time he's right."

"I imagine he's going to break a few hearts," Nita murmured, but she wasn't thinking of Joey. His wasn't the only smile that was irresistible. When she'd returned to the procedure room to discuss Joey's physical therapy regimen with Pia, she'd been aware of Deo's eyes on her the entire time. Part of her, the mindless id that ruled her body and some irrational part of her mind, reveled in the attention even as she chastised herself for responding. "Your family is captivating."

Pia's eyes widened in surprise. "I've got a couple of other brothers besides Joey who are still single if that's your inclination."

"Afraid not," Nita said with a laugh. "Although if a beautiful face was my only criterion, I could be tempted."

"Well, if it's a beautiful face you want, Deo—"

"Deo's gorgeous," Nita said before she could catch back the words. She felt her face warm and added quickly, "But I'm sure she's got a line outside her door already."

"Not as long as you might think," Pia said seriously.

"I'm not actually looking for anyone," Nita said, hoping to derail the uncomfortable conversation.

"Left a girl back home? Providence, right?"

"Nope." Nita struggled not to hear Sylvia's laughter or see her taunting smile. Struggled and failed. *Come on, honey, you know you want me. Why are you fighting me?* "I'm just getting settled into this job and I'll be starting the house renovations soon. Not much time for socializing."

"Once in a while a girl has to have company." Pia squeezed Nita's arm. "It's good for the disposition."

Nita laughed. "Thanks. I'll remember that."

With a secret sigh of relief, Nita waved to Pia and returned to her patients. If she wanted company, it would not be for a casual night in bed with a woman who wouldn't remember her name a week later.

❖

"I'll be right back, sweetie," Tory said, leaning down to kiss Bri on the cheek.

"Okay," Bri said hoarsely, her eyes dry and hot.

Tory ached to scoop her into her arms and cradle her, but as Bri had proven when Reese had been missing, she was strong and brave. And Caroline, who hadn't let go of Bri's hand for the last three hours, would provide all the comfort and support Bri needed.

"You want something? Coffee? Coke?"

Bri shook her head.

"Coke," Caroline said immediately, countering Bri's response. "And some kind of sandwich."

"I'm not hungry," Bri insisted.

"I know you're not, baby," Caroline said, caressing Bri's cheek. "But you haven't eaten anything all day. Don't argue."

Bri leaned her head against Caroline's shoulder and shut her eyes.

"I'll get you both something," Tory said.

Not wanting to be gone too long lest she miss the cardiologist when he came out to report on Nelson's status, she hurried to the elevators. Once in the main lobby, she crossed quickly to the exit and scanned the circular drive that fronted the emergency entrance where Reese had parked her patrol car. Reese leaned against the front of the car, talking on her cell phone.

Tory waited. Watching her while she talked was no hardship. She had always loved to look at her. All too often the demands of daily living prevented them from eating dinner together or even going to sleep at the same time, but she had never been able to look at Reese without being grateful and just a little bit amazed to have her in her life. She never felt it more acutely than now, after Reese had returned from duty overseas.

Reese hung up the phone and held out her hand to Tory. "Any word?"

"Not yet." Tory pulled Reese's arm around her and leaned into her for a quick kiss. Then she stepped back, mindful of emergency personnel coming and going through the ambulance bay doors. "It shouldn't be long now. Is everything all right at the station?"

"Allie and Smith have things under control." Reese hooked one hand around her gun belt. Her face was grim. "Is Nelson going to make it?"

"I don't know," Tory admitted. "He wouldn't have any chance at all if you hadn't been there. If you hadn't—"

"Damn it, Tory. This must have been coming on for a while. He's been complaining of stomach problems for months and I never gave it a thought. He wasn't having indigestion, he was having chest pain."

"Reese, you're not a doctor. I see him practically as much as you do and I never paid any attention either."

Reese's jaw clenched and she looked away. She appreciated Tory trying to make her feel better, but she couldn't help thinking that she was partly responsible. She'd been preoccupied ever since the war started, knowing that she'd be called up to serve in Iraq. And since she'd been back, she'd lost her focus and couldn't concentrate. She saw Nelson every single day, and she should have known something was wrong.

"Nelson could have said something," Tory said gently. "I'm not blaming him, but it's certainly not your fault. You saved his life."

"If he's able to come back to work, how long do you think it will be?"

"God." Tory brushed a hand through her hair, frustrated by Reese's stubborn insistence on taking responsibility for things that couldn't possibly be her fault. "At least six weeks, possibly more. Once he's stabilized, the cardiologist will need to evaluate the extent of the cardiac damage."

"I've talked to the mayor and the district commander. I'll be acting chief until Nelson comes back to work."

Tory took a slow breath. "Of course." She chose her next words as carefully as she could. "Are you okay with that?"

Reese shrugged and smiled ruefully. "Paperwork. I hate it. I'd rather be in a patrol car, but there's no one else with the experience to do it and bringing in someone new would disrupt the entire department during the busiest time of the year. It's my responsibility. I'm fine."

It wasn't the boredom of administrative work that concerned Tory. Reese would be in a command position—not that she wasn't already, every day of her working life. But this would be slightly different, and she couldn't imagine Reese being content sitting behind a desk. What it meant, she imagined, was that Reese would simply be doing two jobs when she was barely recovered enough to do one.

"I know you're the only one for the job." Tory skimmed her fingertips across the ridge of Reese's collarbone. The irregularity from the healing fracture was still palpable. "You're not quite a hundred percent yet, darling. You'll be careful, won't you?"

"Sure," Reese said automatically. "We should get back upstairs, don't you think?"

"Yes," Tory said with a sigh, aware that Reese was naturally most comfortable *doing* something. Anything. Now more than ever, Reese used work as a panacea, or an escape. And once again, it wasn't the time to deal with it. Certainly not today, not when Nelson was fighting for his life. "We should get back."

When Reese took her hand, Tory laced her fingers through Reese's, grateful for the brief connection. It wasn't enough, but it was everything.

❖

Bri jumped up when the cardiologist, still wearing rumpled scrubs, walked into the family waiting room. Other than the four of them—Reese, Tory, Bri, and Carre—only one elderly man occupied the space, sitting off in one corner with a distant expression on his face.

Caroline scooted her arm around Bri's waist and Tory slid close to her other side. Reese stood a few feet away, her expression impassive and her body emanating tightly coiled energy.

"Dr. King," the cardiologist said, looking from Tory to Bri and then back to Tory. "Sheriff Parker is stable. We stented both the anterior descending and the left main."

"That's great," Tory said.

Bri's legs started to shake and she gripped Carre's shoulders tightly, embarrassed to let anyone see how scared she was. She swallowed before speaking. Her throat felt so dry she was afraid her voice would crack. "Does that mean he's going to be okay?"

"The most important thing right now," the cardiologist said kindly, "is that the blockage has been relieved and his heart muscle is getting the oxygen it needs to heal."

"Does that mean you don't know if he's going to be okay?" Bri persisted.

The cardiologist shot a glance at Tory, who said, "Go ahead, Steve, you don't need to soft-pedal it."

"The first twenty-four hours following a myocardial incident are tricky," Steve Olson said. "The heart muscle is irritable because it's been damaged, so arrhythmias—that's an irregular heartbeat—are common, and can be dangerous. Your father's being monitored carefully and we're giving him medication to control cardiac irritability. This time tomorrow, I'll be able to give you a much better assessment."

"When can I see him?"

"The nurses have a few things to do and then you can visit. He's sedated and won't be responsive."

"Okay. I understand," Bri said. "Thanks."

When the cardiologist turned to Tory and began explaining something Bri couldn't understand, Bri whispered to Carre, "I need to talk to Reese."

"Okay, baby." Carre kissed her cheek and let her go.

Bri joined Reese. "I want to thank you for what you did today, for my dad."

"No need," Reese said gently.

"I'm sorry I didn't handle it so well. I—"

Reese shook her head, slung an arm around Bri's slender frame, and pulled her close. She cupped the back of her head as Bri trembled against her. "It's okay. You did fine. I'm proud of you."

Bri's eyes stung and she blinked back tears. It wasn't that she was ashamed to cry in front of Reese. Hell, Reese had seen her when she was messed up and pissed off at everybody. Crying wasn't so bad, although she'd rather only Carre knew that she did it sometimes. Just now, though, she wanted to be as together as Reese was when things got tough. She wanted to be the one everyone believed in. She raised her head and grinned a little crookedly. "I forgot my training."

"Understandable," Reese said gruffly. She loosened her hold and let Bri ease away. "That's the reason there's a chain of command, Bri. It takes practice. Your time will come."

"I want to be ready."

Reese skimmed her knuckles along the edge of Bri's jaw. "You will be."

❖

From across the room, Tory recognized Bri's look of hero worship and was both warmed and worried by it. She knew that Bri could have no better role model than Reese, but she was just coming to understand what a burden that must be for Reese. Not just with Bri, but with the other officers in the department and the young marines she had commanded. What was it like living up to that kind of faith while you were trying to keep death away?

Thinking of the tremendous responsibility of making life and death decisions while faced with the imminent possibility of annihilation, she was reminded of KT and the swaggering self-confidence she always displayed in the trauma unit. When they'd been together, she had allowed herself to forget that KT was not invulnerable or invincible, but rather a woman who suffered every death that she could not prevent and agonized over every decision that might have been made differently.

Tory knew some of that soul-shattering responsibility herself when she made decisions, as she had earlier that day regarding Nelson's treatment. Usually, though, she had a moment or two to collect her thoughts and weigh pros and cons, unlike a soldier in battle or a surgeon faced with exsanguinating hemorrhage. KT had relieved the inexorable stress by reaffirming her prowess in the arms of other women. Reese would never devastate her that way, but Tory did not intend to let her destroy herself, either.

"Sweetheart," Tory said quietly to Reese. "I'm going to stay here for a few more hours. Do you need to get back?"

Reese waited until Bri rejoined Caroline. "I should check in at the station. I need to rearrange the shifts and get some idea of what Nelson had pending." She looked over at Bri. "One of us should be here in case there's a problem, don't you think?"

"I don't want her to be alone if anything should happen," Tory agreed.

"Then I'll come back up tonight in the Jeep and you can take it home. I'll get an officer to take me back in the morning."

"I may stay the night. Call me later and I'll let you know if you should come back out tonight."

Reese frowned and stroked Tory's arm. "You sure you'll be okay? You look beat."

Tory covered Reese's hand with hers. "I'm all right. Tell Reggie I said hi when you see her."

"I will. I'll be back soon." Reese kissed her quickly. "I love you."

"I love you. Be careful."

As soon as Reese disappeared, Tory immediately felt uneasy. It wasn't just that she missed her, which she did, but whenever Reese was out of sight, she was plagued by a pervasive expectation of danger. At moments like this she was forced to admit that Reese's tour of duty in Iraq had made casualties of them both.

❖

"So what do you think of the Doc?"

Deo's eyes narrowed as she regarded her cousin over her beer. "Looks like she did a good job on your hand."

The Squealing Pig was packed as it was every night, but they'd managed to snag a table in the corner near the wide front windows. People brushed against the glass as they passed by on Commercial Street and sounds of the melee outside added to the general din of people crowded around the bar and jostling at tables inside. Considering it was a holiday, Deo had told her crews to knock off early, and she and Joey had come into town for a burger.

"I'm not talking about her medical skills," Joey scoffed, waving to a local who came through the door. "I was thinking of asking her out."

"Come on," Deo said dismissively, hoping to hide her concern. "She's got to have at least ten years on you."

Joey grinned. "You know what they say about older women. I ought to have the stuff to keep up with her."

Deo wanted to smack him and he wasn't even out of line. It's not like they hadn't talked about girls before. She tried to keep it decent, not only because he was her cousin, but because she didn't want him to think that women meant nothing to her. Joey, for his part, was a lot more respectful than most of the guys. Still, hearing him talk about Nita as if she were a potential sex partner made her crazy. She leaned across the table into his face. "She's a lesbian, you nitwit. Forget it."

"So? Maybe she likes tuna on Friday and steak on Saturday."

Deo swatted him in the head. "Asshole."

"Still, you don't know right?" Joey persisted teasingly. "Unless maybe you've already been there?"

"No," Deo grated.

"How come? Did she turn you down?"

Deo clenched her jaws.

"Ho ho!" Joey crowed. "You mean there's finally one woman in town who can resist you?" He punched her arm. "You must be slipping, babe."

"Knock it off," Deo snapped.

Joey's face fell. "Hey. I didn't mean anything by it."

Deo let her breath out slowly and tried to rein in her temper. Jesus, what the hell was the matter with her. Joey was a good kid, and he hadn't said or done anything he hadn't said or done a hundred times before. So Nita obviously thought she was callous and shallow and only interested in a quick lay. So what. Nita wasn't the first person to think she was a fuck-off. Her own parents thought the same thing and worse, and she'd learned to live with that. Yeah, it still hurt, but she kept that to herself.

"Forget it." Deo sipped her beer and feigned interest in the activity outside.

Joey stretched his legs out beside the table and smiled with satisfaction. "So you don't mind if I find out for myself if she's interested in some prime salam—"

"Joey," Deo growled.

Laughing, Joey tilted back in his chair. "She's got you bugged, doesn't she?"

"I never said that," Deo said, but she knew she didn't have to. She *was* bugged. Nita was a beautiful, intelligent, sexy woman who thought Deo wasn't worth the time of day. And for the first time in longer than she could remember, Deo was unhappy with that perception. Sure, it was hard to disappoint anyone or be hurt by them when she asked for nothing and nothing was expected of her. It was also lonely.

"Well, good luck, Cuz," Joey said good-naturedly.

It would take more than luck, Deo knew, and she wasn't certain that she wanted to take the risk. Still, something about Nita almost made her want to try.

CHAPTER EIGHT

Hey," Deo said, working her way through the crowd up to Allie, who stood at the juncture of Standish and Commercial Streets, the busiest intersection in town. "What are you still doing at work? You had the day shift."

"Pulling a double," Allie said, watching an SUV edge its way through the pedestrian-filled street that more resembled a wide sidewalk at nine-thirty at night. She diverted her attention long enough to give Deo an appreciative once over. "You're looking good."

Grinning, Deo returned the look. "I think I might like you in the silky stuff a little better than the leather, but it works."

"You'd be surprised how many girls want me because of the uniform."

"Oh, I'm sure it's not just the uniform," Deo said with a laugh. "Was everything okay this morning? With you being late, I mean?"

Allie grimaced, remembering the chaos that just half a day later seemed a little bit unreal. Bri trembling in her arms was no fantasy, however. Signaling a line of cars to wait, she waved a group of shirtless men in skin-tight trunks that looked suspiciously like underwear across the intersection. "Right after I got in this morning, Chief Parker collapsed—heart attack. He's in the hospital up at Hyannis."

"Oh, man. That's terrible. Is he going to be okay?"

"Nobody's saying very much." Allie sighed and gestured for the cars to move on. "Reese is there now. I'm going up after my shift."

"Tonight? Jesus, you didn't sleep at all last night. You must be beat."

"And whose fault is that?" Allie teased. "I'm okay, plus we're shorthanded. I don't know when else I'll have time. I'm due on shift again tomorrow at ten."

"Well, since I'm the one who kept you awake, the least I can do is drive you up there and back tonight. That way you can sleep while I drive."

Surprised, Allie briefly clasped Deo's hand. "That's sweet. Really. But you don't need to. Last night was totally worth being wiped out today."

"Look, I'd like to. I'm just going to be hanging around at home anyhow."

"No company tonight?" Allie's tone made it clear she wasn't being critical.

"Let's just say I don't have the need." Deo dropped her voice. "Last night took care of that for quite a while."

Allie gave Deo a heated look. "God, you're good."

"I think you mentioned that." When Allie laughed, some of Deo's earlier melancholy evaporated. With Allie, she knew that what she offered was enough, and even if they never slept together again, what they'd shared was still special. "I'll drive you up and wait for you. You take as long as you want. I'll feel better, and the roads will probably be safer if you're not driving half asleep."

"You sure?"

"Yeah. Really."

"Pick me up at the station at eleven, then."

"I'll be there."

"And Deo," Allie said, causing Deo to halt as she started to turn away. "We're cool if it's just a *ride* ride, right?"

"Yeah, totally." Deo winked. "For tonight at least."

Then Deo slipped off into the crowd to the sound of Allie's laughter. As she walked the mile and a half toward her condo at the far west end of Bradford, she reflected on her night with Allie and smiled. Now and then she hooked up with a woman for a few weeks, but more often than not, one or two nights was the norm. She had a feeling with Allie there could be more. Allie seemed to be up for a friendly relationship that involved good sex, and they for sure had the good sex part down. But for some reason, she was okay if the only thing she and Allie ever shared again was friendship. She liked sex, sure, and the connection she felt for those few brief hours when she made love to a woman quieted some dark, angry place inside her. For a little while, she didn't feel alone. But Allie wasn't one of the strangers in town for a week who she could fuck and forget. Allie was a woman she liked, who she was going to run into regularly. Most importantly, she might be a friend. Joey and Pia were about her only friends, and they were family. Maybe sleeping with Allie again would screw up a chance for anything else.

"Jesus," Deo muttered, her hands in her pockets as she strode more quickly along the less congested streets in the West End. "Since when did you worry about whether you're going to sleep with a woman or not?"

And just that fast, she was back in the hallway outside Nita Burgoyne's office feeling angry and baffled as to why Nita wouldn't even accept an invitation to dinner when the look in her eyes said she was interested. In fact, for a few seconds Nita's expression had said she was much more than interested. Just remembering the fiery gaze made Deo flush with heat and shiver with the familiar churning in the pit of her stomach.

Nita had said no—not once, but twice—and that ought to be enough. If Deo needed a few hours with a woman to settle her inner unrest, Allie was most likely willing and if not her, someone else. So why did she want the one who didn't want her?

"Because," Deo whispered, "because I know she's lying."

Nita Burgoyne had said no, but her eyes had betrayed her. No matter what else was going on, Nita was interested. Deo didn't know why Nita refused to acknowledge that, but it was a challenge she couldn't let go of.

❖

When Deo and Allie walked into the crowded intensive care waiting room just after midnight, Bri's face lit up at the sight of Allie. With Caroline in tow, she hurried to meet them. "What are you doing here?"

"Just wanted to see how you were doing." Allie gave Bri a quick hug and smiled almost shyly at Caroline "Hi."

Caroline returned the smile, resting her hand in the center of Bri's back. "I'm glad you came."

"Hey, Deo," Bri said.

"Sorry about your dad." Deo noticed that Bri's eyes were red-rimmed but clear. "How's he doing?"

"The nurses say everything looks good tonight," Bri replied.

When several officers who Deo recognized as members of the Sheriff's Department approached, Deo stepped back while Allie talked to them. Scanning the faces of the others gathered around, she saw Reese and Tory, Reese's mother and her partner, and a couple of other law enforcement officers. With a jolt, her eyes met Nita's. When she nodded, Nita tipped her head briefly in acknowledgment before looking away. Clearly having been dismissed, Deo leaned against the wall and watched Nita. As she had at the party, Nita appeared apart from the others. Not awkwardly or uncomfortably alone, Deo realized, but alone by choice. The circumstance was so different than Deo's own isolation that she couldn't help but be filled with questions. Questions and curiosity and an involuntary surge of sympathy. Alone was alone, and even if by choice, sometimes it spelled loneliness.

Driven by an appreciation for their shared discomfort, Deo sidled through the people who stood talking quietly in pairs or small groups until she reached Nita.

"Long day," Deo said.

"I was just leaving." Nita picked up a leather bag and slung it over her shoulder.

"Stay for a minute."

Nita blinked. "Why?"

"I like your company."

"How much have you had to drink?" Nita asked sharply.

"Two beers, six hours ago."

"Then you have me confused with someone else." Nita stepped sideways and Deo lightly grasped her arm. "What?"

"I don't want to have to chase you down the hall again. It's bad for my ego."

"I don't imagine anything puts a dent in your ego."

Nita's voice held an edge, but the barest glimmer of a smile showed for an instant and then disappeared. It was the first crack in her façade that Deo had seen, and encouraged, she leaned closer and lowered her voice. "Having you turn me down two days in a row hasn't been so good for it."

"It's in very poor taste to make overtures to a woman with your girlfriend standing a few feet away."

"My girlfriend?" Deo said, honestly confused. She followed Nita's gaze to where Allie huddled with Reese and Bri and the other officers. "She's a friend."

Nita sighed. "There's no need to explain, although considering you disappeared with her last night after the party, I'd say your definition of *friend* and mine are slightly different."

"The way I see it, we're just talking."

"Really? You weren't going to renew your invitation for *dinner*? My mistake again, then."

Deo did some fast thinking. She *had* been about to try again, and because she didn't think of her relationship with Allie as anything that would prevent her from doing so, she hadn't considered how it might look to Nita. Hell, when had she ever considered how anything might look to a woman she was interested in? "Jesus, you're confusing as all hell."

"Look," Nita began in a reasonable voice, determined to control a potentially uncomfortable situation that showed no signs of going away. Admittedly, she'd had a visceral response the instant she'd seen Deo enter the waiting area. Before she could contain herself, she had been both happy and excited to see her. That Deo had been with the pretty young brunette from the night before had helped her gain some perspective. There wasn't much doubt in her mind where the bite on Deo's neck had come from. Like a dash of cold water, the sight of the two of them was a blunt wakeup call and a stark reminder of just why Deo was dangerous. "This is a small town and we have a lot of acquaintances in common. We're going to be running into one another all the time. Why don't we just decide right now that the best thing we can do is have a nice casual friendly association."

"I wasn't proposing marriage."

"I know what you *are* proposing. I'm not in the market."

"And if you were, it wouldn't be with me, right?"

Nita shrugged. "No. It wouldn't be."

"Because I'm not your type." Deo made it a statement, not a question.

"I think I already mentioned that."

"How about a contractor? Are you in the market for a general contractor?"

"Excuse me?" Nita said, thoroughly perplexed by not only

the abrupt change in topic but by the fact that Deo seemed to have capitulated with no argument. And that bothered her. Lord, she must be sending out mixed signals because she certainly felt mixed up. She didn't want the woman's attention but it upset her when Deo simply gave up pursuing her as if it were of no further consequence. She hadn't realized how vulnerable she was to any kind of attention from a woman. It had been a long time. Obviously, she needed a date—with someone non-threatening and low-key and normal. Someone whose attention would be pleasant but not distracting, someone with whom she could share something enjoyable but not consuming. Not someone like Deo whose mere presence stirred her up. Not someone like Deo—like Sylvia—who would occupy her mind twenty-four hours a day and keep her body in a state of constant arousal.

"You bought the Captain's house," Deo said, again stating fact. "If you plan on living in it, it's going to take some serious work."

"How do you know about my house?"

"It's my business to know what's happening with the properties in town."

Nita shook her head. "Small-town living will take some getting used to. Yes, I bought it, but I haven't made any decisions yet about what I'm going to do with it or who is going to do it." What she didn't add was that whoever she hired, it certainly would not be Deo Camara. The last thing she wanted was to see her on a daily basis for weeks.

"Rehabbing historic structures is my specialty," Deo said, serious now. "You're going to get the best prices if you go local, and I'm the best there is on the Cape. You'll at least want a bid from me."

"Lord, you really are too much." Nita remembered Pia mentioning the township's regulations regarding what could and couldn't be done to historic buildings and realized she would be better off using a local builder. It was late, she was tired, and she didn't want to argue. In fact, Deo made sense. Compromise. Compromise was something she'd always been good at. "Why don't you send Joey around to look the place over. I'm closing on Friday afternoon and I'll have the keys after that."

"Joey's not experienced enough." Deo grinned. "Besides, he's competition."

"I'm sorry?"

"He wants to ask you out."

Nita gaped. "Joey? My God, he's just a boy."

"He's eighteen," Deo said with a straight face, enjoying seeing Nita off balance.

"He's also a patient."

"He won't be forever."

"Don't be ridiculous," Nita snapped. "You know I'm a lesbian."

Deo lifted a shoulder. "Can't prove it by personal experience."

"And you never will." Exasperated and recalling what Pia had said about their family enterprises, Nita said, "Then send one of your brothers to do the estimate. You must have half a dozen working with you."

Deo jerked as if Nita had slapped her. Beneath her tan, Deo's bronze skin paled and a world of hurt flashed across her face. For a fraction of a second, Nita actually thought she might faint. Without giving it a thought, driven only by her instinct to comfort, she grasped Deo's hand. "What is it?" The fingers lying motionless in her palm were cold and trembling. "Deo?"

"Sorry," Deo rasped, jerking her hand free. "No, no brothers."

"I'm sor—"

"No problem." Deo backed away a step. "Sorry to bother you."

"Deo…" Nita called quietly, but Deo had already spun away. She felt terrible for bringing up something that was obviously still painful. She didn't mind clashing with Deo's arrogance or misplaced sense of entitlement where women were concerned, but she would never have willingly hurt her. "Damn it."

"Everything all right?" Tory asked.

Nita gave a start, then flushed, wondering how much of the encounter Tory had witnessed. She'd always been a private person, and the terrible public humiliation of her relationship with Sylvia had solidified her desire to avoid any kind of display of her personal business. "Yes. Everything's fine."

"Oh, okay. I just thought Deo…never mind."

"I…I unwittingly said something to upset her." She should simply let the matter drop, Nita knew that. But the agony in Deo's eyes had been so deep, so raw, she still ached from having seen it. "I asked her about having brothers."

"I see." Tory sighed. "Her twin brother Gabriel was killed in a boating accident when they were teenagers."

"Oh," Nita murmured, "that's horrible."

"I know," Tory said. "I hadn't been in town very long, but something like that in a community like this affects everyone. I can still remember Nelson calling me down to the harbor. It was the middle of the night, and it was pointless to transport Gabriel anywhere. We tried to resuscitate him right there on the beach...God, we worked on him for almost two hours, and we just couldn't get him back." She shook her head. "I thought Deo was going to lose her mind."

"She was with him?" Nita automatically searched the room, wishing desperately she could find her and say something to ease the pain she had carelessly incited. But Deo was gone, and so was the young officer she'd come in with.

❖

"You don't have to leave," Deo said dully, opening the driver's side door. "I'll just wait in the truck."

Allie climbed in the opposite side and slid as close to Deo as the gear shift would allow. "I need to get back."

"Why don't you try to catch some sleep, then." Deo started the truck and pulled away from the hospital.

"You look pretty bummed out. Are you okay?"

Deo forced a smile. "Yeah. Close your eyes."

Allie gave her a questioning look, but finally gave in and curled up sideways with one hand on Deo's thigh. The small connection felt good, and Deo covered Allie's smaller hand with hers as she drove. Within seconds she could tell from the soft even cadence of Allie's breathing that she was asleep. Route 6 was deserted at one-thirty in the morning, but she was careful of her speed. Allie trusted her, and she wanted to take care of her as she slept.

Forty minutes later she shook Allie's shoulder gently. "How do I get to your house?"

Following Allie's directions, she soon pulled into the narrow drive of a small cottage set on a side street between Wellfleet and Truro. "There you go."

"It's late. Come on inside," Allie said.

"No, you need to sleep." Deo didn't add that she didn't feel like sex. Usually when she was stressed or angry, sex helped. When she was hurt, she mostly wanted to be alone, because being intimate when she was needy made her feel too exposed and uncomfortable.

Without a word, Allie got out of the truck, walked around the front, and pulled Deo's door open. Then she took her hand. "I don't know about you, but I've had a really bad day. I could use some company."

Deo couldn't think of a good reason to say no. She followed her inside the small cottage and into the neat, tidy bedroom at the rear. A double bed sat in one corner, a dresser with a small TV occupied the wall at the foot, and a dressing table with chair filled the far wall.

"Bathroom's across the hall." Allie yawned and unbuckled her gun belt. "You can go first."

On Deo's way back, a naked Allie passed her. She undressed by the side of the bed and climbed naked under the sheets. A few minutes later, Allie crawled in and curled up against her side. Deo put an arm around her and kissed her gently.

"Night," Deo whispered.

Allie drew her leg up over Deo's thigh, murmured something, and fell promptly asleep. Deo listened to the sounds of the unfamiliar house, lightly stroking Allie's shoulder. There were times when she felt like an impostor in her own life, when she couldn't figure out why she was doing what she was doing or why she didn't feel anything when she knew she was supposed to. Allie was warm and soft and Deo knew if she stroked Allie's breast she could wake her, arouse her, and Allie would beg her to make love to her. Her need would become Allie's, and her pain would be transformed into Allie's desire. She could lose herself in Allie's body, in her excitement, in her need, and the places that were numb inside her would fill with Allie's pleasure. If it were any other woman, she wouldn't hesitate, but she couldn't bring herself to use Allie that way.

Allie stirred and kissed Deo's neck. "You okay?"

"Yeah."

"Go to sleep, baby."

"Okay." Deo kissed Allie's forehead and closed her eyes.

Chapter Nine

Time to wake up, baby," Reese murmured as she kissed Tory's cheek.

Tory rolled over on the stiff muddy-brown vinyl couch in the ICU waiting room and grimaced at the cramp in her lower back and the fuzzy headache clouding her brain. "Oh God. I am too old for this." She smiled up at Reese and grasped her hand. "Hi, sweetheart. What time is it?"

"About five-thirty."

"Have you been up all night?" Tory took in Reese's rumpled uniform and the ever darkening circles beneath her eyes. The shadows above her high cheekbones were not new, but it was rare to see Reese in an unpressed uniform. "I thought you were going home to sleep?"

"I stopped by the station and started going through Nelson's inbox." Reese shook her head. "I just started this job and I'm already behind. Any news?"

Tory sat up and skimmed her hands through her hair. Bri and Caroline slept on the adjacent couch, their arms and legs entwined, Bri's face pillowed against Caroline's breast. Even in sleep, Caroline seemed to be sheltering Bri, one hand cupped against the back of her head and her arm circling Bri's waist. Keeping her voice low so as not to awaken them, Tory said, "Our last progress report was around two, and they were having some problems with his blood pressure. The nurses had just started an intravenous drip and promised to let me know if there was any problem."

Reese sat beside Tory and drew her close with an arm around her shoulder. "If everything's okay, I'll take you home. The baby is still with your sister, and Kate will pick her up this morning. You'll be able to get some sleep."

"What about you? Aren't you coming home?"

"I will. As soon as I get the day shift squared away."

Tory wanted to object, but she knew how difficult Reese's task was right now with Bri not working, the Chief absent, and the height of the season upon them. With thirty or forty thousand summer residents plus countless day-trippers crammed into the tiny village, a constant stream of minor accidents, injuries, thefts, bar brawls, and the occasional more serious assault resulted. She stroked Reese's thigh through her khakis. "Promise me you'll try to come home this morning?"

"I'll try."

"I need to go in to the clinic later, too. Nita has been working nonstop all weekend and now this week. I need to pick up the slack."

Reese tilted Tory's face up with a fingertip beneath her chin and studied her. "You can't work if you're exhausted. Close the clinic this afternoon and go in tonight if you have to."

"You're one to talk," Tory protested.

"Baby," Reese said quietly. "I just came back from a tour where I was lucky to get two hours of uninterrupted sleep a night, and even then I was constantly listening for the sound of incoming missiles. Believe me, this is a picnic."

Tory checked to make sure Bri and Caroline were still asleep, then she took both Reese's hands in hers. "I feel like we're constantly moving and I never get a chance to connect with you. And when I do see you, it's never the right time or place to talk about some things."

"What is it?"

"Your father pushed the papers through, right? You're out?"

Reese sighed and Tory's heart plummeted.

"Oh, Reese. You promised you wouldn't re—"

"No, I didn't." Reese freed one hand and caressed Tory's cheek. "I wouldn't do that."

"Then what?"

"I didn't tell you before because I didn't think it made any difference. Officially, I'm on medical leave until September. He's holding the paperwork until then, in case…"

"In case you change your mind? In case you want to go back over there?"

"No—well…" Reese rubbed her forehead, frustrated. "I'm sure that's what *he* thinks. But I didn't have any plans. It's just bureaucratic paperwork and—"

"Then why didn't you tell me?" Tory was glad she had an excuse to speak softly, because she didn't want Reese to hear the tremble in her voice. She was angry and she was hurt, and most of all, she was confused. "You've never kept secrets from me before."

Reese looked stunned. "No! Oh, baby, no." She cradled Tory's face and kissed her. "I didn't think of it that way. Christ, so much has been going on since I got back I just—I'm sorry. I don't know why I didn't think—"

"Okay," Tory said quickly, her anger dissipating at the rising torment in Reese's face. *God, she's so vulnerable right now and I'm not helping.* It frightened her beyond belief that she could be so blind to the fact that Reese was not herself. Reese had been through an experience that would break some people, and yet she refused to even break stride. And despite Reese's insistence that she was all right, Tory knew she wasn't, and she could hardly expect her to behave the way she had before she went away. Wanting to turn back time, wishing that Reese could somehow be miraculously unscathed, was cowardly on her part and incredibly unfair to Reese. "I'm sorry, darling. I know you would never intentionally keep something important from me. It's all right."

"I haven't called him. I haven't done anything, Tor," Reese whispered.

"You said you wouldn't without talking to me." Tory kissed her. "I believe you." She kissed her again. "I'm sorry. I love you. God, I need you so much."

With a muffled groan, Reese pulled her close and buried her face in Tory's hair. "I don't want to hurt you."

"Never. Never," Tory said firmly, caressing the back of Reese's neck. When Reese shuddered, Tory shifted until she was holding Reese. Stroking Reese's shoulders and back, she murmured, "You need some sleep, darling."

Across the room, Bri stirred and sat up. "Did something happen?" She blinked, stared at Reese and Tory for a second, and then looked away. "Sorry."

Reese straightened and rubbed her face. "Hey. Tory's going to check on your dad, and if everything is okay, I'm going to take her home."

"I should get Caroline home too," Bri said as Caroline sat up, murmuring sleepily.

Tory gave an exasperated snort. "If Nelson is stable, everyone is going home." She pointed at Bri. "No arguing. You can't stay here the entire time he's in the hospital. *Everyone* needs to take a break."

Caroline put her hand on Bri's knee. "She's right, baby."

Bri's shoulders relaxed and she leaned against Caroline. "Okay. But I want to see him first."

Tory crossed the room and took her hand. "Come on. Let's go talk to the nurses." She glanced back over her shoulder at Reese. "If you really love me, you'll find coffee."

When Reese stood, an amused grin lifting one corner of her mouth, Tory knew she would do anything in the world to keep her smiling that way. As she threaded her arm around Bri's slender waist, she considered that perhaps love was as simple as the desire to make another person smile.

❖

Deo rolled over to an empty bed and the tantalizing smell of coffee. Her eyes felt gritty beneath her closed lids. Two nights of very little sleep had caught up with her. A subtle shifting of the bed signaled that she was not alone, and she opened her eyes. Allie, naked and smiling, held out a mug of coffee.

"Hi," Allie said before leaning down to kiss her.

It was a good morning kiss, a hello kiss—a nice kiss. Deo pushed up in bed and took the coffee. "What time is it?"

"Almost eight."

Deo winced.

"Late for work?"

"Yeah." She took several healthy swallows of the strong black brew and set the mug aside on the nearby bedside table. "Good thing I'm the boss."

Allie pulled one leg up onto the bed and edged closer until her thigh rested along Deo's. Then she skimmed her palm over Deo's stomach. "Sorry. I don't have to be in until ten so I didn't set the alarm."

"It's only fair. I made you late yesterday." Deo trapped Allie's hand against her middle. She always woke up just a little bit horny and the double whammy of Allie naked and touching her was a lethal combination. Pleasantly lethal, but still a test of her self-control she doubted she would win for long. "How's Chief Parker?"

"How did you know I checked already?"

"You're up. You wouldn't have gone out there in the middle of the night if he didn't mean a lot to you."

"I talked to Bri a few minutes ago. He's not awake yet but he's doing okay."

"That's great." Deo noted the turmoil in Allie's eyes. "You're tight with Bri, aren't you?"

"Bri. Yeah. She's special." Allie laughed shortly. "I guess I have a thing for falling in love with the wrong girls."

Deo stroked Allie's forearm and Allie's hand started moving on her stomach again. "That's tough."

"No. It's okay. I'm only halfway in love with her now." Allie scratched her nails down the center of Deo's stomach and laughed when Deo jerked. "But I'm still a *lot* in lust with her. Kind of like with you."

Allie was beautiful and sexy and Deo was getting harder and wetter by the second. She was losing track of the conversation but she heard the word *love* loud and clear. "With me? You're talking about the lust part, I hope."

"What do you think?" Allie leaned forward and nipped at Deo's lower lip before slipping her tongue into her mouth.

Groaning, Deo grasped Allie's waist and pulled her over until Allie was stretched out on top of her. Allie's thigh rubbed between her legs, producing nearly unbearable friction along the length of her already pounding clit. She slid both hands up and squeezed Allie's breasts. Allie whimpered and sucked on Deo's tongue. They kissed and ground against one another until Deo was on the verge of coming against Allie's leg. Then she dragged Allie further up the bed and captured a nipple in her mouth.

"Oh baby, yeah," Allie moaned, half sitting up as she spread her legs on either side of Deo's stomach.

When Allie rocked her center against Deo's skin, her wet heat scorched Deo's brain and Deo's only thought was to be inside her. She brushed her fingertips over Allie's clit and another flood coated her belly.

"I'm really close," Allie warned, her hips twitching. "Do you want me to come?"

"I want to fuck you."

"Then do it now." Allie gasped and covered Deo's hand, pressing Deo's fingers harder into her sex. "Uh. Good."

Deo rolled Allie over onto her back. Kneeling above her with one hand braced against the mattress, Deo brushed the other hand between Allie's legs and into her. "You're going to be late for work again."

Allie's eyes widened and she arched her back, forcing Deo deeper. "No I'm not," she panted. "You're going to make me come in about five minutes."

Deo shook her head, thrusting hard and fast. "No," she grunted, "two."

"Ohhh," Allie cried, surprise and pleasure playing across her face. "That's the way… oh God, that's… you'll make me…"

"You're so hot inside," Deo groaned as Allie tightened around her. She forgot to breathe and her head went light. Spots danced before her eyes and the roar of the ocean filled her consciousness. Arousal roiled through her like storm clouds in a summer sky, and she thought that if Allie didn't come soon her heart would explode from anticipation. She leaned down and plunged her tongue into Allie's mouth, riding her thumb over Allie's clit as she fucked her faster.

With a muffled cry, Allie bucked and came beneath her, and like lightning exploding from heaven and streaking to earth, the pressure in Deo's belly powered through her and disappeared. She just managed not to fall on top of Allie as she collapsed by her side.

"God, that was good," Deo murmured, her fingers gently slipping out.

"That's," Allie panted, "my line."

"Glad you agree."

Allie slapped Deo's stomach. "Like you couldn't tell. What did it take, about three strokes to make me pop? I can't believe how fast you wind me up."

"*I* wind *you* up?" Feeling lazy and content, Deo slowly turned her head and kissed the corner of Allie's mouth. "You're the one who showed up naked bearing gifts."

"I was trying to be a good hostess."

Deo laughed. "Man, I bet you're popular with the overnight guests."

"I think I should probably be insulted," Allie mused, leaning up on an elbow and casually toying with Deo's nipple. When it hardened, she leaned down and dragged her teeth over it. She smiled when Deo gasped. "But you already know I think you're hot. And I love the way you fuck me."

"If you don't want me to do it again," Deo said darkly, "get your ass out of this bed."

"Who said I don't want you to do it again?" Allie purred. She kissed Deo's nipple sweetly and drew back, her expression growing serious. "I've got a few minutes. Let me make you come."

"I'm good." Deo kissed Allie lightly. "Really. Good."

"Sure?"

Deo nodded.

"Rain check, then."

"Deal," Deo agreed as Allie jumped from bed.

"I'll be ready in ten minutes," Allie called as she disappeared across the hall into the bathroom.

Deo stretched, figuring she had a few minutes to spare while Allie showered. Then she'd drive Allie to the station, grab a fast shower at home, and head over to the main job site. The guys knew what to do so she wasn't worried about work not getting done just because she was a couple of hours late. Thinking about the job brought back her conversation the night before with Nita about her new house.

Nita. Nita was like the thunderclouds that had fascinated her since she was a child, seething with anger and passion and beauty. She had been mesmerized by storms, by the combination of danger and unbearable splendor. She had never wanted to come in off the boat no matter how much it rocked in the wind or how high the seas that lashed over the decks had risen. The fear was thrilling and exciting in a way that nothing else was. She still loved storms. Nita was the first woman she had ever met who hinted at the same power and fury. Thinking about Nita stirred the turmoil in her depths that she had so recently quieted while riding the crest of Allie's pleasure.

She didn't even want to consider that she was fucking one woman to forget about another. With a sigh, Deo pushed back the covers and got up in search of her clothes.

"Something wrong?" Allie asked as she paused in the doorway, toweling her damp hair.

Deo blushed. "No. Just thinking about work."

"Mmm hmm." Allie draped the towel over the back of the wooden chair that sat in front of her dressing table and pulled open the closet door. Extracting a pressed uniform wrapped in plastic, she said, "I'm going to be so busy at work I don't know when I'll see you again. But if you want company…"

"I'll hunt you down like I did last night," Deo said, pulling up her pants. "I'm glad I stayed. Thanks."

Allie grinned crookedly. "I'm absolutely certain I'm the one who should be saying thank you."

Deo shook her head. "No. You're amazing."

"For the record, I feel the same way about you." Allie strapped on her gun belt and regarded Deo seriously. "Sometimes the fact that I can't sleep with Bri and I still want to…it fucks up our friendship. I've been trying to work on that."

Deo waited.

"I hope the two of us can still be friends even though we *did* fuck." Allie sighed. "Jesus, it's really confusing."

"It is, but I know what you mean." Deo kissed her. "We're okay."

"Yeah?"

"Yeah. And for the record, you're fucking hot in that uniform."

Allie wrapped an arm around Deo's waist as they started toward the door. "Well, I'm glad you think so. Because it's the only thing I'm going to be wearing all summer."

CHAPTER TEN

Nita," Tory said, "don't you have an appointment for your walk-through tonight?"

"I rescheduled." Nita set aside the lab report she was reviewing and leaned back in her desk chair. "Are there always this many walk-ins during the summer?"

Tory smiled wearily. "More, usually."

"I can't even begin to imagine how you handled it by yourself."

Tory settled on the small loveseat that Nita had placed in the corner of her office and rested the heel of her sneaker on the edge of a low wooden coffee table. "Before Reese and Regina, I pretty much only worked. I didn't really mind how busy I was then because I didn't have much else in my life."

Nita appreciated what an escape work could be. After the blow-up with Sylvia, she'd worked extra shifts just to avoid seeing her family or friends. Sometime in the year since her life had taken a turn in the wrong direction, she'd come to welcome working fifteen hours a day. She didn't have to think about what a fool she had been. Cowardly, perhaps, but comfortable. Discomfited by the realization, she changed the subject. Something else she had grown adept at when conversations veered too close to harsh truths. "Do you want ice for that ankle?"

"You can tell it's swollen from across the room?"

"I'm not *that* good," Nita said. "But I don't think I've ever seen you sit down before, and I know I've never seen you put your leg up." She glanced at her watch. "You've been on your feet for twelve hours. And that's just today."

"What day is it—Thursday?" Tory shook her head. "The last thing I clearly remember is the ride to Hyannis on Monday morning with Nelson. I haven't lost track of time like this since I was a resident and spent thirty-six hours at a stretch in the hospital."

"Stay there," Nita said as she rose. "I'll get you a cold pack."

Tory leaned back and closed her eyes, grateful not to be moving for just a few minutes. The last time she'd been this exhausted and her leg had acted up so badly that she could barely walk, Reese had been the one to take care of her. Reese had been so matter-of-fact about her injury, so completely without the stifling pity that so many others heaped upon her. She had simply done what needed to be done, and Tory had fallen in love just that quickly.

"Are you awake?" Nita whispered, kneeling down next to Tory.

"Yes, just daydreaming."

"It must have been a nice dream." Nita gently pushed up Tory's jeans and released the Velcro straps on the plastic bivalve splint she wore to stabilize her nerve-damaged ankle. "You had a very happy expression on your face."

Tory laughed. "I was thinking about when I fell in love with Reese. She was doing pretty much what you're doing right now."

Nita glanced up. "Hopefully it was her and not the activity. Because as much as I like you, there's no way I'm taking on Reese Conlon for your affections."

"Don't worry, you're safe," Tory said, appreciating Nita's teasing tone. They so very rarely had the opportunity to talk about anything except work, and it was nice to see a less serious side of her new associate. "I take that to mean that your interest is in women, then? I've never asked."

"Since I was old enough to figure out that I had an interest in anyone." Nita settled next to Tory. "How long have you and Reese been together?"

"A little over five years. I wasn't looking for anyone," Tory mused, "and now I can't imagine life any other way."

"I think that's how it works out when it's right."

Hearing a note of sadness in Nita's voice, Tory said carefully, "No one on the horizon for you at the moment?"

"No," Nita said quickly and dismissively. "Moving here, adjusting to private practice, getting a new house ready to live in…I've got plenty to keep me busy."

"When was your appointment with Elana?"

"Elana? Oh—the realtor. Six. But I knew I wasn't going to make it so I called her to postpone." Nita shrugged. "She said she might still be around for a while, but—"

"It's not that late. You should stop by the real estate office and try to catch her. She's often there in the evening, and you can still do your walk-through."

"We've got at least twelve patients still waiting. I'll stay until we clear—"

"No you won't," Tory said firmly. "I'm going to sit here for five more minutes because the ice is really helping, and then I'll be fine to finish up. I know how much extra work you've been doing all week. And unfortunately, I have another favor to ask."

"Anything."

"I was on the phone with Nelson's cardiologist right before I came in here. In fact that's what I came by to tell you. He's got a fairly substantial aneurysm just distal to the takeoff of the coronaries. They want to operate on him tomorrow."

"Oh God, that's too bad," Nita said. "Of course I'll cover for you. I'm sure we can postpone the closing—"

"Absolutely not. It's scheduled for what...three?"

"Three thirty."

Tory nodded. "Excellent. I'll be back by then. Surgery is scheduled for seven thirty and I'm sure they'll be done by noon. Then I can stay with Bri for a couple of hours after, and I'll still be back here in time to finish up the afternoon hours."

"Are you sure? I know he's like family." Nita hesitated. "And that really matters."

"He is, and Bri is special." Tory laughed. "Sometimes I feel like she's a younger version of Reese, the Reese I never got to meet before the marines really got to her."

"How are you doing?" Nita asked gently. "With Reese home now?"

Tory regarded her curiously. "Most people just assume that her coming home solved everything. Of course, having her here *is* everything."

"I imagine you both feel pulled in a million directions. If Reese is the same kind of marine as all of my family are cops, she probably wants to turn right around and go back."

"God, how did you know?"

"Oh," Nita said with a sigh, "because that's who they are. It's what makes them feel good about themselves. And because they have a very deep sense of loyalty to their fellows. All the things you already know, I'm sure."

"All the things I knew," Tory said hesitantly. "But things I never really appreciated until this happened. She's a little bit at sea right now, and I'm not sure how to help her."

"I'm lousy at advice, but just the same, I've had some experience with this."

"Go ahead."

"It's probably not what you want to hear, but I think if she wants to go back, you need to let her. It may be the only way she can feel whole again."

Tory blinked at the sudden and frightening rush of tears that filled her eyes. "I don't think I can. I don't think I can stand it."

Nita regarded her seriously. "Yes you can. I only had to see you together for a minute to know how much you love her. And that's what love is all about, don't you think? Helping the person you love be who she really is?"

"Even if you lose her?" Tory nearly choked on the words.

"Even then." Nita took Tory's hand. "I'm sorry. I'm not helping."

"No. It's okay. You are." Smiling tremulously, Tory brushed her fingers over her eyes. "It actually helps to talk about what terrifies me. I just can't imagine a day without her. Do you know what I mean?"

"I thought I did, once." Nita rose, her expression carefully blank. "But I was wrong."

Nita took off her lab coat and draped it over her chair. Beneath that she wore a pale yellow short-sleeved blouse, tailored sage cotton slacks, and brown flats. "The nice thing about this town is you can get from one end of it to the other in ten minutes. I'm going to drive by the real estate office and see if anyone's around. And if I can push the closing back even an hour or two tomorrow, I will. Just to give you a little extra time."

"Thanks. And Nita, thanks for the advice too," Tory added softly.

"You're welcome, although I'm not sure how much stock you should put in my opinion." Nita smiled wryly. "I've got a lousy track record with women."

❖

Nita dashed across Bradford in the light rain that had been falling all afternoon and hurried up the three steps to the small porch of Provincetown Realty. Not surprisingly, the door was locked, and when she peered through the large picture window next to the door, the interior was dark. She *was* over an hour late for her six o'clock appointment, and even though she'd gotten the answering machine when she'd called from the clinic, she had taken a chance that someone was working late just the same. Disappointed, she turned away and smothered a small cry when she discovered Deo standing on the steps. Her black sleeveless T-shirt and bleached-to-nearly white jeans were soaked through in patches from the rain, and her hair was even wetter. Her boots were dusty and a long scratch on the outside of her left upper arm appeared fresh. She looked like a woman who'd worked hard all day and, Nita had to admit, the look suited her. She was sexy as hell.

"Something I can help you with?" Deo asked.

"How is it that I've been in town six weeks and until four days ago I'd never seen you before. Now every time I turn around you're there?"

Deo grinned. "Fate?"

"I don't believe in it."

"Lucky coincidence, then, I guess."

Nita stepped back under the sheltering roof as the rain picked up. "You're getting drenched."

Deo tilted her face up to the sky and shook her head like a dog coming in out of the surf. "Feels great. I spent most of the day on a roof. In the middle of July it's about a hundred and ten degrees up there."

"What happened to your arm?"

"Huh?"

Nita frowned and pointed. "You've got a pretty nasty abrasion there."

Deo followed her gaze. "Oh. That. Some idiot didn't bother to pound a nail all the way in."

"When was your last tetanus shot?"

"You're kidding, right?" Deo laughed. "This kind of thing is pretty much business as usual."

"Save me the macho line. That's a setup for infection. I don't suppose you stopped to wash it out, did you?"

Deo pointed to the sky. "God's taking care of that right now."

"More likely St. Jude," Nita muttered.

"You don't like me much, do you?" Deo said amiably, climbing the stairs. She leaned against the post and watched Nita with a half smile.

Nita took a slow breath. "I'm sorry. I don't know you and I've been rude." When she started toward the stairs, Deo sidestepped just enough to block her way. Nita stopped abruptly a breath before their bodies touched. The hairs along her arms stood up as if the air were rarefied. She wondered inanely if Deo was throwing off some kind of an electric charge, because every time she was anywhere near her, her skin tingled. She felt her pulse racing. "That's exactly the sort of thing that annoys me about you."

"What?" Deo asked quietly, leaning closer still.

Deo's mouth was so close to Nita's ear that if Nita turned her head, her lips would brush Deo's cheek. It was all she could do not to move. "You're obviously used to having women fall all over you. You make assumptions that aren't warranted."

"The first time I saw you in the clinic," Deo said, "I looked at you and saw a beautiful woman. I'm sorry I didn't pretend not to notice. That pissed you off, didn't it?"

Surprised at Deo's perceptiveness, Nita nevertheless shook her head. "Believe it or not, that *wasn't* the first time I've ever been cruised."

"I'll bet."

"Let's just say our styles don't mesh and let it go at that."

"So if it wasn't something I *did*," Deo pondered aloud, "then it must be something I make *you* do." Deo grinned and snapped her fingers. "You want me."

Nita snorted and despite herself, she laughed. "God, you are so arrogant!"

"Ah ha. You do laugh." Pleased, Deo pressed her luck. "So, why won't you go out with me?"

Nita rolled her eyes. "We've been through this already. I'm not interested because I already know how the story ends. Women like you aren't interested in making a connection, you're only interested in making a conquest."

Deo's eyes flashed as all traces of humor left her face. "Just what do you base that on? The fact that I'm single and don't hide the fact that I like women?"

Nita flushed. "I apologize. That was absolutely uncalled for. I'm very sorry. I have to go." She tried to sidestep Deo again and, again, Deo moved with her. "Please."

"No you don't." Deo narrowed her eyes. "It's not me at all, is it? It can't be, since you've had your mind made up about me since the minute we met. So who was she?"

"I'm not going to have this conversation with you," Nita said tightly. Deo was far too close to the truth, and not only didn't she want to think about the debacle she'd made of her life, she didn't want Deo to know. She didn't want Deo to know just how susceptible she actually was to Deo's brand of charm. God, how could she be so shallow to want that kind of attention? Why did she crave the intensity of Deo's gaze, why was even Deo's arrogant possessiveness exciting? Why did being anywhere near her make her feel as helpless as a reed bending in the wind. "I don't owe you any explanation. My answer is no—today, tomorrow, and any time thereafter."

"Okay," Deo said mildly. "You don't have to tell me." She jostled the key ring hanging from her belt loop. "I was about to go inside. Do you need something?"

Nita blinked, trying to adjust to the sudden change in topic. Once again, Deo had her off balance. "I don't understand. Do you work here?"

"My office—well, my desk—is inside. I rent some space from my aunt to take care of my billing, store my files, that sort of thing. I don't need much." Deo unhooked her keys. "What do you need?"

"Nothing. I was supposed to do a walk-through on the house tonight because the closing is tomorrow afternoon and I'm not going to be able to get away during the day." She shrugged, frustrated. "But I didn't get away in time today, either."

"So, we'll do it tonight." Deo fit her key into the lock and looked over her shoulder. "Come on inside out of the rain while I find the paperwork."

"Can you do that? I mean—"

Deo grinned. "Elana is my aunt. I stand in for her from time to time. It's no big deal."

"Well, it would help. Are you sure?"

"Yeah." Deo held the door open with one arm and flipped a switch that lit the room with the other. "It'll be fine. And then you won't be pressured tomorrow." Deo leaned against the door, holding it open with her back while she slowly met Nita's eyes. "What do you say? Or are you scared that you might discover you're wrong about me?"

"I'm not the one who's woefully misguided," Nita said sharply as she walked past Deo into the room.

Laughing, Deo followed and let the door swing slowly closed behind her.

CHAPTER ELEVEN

Here," Deo said, handing Nita an industrial flashlight as they stepped into the wide foyer of what once had been a grand mansion standing on a rise above the harbor. The storm had heightened in intensity and precipitated an early dusk. "Watch your step. This house has been uninhabited for thirty years."

Dutifully, Nita clicked on the flashlight and played the harsh white beam over the dark walnut hardwood floors. "It seemed very sound the day I saw it."

"It probably is, but we're going to check out a few places you probably didn't go during the showing." Deo slanted the beam from her light so that the edges bathed Nita's face. In the pale light her skin took on a richer, earthy tone, and her features seemed almost exotic. She was beautiful precisely because her beauty was not conventional. Deo's stomach tightened, but she steadfastly ignored the low-level pulse of arousal. "You can stay down here if you want, and I'll go through by myself."

"I thought this was just a rubber-stamp visit to be sure the roof hadn't suddenly developed a huge hole or something."

"Ordinarily it is, but I'm a certified building inspector and you might as well take advantage of me while you can."

Nita almost laughed. "You are shamelessly relentless. What I don't understand is why you're expending the energy when I'm sure you could find company with no effort at all."

"Maybe I don't like people having unfounded impressions of me."

"People?" Nita tilted her own flashlight and Deo turned her face away, but not before Nita saw the unhappiness in her eyes. "What people?"

Deo grabbed Nita's hand and tugged. "Come on. Let's check out the kitchen."

Recognizing the avoidance ploy because she used it so often herself when there was something she didn't want to discuss, Nita didn't push. Deo was certainly entitled to her privacy, and besides, discussing personal matters wasn't the wisest thing to do when she was trying to keep her distance. Whatever Deo's troubles might be, they weren't her concern.

The wide central hall was divided in the center of the house into two narrower passages by the take off of the central staircase that rose to a second-floor balcony level. As she recalled, the formal living room and dining room were off the right hallway, and the parlor and library were off the left. The large kitchen occupied the entire first floor rear. With only their flashlights to guide them, Nita felt the oppressive atmosphere of the long abandoned house closing in around her. Reflexively, she tightened her grip on Deo's hand. Deo's palm was slightly bumpy—work calluses, she presumed—and very warm. For a fleeting second she imagined how that rough, heated skin would feel chafing over her nipples. The unexpected image and the sharp stab of excitement that shot through her groin made her gasp.

"You okay?" Deo asked.

"Yes," Nita responded sharply, aware that her voice sounded breathy.

"Even though the place has been closed up for years, it doesn't smell damp or moldy," Deo observed, stopping just inside the kitchen. She shone her light over the floor, walls, and ceiling first and then moved on to highlight the wood counters and cabinets. The appliances had all been removed long ago. "No evidence of water damage. That's a good sign. The roof is likely sound and the window casements are probably in good shape."

Nita extracted her hand from Deo's, and immediately the tension in her chest eased. She took a deep breath and chided herself for her mindless response. She had gone far too long without any kind of physical intimacy. That's all it was.

"So what do you think?"

"I'm sorry?" Nita realized Deo had asked her a question while she'd been analyzing her reaction to Deo's touch.

"I was asking whether you wanted to convert the interior to something contemporary or go for a historical restoration."

"If I'd wanted a contemporary house, I would have bought one."

"Well, that makes sense," Deo said, a note of confusion in her voice.

Nita flushed. She was making too much of a brief visceral reaction and allowing it to completely disrupt her control. It was ridiculous. "I want to renovate the house with materials and design that are historically suitable, within reason. I don't intend to walk around the house at night carrying a candle."

Deo laughed. "I think it probably would have been gaslights."

"I consider flush toilets, electricity, central heat and air, telephones, and cable to be essential," Nita said dryly.

"It's going to cost you something to put in the air and bring the electrical system up to today's standards," Deo observed.

"I have considered that." Nita saw no reason to explain that she had money. Her family would take nothing from her now and being single and having gone to medical school on scholarships, she had very little debt. The house was her indulgence.

"I want to check the cellar before we go upstairs," Deo said. "I recommend you wait here."

"To save us repeating this conversation, I'm buying this house and therefore I'm coming with you."

Deo illuminated Nita's face again. "Afraid of spiders?"

Even in the semi-darkness, Nita could make out the mischief in her eyes. She gave Deo a cold stare.

Deo grinned. "Guess not." She reached for Nita's hand once more, and after a second's hesitation, Nita took it. "Stay close, okay? People leave the damnedest things lying around in these empty houses, and who knows what kind of critters might be living down there."

"Charming," Nita muttered, moving closer to Deo in the impenetrable darkness that enclosed her as soon as Deo moved her light away. As she followed, she couldn't help but occasionally brush up against Deo's back. Even if her nipples hadn't tightened at the slightest touch of her breasts against Deo's body, she wouldn't have been able to deny how much she enjoyed the contact. Her blood was practically singing with excitement.

"I don't think anyone's been down here for a while," Deo grunted as she tucked the flashlight under her arm and banged the slide bolt with the heel of her hand. It moved with a rusty groan. After pushing the door open and flooding the stairwell with her bright light, she announced, "All the stairs are here and look like they're in reasonably good shape. Just let me test each one on the way down."

"Maybe we should postpone this until tomorrow," Nita said. "There's no point in taking chances."

Deo pivoted on the top stair, the movement bringing her face very close to Nita's. "Is that what you really believe? Or are you just afraid that you might like it?"

Nita's jaw tightened. "You're in a dangerous position if your intention is to irritate me." She rested her index fingertip lightly in the center of Deo's chest. "It wouldn't take much to knock you down these stairs on your ass."

"I like you when you're angry." Deo let go of Nita's hand and grasped her finger. She lifted it and delicately touched her tongue to the tip. When Nita snatched it away, she laughed. "I don't mind taking risks."

"One more move like that and this inspection is over," Nita said, closing her fist until the tingling in her finger dissipated.

"All right," Deo said softly. "I promise I won't touch you again until you ask me to."

"Then that will be never."

"I do need to hold your hand on these stairs, though," Deo amended and extended her hand.

Nita took it. "As long as you remember it's just business."

"Fair enough."

"And as it happens, I'm *not* wild about spiders," Nita remarked as she followed Deo downstairs. "Feel free to dispense with any webs that come our way."

Laughing, Deo swept her arm over their heads as she walked. "Wait at the bottom of the stairs until I get a good look at what's down here."

Nita had the sense of a large room interrupted at intervals by thick floor-to-ceiling wooden posts. The bright circle of her light illuminated several rough wooden chests overlaid with inches of dust, a chifforobe, several broken chairs, and a rusty oil tank next to an ancient furnace. The floor was hard packed dirt. A faint shimmering illumination at the far end of the room marked Deo's location.

"Anything of interest down there?" Nita called.

"Not much. Looks like someone tried to jack up the—*shit!*"

Nita jumped at the sound of a loud crash. At the same time, Deo's light winked out and a cloud of dust rolled eerily toward her through the beam of light she directed at Deo's location. Quickly, she covered her face and turned away. She felt grit coat the back of her neck and her exposed forearms, but she didn't even consider rushing back upstairs. Something had happened to Deo, and nothing else mattered.

"Deo! Deo, are you hurt?"

At the sound of coughing, the fear squeezing Nita's heart eased.

"Deo?"

"Broke my fucking light," Deo grumbled from somewhere in the darkness.

"Just stand still and keep talking. I'm coming to get you."

"No! There's debris all over the floor."

Ignoring her, Nita started forward, alternating between illuminating the ceiling above her and the floor in front of her. What looked like large chunks of lathe and plaster lay heaped about.

"What happened?" Nita called.

"Someone used a fence post for a strut and it was rotted through. A piece of the underflooring came down. Shine the light at the ceiling and stop walking. God damn it," Deo snapped, "I'll come to you."

Since it made sense for Deo to walk out of darkness toward the light, rather than for her to keep pushing into darkness, Nita did as Deo requested. A minute later Deo, her dark hair and T-shirt white with dust, appeared within the circle of Nita's light. Against the pale powder coating Deo's face, the bright red trickle of blood that ran from her right temple down her cheek looked garish, as if it had been intentionally painted there.

"You're hurt," Nita said, and while her physician's mind told her that the injury could not be serious considering that Deo was walking under her own steam and talking coherently, her stomach clenched with worry.

"A few scratches," Deo said in disgust. "I can't believe I was stupid enough to shake that damned strut. Fucking beginner's mistake."

"When I was in medical school," Nita said quietly, "the lover of one of the residents was killed in an accident almost exactly like this." Tentatively, she touched Deo's cheek next to the thick red rivulet of blood. "Except in her case, a beam hit her in the back of the neck and killed her instantly."

Deo raised her hand as if to take Nita's, then let it fall. "Freak accidents happen. Most of the time you get a few bumps, a couple of scrapes, and you forget about it a minute later. I'm fine."

"We'll need to get that cleaned up and make sure you don't need sutures." Nita backed away, not wanting to think about the surge of panic she'd experienced when she thought Deo might have been seriously injured. It didn't mean anything. She would have felt the same for anyone she was with.

"I want to finish going through the house."

"Absolutely not," Nita said with finality. "You're already injured, plus you're filthy. You need a shower and I need to look at your face."

"I'm not going to get your house any dirtier than it already is, Nita."

"Don't be ridiculous. You know what I'm talking about."

"And we're here now, and I just want a quick tour of the upper floors and a peek in the attic." Deo turned Nita toward the stairs. "Besides, the weather is supposed to clear tomorrow and I want to take a look under the eaves while it's raining. The situation down here isn't enough to hold up the closing, but if you've got a leaking roof, you want to know about it now."

With a sigh, Nita started climbing. "Ten more minutes."

"Twenty and you've got a deal."

Against her better judgment, Nita agreed. Happily, the rest of the house was sound, and they reached the narrow stairway leading up to the widow's walk without further incident. The sound of rain drumming on the roof was so loud, Nita was forced to lean close to Deo or shout.

"It's pouring out there. You can save that for another day."

"No way," Deo said. "That's one of the best parts of this house. Besides, I need a shower. You can stay—"

"Let's go then," Nita grumped. Carefully, she negotiated the twisting stairs and waited on a small landing while Deo loosened yet another rusty latch and threw open the door that led out to the railed walkway that circled the highest portion of the roof. As she stepped out into the rainy night, she gasped.

"Oh my God," Nita whispered. "It's gorgeous."

The town lay spread out below them, curving along the harbor. Sailboats and yachts rocked in the harbor, their running lights sending skittering shafts of gold across the inky surface. Despite the rain, a half moon peeked from behind the cloud cover and cast its pale timeless glow over the scene. For an instant, Nita imagined herself a woman searching the sea night after night, waiting in the dark for her lover to return.

Deo watched Nita take it all in, struck by the way her features softened and a sad smile played across her mouth. She was every bit as beautiful as the night.

"Glad you came up here?" Deo asked quietly.

Nita turned. "Oh yes. I think I'll come up here every night."

"I don't blame you. I would too."

"Turn your face up to the sky," Nita said, her throat suddenly thick. Deo's dark hair lay in tendrils over her cheeks and neck. Her body was silhouetted against the moonlit sky, strong and tight and powerful. Nita wanted to run her hands over her sculpted shoulders and down her bare arms. She wanted to slide her palms beneath the thin T-shirt and cup the soft swell of her barely perceptible breasts. She wanted, and the wanting felt good even though she knew there was no more basis to it than a primal urge programmed somewhere in the depths of her brain. She hadn't been able to resist touching Sylvia, and she had paid for that weakness with a huge part of her heart and soul. She would not make the same mistake again.

"What?" Deo asked, trying to decipher the look on Nita's face. For an instant she thought she had seen desire, but now she saw only sadness. Remarkably, it was the sadness that made her reach out more than the fleeting desire.

Nita held up her hand and forestalled Deo's motion. "Shower, remember? Tilt your head back and let the rain wash you clean."

Wondering if it could really be that simple, Deo closed her eyes and surrendered to the storm.

❖

"Nelson," Reese whispered. "You awake?"

Nelson Parker turned his head slowly on the pillow, clearly struggling to focus. His voice was raspy and faint when he spoke, a mere echo of his normally deep vibrant baritone. "Reese."

Reese reached over the aluminum railings that separated her from him and rested her hand on his bare forearm. When he tried to raise his arm he could barely move it and his weakness struck her even more powerfully than seeing the tubes and other monitoring devices attached to and exiting his body. "How are you feeling?"

"Dog shit."

"Yeah, I imagine." Reese grinned and Nelson's mouth flickered in a smile. "I won't make it here before your surgery in the morning, so I'll see you sometime tomorrow afternoon when you wake up."

Nelson nodded almost imperceptibly. "Busy?"

"The usual."

"Bri."

Reese reached for the oversized Styrofoam container filled with water and positioned it so Nelson could reach the straw without lifting his head. She waited while he drank and then put the cup back on the narrow television table next to the bed.

"Lot to ask…" Nelson swallowed, and when he spoke again his voice was stronger. "Have to ask you to look after her if things don't go well tomorrow."

It never occurred to her to say anything other than the truth. To do anything less would be to deny him the respect he deserved. She knew he might die. So did he. It wasn't dying that mattered, but how one did it. "I will. She's strong, Nelson. She'll be all right."

"She here?"

"Can't get her to stay away." Reese grinned. "Between Tory and Caroline they've gotten her to go home a few times to shower and change her clothes."

"Damn stubborn kid," he said, his eyes shining.

"We love her. She'll always have a home with us—both her and Caroline." Reese squeezed his arm. "You don't have to worry about her. What you need to do is everything you can to stick around for her. That's the mission."

"Sounds easy."

"Shouldn't be too hard." Reese slid her hand down until her fingers lay in Nelson's palm. He closed his around hers. "I'll see you tomorrow, Chief."

"Roger."

Reese walked out into the hall and found Bri waiting just outside the door. Caroline was with her, her hand tucked into the back pocket of Bri's leather motorcycle pants. "Your dad needs to get a good night's rest, so why don't you say good night to him. You'll see him in the morning."

"Okay." Bri's voice was slightly unsteady.

"Tory says the surgery will make him stronger." Reese briefly clasped her shoulder. "That's what he wants."

"I know." Bri glanced at Caroline. "You coming in with me?"

Caroline gave her a look. "Like I wouldn't?" She kissed her cheek. "What a blockhead."

When they disappeared into Nelson's room, Reese returned to the ICU waiting room and slumped onto the sofa next to Tory. It was only a little after nine p.m. and she shouldn't be tired, but she was.

"Bri okay?" Tory asked, taking Reese's hand.

"She'll stand," Reese replied.

"She's scared."

"Yes." She raised their joined hands and brushed her lips over Tory's. "But scared or not, she'll be okay, because it's not the fear that matters, but what you do about it."

"Well, there's not much more we can do here until tomorrow." Tory rose with Reese's hand still in hers. At Reese's look of surprise, she said, "And I need you tonight."

Reese stood and eased her arm around Tory's waist. "Let's go home."

Chapter Twelve

Follow me home," Nita said, leaning into the open window of Deo's truck. "I want to look at your face in decent light."

"It's nothing, I can tell." Deo would have welcomed the invitation under other circumstances, but she didn't want Nita viewing her as just another patient. Nita had been warm and relaxed with Joey at the clinic but had held herself back from everyone at the party that same night. Even in the ICU a few nights ago, she hadn't really been part of the group. It wasn't hard to see that Nita was more comfortable relating to people from a professional distance, and distance wasn't what Deo had in mind. "I've had worse."

"That may be," Nita insisted, "but it was my house that fell on your head, and I want to be sure you're all right."

"It's not your responsibility."

"Please," Nita said softly.

Deo sighed and sagged back in surrender. "Jesus, and you call me relentless."

Nita stepped back, smiling faintly. "I'm subletting a place in the East End across from Angel Market."

"I'll meet you there," Deo said.

Less than ten minutes later, Deo parked in the empty lot beside the darkened gourmet grocery store and crossed the street to where Nita waited on the sidewalk. She followed her down a narrow gravel walkway between two buildings to the entrance of a familiar ground floor rear apartment. A small wooden deck led to sliding glass doors that opened into a compact kitchen. Nita turned on the light and Deo stepped inside.

"How do you like this apartment?" Deo asked.

"It's great. The space isn't that large, but it's very well designed and they really thought of everything when they—what?" Nita asked as Deo grinned.

"There's no better recommendation than a satisfied customer." Deo slid her hands into her pockets and shrugged. "My crew renovated it. I did most of the design myself."

"It's very good work."

"Like I said—no better reference. Since I've already done the inspection on your house, I can work up quotes for the renovation—"

"Aren't you getting a little ahead of yourself?" Nita interrupted irritably. "I haven't requested a job estimate from you yet."

"Well, you will."

"Oh, you think so." Nita snorted. "*Usually* I like a confident woman, but you take entitlement to an extreme."

"Are you saying I'm spoiled?" Deo teased.

"Aren't you? When's the last time anyone took serious issue with you?"

Nita's criticism stung, and without thinking, Deo said, "Does getting thrown out of your own house at seventeen count?"

Immediately, Nita's voice softened and she gently clasped Deo's forearm. "What happened?"

Deo shrugged, wanting to change the subject, but the sympathy in Nita's eyes and the tenderness of her touch seduced her into revealing more than she usually would with anyone, even a woman whose bed she shared—or hoped to. "My father beat me until I was half dead and then threw me out on the street."

"Why?"

"Because I killed his only son." Deo shoved the door open and strode out onto the deck. She was already halfway up the alley when Nita's voice reached her.

"Deo, please don't go. Deo?"

Enticed by the concern in Nita's tone, Deo slowed but didn't look back. The rain had let up until just a fine mist hung in the air. Moisture beaded on her cheeks like the memory of long-ago tears. "Look. I don't want to talk about it."

"You don't have to," Nita said from very close behind her.

Deo shivered at the light touch on her shoulder.

"We all have our secrets," Nita said quietly. "I'm sorry I forced you into revealing one of yours."

"Usually women want to hear your secrets," Deo said curiously, turning to face Nita in the semi darkness. "Isn't that what intimacy is supposed to be all about? Sharing secrets?"

"Quite possibly," Nita said steadily. "But I'm not interested in intimacy. I'm interested in looking at that laceration on your face."

Deo smiled crookedly. "I'm really the perfect person for you to sleep with."

Nita frowned. "I'm not even going to try to follow your logic. Come back inside."

"I'm not interested in intimacy either, and I won't try to make you tell me your secrets," Deo said as she fell into step beside Nita.

"I don't have any secrets worth telling."

"Sure you do," Deo said softly. Nita might use her professional cloak and personal reserve to keep people at a distance, but Deo had caught glimpses of the tenderness and passion she tried to hide. Nita would not be alone unless someone had taught her that love was dangerous. But *she* was not the person to change Nita's mind about that. They were alike that way, her and Nita—connection meant caring, and caring meant pain. "But like I said, I'm not pushing."

Nita decided that ignoring her, as impossible as that was most of the time, was the best approach. "Follow me down to the bathroom."

Nita directed Deo to sit on the closed commode while she retrieved antiseptic, steri-strips, and other supplies from a tall narrow cabinet next to the sink. Although well laid out with a spacious shower and vanity, the room was still small, and there wasn't much space for them to maneuver around each other. As Nita bent down, Deo's leg brushed her ass, and that brief unintentional caress shot straight through her. Pretending she hadn't gotten instantly wet, Nita stood and tilted Deo's head up with her fingers beneath her chin. Deo's skin was damp from the rain and the silky smoothness made her think of the way a woman's body misted just before she came. This close, she could see the small gold flecks in Deo's irises, and she imagined the way they would darken and swirl just before…

"Close your eyes," Nita said hoarsely.

Once released from the hypnotic pull of Deo's gaze, Nita used a cotton swab to clean the laceration that paralleled Deo's hairline. Concentrating on the familiar task helped her ignore the buzzing in the pit of her stomach. She brushed Deo's wet tangled hair away from the cut and resisted the urge to run her fingers through it. "The laceration is long, but not too deep."

"Told you that," Deo said, automatically spreading her legs so that Nita could get close enough to work. The solution Nita swabbed on the cut stung, but that sensation was quickly obliterated by her awareness of Nita's body almost resting against hers. The insides of her thighs rubbed against Nita's legs and a wave of heat shot through her. She couldn't tell if the torrent of warmth was coming from inside her body or from Nita, but she was aware that the fingers on her face had stopped moving.

Deo opened her eyes and found Nita staring at her, and there wasn't a doubt in her mind as to what she saw in Nita's eyes. Slowly, carefully, she slipped her hands around Nita's body and cupped her hips. When Nita didn't draw way, she gently pulled her closer until Nita's crotch nestled against her belly. She was suddenly so hot and so hard she thought she would explode, but she held absolutely still. Some sixth sense warned her that Nita must make the first move.

"Let go," Nita whispered as the heat from Deo's body flooded hers. She couldn't step away, not with Deo's hands on her.

"You don't want me to do that," Deo murmured.

"I do," Nita insisted, knowing it was herself she was trying to convince. Deo's breasts rose and fell quickly and her nipples had tightened beneath the still damp T-shirt. Entirely against her own volition, Nita's fingers crept around the back of Deo's neck and spread through her hair. With a soft groan, Deo pressed her face against Nita's stomach. The top of her head glanced over Nita's nipples, and Nita trembled with another wave of arousal. She had very little time. Deo's breath against the thin fabric of her blouse seared her skin and she wanted Deo's mouth roaming over her body. She would burn for her, she knew, igniting beneath Deo's hands until all that remained was ashes. She would never survive the inferno again.

Eyes closed, lips parted, Deo moaned against Nita's stomach. "Nita, please. I need to touch you."

Trembling, Nita gathered all her strength and pushed away. "You have to go."

Deo dropped her hands onto her thighs, palms up, her fingers curved in supplication. Panting, she nodded wordlessly.

Surprised but grateful, Nita took another step back. Amazingly, her voice sounded almost normal. "Keep that cut covered while you're working. It should be fine."

"Right," Deo said, rising unsteadily to her feet. "Thank you."

Unable to look away from Deo's flushed face, Nita reached behind her for the bathroom door and pulled it open. Then she pressed against it so Deo could pass. She was careful that their bodies did not touch. Like an automaton, she followed Deo to the kitchen and watched her wrench open the glass doors. A breeze smelling of sea and summer rain wafted through the kitchen. A fleeting image of the two of them naked, lying before an open window making love until dawn while the fresh clear air washed the past away, skittered through her mind.

"I'm sorry," Nita said softly.

"For what?" Deo's breathing was ragged.

"I shouldn't have touched you."

"Does it make any difference that I wanted you to?"

Nita shook her head. "None at all."

"I'm leaving because you want me to," Deo said, "not because I want to."

"I'm grateful."

"Don't thank me," Deo said harshly. "Next time I won't be as accommodating."

"Please go. This won't happen again."

"That's where you're wrong." Deo stepped outside, closed the door, and disappeared.

Wrapping her arms around her middle, Nita leaned against the counter and wondered how things had gotten so out of control so quickly. Then she tried to tell herself it could have been worse. Deo might have awakened her libido, but thankfully she still had control of her common sense. She hadn't been with anyone since Sylvia. In the months since, she had so ruthlessly crushed her desire, so completely disavowed her own need, that she was rarely aware of sexual desire. She hadn't even masturbated since she had finally purged her system of wanting Sylvia every moment of the day and night. Now a pulse beat heavily, insistently, between her thighs, and she knew she would come with the lightest touch.

The pressure was nearly unbearable, but she wouldn't satisfy herself, not when she wasn't sure whose face she would see as she orgasmed. Sylvia or Deo? Was either any safer than the other?

❖

Too agitated to go home to silence, Deo walked. Driven by the churning in her stomach and the hot thrum of need coursing through her blood, she didn't notice passing faces or register the occasional bump on her shoulder as she threaded her way through slow moving clumps of casual strollers. Over the years, she'd learned to recognize lust in all its various guises—mindless, playful, urgent, detached. She'd made love to women who were so insatiable she'd nearly dropped from exhaustion before they'd had enough. Strangers had fucked her in the dark until she couldn't remember her own name. Never once had she seen a look of such undisguised hunger and desperate vulnerability as she'd seen on Nita's face tonight. It was plain to see that Nita wanted her and feared her in equal measure, and knowing that twisted her up like a giant claw ripping at her insides.

Rebelling at the idea that Nita expected her to hurt her, Deo strode faster. Her body was in rebellion too, adrenaline pumping, her loins pounding with lust and need. She wanted to pour her longing and loneliness into a woman's body. Even more than she wanted to come herself, she wanted a woman coming beneath her, crying out in ecstasy.

The blaring sound of a car horn brought her up short, and she jumped out of the way of the car she'd walked in front of. Shaking her head, she focused on her surroundings for the first time and saw that she was in front of the Vixen, one of the hot spots for lesbians on the prowl. It wouldn't take long to find a woman in there to empty herself into, or she could call Allie. Allie gladly took what she had to give, and because of that, she could relax enough to let Allie pleasure her. If she didn't find release, she would never be able to sleep. Her head and her groin were in a race to see which would detonate first.

Stranger or friend. Which should she choose, which should she use?

With a sigh, she crossed diagonally to the Squealing Pig and pushed through the door.

"Beer," she said tersely to the bartender. With any luck, she could drink the edge off and forget who she really wanted to fuck.

❖

"Let's go to bed," Tory said, sliding her arms around Reese's waist from behind as Reese gently lay Reggie into her crib and tucked the covers around her.

Straightening, Reese turned and kissed Tory's forehead. "Good idea."

Tory took Reese's hand and led her across the hall and closed the bedroom door behind them. Once inside there was only moonlight to guide them, but after the rain had stopped, the wind had blown the clouds away and the night was bright enough to see by. She unclipped Reese's tie and laid it on the dresser just inside the door. Then she began unbuttoning her shirt.

"Have I ever mentioned how much I love to undress you?" Tory murmured.

"Once or twice." Reese said thickly, reaching down to gently tug Tory's blouse from her jeans.

"It's the first time all week we'll actually be going to bed together." Tory pushed Reese's shirt off and let it fall, then pulled up her T-shirt. Reese obliged by raising her arms and Tory stripped her. Her silhouette in the moonlight was a breathtaking combination of hard planes and subtle curves, her body almost too sharply honed. Tory brushed her hands over Reese's chest, lingering on the subtle swell of her breasts. "God, you're beautiful."

Reese trembled, her breath coming faster. "It's late and you'll need to leave early to get back to the hospital in the morning."

"I know what time it is." Tory trailed her fingers slowly down Reese's stomach to her fly and opened her pants. Hooking both thumbs around the waistband and catching Reese's briefs in the same grip, she pushed them down. "Kick off your shoes."

"Tory," Reese whispered, an edge of uncertainty in her voice.

Kneeling, Tory worked Reese's clothing off one leg and then the other until she was nude. Then she leaned forward and pressed her face against Reese's abdomen, encircling her hips with both arms. She kissed the base of her stomach and ran her hands lightly over Reese's ass. "You can't know how much I missed you. Even with you home again, it catches me in the middle of the day. This ache I have for you." She tilted her chin up but she couldn't see Reese's expression, only the distant shadow of her face. "I need you inside me tonight."

Reese groaned quietly and cupped Tory's face with both hands. "Baby, I'm not sure..."

Tory rubbed her cheek over the soft delta between Reese's legs and pressed a kiss to her center. Then she rose and wrapped her arms around Reese's neck. "Don't be afraid."

"When…when I touch you I feel like I'm running, running for my life and you're all that can save me."

"You're not lost, darling." Tory guided Reese's hand to her breast. "And I'm right here."

Shaking, Reese kissed her tenderly, with infinite care, and slowly unbuttoned her blouse. She reached one hand behind and released Tory's bra as Tory skimmed off her jeans and panties. With her mouth against Tory's neck, Reese circled her waist and pushed her toward the bed. Tory went down on her back and Reese followed, her thigh between Tory's legs. Her voice was hoarse and tight. "Here with you like this, I know who I am."

"Then be with me. You can't hurt me." Tory shifted until Reese was between her legs and then hooked her calves over Reese's thighs. She kissed her, drawing Reese's tongue into her mouth, and rocked her hips in invitation.

Reese gave herself to the heat of Tory's mouth and the call of her body. When she felt her control slip and the choking need that verged on desperation surging through her, she tried to pull away, but Tory only held her more fiercely.

"Don't go," Tory whispered, cradling the back of Reese's head in one hand and grasping Reese's wrist with the other. She pushed Reese's hand between them, down over her belly. "Be with me. Be in me. I need you."

"I love you," Reese gasped, sliding into her, submerging herself in the solace only Tory could provide. "Tory. Tory."

"Always…" Tory arched to take her deeper. "Always right here."

Reese pushed Tory to the edge, thrust after thrust, until she was about to crest, and then grew still inside her. When Tory cried out, imploring her not to stop, Reese whispered, "I will never leave you."

While Tory trembled on the brink, Reese slid down the bed and took her into her mouth. As Tory came, she grasped Reese's free hand and their fingers entwined.

Tory held her inside as long as she could, and continued to hold her hand after Reese slipped from her and lay panting with her cheek pillowed against Tory's stomach. Tory traced the wedding band on Reese's finger while she stroked Reese's face, thinking about her promise to love and cherish.

"I wish I could give you everything you need," Tory whispered.

"You give me more." Reese moved up the bed to take Tory into her arms. She cradled Tory's head against her shoulder and kissed her. "You give me things I never knew I needed. More than I ever dreamed of having."

"Sometimes I feel selfish."

"No." Reese sighed. "You aren't. You never have been. It's me."

Tory raised her head. "You know what? Our life has been upside down since April, and this week has been really hard." She kissed Reese firmly. "I'll give myself a break if you'll do the same."

Reese laughed. "Is this like a timeout for grown-ups?"

"Something like that." Tory ran her fingers through Reese's hair, then curled up against her again. "We're together, and we always will be, no matter where either of us may be. For now, that's all that matters."

"That's everything." Reese pulled the covers over them and held her tightly. "I'll see you in the morning, baby."

Holding to that promise, Tory fell asleep to the sound of Reese's heartbeat.

Chapter Thirteen

"Oh man," Bri moaned, curling onto her side as she reached down to caress Carre's face with trembling fingers. Her head still buzzed from waking up in the middle of an orgasm. "Babe, what are you doing?"

"Making you feel good."

"Why aren't you asleep?"

"Because I woke up and I thought about us being at the hospital all week and that we'll probably be there most of the weekend, and I wanted to take care of you." Caroline rubbed her cheek against Bri's belly. "You wouldn't let me last night, remember?"

Bri combed her fingers through Carre's hair. "I didn't think I could come. I've been so twisted up all week, I wasn't even horny."

"You didn't *think* you were." Caroline scooted up on the bed and pulled Bri's head against her breasts. "But baby, you're always horny. Besides, it's good for you. It always relaxes you."

"Is that what you call it?" Bri closed her eyes briefly and pretended that it was just the two of them together with nowhere to go and nothing to fear. But she could only hold on to the dream for a few seconds. "What time is it?"

"Four thirty, about. It's still dark outside." Caroline rubbed Bri's shoulders. "We should leave in about an hour. You go ahead and sleep some more. I'll wake you up."

"Don't know if I can."

"You okay?"

Wordlessly, Bri nodded, tightening her grip on Carre. She'd been in scary situations a few times at work—the fire, the shootout in the dunes, the drug bust that went bad. She'd been scared, sure, but even that night when she'd been dragged into the brush and beaten, she hadn't felt this powerless. She'd always fought back. "I think something bad might happen, and I don't know what I'm supposed to do."

"Remember what your dad said last night. That he wasn't going to worry about you because he knew you were strong."

"Yeah," Bri mumbled.

"Being strong doesn't mean you can't be scared." Caroline tilted Bri's face up and kissed her eyes, then her cheeks, then her mouth. "And you don't have to be strong all the time, baby."

"Oh fuck," Bri blurted as the tears came and she couldn't stop them. Carre rocked her and made soft little sounds of comfort, and Bri clung to her like she couldn't ever remember holding on to anyone before. Maybe she had, when she was little—before her mother died, before the house grew silent and her father so sad—but she couldn't remember. Then she was a teenager and she was fighting everyone because she was different, and everywhere she turned someone said she couldn't be who she was, and she had to be strong because Carre risked so much in loving her. And now—now she was grown, and she wanted to be strong like Reese was strong—strong and brave no matter what happened. But she didn't feel strong.

"I don't know…" Bri gulped and willed herself to stop crying. "I don't know how I'd make it if I didn't have you."

"Oh baby," Caroline murmured, stroking Bri's hot, damp face. "Don't you know by now I need you to need me? Just like I need you." She kissed her forehead. "You are such a blockhead sometimes."

"I'm trying so hard, but I'm never going to be like Reese." When Carre drew back, there was enough morning light filtering through the skylight in their second floor apartment that Bri could make out the frown on her face. "What?"

"Do you think Reese is strong all the time?" Caroline shook her head. "Don't you get that part of the reason Reese *seems* so strong is because she has Tory? Jeez, all you have to do is watch them."

Bri remembered waking up in the ICU waiting room and seeing Tory holding Reese. Comforting her, pretty much like Carre was doing now. Thinking that Reese wouldn't want anyone to see her so vulnerable, she had looked away. She hadn't wanted to embarrass Reese, but maybe she had been wrong in thinking that she would. She wasn't ashamed to have Carre hold her. She just felt lucky.

"How come you know these things and I don't?" Bri complained, rubbing her face against the inside of her arm to wipe away the last of her tears.

Caroline laughed. "Because we're made differently and different things are important to us."

Bri frowned. "I don't get it."

"I know, baby," Caroline said gently. "It doesn't matter as long as you know that I don't always need you to be strong and I need to feel strong for you too sometimes."

"If anything happens to my dad I don't want anybody around except you." Bri took Carre's hand. The tears were close again. "Okay?"

"Reese and Tory love you, baby." Caroline kissed Bri until Bri relaxed into her arms. "I'll be right there, I promise. But you can't shut them out."

"Thank you for…you know. Being with me."

"You're gonna make me mad if you say that again." Caroline pulled Bri on top of her and held her tightly. "There's only one thing I want you to say to me. You know what it is."

Bri rested her forehead against Carre's and whispered, "I love you so so much."

❖

"You made it," Nita exclaimed as Tory hurried into the office at just after three in the afternoon. "You'd better sit down. You look exhausted."

"I only slept a few hours last night, but I actually felt rested when I woke up this morning." Tory dropped onto the sofa with a grateful sigh. "It's just been a tense day."

Nita frowned. "Problems with Nelson's surgery?"

"He came through the procedure with no major problems, but the surgeon said he saw a little more bleeding post-op than he'd like. They're just watching him for now."

"Maybe you should head back, then."

Tory shook her head. "There are some things I have to do here. Reese will be there in an hour or so. We've got it covered." She pointed a finger at Nita. "Besides, you have a closing to go to. So—go."

"You're sure."

"Positive. Call me later."

Nita shrugged off her lab coat, hung it on a coat tree inside the door, and grabbed the soft brown leather shoulder bag that doubled as her briefcase. Murmuring her thanks, she hurried out.

The few moments it took to drive into town were the first free minutes she'd had all day. Unfortunately, the first thing she thought of was Deo. There was no reason to think that Deo would be at the closing, for which she was glad. A day or two without seeing her would put everything into perspective. She was only temporarily off-balance because she hadn't expected to meet anyone who stirred her up the way Deo had. Nothing to worry about.

So, she'd met an attractive charming sexy woman who had turned her on. So what? So what if she'd tossed and turned for an hour the night before, too keyed up to sleep, unable to purge the memory of Deo's warm breath against her stomach from her mind. So what if she'd awakened for the first time in months with a hum of arousal singing through her blood. All perfectly normal, perfectly natural. No crime in acknowledging involuntary responses she had no plans to do anything about.

Case closed.

❖

"How does it feel to be a homeowner?" Elana Torres asked, handing Nita the keys with a warm smile.

"Wonderful," Nita replied automatically, and on one level, she *was* thrilled. The house had charmed her from the beginning with its history and faded grandeur, and she looked forward to restoring it. The project would occupy her free time, what little of it there was, and in the end, she would have something exceptional of her own to show for it. But undercutting the excitement was a thread of sadness that she was doing this alone. Her first home, a significant dream realized, and she had no one special with whom to share the pleasure.

Elana handed Nita a thick manila envelope. "Deo asked me to give this to you. She said to tell you the renovation estimates just cover the major structural elements. The finishing details take more planning, depending on what you have in mind."

"I, uh…" Nita stared at the envelope but didn't take it. She had the irrational thought that if she touched it she might feel the rough brush of Deo's callused palm over her body and give herself away with some small movement or sound.

"Deo's family, as you know, but I can also recommend her without reservation," Elana added. "Still, I put contact information for one of the other local contractors and a company from Barnstable in with your settlement papers in case you want to get competitive bids."

"Yes. I suppose that would be a good idea."

"Call soon. At this time of the year, everyone is booked solid. I'll do what I can to help set up the appraisals, if you like."

Of course, Nita thought, *summertime is the height of the building season*. But Deo had taken the time to write up the estimate. She wondered when. "Deo put this together awfully quickly."

"She was in here crunching numbers when I arrived at six this morning." Elana smiled. "She's never been one to let grass grow under her feet."

Nita stifled a comment about fast workers and accepted the envelope. It could take weeks to even schedule an appraisal with someone else, and longer still to get the renovations started. And somehow, she didn't think that Deo's comment about being one of the best in the business was an idle boast. Her own sublet was proof of that. Annoyed that she was allowing a transient *situation* with Deo to compromise what should be a professional undertaking, she asked, "Do you have local references I can check? She's already seen the house, and—"

"Deo always includes references at the end of her estimates. If you need any other information, just call me. Most of the businesses in town use her, and there's never been a single complaint."

Blushing, Nita said hastily, "Really, I'm sure she's excellent. I didn't mean to imply otherwise."

"Don't think anything of it," Elana said. "It's an important decision, and I'm sure you want to have the right person do the work."

"Yes. I do. Well," Nita bounced the keys in her palm. "I think I'll pay my new house a visit."

"Welcome to town." Elana extended her hand. "Call me if you need anything. Remember, you're one of us now."

❖

One of us. Nita leaned against the balustrade on the widow's walk and surveyed the harbor from atop her new home. With still two hours until sunset, the evening had taken on a golden blush, and the white sailboats and yachts floated like pristine clouds atop the deep blue surface of the water. So high above the street, the breeze was cool and brisk, raising goose bumps on her sun-heated skin. *One of us.*

She could still hear her brother's angry words. "How could you, Nita? He's one of us. You don't fuck with one of us."

She hadn't needed her brother's fury or her father's cold disdain or her sister's shocked criticism to understand that the thin blue line was unassailable. She'd known it all her life. Every member of her family took pride in it, and she had broken the line. Ignored the code, disrespected the fraternity, sullied the family honor. She was no longer one of them, cast out for her transgressions.

"All for what," she murmured for the thousandth time, but she knew the answer. Sylvia. Beautiful passionate, possessive Sylvia. Sylvia, with her hot demanding hands and her sweet seductive mouth. Sylvia. God, she could still taste her.

"Hey!" Deo yelled up from the street. "Don't lean on that!"

Shaking her head, feeling as if she were awakening from a dream, Nita stared down the three and a half stories to the sidewalk. Deo stood with her legs apart and pelvis tilted forward, hands on hips, glaring up at her. Despite the height, Nita could make out streaks of dust on her neck and the sweat that sheened on her bare arms. In an instant, memories of Sylvia disappeared and Nita was grateful.

Recognizing the gratitude for what it was, the mindless substitution of one desire for another, she defiantly grasped the iron railing and shook it. Despite the protesting creak she heard as she rocked it, she shouted back, "It's perfectly fine."

"Cut it out! Jesus, Nita." Deo shoved open the scrolled iron gate that separated Nita's small front yard from the narrow brick sidewalk and stalked toward the house.

Nita lost sight of her, but she didn't have any trouble hearing her.

"Let me in," Deo barked.

For one second, Nita considered ignoring her. Then, embarrassed by her reluctance to confront a woman just because she was attracted to her, she abandoned her perch above the town and unhurriedly made her way downstairs. When she opened the door, she felt completely calm.

"Yes?" Nita said.

"Jesus Christ, Nita," Deo repeated heatedly. "Do you want to kill yourself? You've got to be careful around this place until we've gone through it completely."

"There is no *we*," Nita responded levelly. "And I *was* careful."

"Leaning over that railing is not careful! If you had fallen…" Deo tried to rein in her temper, but she was still running on nerves after glancing up to see Nita precariously positioned on the widow's walk, a look on her face that said she was a million miles away and not paying any attention to what she was doing. Deo envisioned the bolts pulling loose from the water-softened wood, the railing crumbling, and Nita falling. Falling and lying crumpled on the grass, her eyes open and empty. She shivered. "Fuck."

"I appreciate your concern." Recognizing Deo's anxiety—surprised and oddly touched—Nita asked more gently, "What are you doing here?"

"I'm working a job not far from here, and I figured you might stop by here after the closing." Deo shrugged. "I thought we could get a look at the place while it was still light and talk about the work schedule."

Nita tried to suppress a smile and almost succeeded. "I don't remember accepting your proposal."

Catching the smile, Deo leaned against the door frame, her fear and anger giving way to pleasure at the slight chink in Nita's formidable armor. "Did you look at it?"

"Yes." In fact, it was the first thing she had done when she arrived at the house. She'd walked through the dusty, barren rooms studying Deo's notes, imagining the ornate ceilings restored, the woodwork and floors sanded and refinished, the wainscoting and scrolled chair rails replaced. "I still need to call your references."

"Don't trust me?" Deo teased.

"Not a whit."

"Going to let me in?"

No, Nita's common sense screamed. *No. No no no.* Reminding herself it was a simple business transaction, she stepped back. "I can't live here without plumbing and electricity."

"You need a kitchen."

"I can live very well on take out."

"For food, maybe. What about coffee in the morning?" Deo followed Nita down the wide central hall, admiring the way Nita's rear filled out her navy slacks. Her cream colored blouse was the perfect complement to her coffee complexion, and Deo thought once again how beautiful she was.

"By the way, I think you missed something," Nita said.

"Impossible."

When Nita stopped abruptly and turned, Deo almost bumped into her. They were so close she could smell Nita's earthy floral perfume. Her stomach tightened in the way it did when she was getting hard, and she shuddered with the unexpected surge of arousal.

Nita nearly recoiled at the sexual charge pouring from Deo's body. The force of Deo's attraction was so tangible she expected to see it materialize, a beast clawing its way to freedom and hunting her down. But rather than run, there was a beast of her own straining to charge back—aching for the frenzy of mating that left only wreckage in its wake.

"There's a water mark on the ceiling under the stairs," Nita said hoarsely, pointing back over Deo's shoulder. "It's not on your report. You probably couldn't see it the other night."

Swallowing, forcing down the urge to grab Nita and kiss her the way she'd wanted to kiss her the night before, Deo looked where Nita indicated. Frowning, she pulled her jackknife from her pants pocket and scraped at the plaster in the stairwell. When it flaked away, she pressed her fingertip to the small gouge. It was dry. "An old leak. They probably fixed it but never bothered to repair this. Good pickup."

"Thanks. So," Nita said, backing up a step. "Want to finish the tour?"

"Sure." Deo didn't move. Neither did Nita. *What about me, Nita? Want to finish me? Just a kiss, just a touch. I've been ready since last night.*

"Assuming your references check out—"

"They will."

"Assuming they do," Nita said firmly, "when can you start?"

"It will take a few days to get materials lined up. Sometime next week."

"How long before I can move in?"

Deo shrugged. "Can't tell until I see what kind of surprises we find. There are always surprises with this kind of job."

"Ballpark."

"It depends on if you're willing to rough it or not."

"I don't need pampering."

"But do you like it?" Deo asked softly.

"A condition for you doing this job," Nita went on steadily, "is that you cease your pointless flirting."

"Do you want that in the contract?"

Nita laughed and shook her head ruefully. "How good is your word?"

"I don't make promises I can't keep."

"Then your word will do."

Deo shook her head. "Sorry, I can't oblige."

"Why?" Nita asked, half aggravated and half intrigued.

"You know why."

Nita's pulse pounded as if Deo's hands skimmed her body. She didn't bother denying the attraction. They'd both know she was lying.

"I forgot," Nita said. "It's second nature to you."

"I don't mind if you want to pretend that's all it is." Deo regarded Nita seriously. "No more exploring this place by yourself, especially once we start working. I'll meet you at any time and take you through personally."

"That won't be necessary. But I appreciate it."

"Consider it part of the service." Deo grinned.

"Come on, let's finish up." Nita turned away, refusing to allow herself to succumb to the lure of Deo's attraction. "I'll call you when I've made a decision."

"I'll be waiting."

The words, even though she knew they were empty, sent a ripple of pleasure through Nita's core. She was so aroused she knew that denying herself release tonight was not going to be possible, and she didn't know whether to rejoice or repent.

Chapter Fourteen

"Hi," Allie said breathlessly as she rushed into the waiting room and kissed Bri on the cheek. At nine p.m. on Saturday night, the waiting room was nearly empty. "Sorry I didn't make it yesterday—hi Caroline—we had a three car pileup on Six last night that took us hours to sort out—how's the chief?"

"Pretty good," Bri said. "He still has that breathing tube in so he can't say anything, but he blinks when I talk to him so I know he's okay."

Allie dropped into one of the dark green vinyl chairs and let her arms flop over the sides. She'd changed out of her uniform into low-cut jeans and a scooped neck short-sleeved cotton top that came just to her bellybutton, and it felt great not to be working for a few hours. "That's good. Everybody's asking for him. Tell him that, okay?"

"I will. You didn't need to drive all the way up here, you know. You called yesterday after the surgery."

"I know, but…" Allie blushed and glanced at Caroline, who stood with one hip cocked against Bri's and her arm around Bri's waist. The possessive stance wasn't conscious, but Allie got the message just the same. "It feels like we're more than just people who work together, you know?"

Bri nodded. "Yeah. I do."

Caroline kissed Bri's cheek and stepped away. "I'm going downstairs to get us something to drink, baby. Allie, you want something?"

"No. Thanks. I'm not going to stay that long."

"Okay. Back in a few."

"Got a date?" Bri perched on the wide arm of Allie's chair and braced an arm against the back.

"Ha. I wish." Allie leaned back to look up, her cheek nearly touching Bri's hand where it rested on the vinyl. "I don't have anything lined up, and if I did, I think I'd be too tired to do anything about it."

"What about Deo?"

"Oh yeah. Deo." Allie eyed Bri. "So much has happened this week I forgot you were bent out of shape about her. What gives?"

"I asked you first."

Allie lifted a shoulder and gave Bri a lazy smile. "She's hot. I mean like touch me and I go off like a bomb hot."

Bri rolled her eyes. "I kinda got that from watching her feel you up on the street in front of Spiritus."

"She wasn't and so what if she was?"

"That's a low-life move. You're too good for her."

"You don't even know her, and for your information, she *refused* to fuck me on the street when I asked her to." Allie sighed in exasperation. "We're fucking, Bri. She's fun to be with, and she makes me come like there's no tomorrow. End of story."

"Deo's got a rep for never staying around long, so just…be cool, okay?"

Allie sat forward and rested her hand on Bri's knee. "Listen, stud, I know what I'm doing, okay? But thanks."

"I'm coming back to work on Monday," Bri said.

"Yeah?" Allie brightened. "That would be great. Are you sure?"

"As long as my dad is still doing okay, I want to. I don't feel right just sitting around here. Especially with how busy all the rest of you are covering for me, and Reese doing double duty with my dad out."

Allie squeezed Bri's hand. "You should be here. Everyone understands."

Bri grinned and shook Allie's hand playfully. "What's the matter? Don't you miss me?"

"Oh yeah," Allie laughed. "I really miss you bitchin' about me being late and complaining about who I fuck."

From the doorway, Caroline said wryly, "That's a sign she likes you." She crossed the room and held out sodas to both Allie and Bri. "I got you one Allie, just in case."

"Thanks." Allie released Bri's hand and took the bottle. "I haven't been out of my uniform all week and it's time to go dancing. I'll drink this in the car on my way home."

"I'll call you tomorrow and let you know if I'm coming in for sure," Bri said to Allie as she hooked a finger through the belt loop on Caroline's jeans.

"Okay. See you." Allie waved and hurried out.

As she took the stairs down to the lobby, she twisted off the top of her soda and pulled down a long swallow. Nice of Caroline to bring it—nice of Caroline to put up with her creaming over Bri, too. Jesus that was embarrassing, especially since she knew Caroline knew, even if half the time Bri was clueless. Girls always knew these things.

She was tired. Tired of working. Tired of walking on eggshells around Bri, never knowing when she'd look at her and want her in ways she shouldn't. Tired of wishing the women she slept with were more than bed partners. And so damn tired of wishing Ashley would call her.

With a mental snarl, she flung herself into the car, keyed the ignition, and tore out of the parking lot. None of that was going to change tonight, and there was nothing wrong with a little company to take her mind off what bothered her.

❖

Nita was restless. For the first day in a week and a half, she hadn't worked. Tory had insisted she take the weekend off. Feeling at loose ends all day, she'd been painfully reminded of just how little connection she had established in her new community, and how much she had allowed work to take the place of pleasure in her life. Determined to change that, she'd walked through town to her new house, and the sun and the enthusiasm of the crowds and the breathtaking glimpses of the harbor that teased her through the narrow alleyways between buildings had banished some of her discontent.

Once at the house, she'd immediately lost herself in the excitement of imagining how it would look when it was restored. Even when she realized she was making mental notes of things she wanted to discuss with Deo, far from being derailed, her anticipation grew. Buoyed by the uncharacteristic surge of happiness, she extracted the estimate from the manila envelope she had left lying on the counter in the kitchen the day before and impulsively dialed the phone number on the report. She got an answering machine, which was what she expected, and left a message accepting the proposal.

Now, ten hours later, she wondered if she'd made a mistake encouraging a situation where she'd see Deo regularly. Especially, she thought with a whisper of chagrin, after the night before. She had been so keyed up, so physically agitated, she'd finally relented and made herself come. It hadn't taken much, either time, just a few long firm strokes and a little teasing pressure and the orgasms burst inside her like a rocket flair, brilliant and bright. And as she moaned and twisted, she'd felt Deo's hot breath against her skin.

Nita twitched and stared at the book in her lap. She had no idea how long she'd been sitting in her living room, replaying the events of the day. Urgency coiled in her depths and she knew she was wet. She needed a diversion or she was going to have to masturbate, and she feared anything she could do was not going to be enough to satisfy. She had hoped to smother the consuming need she had to take and be taken by denying it, but instead, she'd only stoked the fury.

"Enough," she muttered, surging to her feet. She needed to hear voices other than those in her head or she was going to go crazy. She'd walk, even though walking was not what her body craved.

❖

Deo pushed the whiskey glass back and forth on the bar in a slow half circle, back and forth, back and forth, replaying the message in her mind.

"Deo, hello. It's Nita Burgoyne. I've decided to accept your proposal. Call me and let me know when you can get started."

She'd rewound the tape and played it five or six times in succession, feeling foolish as her belly churned and heated at the sound of Nita's voice. Mentally, she edited the tape. *"Deo, it's Nita. Call me."*

"Pathetic," Deo muttered. She had never mooned over a woman this way, not even when she was a teenager. She'd always had plenty of interest in sex, but there was never anyone she *had* to have. Never anyone whose voice she hungered to hear on the phone or whose face she desperately sought in the crowd.

At sixteen, she had just been figuring out that she wanted girls, and only girls. By seventeen, she had kissed more than a few and managed a couple of fast fumbles under the pier, and then her life had blown apart. Literally. And then all she wanted was to forget. Quick couplings in the dark, lots of them, had worked for a while. If it hadn't been for Pia standing by her, and Pia's parents giving her a place to live until she could manage on her own, she might not have made it. Eventually, she'd worn the edge off her pain and wounded rage and, by eighteen, had settled into a rhythm of one night stands and friendly but emotionless encounters. When her father, at her mother's insistence, had offered to help her get started in business, she had wanted to refuse. But Pia had urged her to accept for the sake of their families.

Hasn't everyone suffered enough? Pia had said, and Deo swallowed her pride and accepted his help and within two years had paid back every penny. Now they had an uneasy truce. She didn't spend much time around him, and if he started drinking, she left before his festering anger bubbled to the surface.

Her life worked, even if now and then she had the uneasy sense there should be more. Then Nita came along and disrupted the pattern she'd gotten used to. At first meeting, she'd responded to Nita with her hormones, just as she always did, and Nita's automatic dismissal had been a pleasant challenge. But it wasn't the challenge of conquest that kept her interested. Every time they were together, even for a few minutes, she caught glimpses of the deep passion and pain that Nita struggled to hide. *Those* emotions she knew something about, and that's what intrigued her most of all.

"Hey, hot stuff," Allie purred, wrapping her arms around Deo's neck and pressing up against her back. She kissed her ear. "How you doing?"

Deo shifted on the bar stool and kissed Allie lightly on the mouth. "Not bad. You?"

"I'm better now." Allie skimmed her hand down Deo's back and curled her fingers beneath the waistband of Deo's jeans. Then she leaned over the bar and waved at the bartender. "Georgia, honey! *Please* give me a beer before I die."

"Rough day?" Deo asked.

"Rough week." Allie twisted sideways in the narrow space between Deo's stool and the occupied one next to it and snuggled her crotch against Deo's thigh. "We're shorthanded. Tourist season. The usual. The chief is doing okay, though."

"That's great." Deo tipped the contents of her glass down her throat and then held out the empty toward the bartender, who slid a sweating bottle of Molson's across the bar to Allie. "Fill me up."

"So," Allie said after taking a swallow of her beer. "I could really get into fucking for the rest of the night. Interested?"

Grinning ruefully, Deo wrapped both arms around Allie's waist and leaned her forehead against Allie's. No excuses. No lies. Not with her. "I don't think I'm there tonight, babe."

Allie leaned back, her pelvis still pressed to Deo's leg, and regarded her with a frown. "You okay?"

"I don't know." Deo shrugged. "Maybe I'm just tired."

"You know, there's nothing like a really good fuck to make you forget all the shit in your life." As she spoke, Allie worked her hand up the inside of Deo's thigh and cupped her crotch. Unerringly, she pressed her thumb against the base of Deo's clit and circled slowly. "And you know it will be good."

"Oh, Jesus." Deo stiffened all over as her clit went rigid. "It's already good."

Watching Deo's face, Allie eased up a little. "It's not really what you want, though, is it?"

"Allie," Deo whispered.

"I know what you look like when it's what you need." Allie patted Deo's crotch and kissed her. Then she removed her hand. "You going to be okay?"

"Yeah. You?"

"Sure." Allie glanced around the crowded room. "I might still get that fuck tonight, or I might just go home and sleep. Either way, we're good."

Deo drained her whiskey, kissed Allie's cheek, and slid off the stool. "Thanks."

Almost to the door, Deo saw Nita standing off to one side in the shadows and worked her way over to her.

"I got your message about the job," Deo said.

"Good."

"I'll give you a call Monday afternoon or Tuesday with a work schedule."

"Fine."

Deo frowned at Nita's icy tone. "What?"

"Nothing."

Deo's head hurt and her crotch ached. Her patience was nonexistent.

"Damn it, Nita, if you're pissed off at someone, don't take it out on me."

"You ought to be in a better mood seeing as your girlfriend just gave you a hand job at the bar," Nita said acerbically. She couldn't believe she'd let Deo get into her head the way she had when Deo clearly had nothing more on *her* mind than a quick fuck.

"Not that it's any of your business," Deo snapped, "but she isn't. And she didn't."

Before Nita could reply, Deo turned on her heel and stormed out the door.

"Good," Nita muttered to herself. "Go."

Then, before her judgment could overrule her instincts, she slammed her beer bottle down on the nearest table and hurried after her. Her anger and self-loathing weren't Deo's fault and never had been.

"Deo!"

Deo didn't stop but abruptly cut across a small parking lot to an adjacent street that was little more than an alleyway. Nita caught up to her halfway up the dark narrow passageway and grabbed her shoulder from behind. "Deo."

Deo spun around. "What do you want?"

No street lights. Only moonlight. Deo's face was all sharp planes and secret shadows. Her voice was harsh and undercut with pain. Nita grasped her muscular upper arms, pushed her back against a shoulder high stone wall, and drove her body against Deo's.

"This." Nita thrust her tongue into Deo's mouth and was instantly swallowed by the heat. She moaned at her first taste of Deo—whiskey and wanting and danger. Deo's breasts were a tauntingly soft counterpoint to her hard stomach and thighs. God, Nita could barely breathe she was so hungry for her. She sucked Deo's tongue and frantically rubbed her crotch into Deo's.

Blindsided, Deo reacted by instinct. She grabbed Nita's ass and dug her fingers in, urging Nita to pump faster between her spread thighs. When Nita yanked Deo's shirt from her jeans, shoved both hands up underneath, and squeezed her breasts, Deo's clit expanded and pulsed. She jerked her head away and Nita whimpered a protest.

"Keep it up and I'm gonna have to come," Deo warned, trying to focus enough to see if they were still alone in the dark bend of the lane.

"Oh yes," Nita grated, pinching and twisting both nipples hard. "Yes."

"Fuck it." Deo's vision wavered and she closed her eyes. Only the wall at her back and the weight of Nita's body pinning her to it kept her upright.

Nita plunged her tongue back into Deo's mouth, distantly aware of Deo groaning, coming or trying not to, she couldn't tell—all she knew was the fearful pounding low in her belly. She keened as it clawed at her, tearing her insides to shreds. Then, mercifully, the spasms erupted deep in her sex and, throwing back her head, she shouted triumphantly. "*Yes*."

Nita orgasmed twice in rapid succession, riding one peak right into the next, her mind wiped clean by blazing sensation. At last, she sagged against Deo and fought to control her rioting body. If she kissed Deo again right now she thought she might come just from tasting her. She had to stop before she tried to strip her naked on the street. Deo's arms trembled around her waist, and her chest heaved as if she were drowning. The part of Nita's mind still functioning recoiled at the irony—she had meant to walk off her relentless lust for Deo, but she'd ended up assuaging it with Deo's body.

"I'm sorry," Nita murmured, pushing herself upright. "You didn't ask for that. That was inexcusable of me."

"I'm not complaining," Deo gasped. "I'm not even sure what happened."

"Did you even come?"

"I don't know, I think so." Deo's head was still reeling, and she felt as if she had been hardwired into Nita's nervous system and then electrocuted. "When you came it felt like I was coming, too, but I don't know if I really was. Jesus, what did you do?"

"It's been a long time. I lost control."

When Nita tried to pull away, Deo tightened her grip on Nita's hips. "What happened to you never wanting to be in the same country as me?"

"Apparently, I was mistaken."

Deo waited until two shadowy figures, laughing softly, passed by arm in arm. "Who is Sylvia?"

"What?" Nita's face flamed when she realized she must have called Sylvia's name. "I owe you a tremendous apology. I'm very sorry."

"It happens," Deo said with a nonchalance she didn't feel. She'd worried a time or two that she wouldn't remember the name of the woman under her or inside her, but she'd never cared enough about anyone to cry her name in those few moments of complete and total surrender. Feeling irrationally jealous, she pulled Nita back between her legs. "I get that she's a lover. What else?"

"It's not relevant." Nita gripped Deo's wrists and pushed away. To her surprise, Deo released her. Free, she had nowhere to go and, instead, stayed where she was.

"Don't you think I deserve a little more than that, seeing how I just stood in for her?" Deo tucked in her shirt and started to walk toward Bradford.

Where Nita expected anger, she heard resignation, and that made her feel almost worse than anything else that had transpired in the last few disastrous moments. She owed Deo an explanation, since she wouldn't accept an apology, and she fell into step. "She's an ex-lover."

"That part I figured out."

Nita hesitated. She hadn't told anyone, ever. Because she couldn't. And Deo was the last person she wanted to tell, because she hadn't been thinking about Sylvia. Not consciously. It hadn't been thoughts of Sylvia that had kept her awake the last few nights and it hadn't been Sylvia in that bar making her half crazy because another woman had her hands all over her. That had been Deo. And only Deo. But she knew the two were tangled up in her mind, and worse, in her body. She was grateful for the dark, because all she could see was the glint of moonlight in Deo's eyes and the outline of her face. And she was thankful that Deo would not be able to see the shame in hers.

"Sylvia is the wife of my brother's partner and the biggest mistake I ever made in my life."

"Wait...your brother's gay and his partner has a wife?"

Nita laughed mirthlessly. "No. My brother's a cop and his partner on the force is Sylvia's husband."

"That sounds like a tricky situation."

"It's a cardinal sin. No one messes with a cop's wife. If I'd been a man, they probably would have taken me somewhere and beaten me until I wished I were dead." Nita sighed. "Since they couldn't do that, they cast me out."

"Your brother?"

"My whole family. They're all on the force and they all know. Half the force knows. Sylvia and I were…indiscreet." Sylvia had demanded sex when they were at a retirement party for one of Nita's father's friends. She couldn't say no, she'd never been able to say no, and Sylvia's husband had walked into a downstairs bathroom while Sylvia was taking her against the wall. Sylvia hadn't stopped fucking her despite her husband's outraged shout, and Nita had climaxed while he watched. "We all pretend it didn't happen, but everyone is happier if I keep my distance."

"Jesus. What about her? You still see her?"

"God, no. Even without the uproar from my family, Sylvia… Sylvia told her husband *I* had seduced *her*. He believed her, because he loved her."

"I guess you did too."

"Believed her, or loved her? Neither." Nita stopped walking. She had said all there was to say. She had been unable to resist what Sylvia made her feel, and after tonight she couldn't even lie to herself any longer. She still hungered for it. The wild passion, the consuming pleasure, the mind-melting burn of orgasm as it swept through her. Her weakness humiliated her. "I don't expect you to do the renovations now."

"Why not?" Deo studied Nita in the light of cars passing behind them. "I'm not angry."

"You should be."

"Why? Because we fucked when we both wanted to?" Deo shrugged, feigning calm. If Nita walked away with this between them, she'd never get close to her again, and she wanted to now, more than ever. Not just because of the sex, which had been unlike anything she'd ever experienced. But because she knew what it was like to pull a family apart, to be pushed aside and abandoned in payment for her sins. "That's business. This is what it is."

"What it is, is over."

"All right," Deo said, forcing herself to leave when she wanted to protest. When she wanted Nita naked in her bed, calling *her* name when she went blind with pleasure. "I'll call you when I'm ready to start work."

Nita watched Deo walk away and want twisted through her. She despaired of ever forgetting the feel and taste of her. Hard muscles and tight-nippled breasts. Hot whiskey and sunshine. *Oh God, what have I done?*

Chapter Fifteen

Tory tucked the chart from the last patient under her arm and paused when she saw the light filtering from beneath Nita's closed door. It had to be close to ten p.m., and despite taking the day shift all week, Nita had been in the office every night until after Tory had left. It had been so busy, they had done little more than pass one another in the hall, but the few times they'd spoken, Tory had noticed that Nita seemed tense and preoccupied. It wasn't her nature to interfere, but she hoped they were becoming friends. She knocked on the closed door.

"Come in," Nita called.

"It's just the middle of July," Tory pointed out with a smile. "If you keep it up, you're not going to make it to Labor Day."

"I don't think paperwork is going to kill me," Nita said, "although there have been times I've wanted to kill myself if I had to fill out one more insurance form."

Tory laughed and settled into the chair across from Nita's desk. "I know. I just wanted you to know I don't expect you to work eighteen hours a day. You're doing a great job. I'm really glad you're here."

"Thanks." Nita flushed with an unexpected surge of gratitude at the affection in Tory's voice. Until the debacle with Sylvia the year before, her sister Lena had been her closest friend and confidant. Now when they spoke at all, it was strained and coldly formal. "So am I. I know we don't have to decide anything right away, but I already know I want to stay."

"Good. Then we agree." Tory tapped the file against the edge of the desk and pretended to frown. "In which case I definitely don't want you overworking. It's Friday night. Shouldn't you be taking advantage of all the hundreds of women in town?"

Tory's tone was playful rather than suggestive. Still, Nita stared down at the desk to hide her reaction, because she had been considering just that for the last few hours. The brief, frantic sex she'd had with Deo had completely turned her inside out. She couldn't stop thinking about it, about *her*, and she was as terrified as she was on edge. It was just like the way it had been with Sylvia. She craved the taste of her, the feel of her, and she was constantly aroused. She'd talked to Deo on the phone twice during the week to approve the purchase of materials, and just the sound of her voice had left her wanting to come. It was worse in person. She'd seen her once when she stopped by the house in the evening. She hadn't expected Deo to be around that late but she had still been there, checking on the early stages of the project. The sight of her had made her wet and, afraid that Deo would read the lust in her eyes, she'd made some excuse and escaped as soon as possible.

Tonight she had been thinking that if she wore herself out with someone else, a stranger, she could get Deo out of her system. Maybe that's what she should have done with Sylvia, instead of allowing Sylvia to control her. Instead of meeting Sylvia in some roadside motel every time she called, instead of letting Sylvia walk into the hospital and fuck her in an empty examining room or stairwell or supply closet any time she wanted. Instead of biting into her own flesh to still her screams while Sylvia went down on her at a family barbecue with Sylvia's husband just outside the open bedroom window, playing baseball with her brother and the other cops. Sylvia had craved the risk and Nita had craved Sylvia's relentless, insatiable hunger for her.

Shuddering from the memories, she said hoarsely, "Maybe. Maybe I should."

She must have given something away in her voice, because Tory tilted her head and regarded her with concern. "Something wrong?"

"No." Nita feigned a smile. "A case of the blues, that's all. I think I'll feel better when I'm settled. I feel like my entire life is packed in boxes."

"Are things underway at the house?"

"Yes," Nita said curtly, and then, realizing how that sounded, went on, "Deo has a crew working outside on the roof and the windows and another inside redoing electrical." She hoped her voice hadn't trembled when she said Deo's name, because she hadn't felt quite steady. "Before long, I'll be able to live there."

"You're not going to try living there while they're still renovating, are you? God, Reese tried that when she first moved here, and after a few weeks the constant disruption really started to get to her." Tory smiled. "Fortunately, I got her to move in with me."

"I'm sure that wasn't difficult," Nita said, hoping to change the subject.

"Harder than you might think. I wasn't too trusting of relationships at the time and Reese…Reese had never been in one." Tory shook her head. "God, we were a pair."

"It's funny," Nita mused almost to herself, "when you see a solid couple you think that things have always been that way. That they never had issues to work out."

"We're solid," Tory said. "As solid as any two people can be, but we certainly have issues." She sighed. "I never expected Iraq. I don't remember Vietnam, and who really imagines a war like this?"

"Where are things with that now?"

Tory grimaced. "Nelson's illness has just about eclipsed everything else, and now Reese is working double and sometimes triple shifts. We haven't really talked about it."

"Maybe that's a good thing." At Tory's surprised glance, Nita shrugged. "Reentry must be terribly disorienting. One minute, she's half a world away in the middle of a war. Added to the pressure of keeping other people from being killed, she must have been worried about her responsibilities to you—and then she's wounded and captured. A few days later she's home again. God, my head is swimming even thinking about it."

"You're saying that the best thing for her is just that she's home," Tory mused aloud, although she was really talking to herself. "That she gets used to being here, back in her life, *our* life, for a while before she…*we*…make any decisions."

"I think so." Nita leaned forward. "Even though she's terribly busy, I imagine it feels good to her to be surrounded by people she loves, doing the work she loves."

"Why didn't I see that?" Tory said reproachfully.

"Because she scared you to death and you thought you were going to lose her, and none of us sees too clearly when we're terrified."

"I think you're good for me." Tory smiled and wagged her finger at Nita. "Now you have to stay."

"I'd like that," Nita said softly, feeling just a little bit better for the last few moments of connection. She hadn't realized how much she'd missed that.

"So? Are you going to get out of here before it's too late to go out and have fun?"

Laughing, Nita threw up her hands. "I'm going. I'm going."

"Good," Tory said, rising. "Let loose a little."

"Whatever you say," Nita said, laughing too.

"I don't want to see you back here until Sunday afternoon," Tory said on her way out of the room.

When Nita contemplated the next thirty-six hours, she wondered how she would fill them. Of one thing she was certain. Letting loose was the last thing she wanted to do.

❖

Tory arrived home an hour later, and the house was dark. Her heart sank as she climbed the stairs to the rear deck. Reese must be working an extra shift again. She wondered how long Reese could keep up the relentless pace without folding. Even *her* formidable will and strength couldn't hold up forever.

"You need to stop worrying so much," Reese's voice came to her through the dark.

"You can't see my face, and I know I'm not talking to myself," Tory said, now able to make out the image of her lover reclining in a lounge chair. Already, her heart felt lighter. "So how do you know what I was thinking?"

"You were sighing." Reese reached out to her.

Tory laughed and clasped Reese's hand. "Up. If I lie down there with you, I'm going to fall asleep or want to make love. Unfortunately, I'm tired enough for the first and too tired for the second."

"I'm not sure I followed all of that," Reese said, unfolding her length from the chair and rising. She slipped her arm around Tory's waist. "But I got that you're tired. Want a glass of wine and a soak in the tub?"

"Oh God, that sounds good," Tory murmured, resting her cheek against Reese's shoulder. "Yes to the wine, but can I have it in bed?"

"Leg still bothering you?"

"A little."

"Then why don't you go upstairs and I'll be up in a few minutes with your wine."

Tory kissed her, lingering on her mouth and lightly teasing just inside with her tongue. "Thank you."

A few minutes later, Tory stretched out in bed and murmured appreciatively as Reese handed her a glass of red wine. Sipping slowly she watched with pleasure as Reese stripped and joined her beneath the sheets. "How's Reggie?"

"Talking up a storm." Reese took the glass when Tory offered and tasted the wine. "Words are right around the corner. It's amazing." She watched the red wine swirl in the glass. "She changes so quickly. I would have missed so much if I'd been gone longer."

Tory turned on her side and smoothed her fingers through Reese's hair. "Your mother told me your father was gone most of the time when you were this age. It must have been very hard for him."

"Maybe. I'm sure part of him was happy doing what he was trained to do. Not being deployed to Iraq this time is driving him crazy."

"I guess I don't quite understand anyone wanting a war," Tory said quietly.

"Wanting to test yourself, to do what you're trained to do, isn't quite the same thing as wanting a war," Reese said, "although I know it probably sounds that way."

"It's a distinction that's very hard to grasp." Tory stroked Reese's arm. "But you didn't want war, and you're as much a marine as he is."

"Thanks." Reese leaned close and kissed Tory briefly. "I'm a peacekeeper, and that's different than wanting to engage the enemy. I never needed a war to do what I thought was important."

"You're a peacekeeper here," Tory pointed out. "Not only do you keep your community safe, you help train the young to be strong and self-confident and self-reliant. You're a role model for young women and men just like Bri. This community needs you."

Reese cupped Tory's cheek and kissed her. "One thing's for certain. I don't want Nelson's job. A few weeks of dealing with the paperwork and bureaucracy is enough to convince me of that. I need to be on the streets."

"Until Nelson is back on his feet, you can't do both jobs." Tory held up an index finger in warning. "I mean it. There's nothing you can say that will convince me otherwise. As long as you're acting chief, you need to cut back on the street patrols. Please. Before you get hurt."

Reese grimaced, but nodded. "All right. We're starting to get things running smoothly again, especially now that Bri is back on duty."

"How is she doing?"

"She's a little distracted, a little tired, but Allie's watching out for her. She's okay."

"Good." Tory took the glass, finished the wine, and set the glass aside. "Nelson will be home in a few days and that will make it easier for her."

Reese rested back against the pillows and drew Tory into her arms. She kissed the top of her head and stroked her hair. "Speaking of fathers, mine called today."

Tory struggled not to pull away. She smoothed her fingertip along Reese's collarbone, noting that the swelling at the site of the fracture was better. "Oh?"

"There's a post open in his department at Strategic Planning in DC. He thought I should take it when my medical leave is over."

"DC." Tory willed herself to think—think, not react. "Not Iraq."

"No, not Iraq. Tory—"

"DC isn't so far. You'd get home sometimes, right? Or we could come—"

"Baby, I'm not going."

"I know it's a desk job and you hate that, but—"

"I told him I hadn't changed my mind," Reese said before kissing Tory into silence. She drew Tory on top of her and spread her fingers through Tory's thick auburn hair. "I told him I wanted him to finalize the paperwork for my discharge."

"Be careful of your collarbone. I'm too heavy to be on top of you just yet."

Reese laughed and kissed the tip of Tory's chin. "You're not heavy, but you are very sexy. How tired are you?"

Tory tilted her hips into Reese's crotch. "I'm waking up."

"So am I."

"Did he argue?"

"He said we'd talk again." Seeing the look of concern flash across Tory's face, Reese said quickly, "It's okay. He'll do whatever I want. He's just going to take a little convincing."

"I love you," Tory said softly. "I will support you in anything you need to do."

"I know." Reese caressed Tory's back and cradled her butt. "Right now, I need you."

Tory leaned up and turned off the light. Then she settled once again on top of Reese. "Darling, you never need to ask."

❖

Nita walked past the Vixen without a glance. At midnight on Saturday night, Deo was undoubtedly there if she hadn't already found company for the evening. Nita didn't want to chance another encounter, because she could never be certain how she was going to respond to her. She couldn't afford a repeat of the previous weekend's performance. Her life hadn't felt this off-kilter since the early days of her relationship with Sylvia. She could barely think, she couldn't eat, she couldn't sleep.

Ten minutes later she paid her cover and worked her way through the throngs of dancing, laughing women at the Pied. It was a little smaller but had the advantage of an outside deck right on the harbor and, after securing a drink at the bar, Nita walked outside and leaned on the deck rail. Sipping her drink, she let the sea breeze cool her heated skin. She was warm from the walk through town and her thoughts of Deo.

As disconcerting as it was to be plagued by the insistent thrum of unsatisfied arousal, she felt alive in a way she hadn't for months. And despite her regret over giving in to her urges with Deo, she wouldn't lie to herself and say that it hadn't been wonderful. For one blazing instant, riding the crest of nearly unbearable pleasure, she had felt completely free.

"Excuse me, but I was wondering if you'd like to dance?" a woman asked from quite nearby.

Nita didn't recognize the short-haired blonde with the pleasant smile, which was good. She had come out looking for a diversion, and she preferred to find it with someone she wasn't going to be seeing around town on a regular basis. "Yes. Yes, I would."

The tempo of the first dance was fast and the music too loud for conversation, but Nita managed to get a name and a few other snippets of vital information, the most critical of which was that Beth was in town for the week on vacation. One song segued into another until eventually the rhythm slowed enough that they could dance close. Twice in less than a week Nita found herself with her arms around a near stranger after having gone months without touching another woman. Beth was an inch or two shorter than Deo and thinner, lacking her hard muscles, but curving in all the right places. Nita enjoyed the swell of soft breasts moving against her own and the subtle press of Beth's thigh between hers as they danced. She was pleasantly aroused but in no danger of losing control again. When Beth deftly maneuvered them into a corner of the room and kissed her, Nita found Beth's soft lips and gently probing tongue enjoyable, but she felt none of the urgency she had with Deo. After a minute or two when Beth moaned softly and tightened her hold, Nita gently pulled away.

"I think I need to slow this down," Nita murmured.

"Sorry," Beth said breathlessly. "I don't usually—"

"Don't apologize. I'm not the least bit upset." Nita smiled. "I enjoyed the dance and the rest of it."

"Any chance we might get together sometime this week?"

"Give me your number. I'll call if I can."

"I don't have anything to write with," Beth said.

"Don't worry, I have a very good memory." After Beth recited the figures, Nita repeated them mentally, then kissed Beth lightly. "Thank you. And thank you for the dance."

Pleased that her restlessness had dissipated, Nita decided she'd achieved her goal and made her way to the exit. She had just stepped out into the narrow passageway that led to the street when Deo caught up to her.

"I take it the blonde wasn't to your liking?" Deo said.

Nita slowed, taking in Deo's tight white tank top, form-fitting black jeans, and boots. The shirt left nothing to the imagination, and even in the murky light cast by the neon signs on the street, Deo looked sleek and sexy. In one beat of her heart to the next, Nita became completely aroused.

"On the contrary," Nita said coolly, desperately trying to smother the flames licking at her insides. Several women left the bar together and she stepped off the wooden walkway to let them pass. Deo followed until they stood in the shadows of the building. "She was very pleasant."

"Pleasant." Deo said the word as if she were speaking of something that should be crushed under her boot. "You don't want pleasant."

"You don't know what I want."

"Sure I do." Deo leaned into her until their bodies touched. "You want the burn. You want the fire." She stroked Nita's cheek with one finger. "So do I. Come home with me."

"No."

"Why not? You came out looking for more than a kiss, and I never got a chance to touch you last week." Deo skimmed her hand lower, tracing Nita's throat with a gentle caress.

Nita's heart felt as if it might pound out of her chest, and she was glad Deo couldn't see her face very clearly. She doubted she could hide how badly she wanted Deo to keep touching her. "I told you, it was a one time thing."

"I don't consider a quick grope anything more than an invitation. I want to make love to you all night," Deo said. "*Then* maybe it will be a one time thing."

"I'm sorry." Nita stepped around Deo. "Good night."

"I need to go over some things with you at the job site," Deo said, grasping her arm. "You can't keep avoiding me."

"Fine." Nita pulled free. "I'll be by sometime this week. If I get time."

"There will be plenty of people around. You don't have to worry."

"You don't worry me." Nita turned and walked away, aware that Deo was watching her. No, Deo didn't worry her. What worried her was how desperately she wanted Deo's hands on her. Walking toward home, she knew that she faced another restless night and she had just said no to the only person who could have given her some relief. She'd said no because she had so very badly wanted to say yes. A mindless yes had nearly destroyed her once, and she could not let it happen again.

Chapter Sixteen

When her office phone rang, Nita gulped down the last of her soda and snatched up the receiver. "Burgoyne."

"Nita," Randy said, "it's Deo Camara again."

"Tell her—" Nita hesitated, feeling guilty about forcing Randy to make excuses for her. Deo had already called twice that week, and she'd ducked the previous calls with the message that she was with patients. Then she had conveniently not called back. "I'll take it."

A second later, Nita said, "Hello."

"It's Deo."

"I know." Nita couldn't help herself. She tilted her head back and closed her eyes. The sound of Deo's voice filled her with pleasure, and since Deo couldn't see her, she had no reason to hide her response.

"What time do you get off work?"

"Around seven, if no emergencies come up. Why?"

"I need you to do a walk-through with me," Deo said.

"Can it wait until the weekend? I'm off on Sunday."

"No. We should have done it two days ago but you've been avoiding me."

"I'm not—"

"Yes, you are."

Deo sounded both edgy and sexy, and an image of Deo in the tight white tank top that showed off her muscles and breasts came quickly to mind. Nita shivered with a full body memory of Deo gasping with excitement while they rocked against one another. Recalling how she had rushed to orgasm in Deo's arms, Nita's body quickened instantly, and she had the exhilarating, absolutely petrifying thought that if Deo kept talking she might come just sitting there.

"I can stop by your office if it's inconvenient for you to co—"

"No!" Nita couldn't see Deo at work. She wouldn't be able to concentrate for the rest of the evening. Worse, she couldn't trust herself.

Her plan to diminish Deo's unsettling impact on her by avoiding her had backfired. With each passing day, she thought of her more frequently. And the *nights*. Her nights were a nightmare of erotic dreams and feverish sleep.

"I'll meet you." Nita glanced at her watch. For a Thursday night the patient load was light, and there was no telling what Friday would bring. "I can be there in an hour and a half."

"That's fine. Thanks."

Nita hung up and rested her face in her hands, drawing deep breaths while she willed her traitorous body to calm. After a minute, she slumped back in her chair and opened her eyes. Tory stood in the doorway watching her.

"Bad news?" Tory asked with concern.

Nita laughed shakily. "No. No, that was Deo—something about the house."

"How's it going?"

"Fine. Fine."

"Deo is supposed to be very good."

Nita feared that Tory could tell she was blushing from across the room. When Tory moved further into the room and closed the door, Nita was certain of it.

"The last couple of weeks I got the sense something was bothering you," Tory said. "Do you want to talk about it?"

"We've got patients," Nita said.

"We've always got patients. Ten minutes won't change anything."

"It's nothing. Just stress—the house, you know."

"Uh-huh. The house."

Nita chewed her bottom lip. She had never told anyone what was happening with Sylvia. Who could she possibly have told who wouldn't tell her exactly what she'd been telling herself—getting involved with Sylvia was insane. It was a recipe for heartbreak. Worse, it was wrong. All the time her life had slowly been consumed by her affair with Sylvia, she had become more and more alone, until all she had left was thwarted desire.

"Deo is very attractive," Nita said quietly.

"Deo Camara is gorgeous." Tory sat down, looking as if she had all the time in the world. "Is she hitting on you?"

"Now why would you ask that," Nita said sarcastically.

Looking surprised, Tory said, "Because you happen to be very attractive too, and I imagine Deo has noticed."

"Apparently Deo makes a habit of hitting on women."

"I don't know her well enough to say," Tory said. "I doubt she lacks for company, considering that she's young and single and seems to be very nice."

"Not to mention the gorgeous part."

"Yes. There is that too." Tory paused. "And you're not interested?"

"No," Nita said after a long second. "I am."

It felt good to say it out loud, even if she had no idea what it meant. It felt good not to be alone with the feelings.

"You don't sound happy about it."

"I don't have time for the kind of upheaval a woman like Deo creates."

Tory frowned. "What kind of upheaval?"

"The distraction, the obsession. The…the…God, I don't know. I can't think."

"Sounds like you've already got the distraction part," Tory said with a small smile.

Nita laughed shortly. "Oh God, I do."

"You're attracted to her, but you're not sure you want to be."

"No. I'm quite certain I don't want to be." Nita stood and picked up the closest file. "As long as I remember that, I'll be fine."

"All right. That might work." Tory rose and gave Nita a quick hug. "If you ever want to talk, let me know."

"Thanks. I…just thanks."

❖

Deo paced on the wide front porch of Nita's house. Maybe Nita wasn't coming. Nita obviously didn't want to see her, but she just couldn't take the hint. Hell, Nita had gone out looking for sex with a stranger rather than take Deo up on her offer to go another round. That should have hammered home the message that Nita wasn't interested. But after slowly going crazy all week when Nita wouldn't return her calls, she had finally pushed her into a meeting. Totally unlike her. Then again, nothing about her reaction to Nita was like her.

It would have been so much simpler if she didn't know that Nita wanted her. Contrary to what everyone thought, there were plenty of women who weren't interested in her, and she didn't chase after them. She never made it a secret that she wasn't interested in anything resembling a long-term relationship, and that was enough to send most women running in the opposite direction. Now and then she misjudged and ended up going home with someone who *said* she only wanted a casual thing, but really believed she could change Deo's mind after a date or two. When that happened, Deo extricated herself as quickly and painlessly as she could.

But whatever else was going on with Nita, Nita wanted her body, at least. That had been amazingly and very pleasurably obvious for those few incinerating moments in the dark. Ordinarily, when Deo got the sense that a woman didn't want a repeat, she let it go. This time she couldn't, and not being able to get Nita out of her mind not only pissed her off, it confused her. Sure, she wanted Nita in bed again. Christ, who wouldn't. She was beautiful and sexy, and she set Deo off like a 220 volt blast straight to the groin. But it was more than possibly the best sex she'd had in her life that kept her thinking about Nita, that had her craving the sound of her voice and the lightest touch of her fingers all day long and half the night. When Nita told her about Sylvia, Nita couldn't hide how much she hurt. And she hurt in a way Deo understood. Passion and pain ruled Nita with equal measure, and Deo was drawn to both.

She braced her hands on the railing and watched the crowds passing by beyond the iron gates at the end of Nita's flagstone sidewalk. Men in groups, mostly shirtless, jostling and cruising. Women, usually in couples, many pushing strollers. Straight families, the kids oblivious to the passing spectacle and the parents trying to act as if being surrounded by same-sex couples was ordinary. All different, but still families of a sort. When she allowed herself to stop working and screwing until she was too tired to do anything else except drop into bed, Deo wondered what her life would have been like if she hadn't lost hers. And those pointless ruminations were exactly what drove her to fill her days with work and her nights with women.

The rusted wrought iron gate creaked open and Nita slipped through it. With the setting sun at Nita's back, Deo couldn't see her face clearly, but the air shimmered around her as she glided toward her. Her dark hair flowed loosely around her shoulders, and she lifted a hand to push the wind-blown strands away from her face. She was beautiful in the unselfconscious way of women who had no idea how truly beautiful they were.

"Sorry I'm late." Nita stopped at the bottom of the broad wooden stairs to take in Deo as she leaned with her forearms on the railing. Her T-shirt was damp at the neck and her hair looked wet. Nita had noticed several of the workmen dousing their heads and shoulders with a hose, washing away the grit at the end of the day, and she imagined that Deo had done the same. She could see Deo, the hose coiled in one hand, tossing her head back while water cascaded from her face. In the next breath, she envisioned Deo's face above her in bed, sweat dripping from her jaw onto Nita's cheeks as they rode each other. The image was so intense she nearly moaned.

"I thought you weren't coming," Deo said, trying to read what she saw in Nita's face. For a minute she thought Nita was going to turn and walk away.

"I was just about to head over here," Nita said breathlessly, "and we had an emergency. Tory is going to be seeing patients for another few hours as it is, and I couldn't leave her with an add-on, too."

"Something serious?"

Nita climbed the stairs, thankful that discussing work helped ground her. Her heart rate was slowing toward normal, and she could actually look at Deo without imagining how Deo would feel stretched out on top of her, naked. Almost. "A two-year-old with a peanut in her ear."

Deo laughed and led the way into the house. "Ouch. I bet that was fun."

"She was actually fine. It was her mother who was stressed, which is usually the case."

"I'll bet." Deo flipped a switch and a temporary overhead light, *sans* fixture, came to life. "Voilà."

"Very nice," Nita replied, admiring the dangling bare bulb. "Quite an improvement."

"Thank you," Deo said with a small bow. "So how did your patient manage to get the peanut stuck in her ear?"

"Compliments of her four-year-old brother."

"Ah, now I see." Deo walked into the kitchen, caught up in the easy conversation. Without thinking, she said, "I stuffed a bb up my brother's nose when we were four. They had a hell of a time finding it."

"I imagine." Nita was fascinated by the glimpse of pure pleasure that suffused Deo's face. She had so rarely seen her so unguarded. She looked young, carefree, happy. Then, the light in Deo's eyes died and she looked away. Without a second's thought, Nita grasped her hand. The scar that snaked across the top stood out starkly against her tan. "I'm sorry."

"For what?" Deo asked hoarsely.

"About your brother."

"Yeah. Well." Deo wasn't certain why she had even mentioned Gabe. She never talked about him. No one did, at least not when she was around. Maybe it was just easier to confess while standing in the middle of the century old kitchen with the fractured rays of sunlight slanting through the wavy glass windows, feeling as if she had been transported to another time. Nita's voice was so gentle, her fingers so warm and so soft. No one ever touched her just to soothe her pain.

"Gabriel," Deo heard herself say. His name felt strange on her tongue, as if it was a foreign language she'd forgotten she knew how to speak. "We were twins."

"Ah, God. It's terrible to lose a sibling, but a twin. I think that's even worse."

Deo's expression hardened and she pulled her hand away. "No. What makes it worse is when you kill him. Let's finish this up. I'm sure you have better things to do."

"Deo," Nita said as Deo turned away, unable to bear the terrible sorrow she glimpsed in Deo's face. "I understood it was an accident."

"From who?"

"Tory."

"It wasn't. I was there, I should know."

When Deo made no move to walk away, but instead stood staring out the window into the overgrown garden that overran a small flagstone patio, Nita stepped beside her and rested her hand on Deo's shoulder. In profile, Deo's face might have been carved from granite. "What happened?"

Beneath Nita's fingers, Deo's torso rose and fell with her quick shallow breaths.

"We were at a party. Most of the kids were a year or two ahead of us. Everyone was drinking and…he walked in on me and another girl when we had gotten to the point where we couldn't lie about what we were doing. I hadn't told him I was gay and he was pissed. I don't know if it was because I hadn't told him or because he was ashamed of me."

Nita felt Deo shudder but resisted the urge to put her arm around Deo's shoulders. She was afraid if she pulled Deo too far from her reverie she'd stop talking. "What did he say?"

"Nothing. Well, he cursed me out, and then he stormed out." Deo laughed brittlely. "Of course he was drunk, and he never could drink much. I caught up to him down at the harbor just as he was un-mooring the skiff we kept docked there. It was the middle of the night and a big storm was coming in. The waves were already too high for that size boat, but he wouldn't listen. I barely managed to jump in before he pulled away from the dock."

Deo stretched her arm along the window casement and rested her forehead against it. Nita couldn't see her face, but she didn't need to. She could hear the anguish. She gently rubbed small circles in the center of Deo's rigid back.

"He had always been a crappy pilot and loaded...forget it. He couldn't take the waves and we were foundering. I tried to make him give me the wheel, but I could hardly keep my feet under me. Then we went over and…" Deo choked and her shoulders heaved.

"Just take your time," Nita murmured.

"At first I couldn't find him, but somehow I grabbed onto his shirt. He didn't answer me when I yelled his name, and I couldn't see his face." Deo rubbed her eyes with one hand. "It took me so long to get him to shore. And then it was too late."

Nita was no stranger to pain. She consoled those who had lost loved ones all the time, aching for every one of them while she offered pitifully inadequate words of comfort. She held herself back then because she had to, because the distance allowed her to do what she was best at. But she couldn't bear to stand by helplessly while Deo suffered. Ignoring the alarm bells clanging wildly in her head, she threaded both arms around Deo's waist and pressed a kiss to the center of her back. "I'm so terribly sorry."

With a muffled groan, Deo spun around and pulled Nita into an embrace. But instead of kissing her, which is what Nita expected, Deo buried her face against Nita's neck. Holding her, Nita stroked the back of her head and rocked her gently, as she would a child.

"It's all right. It's all right," she whispered, even though she knew it wasn't. Words would not heal this wound.

After a few moments, Deo backed away. "I'm sorry."

"There's no need to apologize."

"I don't know why I told you that."

"I'm glad you did."

"Why?" Deo demanded. Anger warred with gratitude. She didn't want to talk about Gabriel, she didn't want to think about him. She didn't want to admit how good it felt to be held, and not blamed.

"Because I know how hard that was for you and I'm…I'm honored that you told me." Nita reached out to touch Deo's face, then stopped at the last second. They'd already gone too far.

"He wouldn't have been in that boat if it hadn't been for me. And if I hadn't let him pilot it, we wouldn't have capsized. He drowned because I fucked up."

"It was a horrible *accident*." Nita knew her words wouldn't change Deo's mind or assuage her guilt. "I'm so very sorry."

"Yeah." Deo let out a long breath. "Look, do you mind if we do this tomorrow?"

"No, of course not."

"I'll call you."

"All right." Nita followed as Deo strode rapidly ahead of her down the hall toward the front of the house. Deo held the heavy wood door open so Nita could step out onto the porch.

"I'd appreciate it if you would forget this happened," Deo said.

"I won't mention it to anyone." Nita already knew there was no way she could forget it. She could still feel Deo in her arms.

"Thanks." Deo closed and locked the door, then circled Nita without touching her. As she hurried down the front steps, she murmured, "Good night."

"Good night, Deo."

Nita watched Deo slip through the iron gate and disappear into the crowds. She wondered if there was a woman Deo would go to for comfort or just to help her forget her pain for a few hours. Slowly, Nita made her way down the walk, too weary and too raw to even pretend she didn't want to be that woman.

Chapter Seventeen

"Bri," Allie said, rolling down the window to get a better look at the figure hunched over on the edge of the pier, "pull over there."

"What have you got?" Bri eased the patrol car to a stop and squinted to see through the light rain that had begun falling just after midnight.

"There's someone leaning against the piling and it looks like they're about an inch from falling into the bay."

"Better check it out."

Allie stepped out of the car and flicked on her flashlight, then waited until Bri did the same before cautiously approaching the person, whose face was turned away. "You there, on the pier. Sheriff's department. You want to slide back from the edge?"

When the person gave no indication of moving, Allie played her light over the figure, looking for anything that suggested a weapon or other sign of danger. Closer now, she recognized the broad shoulders beneath the soaked T-shirt and the familiar line of her jaw. "Deo?"

Bri approached from the opposite side, and she and Allie reached Deo at the same time. Allie made a motion for Bri to wait and then squatted down next to Deo. "Hey, baby. What are you doing out here?"

Slowly, Deo turned her head. "Chasing ghosts."

"With what? Tequila?"

"Not for a few hours."

"Did you drive?"

Deo shook her head. "Walked."

"If you fall asleep you're going to end up in the harbor," Allie teased, studying Deo's face carefully. She seemed dazed, almost disoriented. "Take my hand so I can help you up."

"I'm okay." Deo braced one hand against the huge wooden piling and tried to get her feet under her. She swayed dangerously out over the water ten feet below them, the surface nothing more than a shiny black slick in the moonlight.

"Whoa," Allie said, yanking Deo's T-shirt and nearly toppling forward herself. "Steady."

Bri grabbed Deo from behind, hooked both hands under Deo's armpits, and dragged her back from the edge. "Jesus, Camara, you want to take Allie into the water with you? What the fuck are you doing?"

"Easy, Bri," Allie murmured, climbing to her feet.

"Sorry." Deo blinked rapidly. "Sorry."

"Get up." Bri lifted and Deo pushed herself to her feet. She wavered for a few seconds, then got her balance.

"I'm not drunk," Deo said, although her voice was thick, almost slurred.

"How much did you have to drink earlier?" Bri's expression was stony.

"A few shots. Just tired."

"Where's your truck?"

"Home."

"Come on, Deo," Allie said gently. "Get in the cruiser. We'll take you home."

"I'll walk. Clear my head."

Allie glanced at Bri who shook her head. "It's an ugly night and that's a long walk. Besides, this will give us something to do."

"I'll be okay."

Bri gripped Deo's arm. "Get in the cruiser, Camara. We're driving you."

Deo hesitated, then followed along as Bri escorted her to the patrol car. Once in the back seat, she leaned her head back and closed her eyes.

"Deo," Allie said softly five minutes later. "We're here."

"Thanks," Deo said after Allie got out and opened the door for her.

"You okay, baby?" Allie said softly.

"Yeah."

"You want me to come by later?" Allie ran her fingertips over Deo's chest. "Maybe just to talk?"

Deo covered Allie's hand with hers and squeezed gently. "Thanks. I'm just gonna crash."

"Sure. Just remember, you can always call."

Allie stepped back and then waited outside the cruiser until Deo unlocked the door and disappeared inside.

"We can swing by again," Bri said when Allie settled back into the front seat, "if you're worried about her. Make sure she doesn't take the truck out anywhere."

"She's probably in for the night, but if you don't mind—"

"Hell, Allie, I don't mind. She looks fucked up tonight. Is there some kind of trouble between you two?"

"No," Allie sighed. "I haven't seen her for a couple of weeks. I mean I've *seen* her, but not that way. We're really not an item."

"You want to be?" Bri asked as she headed back down Bradford to the center of town.

Allie was quiet for a minute. "I think if we were still fucking, I'd want to be, because I like her, you know?" She shifted on the seat a little and grinned at Bri. "She's like you. All dark and broody. I'm a sucker for that."

Bri laughed and kept her eyes on the road. "Yeah, right. So why haven't you gone after her?"

"She's not all broody over *me*, and I think I'm gonna hold out for a girl who is."

"I don't get that," Bri muttered.

Allie reached across the space between them and patted Bri's thigh. "I know you don't. But Caroline does."

❖

When the sunlight hit Deo in the eyes at six a.m, she rolled over with a groan and buried her face in the pillow. Cautiously, she took stock. Headache. Queasy stomach. Scratchy eyes. Not enough sleep. A little too much to drink. She hadn't set out to get drunk and quit drinking when she realized she was on her way, but the whole night was something of a blur. She should not have talked to Nita about Gabe—every time she thought about that night the guilt fucked her up.

She flipped onto her back and guardedly opened her eyes. Other than the fact that it felt like someone was sticking hot needles into her eyeballs, she figured she'd live. For a long time after Gabe had died, she hadn't really wanted to, but some part of her wouldn't give up. Plus, Pia would have kicked her ass if she'd done something stupid. So she'd shut down the parts of her that hurt and tried not to look back.

Then, something as simple as a childhood memory had brought it all back with perfect clarity. That happened sometimes, and it was always bad. This time was different. Nita had listened and whispered, *It's all right.* Deo knew that was a kind lie, but it felt good to have someone say it anyhow. Pia had tried, all those long years ago, but Deo had never believed her. She didn't believe Nita either, but knowing that Nita believed it still eased some of the hurt inside.

So maybe the jackhammer tearing up the inside of her skull was worth it after all. With a groan, she rolled out of bed and headed for the shower. On her way, she remembered Bri and Allie bringing her home. She'd have to call Allie and thank her.

Allie. Allie was sweet and sexy. Why not Allie? Why couldn't she be losing sleep over Allie? They were good together, and it would be simpler. Easier. She reached into the shower, twisted the faucet to cold, and stepped in. Gasping, she toughed it out until the cobwebs dissipated and her head felt clearer.

Not Allie—maybe because it *would* be easier. Easier maybe, but not as honest. And she liked Allie too much for that.

❖

Nita looked at her watch for the third time in five minutes and told herself for the tenth time in the last fifteen that she was making a mistake. She should not be sitting in front of her new house at six-thirty in the morning waiting for Deo Camara to come to work. She should not have lain awake half the night worrying about her, either. And she *certainly* should not have called her at two in the morning. Thankfully, Deo hadn't been home, and she hadn't left a message. What would she have said?

Hi, I'm calling you in the middle of the night because I can't sleep, and I can't stop thinking about the pain in your eyes.

Oh yes, that would have been perfect. Of course, discovering that Deo wasn't home only gave her an entirely new set of circumstances to lose sleep over. Who was holding her, consoling her—offering her pleasure to banish the pain? Imagining someone comforting Deo was every bit as difficult to tolerate as the visions of someone caressing her, making her cry out, making her come.

"This is crazy, and you're going to make yourself crazy," Nita muttered. She reached for the keys but before she could start the engine, Deo pulled in to the curb in front of her. Nita took a deep breath and watched Deo climb out of the truck. White T-shirt, khaki pants, work boots. Her hair still wet—her hair always seemed to be wet and every time Nita saw it, she wanted to drive her hands into it. Deo had circles under her eyes, and Nita didn't doubt that the shadows extended all the way inside.

Before she could talk herself out of it, Nita opened the car door and stepped out. "Good morning."

Deo walked cautiously forward. "Hi."

"I…uh…thought I'd get a look at the place during the day." Nita couldn't bring herself to say *I wanted to see you. I hate how much you were hurting last night.* "I know you're probably very busy right now and I won't keep you—"

"No, that's okay. The guys won't be here for at least half an hour." Deo came alongside Nita's car and stopped a few inches from her. "Do you want to go inside?"

"Sure, I—" Nita halted as a patrol car stopped in the street beside them and an officer stepped out. She didn't immediately recognize her, but it was clear that Deo did, judging by her surprised expression. When Nita looked closer, she realized who it was. Deo's *not* girlfriend. "Maybe we'll do this another time."

When Nita opened her car door to leave, Deo grabbed the top edge and held on.

"No," Deo said, "I won't be a minute. Don't go."

Nita hesitated, aware that the officer was standing a few feet away, observing the exchange. Deo hadn't taken her eyes from Nita's face and Nita couldn't look away from her. Her throat felt tight and dry. "Okay. I'll wait on the porch."

"Wait right here." Deo turned toward Allie. "Hi. Just finishing your shift?"

"Yeah, we're on our way in right now," Allie said. "We saw your truck was gone from the condo. You're here early."

"The forecast is calling for rain again tomorrow," Deo said. "You know how it is."

"I know. Contractors have to work while the sun is shining." Allie glanced up at Nita's house, then nodded to Nita. "It's looking good."

"Yes, thanks," Nita said.

"Thanks for the ride home last night," Deo said.

"No thanks needed." Allie slid back into the cruiser. As the cruiser pulled away she called out the window, "Be careful up on that roof today."

"Always." Deo waved after the cruiser, still holding Nita's door open with the other arm. Then she turned in Nita's direction. "Ready to go inside?"

"You sure it's no trouble?"

"None at all," Deo said, closing Nita's door. She led the way up the flagstone walk and inside. "There's something I want to show you in the master bedroom."

Nita followed up the wide twisting staircase to the second level. A balcony ringed the foyer below. The center room was the master bedroom, and when she walked in, she had an image of a four poster bed, an antique armoire, and a rich oriental carpet covering the wide plank floors.

"It's such a beautiful room."

"It is," Deo said. "The window seat on the back wall was designed to offer a view to the rear gardens." Deo indicated the narrow, multi-paned windows above the wooden seat that had at one time been covered by plush pillows. "Unfortunately, these window casements are shot and need to be replaced. Too much water damage."

"All right."

Deo leaned against the wall next to the window seat. "I was wondering if you might like a balcony outside your bedroom. I can take out the window seat, replace the windows with French doors, and put a balcony across the rear to overlook the garden. Nothing too big, just enough for a small table and chairs. You've got a bit of a harbor view and the sunset should be spectacular from here."

"Oh," Nita whispered. "That would be wonderful."

"Okay, then. I'll bring by a catalog so you can pick out the doors."

"You choose something. You know what suits the house." Nita started to sit on the window seat, but Deo stopped her with a hand on her arm.

"Dusty. You'll get your good clothes dirty. Hold on a second." Deo pulled a navy blue bandanna from her back pocket and wiped off the window seat. "There."

"Thank you." Nita flushed at the attention. "The gardens are going to need work."

"If you want a professional landscaper, I can suggest someone. Pia is really good too, if you just want ideas."

"I'll ask Pia when I get ready."

"So…do you want to take a look at the roof?" Deo asked.

Nita tilted her head back against the wall. "Not really. Whatever you're doing up there, I'm sure it's what needs to be done."

Deo grinned. "Trusting."

"About some things." Nita studied Deo's face. "How are you doing?"

"I'm happy with the way things are coming along. No big surprises yet."

"I didn't mean the house."

Deo shifted and looked out the window. "I'm fine."

"You look tired."

"I shouldn't go out to play on work nights."

Nita pushed aside the fleeting image of Deo in bed with a woman. "Did you get into trouble or do you always have a police escort home?"

"One drink too many. It's a small town, and the police really do serve as well as protect."

"I'm glad." Nita knew she shouldn't push, but from the way Deo's hand was balled into a fist and the rigid way she held her body, she was more than tired. She was hurting. "Is it because you told me about your brother?"

"What?" Deo asked in a raspy voice.

"The reason that you're so upset?"

Deo looked down at Nita, her eyes too shuttered for Nita to read. "I don't want to talk about it."

Nita stood up. Deo was very close, just inches away. Her legs trembled and it was hard to catch a breath. "We don't have to talk about it." She skimmed Deo's forearm with her fingers. "Perhaps with Pia. If you talk about it, a little bit, whenever you can, after a while it might not hurt so much."

"There are better remedies," Deo said darkly.

"Drinking only works for an hour or two, and the payback is hell." Nita smiled tremulously as something raw and dangerous surfaced in Deo's eyes. A wave of heat engulfed her, and she made no move to escape.

"*This* works every time." Deo grasped Nita by the shoulders and kissed her, pushing her back until she was pressed against the wall with Deo's weight upon her.

Nita wrapped both arms around Deo's shoulders and opened to her, absorbing her hunger through every pore. Her body ignited and she moaned. Deo caressed her breasts as she delved inside her mouth and Nita shuddered. She wanted Deo inside, so badly she was ready to beg. *Fill me, I'm starving. So hungry. So empty.*

Deo broke the kiss and buried her face in Nita's hair. "Nita. I'm going crazy for you. It's nuts."

"I know," Nita gasped. "Maybe we just need to burn it out of our systems." She slid her hand down Deo's back and cupped Deo's ass, pulling her hard into the vee between her legs. The jolt of pressure was exhilarating. "I can't stop thinking of you inside me."

Deo groaned. "Let's go to my place. Now. If I don't touch you I'm going to end up punching walls."

Nita grabbed Deo's hand and pressed it between her legs. "Touch me now."

"Nita," Deo gasped. She kissed Nita's neck, her jaw, her mouth. "We can't. Not here."

"Just a second. Only take a second," Nita urged, opening the waistband of her slacks. "God, I need you."

"Nita…wait." Deo shivered, her lips against Nita's ear. "I want more than a two minute fuck."

Sylvia's voice sliced through her mind. *Let me touch you, baby. It'll only take a second. Let me make you come. You know I love a fast fuck.*

"Oh my God," Nita whispered. Sylvia pushing her against the wall in the stairwell, her hand inside her scrubs, inside her, thrusting deep, fast, until she was coming, coming and crying and wanting more. Sylvia taking her in a frenzy after they'd been forced to spend the evening pretending they were mere acquaintances. Sylvia had taught her that the hunger was all there was, and a moment's satisfaction was all she would ever have. "My God, I can't do this again."

Nita pulled away, needing to brace one arm against the wall to steady herself. She couldn't look at Deo. "Please. Give me a minute. Just…please go."

"Not until you tell me what's wrong."

"I can't."

"Christ, you were just begging me to fuck you. What happened?"

"I came to my senses."

Deo grit her teeth. She wanted to grab Nita and shake her, or kiss her until she went soft and hot in her arms again. "Bullshit. What happened? Do what again? Is this about her?" When Nita didn't answer, Deo's head pounded with anger and the remnants of raging lust. "Jesus, what the fuck did she do to you?"

Nita shook her head. "It wasn't her. It was me. I let her."

"Let her do what? Teach you a minute was all you could have?"

"A minute is all I want."

"Fuck that. That was all she was willing to give you." Deo cupped Nita's chin in her hand and forced Nita to look at her. "I don't mind a quick, hard fuck. In fact, every time I see you that's exactly what I want." She rubbed her thumb over Nita's mouth. "But it's going to take more than that to burn you out of my head. All night, remember? That's the deal. That's what I want."

"One night?" Nita whispered, closing her slacks with trembling hands.

Deo kissed her. Long enough and hard enough to bring back the need, then she eased away. "That's what I said."

Nita's body ached. Sylvia's face, her voice, the touch of her hands shimmered through her memory. When she met Deo's intense eyes, the heat seared the other images away. "Touch me. Touch me so I know it's you."

"I'll make sure you know who it is," Deo murmured. Then she cupped Nita's face in her palms and kissed her again, slowly, deeply, tracing her forehead, her cheekbones, her jaw with the tips of her fingers. She caressed her until Nita relaxed against her body, her frenzy turned to yearning. "That's better. Now remember that."

Nita rested her cheek against Deo's shoulder as her heart pounded wildly against Deo's breast. "I will."

"Good. What time do you get off work tonight?"

"With luck, seven."

"I'll be there."

Chapter Eighteen

Nita pushed open the examining room door and smiled at Joey Torres, her heart lurching just a little at her first glimpse of the dark eyes and rakish grin that were so like Deo's. She nodded to Pia, who leaned against one end of the examining table. "Hi Joey. You must really rate, having your physical therapist come with you to get your sutures out."

Pia ruffled Joey's hair. "He's a big baby, and since my mother is tied up, I promised I'd come hold his hand."

"She's lying," Joey protested. "She just doesn't trust me to tell her your decision about when I can go back to work."

"It's not me!" Pia objected. "It's Deo!"

"Yeah, and you always side with her!"

"Mmm hmm," Nita said, half listening to the sibling banter as she released the Velcro straps on Joey's splint. The door opened behind her, and she glanced over her shoulder, expecting to see Sally. She hesitated for just a second, Joey's hand cradled in hers. Deo stepped a few feet into the room and slid both hands into the pockets of her work pants. She appeared the slightest bit uneasy.

"Yo, Deo," Joey said. "Just in time!"

"Oh good, I was afraid I'd missed the party." For all her bantering tone, Deo regarded Nita seriously. "Randy said I could come back. Is that okay?"

"It's fine." Nita shifted slightly so Deo was out of her field of vision and refocused on Joey's hand. She couldn't quite concentrate when Deo was in sight. "The incisions look excellent. We'll get your sutures out, but you're still not ready to go without the splint."

Behind her, Deo groaned. "So he still needs to sit around on his ass doing paperwork?"

Nita smiled but didn't look at her. "I'm afraid so."

"What a deal," Deo muttered.

"Joey," Nita said, "do you want to lie down while I remove the sutures?"

"Nah, I'm fine."

While Nita removed Joey's sutures, she discussed his therapy plan with Pia. The entire time she worked, she was aware of Deo peering over her shoulder. Every now and then, warm breath wafted across the side of her neck, and by the time she finished, her entire body tingled.

"There you go," Nita said. "Let me see you in a month, Joey. Keep up the program that Pia outlines for you, and I think we'll be able to get you into a smaller splint then. Pia, are you good with that timing?"

"So far. If anything changes, I'll let you know." Pia slung her arm around Joey's shoulder and kissed his cheek. "You were so brave."

"Cut it out," he complained, but he was grinning.

Pia laughed. "Come on, I'll take you for ice cream."

Deo snorted. "Is he going to get a balloon, too?"

"When you stop at the desk to make your next appointment," Nita said gravely, "Randy will give you a lollipop."

"Cool," Joey said, jumping down from the table.

"Be sure to bring him back to work," Deo grumbled to Pia. "We've still got plenty of ordering for him to do."

"Don't worry, boss," Pia said, patting Deo's cheek. "I'll deliver him in an hour or so."

Nita straightened after finishing her chart note and discovered that the room was empty except for Deo. The door to the hall was closed and they were alone. Deo watched her from a foot away, the expression in her dark eyes even more intense than usual. Reflexively, Nita took a step back and her hips bumped into the examining table. "I didn't expect you."

"I know." Deo stepped closer. "How's your day going?"

"All right. Fine. Busy."

"Mine too. Except I can't concentrate because I keep thinking about kissing you."

Nita held the chart up between them, feeling the beginnings of panic. "Don't touch me."

"Why not?" Deo asked, her voice low and husky.

"Because I'm working and I can't do this here."

"Do what?" Deo frowned.

"We can't…" Nita glanced at the door. It wasn't locked. "Anyone can come in. I can't."

"Nita, it's okay." Deo eased back. "I just wanted to see you. I'm not going to try anything."

"I'm sorry. I just…" Nita grasped Deo's hand. "I'm glad to see you."

"Remember what I told you this morning—what I think about every time I see you?"

Nita nodded. *I have nothing against a quick, hard fuck. In fact, every time I see you that's what I want.*

"Just because I want my hands on you doesn't mean I'm going to force you," Deo said.

"You wouldn't be forcing me," Nita whispered. Deo's hand was hot, so hot. She could feel Deo's fingers brushing over her breasts, twisting her nipples, teasing between her thighs. She ached and her breath shuddered in her chest. She wouldn't say no. "You wouldn't have to."

"But it's not what you want, is it?"

"No. Not here."

"I know." Deo freed her fingers from Nita's grip. "I'm sorry if I've upset you."

"You haven't." Nita smiled shakily. She couldn't pretend that Deo's interest, her attraction, didn't feel good. It did. It felt wonderful. "I'm glad you came by. I'm glad you wanted to see me."

Deo grinned. "Good. So, I'll be back at seven. I'm taking you to dinner."

"Are you?"

"Yes. I know this little restaurant. Very private, great food. You'll like it."

"Pretty sure of yourself."

"About some things." For a moment, Deo looked uncertain. "I *will* see you tonight, right?"

"Yes." When Deo started to turn away, Nita grabbed her hand again and stopped her. Then she kissed her. She had wanted to kiss her since the instant she'd seen her, but she had been afraid. Afraid of where it would lead. Afraid of losing control. Afraid of the wanting overpowering her reason. But Deo hadn't pushed her, and now she wasn't afraid. Deo's lips were soft and warm, her tongue a gentle sigh in Nita's mouth. Desire blossomed full and rich in her depths, and she welcomed it. Far sooner than she wanted, she drew away. "See you at seven."

"Hell, Nita. If I think about that while I'm up on the roof, I'll fall off." Deo's chest rose and fell rapidly and her eyes glittered with arousal.

Nita tapped Deo's chest with one finger. "Then don't think about it."

"Yeah, right. I won't breathe, either."

Laughing, Nita pushed her toward the door. "Go. Stop distracting me."

Deo opened the door, then grinned over her shoulder. "Don't lie. You like it, right?"

Maybe, Nita thought, *maybe I do*. Shaking her head, she pointed to the hallway. "*Go.*"

With a laugh, Deo disappeared.

❖

Deo wiped the sweat from her face with the bottom of her T-shirt, then clambered down the scaffold and headed around the side of the house into the front yard. Pia and Joey ambled toward her from the street.

"Two hours," Deo said. "You can eat a lot ice cream in two hours."

"Oh, stop being such a tyrant," Pia said. "I got him back in plenty of time to do all the paperwork you need. Besides, it's my mother's birthday party this weekend and we had to pick out a present."

"The list of the paint and drywall we need is in the kitchen," Deo said to Joey. "We have to get the orders faxed out today."

"Aye, aye, Captain," Joey said, giving a mock salute. He dodged as Deo tried to swat him and hurried off laughing.

"You're coming to the party, right?" Pia said.

Deo looked away.

"You have to."

"I know." Deo sighed. "I'll stop by for a few minutes, okay?"

"My mother adores you, and she'll be heartbroken if you don't come. My father will keep an eye on how much your father's drinking.

It will be okay." Pia slid an arm around Deo's waist. "And I need you there. Otherwise, I'll drown in testosterone."

Deo laughed. "What about KT? Won't she be there?"

"She's going to try, but she's on call the night before, and sometimes she doesn't get out when she expects to. Besides," Pia nudged Deo's hip with hers, "KT makes my bones melt, but she rates right up there with my brothers on the macho scale. She'll probably spend the afternoon talking sports with Joey and Antonio."

"What do you think I'm going to be doing? Discussing floral arrangements?"

"At least I can count on you to hang with me."

"Okay, okay. I'll come."

"You can always bring a date."

Deo rolled her eyes. "Yeah right."

"Still seeing Allie?"

"Not that way. We're friends, that's it." Knowing where the conversation was headed, Deo tried to extricate herself from Pia's grasp. "Look, I have to get back to work."

"Uh-huh," Pia said, grabbing the bottom of Deo's T-shirt and twisting it in her hand. "What aren't you telling me?"

"Nothing. Not a thing."

"You looked just like this when you were up to your eyebrows in Calley O'Reilly a week before she was supposed to marry Jimmy Jones. You didn't want me to know you were fooling with her because you knew I'd kick your ass."

"She was a dyke," Deo protested. "She didn't marry him, did she? And now she has a pregnant wife and so does Jimmy. It all worked out just fine."

"That's not the point. Jimmy wanted to kill you." Pia dragged Deo over to the porch and pulled her down onto the steps "You couldn't hide the good stuff from me then, and you still can't. Who is she?"

Deo wanted to say no one, because technically it was true. She and Nita hadn't slept together and they certainly weren't dating. But denying her didn't feel right. "I'm sort of in the middle of this…thing, right now. It's just temporary."

Pia frowned. "A temporary thing. Define thing."

"Jesus, Pia. Gimme a break, will you. I have to go back to work."

"You're the boss. You should be sitting in a lounge chair under a tree telling the boys what to do. You can spare me fifteen minutes." Pia rested her hand on Deo's leg. "You look like shit, by the way. What's going on?"

"I just had a rough night." Deo stared hard at a sliver of blue water that was visible between two houses across the street. By day, the harbor looked beautiful, by night, its dark surface reflected her tormented memories. "I told Nita about Gabe, and it kind of twisted me up. That's all."

Pia took Deo's hand and drew it into her lap. "You told Nita."

"Yeah."

"You're seeing Nita?"

"Not exactly," Deo said quietly.

"Sleeping with her?"

"Not exactly."

"What does that mean? Heavy petting?"

Deo laughed. "We kind of have this thing."

"You said that already, sweetie. Your vocabulary is a little lacking today."

"I can't get her out of my head, and if I don't get her into bed soon I'm going to do more than fall off the roof."

Pia squeezed Deo's hand. "I thought there was something when I saw the way she looked at you this afternoon."

"What way?" Deo studied Pia intently.

"When you first walked in she got really still, for just a second, and looked at you…how should I say this. Like she wanted to swallow you whole."

Deo groaned.

"How long has this *thing* been going on?"

"I don't know. I think maybe since the first time I saw her."

"Uh-oh."

Deo closed her eyes. "You got that right."

Pia kissed Deo's cheek. "She's beautiful. And I really like her."

"It's not like that."

"Deo, sweetheart," Pia murmured. "If you told her about Gabe, then this is like nothing you've ever experienced before. You know that, right?"

"I'm not like you, Pia. I don't do relationships."

"I know." Pia stood up and dusted off the back of her slacks, then smiled at Deo. "Of course, you've never had any reason to before. Bring her to the party this weekend."

"No fucking way."

"Never say never," Pia called back over her shoulder. "Love you."

"Yeah," Deo muttered, wondering how it was Pia always got her to tell her everything. Even the things she didn't want to admit to herself.

❖

"Can you believe it?" Tory said to Nita as they walked up the hall together, leaning into the examining rooms and turning off the lights as they went. "We're actually done at a decent hour. Both of us."

"I think this is the first time that's happened in almost two months." Nita shrugged out of her lab coat and stepped into her office to hang it on the coat tree. She had an hour before she was due to meet Deo, and she was inordinately pleased that she could go home and change into something more casual than what she wore to work. It seemed foolish, because they weren't actually having a date.

"I don't know about you, but I'm going to make the most of it." Tory waited while Nita collected her bag. "I'm going to find Reese and make her take me out to dinner. How about you? And don't tell me you're going to stay home and read a book."

Nita flushed, imagining herself saying, *I'm meeting a woman for sex.* "I'm having dinner with Deo. To talk about the house."

"Ah. A business dinner."

"Yes," Nita said quickly. It *was* a business dinner of sorts. They were going to deal with the unfinished business between them. Clear the air. Scratch the itch that had been driving them crazy. Driving her crazy, at any rate. She still wasn't certain why Deo would bother when there had to be any number of women who would likely volunteer to scratch her anywhere she needed it.

"I hope she's taking you to Porto's. It's her cousin's restaurant. Really hard to get into during the season."

"I'm beginning to think that Deo has a family member available to fill every need." Nita laughed as she and Tory entered the deserted waiting area. Randy was still behind the reception counter working on the computer.

"Don't stay too late," Tory called to him.

He waved. "Don't worry. I'm out of here in five minutes. I can still catch the last hour of the tea dance."

Tory held the door open for Nita, then followed her out into the parking lot. "I hope you have a great time tonight."

"It's not a date," Nita clarified.

"I haven't forgotten that conversation we had about a certain gorgeous someone you weren't really attracted to," Tory teased gently.

"Oh God," Nita said, stopping by her car. "I don't know why I'm pretending with you. I haven't the slightest idea what I'm doing with her."

"Maybe that's good," Tory said. "Maybe it's better not to have expectations, either good or bad. That way, whatever happens will just be true."

"Wouldn't that be nice," Nita whispered as she slid into her car. She rolled down her window and waved as Tory unlocked her Jeep. "Have fun with your sheriff."

Tory grinned. "That's my plan."

Chapter Nineteen

The station house was empty except for Gladys, sitting behind the semi-circular counter that held several computer screens and the radio equipment.

"Hi Gladys," Tory said. "Reese around somewhere?"

"In the office," Gladys replied, inclining her head toward the closed door behind her. "I hope you came to kidnap her."

"You're reading my mind."

"Good, because as much as I love her, I'm getting tired of her company."

"I'll take her off your hands for tonight, at least." Tory saw by the large plain-faced clock on the wall that it was closing in on six-thirty. Gladys usually left two hours earlier. "Shouldn't you be getting out of here too?"

"I will, as soon as one of the boys shows up to relieve me."

Tory wagged her finger as she pushed through the wooden gate and threaded her way between the desks towards the chief's office. "I know everyone's working overtime, but I'm counting on you to set a good example for this crew."

"You know damn well that if Reese works eighteen hours a day so will everyone else, even if she doesn't tell them to."

"Well I'm going to take care of that problem right now. She won't be back tonight."

"Good."

Tory tapped on the door which said Nelson Parker in bold black letters and walked into the unadorned ten-by-twelve-foot office. Reese was behind the desk, her tie askew and her eyes red rimmed. She looked more harried than tired.

"Hello darling."

Reese dropped her pen and leaned back in her chair, a welcoming smile on her face. "This is a nice surprise."

"Busy?"

"I can probably spare you a minute."

"Oh, you think so?" Tory circled the desk, grasped the arms of Reese's swivel chair, and kissed her. Once certain that she had Reese's attention, she slid onto her lap and wrapped her arms around Reese's neck. Reese gripped her waist, groaning softly as Tory slowly and thoroughly explored her mouth. After a minute, Tory realized her plan to seduce her lover into leaving work was about to backfire. They hadn't made love in a few days, and the kiss was quickly getting away from her and turning into something far more serious. Reese felt so good, her body so tight and hard, her lips so soft, so hot. Tory wasn't thinking about dinner anymore, she was thinking about Reese's mouth on her, teasing her until she was too helpless to do anything except come. Tory pulled back, breathing hard.

"I think I need more than a minute."

"Christ," Reese muttered. "Kiss me again like that and I'm not even going to need thirty seconds."

Tory laughed and massaged Reese's shoulders while gently rolling her hips in Reese's lap. "I have every intention of kissing you again like that." She brushed a quick kiss over Reese's mouth. "In fact, I'm going to do a lot more than that. After you take me to dinner."

Reese growled and buried her face in Tory's neck. As she bit slowly on the muscle that shadowed the pounding pulse in Tory's neck, she skated both hands up Tory's sides and over her breasts. Tory gasped, feeling herself get wet. Twisting her fingers through Reese's hair, she dropped her head back and closed her eyes.

"Don't get me too excited, darling, please," Tory whispered, rocking her ass harder into Reese's crotch.

"Why should I be the only one going crazy?" Reese grunted. She found Tory's nipple and pinched rapidly.

"Oh God, Reese…don't. You know how much that makes me want to come."

Reese tugged Tory's earlobe with her teeth, then skimmed the tip of her tongue along the shell of her ear. "I love it when you need to come. I love the way you rub against me, the way your breath catches in your throat. I love the small sounds you make when you start to swell and pound inside, almost like it hurts, but I know it doesn't."

"Stop it." Tory pushed Reese's hands away. "That's so wonderful I can't stand it."

Laughing, Reese wrapped her arms around Tory's waist and kissed her throat. "Didn't you come here to seduce me?"

"Into taking me to *dinner*. I wasn't planning on having an orgasm in your office." Panting softly, Tory rested her cheek against Reese's shoulder. "Sex was supposed to be dessert."

"Let's make it the appetizer. Then we'll pick up the baby and get takeout."

"Yes," Tory murmured, nuzzling Reese's neck. "Yes, soon. I just need a minute to settle down so Gladys doesn't take one look at me and know what we've been doing."

"Don't settle down too much," Reese warned, stroking Tory's hip. "I'm taking you straight home to bed."

"Mmm," Tory sighed. "Will you make love to me until I scream?"

Reese's expression darkened and her voice dropped impossibly low. "Until you scream for me to stop."

No longer caring about anything except giving herself over to the connection she shared with Reese and no one else, Tory rose, her legs shaking as she clutched Reese's hand. "Now. Take me home now. I need you."

❖

When Deo's phone rang at quarter to seven, her stomach sank. Nita was calling to cancel. She'd worried all day, despite their brief conversation during the afternoon, that in the cool light of day Nita would change her mind. It was one thing to give in to passion in the heat of the moment, and quite another to view it as something you wanted, something you wanted with another person, and to allow it to happen.

Truth be told, she was nervous herself. Usually when she ended up in bed with a woman it was because she clicked with her by chance—she wanted company, and so did her bedmate, or she was twisted up inside, running on adrenaline, needing release, and a woman was there, offering a few hours of pleasure. She'd never thought about a woman the way she thought about Nita, day in and day out, remembering the way she looked or something she'd said or the slightest touch. She never thought about a woman and wanted her enough to say, *Be with me tonight.*

"Hello?"

"Deo, it's Nita."

Deo held her breath.

After a moment of silence, Nita said, "Are you there?"

"Are you canceling?"

"Do you want me to?" Nita said softly.

"No. No, I don't."

"I got done early and I'm home. Can you pick me up here?"

The tightness in Deo's chest eased. "I'll be there in ten minutes. Do you mind walking from there? It's not far."

"That would be nice. I'll see you in a few minutes."

Deo disconnected, shoved the phone into her pocket, and grabbed her keys. She wanted to get there, get to Nita, before something happened to change everything. Rather than fight traffic, she swung around the far West End and drove up 6 faster than she should have until she could cut back into town. She parked on a side street around the corner from Nita's and hurried down to Commercial. When she rounded the corner, she slowed. Nita waited on the sidewalk in front of her house. She had changed into casual black slacks with low heels and a cream colored silk blouse. Her hair was loose and the same brisk wind that lifted her hair in thick dark waves molded the silk to her body, outlining her breasts. Deo imagined the weight of Nita's breasts in her hands and stumbled. Just at that moment, Nita turned in her direction. Her face softened as she laughed.

"Hi," Deo said.

"Good evening." Nita looked Deo up and down. Tonight, loafers replaced her work boots, and her navy blue polo shirt and tight blue jeans left nothing about her muscular body to the imagination. On impulse, she took Deo's hand. "You look great."

"So do you." Deo kissed her lightly. "Better than great."

"I'm starving," Nita whispered, afraid if they didn't move soon she would simply pull Deo down the path behind them and into her apartment. And then all pretense that they were doing anything other than preparing to vent their pent-up sexual frustration would be lost. She wanted her, and she couldn't hide it. What she saw in Deo's eyes convinced her she wasn't alone. "Are we still going to dinner?"

"Yes." Deo's voice was hoarse. "We are."

Nita nodded and fell into step as Deo led the way. At just before seven, the sun still held some heat and the ocean breeze was welcome. The streets were crowded, the atmosphere jubilant, and Nita realized she hadn't been on a date—an evening out with a woman whom she found attractive and interesting—in years. Swiftly, she reminded herself that this wasn't a date. She couldn't allow herself to think otherwise.

"Are we going to Porto's?"

Deo looked surprised. "Yes. You know it?"

Nita shook her head. "No, but Tory said it's wonderful. That your family owns it."

"My aunt and uncle on my father's side."

"What if I told you I wasn't going to sleep with you tonight."

Deo's pace didn't slow. "I'd tell you to try the lobster fra diavlo. It's the house special." She stopped as they turned a corner into one of the narrow side streets and pulled Nita around to face her. She kissed her, more deliberately than she had a few minutes before. "I'd tell you that I like to look at you. I think you're beautiful." She cradled Nita's face and kissed her again, leaning into her until their bodies just barely touched. "I'd tell you that I want to make love to you so much I hurt, all the time, but if all you want is dinner, we'll sit and talk over glasses of port until my cousin throws us out. Then I'll walk you home and say good night." Deo kissed her again, tracing her tongue inside Nita's lower lip. Nita tasted sweet and warm. Then she pulled back and caressed Nita's shoulders and down her arms. "So what are you telling me?"

"The very first time I saw you I imagined you touching me." Nita stroked Deo's face. "And every time since. I imagined it, but I didn't want it. I don't know what I want tonight."

"Try the lobster fra diavlo." Deo started walking again, Nita's hand firmly in hers.

❖

Lying on her stomach with Reese stretched out along her back, Tory thrust her hips up and moaned when Reese rocked against her. Reese's cheek was damp against the back of her neck, and Reese's grip on her hands was so tight her fingers ached. The weight of Reese's body pinning her down was at once comforting and exciting. Tory held her breath, listening to Reese's labored gasps, her own arousal at a fever pitch. Just when she was certain Reese would climax, Reese lifted up and away.

"Don't stop, darling, I want you to...oh God." Tory lost the words as Reese cupped her from behind, alternately entering and then stroking her. As Tory hurtled toward orgasm, she was dimly aware of Reese pressing rhythmically against her hip and whispering her name. "Inside me," Tory moaned, "inside me...be inside me when I come."

With a muffled cry, Reese pushed into her. As Tory slipped into orgasm, she sensed Reese follow. She held onto the pleasure as long as she could, sliding up and down Reese's fingers, milking the rippling contractions until she collapsed into a boneless puddle. Reese groaned and rolled off. Tory spooned her backside into the curve of Reese's stomach and sighed with contentment.

"I hate to be unoriginal," Tory murmured, "but that was so good."

Reese chuckled and moved Tory's hair aside to kiss her neck. "Sorry it was so fast. I can't seem to wait these days."

"It wasn't too fast." Tory turned onto her back and cupped Reese's jaw. "I don't want slow and easy. I want to feel you everywhere at once, as deep inside as you can get. I need that too." She kissed her. "Slow and easy will come when we're both ready."

"I need you all the time."

"I'm not complaining."

"Being away from you shook me up," Reese said, her expression distant. "I was too busy all the time to really think about it, but nothing felt right. Inside. You and Reggie, you're my reason for everything."

"Before you had us, being a marine was everything." Tory draped her leg over Reese's and curled closer. "You wouldn't have come here five years ago if you hadn't been looking for something else you needed. I like to think it was us."

"Believe me, it was."

"Maybe it was so hard over there because you expected to feel the way you did about being a marine before you had us. I bet lots of the other marines felt just like you, being away from their families. You just never had any practice at it before."

"I don't think my father ever felt the way I did," Reese said flatly.

"You can't be sure of that, but if it matters, maybe you should ask Kate."

"It doesn't matter. I'm not him." Reese pulled Tory on top of her and kissed her. "Maybe I'm not the marine I thought I was, but I'm so much more because of you."

"Darling, you are a fine marine. And a wonderful lover. And a great mother. And a perfect partner." Tory kissed Reese's throat, then her breast, then down the center of her abdomen. She rubbed her cheek against Reese's lower belly. "I adore you."

Reese combed her fingers through Tory's hair and lifted her hips to guide Tory between her thighs. "Take me slow and easy this time."

"I'd love to," Tory whispered, brushing her lips over Reese's clitoris.

Reese closed her eyes and sighed as Tory drew her between her lips. Light as bright as rocket flares burst behind her eyelids as Tory tongued her, and the heat spreading through her belly and thighs was like the desert, scorching her. But this time she burned not with uncertainty and apprehension, but with the sure and certain knowledge of who she was and where she belonged.

Reese's cell phone rang, and Reese cursed. She was seconds from orgasm. When she tried to twist and reach for it, Tory pressed a hand against her belly and held her down, relentlessly teasing her with her mouth and tongue.

"Baby," Reese moaned as the phone continued to ring and the pressure became so intense her stomach spasmed. She was so close and she needed the release so badly. The phone kept ringing. "Baby I should…" Tory pushed down on her stomach and entered her with her other hand and Reese went rigid. In the next breath, she came.

When Reese opened her eyes, her face was pillowed against Tory's breasts. She didn't remember Tory moving, didn't remember Tory pulling her into her arms. She didn't remember starting to cry.

"It's all right, darling," Tory soothed, stroking Reese's face. "I promise, everything is all right."

"I love you."

"Mmm, I know. That's *my* everything."

"The phone—I should check…"

"I know." Tory leaned across Reese for the phone. With one arm around Reese's shoulders, she handed it to her.

Still trembling from her orgasm, Reese checked the last number. "It's Bri."

"Delegate. I'm not done with you yet."

Grinning, Reese called back. "Conlon." Listening, she tensed and sat up. "I'll be right there."

"What is it?" Tory asked as Reese disconnected and stood up.

"Are you on call tonight?"

"No, Nita. Why?"

Reese grabbed her pants and pulled them on. "Because I might need someone to give an official time of death. Bri's got medics working on someone right now."

"Do you want me to come with you?" Tory got out of bed and pulled on her robe.

"No. Go ahead and get the baby. It might take a while to sort this out. I'll call Nita if I need her."

Tory kissed Reese. "You okay?"

"A lot better than I was an hour ago." Reese kissed her again and hurried toward the hall. "You should go ahead and have dinner. I love you."

"Be careful." Tory sank down on the side of the bed, her body still craving Reese's touch. Despite missing her already, her heart felt lighter. Reese had cried— something she almost never did. Tory couldn't help but feel that these tears were just what they both needed.

❖

"So?" Deo said. "What do you think?"

"I want to marry your aunt," Nita said, after savoring another bite of fra diavlo. "God, this is good."

Deo laughed. "Told you."

"I definitely made the right choice."

"You mean dinner over wild sex with me?" Deo teased.

Nita pretended to look thoughtful. "Well, I don't suppose there are many women who could…cook like this."

"That's cruel." Deo reached across the table and took Nita's hand.

"Don't I get a reward for introducing you to this culinary delight?"

Nita regarded their joined fingers. Deo's were rough, marred here and there by small nicks and scrapes, but her touch was amazingly gentle. Like the woman herself. She rubbed her thumb carefully over the scar on Deo's hand, then she looked up to find Deo studying her intently. "What would you like as your reward?"

"To hold you," Deo said instantly. "To make love with you. No rush. Just us. As fast or slow or hard or soft as we wanted. Jesus, Nita, please, I…"

"Shh. I don't want you to beg."

"I don't mind," Deo said. "And I have no idea why I don't."

"I don't want that kind of power over you," Nita said firmly. "I've been there. It doesn't feel good."

"Why didn't you leave her?"

"Because she said she needed me," Nita said bitterly. "Me and only me. Because I'd never been enough for anyone before, and she made me believe I was the only one who could make her happy." She shook her head. "Pretty pathetic."

"Did she make you happy?"

"No," Nita said after a long moment. She took a breath, refusing to lie despite hating the truth. "But while she was inside me, owning me, telling me no one could ever take my place, I felt worthwhile."

"That's powerful," Deo murmured.

"Yes." Nita tried to pull her hand away, embarrassed, but Deo wouldn't let her. "I was addicted to the way she made me feel. We'd been lovers on and off since I was twenty, but she could never admit to being a lesbian. I swore I'd stop when she got married, but she'd come to me, wild for me, and I couldn't say no."

"But you finally broke it off."

Nita laughed bitterly. "I didn't have much choice once everyone knew."

"And she never called?"

"Oh, she called. She called for months, begging me to meet her. Just to talk. But I knew what would happen." Nita filled her wine glass and swallowed deeply. "That's a big reason why I took this job. A new place, far enough away so we wouldn't bump into each other. Too far for a rendezvous."

"Do you still want her?"

"No. No, I don't."

"Good."

Nita smiled ruefully. "That's it?"

Deo shrugged. "She had a hold on you. It happens. Sometimes I think it's not the hold that hurts, it's what people do with the power that it gives them. She wasn't worthy."

"You're a very interesting woman, Deo. Why don't you have a lover?"

"I..." Deo broke off, her face flushing as her cousin stopped at the table.

"Sorry," Lucia said brightly. "I didn't mean to interrupt. Can I take your plates and bring you some dessert or a little port?"

Deo looked at Nita.

"Dinner was wonderful," Nita said, her eyes on Deo. "But I think I'll pass on the port tonight."

Deo grinned. When her cousin had collected the dishes and moved away, she asked, "Does that mean we're not going to close this place?"

"Actually, I thought we might spend the rest of the..." Nita broke off as her cell phone rang. "Sorry. I'm on call. Just a second."

Nita found her phone in her purse. "Hello? Yes. I'm sorry, where? All right, yes. About ten minutes." She put the phone away. "I'm so sorry. I have to go."

"Where?"

"The sheriff needs me down at the Coast Guard station."

"I'll walk you down."

"No, I don't think you should. I'll be fine."

"Why not?"

"Really, Deo. That's not necessary." Nita could tell Deo was going to insist and lying to her was out of the question. "There's a body on the beach—probably a drowning. You don't need to see that."

Deo leaned across the table. "I don't need you to protect me from anything."

"Maybe not. But I want to."

"You're a very surprising woman yourself, Dr. Burgoyne," Deo murmured. "Will you call me later?"

"Are you going home? The night's still young," Nita said, trying to sound lighthearted. She loathed the thought of Deo ending the evening in bed with another woman.

"Believe me, no one else will do." Deo stood as Nita rose and kissed her. "And that's not a line, or a power trip. It's just the truth."

CHAPTER TWENTY

Reese angled the umbrella into the wind and tried to shield Nita as she knelt over the still form on the ground. The wind had picked up noticeably in the last few hours, and whitecaps roiled the normally sheltered water of the harbor. Headlights from several emergency vehicles, including her cruiser, crisscrossed over the small group huddled around the body. Beyond, the night was starless.

"Time of death 9:53 p.m.," Nita said without looking up. "I'm going to take blood right now for a tox screen. Can someone get me a syringe and some ice?"

"Coming up, Doc," one of the EMTs said. "We pulled some earlier when we started the IV."

"Good, I'll make a note for them to run both of them in Hyannis when they do the post. Some substances degenerate quickly with time." Nita ignored the water dripping into her eyes and off her jaw onto the pale, still face below her. Someone's son, possibly someone's brother. She thought of Deo as she accepted the syringe from the medic, palpated the thick sternocleidomastoid muscle in the neck, and slid the needle into the jugular vein. She tried not to imagine Deo looking down at her brother's lifeless face. "Any idea what happened?"

"Bri and Allie are still looking for witnesses," Reese said. "The first anyone noticed him was when he washed ashore. Think he could've come off a boat somewhere further out to sea?"

"I hate to speculate without doing a thorough exam," Nita said, straightening, "but from what I can see of his face and hands, he's not torn up at all. That suggests he hasn't been banging around in the water for very long."

"Yeah, that's what I thought too."

Nita dropped her gloves into a large red plastic biohazard bag and accepted the clipboard with the incident report from the EMT. After dashing off her findings, she handed it back. "Do you need me for anything else here, Sheriff?"

"No. The rest of it will have to wait until they get him to Hyannis. Thanks for coming out."

"No problem. I'm sorry it turned out the way it did."

"Me too." Reese guided Nita up the muddy slope with a hand on her elbow. "You need a ride home?"

"That would be great. Thanks." Nita sluiced water from her face with both hands. Her clothes were soaked, and her silk blouse clung to her in cold sheets.

"I'll have Bri drive you." Reese lifted up the yellow crime scene tape which Bri and Allie had hastily erected around the scene when they answered the call. "I've got a jacket in the car. You must be freezing."

"I'll take you up on tha—" Nita fell silent as Deo materialized from the small crowd of onlookers that had gathered outside the tape while she had been working. "What are you doing here?"

"I thought you might need a ride," Deo said. "This weather is getting worse by the second."

"According to all reports," Reese said, "we're looking at a lot worse in the next five days. Big storm coming up the coast."

"Bad for fishing," Deo said, glancing out toward the harbor before moving closer to Nita. "My truck's just up the street."

Nita turned to Reese. "Thanks, Sheriff, but your officer doesn't need to taxi me anywhere. Deo can take me home."

"All right. Thanks again." Reese touched her cap and headed back down to the scene.

"How long have you been here?" Nita asked, aware of people watching her as she made her way up the beach.

"A few minutes." Deo slipped her arm around Nita's waist. "By the time I got to my truck it was really coming down, and I knew you were walking. Do you mind?"

"I wish you hadn't seen this. Are you all right?"

"Yes."

"No bad memories?"

Deo hesitated. "I don't remember all that much." She opened the Defender for Nita and held the door as she climbed in, then went around and got behind the wheel. "I remember people shouting and I remember being cold. So cold that I thought I'd never get warm."

Nita slid as close as she could and put her hand on Deo's thigh. "You're cold now, too. And soaked."

"I'm used to it." Deo started the truck and pulled out onto Commercial Street. "The lights were in my eyes, red and blue and white flashes, and I couldn't see anyone clearly, just shapes. It almost seemed as if I might be dreaming. I hoped I was. One of those bad dreams that feels so real while you're having it, and then you wake up and you're so happy it was just a dream." She took a shaky breath. "But I didn't wake up. Gabe was gone and everything changed."

"I'm sorry. So sorry," Nita murmured, stroking Deo's hand where she clenched the steering wheel.

"Thanks," Deo said roughly, grasping Nita's hand and threading her fingers through Nita's. "My condo is right around the corner. It might be July, but I think a fire would be nice right about now." She glanced at Nita. "After a hot shower."

Nita's stomach quivered and she forgot about being cautious. The specter of death, so final, so brutal, still hovered around her. She was cold and sad and Deo offered her heat and a moment's forgetting. It was enough.

"Yes." She leaned across the space between them and kissed Deo's neck. "That sounds perfect."

❖

"First things first," Deo said, closing the door to her condo. She pointed across the living room, which was furnished with a tan sofa, matching chair, and a low glass table in front of a slate stone fireplace. "The bedroom is up those stairs—first door on the right. You can take your clothes off in there."

Nita raised an eyebrow.

"Your *wet* clothes." Deo pulled her own dripping polo shirt from her jeans. "I'll bring you something dry. You can shower in my bathroom up there. I'll use the one down here."

"If you take that shirt off now," Nita warned, "neither one of us is getting a shower."

Deo hesitated, her shirt pulled high enough to expose her stomach and the curve of her breasts. "That sounds like a dare."

"No," Nita murmured, smoothing her palm over Deo's stomach.

"That's a promise. God, I love your body."

Deo shivered as Nita continued to caress her. "Nita. I'm wound up like a top."

"Really." Nita wrapped her arms around Deo's neck and kissed her. They were both soaked, but the heat of Deo's mouth and the promise of her touch warmed her all the way through. When Deo ran both hands down her back and then cupped her ass, she felt herself surge dangerously toward the boiling point. She didn't want it to be that way, fast and furious and desperate. Not tonight. Not for this one night. Tonight she needed it to be different. Despite all her instincts crying out to sate her desire, and quickly, she drew back. "I'm going to get out of these clothes."

Breathing hard, Deo nodded wordlessly.

"Maybe you can start the fire after you shower." Nita kissed Deo lightly.

"Fire's already started," Deo muttered.

Laughing, Nita headed for the bedroom. When she found it, she closed the door, half wishing that Deo had followed and grateful that she hadn't. Her hands were shaking as she unbuttoned her blouse. They were going to have sex. She knew that. She knew that Deo knew it. It wouldn't be the first time she had kept an appointment for sex. She had gone places to have sex before, so many times she'd lost count. Roadside motels. Borrowed apartments. Abandoned on-call rooms. Assignations for pleasure that left her feeling empty and alone.

Sylvia was almost always there first, and she would often take Nita the instant Nita walked in—a second's frantic coupling against the door and then Sylvia would be inside her or on her knees, claiming her with her mouth. Nita was usually already so aroused just from anticipating Sylvia's onslaught, hungering for the connection during the days and weeks when they had no contact—not even a phone call—that she would rarely be able to hold back for more than a minute or two. She would come screaming, all the while wondering why she felt no satisfaction. Once was never enough for either of them, and for half an hour or forty-five minutes Sylvia drove her relentlessly through one orgasm after another until Nita was too weak to move. All the while, Sylvia insisted that Nita was *hers*, that Nita was everything she needed, everything she wanted—her heart and her soul. And Nita let herself believe.

Sighing, Nita slipped into the shower and prayed that the heat would penetrate to the cold place deep inside. She didn't want to think of Sylvia, not tonight, not ever. When she stepped out, she found a thick white robe folded on the vanity and wondered when Deo had placed it there. She wondered, too, if Deo had looked at her through the steam-streaked glass doors and ached for her the way she ached. She finger-combed her hair and pulled on the robe, tying it loosely at the waist.

Halfway down the stairs, Nita felt the heat. Inside a fire blazed while outside the storm raged, wind driving the rain with such force it sounded as if stones pelted against the skylights and glass doors. Deo lounged in the chair in front of the fireplace, two glasses of wine on the table beside her. Her short black robe came to mid-thigh and dipped into the valley between her legs. Trying to pretend she wasn't going out of her mind waiting for Deo to touch her, Nita strolled to the chair, leaned down, and kissed Deo.

"Thanks for the robe. And the fire."

Deo tilted her head back and held out her hand. "You're welcome." She tugged Nita around to sit on her lap and nuzzled her neck. "I love it when your hair is down."

"I can't do anything else when it's wet like this, but I like the way it feels." Nita caressed Deo's neck and traced the curve of Deo's breast underneath the material that slanted between her breasts. "I like the way you feel too."

Nita lowered her head to kiss her just as Deo tilted her face up, and they came together with a hungry clash of mouths and tongues. Deo's hands were on her shoulders, then her waist, then inside her robe stroking her belly and her hip. Feasting on Deo's mouth, answering her teasing tongue with strokes of her own, Nita was very quickly almost as far gone as she had been that night outside the bar when she hadn't been able to stop herself from coming in Deo's arms. Another few minutes of Deo's tongue thrusting inside her mouth or the barest brush of Deo's finger between her thighs, and she was going to climax.

"It's too soon," Nita gasped. "God, too soon."

"You need to tell me now," Deo murmured, parting Nita's robe a few inches and kissing the center of her chest, "if you don't want to make love." She groaned as Nita's fingertips glided over her nipple. "And you might need to get off my lap, too."

"I understand. I'm sorry." Nita gripped the wide arms of the chair and pushed herself off Deo's lap. Watching Deo's expression falter, she quickly knelt between Deo's legs and pushed the robe open with both hands. Leaning to kiss the inside of Deo's thigh, she murmured, "Maybe I'll be safer down here."

"I don't think so." Deo caressed Nita's face, her fingers shaking. "I'm really in trouble."

"No you're not." Gently, Nita spread her fingers along the taut muscles that framed the vee of Deo's sex and kissed her. She tasted sweet and rich and Nita licked delicately along the furled folds to the prominent ridge in their center. When she found a spot that made Deo twitch and moan, she played with it, pressing with the very tip of her tongue. Back and forth. Back and forth. Back and forth and around.

"Please," Deo whispered, her legs twisting as her muscles clenched tighter and tighter. "Please stop. I can't take you doing that any more. I'll come right in your mouth."

Nita gripped Deo's thighs firmly to stop her from pulling away. Deo was hard, throbbing, hot, and Nita needed more. She sucked, sliding Deo's clitoris in and out between her lips, and Deo groaned, a broken, hopeless, unbelievably beautiful sound. Reaching up, Nita caressed her tense belly and said with her mouth against Deo's clit, "I can't believe how hard you are. Stop fighting it. I *want* you to come."

When Nita slipped her fingers just inside and went back to sucking her, Deo jerked forward, clutching Nita's shoulders. "I'm going to come. Don't stop. Jesus. Jesus, lick right there, oh…just don't stop."

Nita wrapped both arms around Deo's waist as Deo rode her mouth. She wished she could still her own heartbeat so nothing interfered with her absorbing every sound and movement of Deo's body as she climaxed. Finally, Deo groaned and collapsed back into the chair. Nita couldn't let her go, but covered her sex with light kisses until Deo pushed feebly at her face.

"Give me a minute," Deo murmured. "Too sensitive right now."

"You are so amazing." Nita gazed up the length of Deo's body. Deo was golden in the firelight, her skin shining with sweat and pleasure. Nita was aware of time passing, of the night hurtling toward dawn, and she needed more. Carefully, she eased inside her, moaning when Deo closed down around her fingers. "That's it. Beautiful."

"Nita, God, what are you doing? I don't…oh God…I can't…"

"Shh," Nita soothed, pulling out and pushing back in a little at a time, carefully avoiding Deo's swollen clitoris. "Just relax. Just hold me inside. You don't have to do anything."

Deo stared down at Nita helplessly. "Feels so good."

"I can tell." Nita smiled, watching Deo's face as she slowly fucked her. "I want to make you come all night."

"Can't," Deo muttered. "Want to, but…"

"Stroke your clit. Show me what you like." Nita kept her tempo slow, her strokes gentle.

"Let me make you come," Deo protested, grasping Nita's wrist.

"Not yet. I'll come fast, and I don't want to. I want this. Please. I want you."

Deo relaxed and pressed two fingers against the base of her clit. "It will take me a while."

"That's all right. I've got all night." Nita winced inwardly at the irony. All night. All night, and she needed every minute and so many more. Her clitoris pounded, and she was wet, so wet. But it wasn't her orgasm she wanted as she watched Deo circle and stroke and pinch her thickened clitoris. Deo's pleasure was sweeter than anything she'd ever experienced. "Does it feel good?"

"Yes," Deo hissed through gritted teeth. "Getting so hard again."

"Are you going to come?"

"I…don't…know."

Nita matched her strokes to the speed of Deo's hand, picking up as Deo circled faster. Minutes passed and Deo moaned, her motions frantic. Sensing Deo's need, Nita massaged Deo's other opening with her free hand and slid a finger through the firm muscle.

"Oh God," Deo cried, her body bowing. "Oh God you're going to make me come."

"Yes," Nita whispered, thrusting with both hands as Deo finished herself with a low, tortured moan. "Yes, yes, yes."

Deo's head fell back against the chair, her arms dropping limply to her sides, her breasts and stomach heaving as she fought to breathe. Nita gently withdrew and pillowed her cheek against Deo's stomach. "When you come, I feel like something inside me is going to burst. You're so beautiful I can't stand it."

"I want us to go to bed," Deo groaned. "I want to touch you. Please Nita. Please let me touch you."

"I need you to." Nita kissed Deo's stomach. "I want you to."

Deo reached for the wine beside them and handed a glass to Nita. She drank deeply from her own and rose, hoping her legs would carry her upstairs. She gripped Nita's hand and drew her along beside her to the stairs. "I've never come like that before."

"No?" Nita circled Deo's waist as they climbed the stairs. "I've never made love to anyone that way before. I'm so hungry for you."

"You sound sorry," Deo whispered, pushing open her bedroom door. Just inside, she turned on a small table lamp that left most of the room in shadow.

Nita shook her head firmly. "No. Not sorry at all."

Deo emptied her wine glass and put it on the bedside table. She held out her hand for Nita's and placed it beside her own. Then she untied her robe and let it fall. She watched Nita's gaze travel over her body and her nipples hardened at the heat in Nita's eyes. "Will you take off your robe?"

"Yes." Nita untied the sash and shrugged it from her shoulders, willing her body to quiet.

"Oh," Deo murmured, resting her hands on Nita's shoulders. "So much more beautiful than I dreamed." She traced her thumbs along Nita's collarbones and then smoothed her palms over Nita's chest until she cupped her breasts. Nita's nipples were hard, dark shadows against her smooth light brown skin. Lifting Nita's breasts in her palms as she had imagined so many times, she licked first one nipple, then the other.

Nita grabbed Deo's arms to steady herself as her thighs trembled. "Suck," she implored hoarsely. "Suck them."

Deo wrapped one arm around Nita's waist and pulled her backwards toward the bed, carrying her down with her as she settled onto her back. Nita braced herself above Deo's body as Deo continued to torment her breasts with her teeth and lips and tongue. It was too much, too good. Nita straddled Deo's thigh, riding her clitoris over the hard muscle.

"I'm going to come," Nita warned, "I'm going to come. Oh God, Deo."

"Wait," Deo murmured, rolling Nita over and easing her leg from between Nita's, breaking their contact. "Wait if you can. If you can't, it's okay."

Nita's breath sobbed in and out of her chest and her hips thrashed helplessly. "Touch me. Will you please touch me?"

Deo leaned on one elbow and kissed her, caressing her breasts and her belly and lightly between her thighs, her fingertips gliding over Nita's clitoris and then away, again and again. Nita dug her fingernails into Deo's back, clinging to her as she struggled to hold back the feral need that beat at her for release. Deo's tongue was soft and gentle, her callused hands everywhere, painting her body with exquisite tenderness. Gradually, the fire Deo kindled transformed into a deep consuming blaze that spread through her blood and muscles, obliterating everything in its path.

"I'm coming," Nita sighed, surrendering as her orgasm rolled over her, leaving nothing behind but pure satisfaction. As she peaked, Deo filled her and she jolted into another, harder climax. Wild with unexpected pleasure, she screamed Deo's name.

Chapter Twenty-One

As Nita roused from sleep, she registered the totally foreign sensation of lying on her back with a warm body curved along her side. Before her still cloudy mind could decipher what that meant, she became aware of something even more extraordinary. Her skin tingled from her throat to her knees and three distinct points of pleasure beat in time to her heartbeat. Her nipples were painfully, delightfully hard, and her clitoris was disturbingly but quite wonderfully tense.

"I know you're awake," Deo murmured, circling Nita's nipple with her tongue.

"What are you doing?" Nita breathed, keeping her eyes closed. She held very still. Whatever was happening, she didn't want it to stop.

"Fulfilling a fantasy." Deo sucked the other nipple then trailed her tongue down the center of Nita's body and dipped into her navel. "I want to taste every part of your body. I'm about halfway there." Deo kissed the top of the crisp, neatly trimmed black triangle at the base of Nita's abdomen and smoothed her palm along the sleek length of Nita's thigh. "You're unspeakably beautiful."

Nita lifted her hips, she couldn't help it. "I'm unspeakably aroused."

Deo inched lower, and Nita felt first a teasing breath and then Deo's lips slide smoothly down her clitoris. "Oh my God."

"Mmm." Deo lingered a second, sucking gently, before shifting her body between Nita's legs. She licked the inside of her thighs, then kissed her way lower. "Very sexy knees."

"Deo," Nita moaned, pushing herself up on her elbows. She opened her eyes, and everything clenched at the sight of Deo reclining between her legs, naked and gorgeous in the misty dawn light. Her wide shoulders dipped down to a shallow valley below the rise of her round, firm ass. Nita had a swift vision of rubbing her sex over Deo's ass until she came. Her clitoris twitched and she moaned again. "Just looking at you makes me wet."

"Good. I want to make you as crazy as you make me."

Deo's gaze met hers, and the hunger in her eyes made Nita's stomach twist. She pressed three fingers to her clitoris and felt it protrude. God, she was so excited. "Can you see what you've done?"

"I said you were beautiful." Deo massaged the tops of Nita's feet, then stroked upward over her calves and finally pushed her legs apart until her thighs were stretched tight. She lowered her head and opened Nita with her thumbs. "And you're very ready."

"Wait," Nita said urgently, pressing her palm to Deo's cheek just before Deo reached her with her mouth. "I won't be able to keep from coming if you put your mouth on me now."

"That's okay."

"No it's not. I want you on top of me." Nita tugged Deo's hair. "I want *you* in my mouth while you lick me. Now. Come on."

Deo's expression turned ravenous, and her lips parted in a near growl. Swiftly she reversed her position and lowered herself above Nita's face.

"Don't touch me yet," Nita murmured, wrapping her arms around the outside of Deo's muscular thighs. Then she delicately licked her. Deo jerked and Nita smiled. "Don't touch me until I tell you that you can."

"Nita," Deo snarled, rubbing her cheek over Nita's sex. "You're so wet for me."

"I'm not the only who's wet," Nita whispered. She stroked the flat of her tongue between Deo's lips and over the surface of her exposed clitoris. Deo's thighs trembled. "You like that, don't you?"

"You know I love it." Deo kissed Nita's clitoris.

"Deo, don't."

"I want to suck you."

"No," Nita gasped. "Not yet." She fluttered her tongue under Deo's clitoris and Deo swelled and pulsed. "Tell me if you're going to come."

"A minute—not much longer. I'm getting close. Oh Jesus—I'm not kidding."

Nita licked her again and teased the spot she had discovered the night before. Deo shivered and writhed and Nita felt another kiss brush over the top of her clitoris, harder this time. It felt so good. "Careful. I don't want to come."

"Yes you do," Deo groaned. "Please. Let me suck you."

"No." Nita struggled to hold back the pleasure that threatened to burst free and concentrated on Deo, licking and kissing and teasing until Deo was so hard and so wet she knew Deo would come any second if she didn't stop. She pulled her mouth away. "Quick. Come up here—I want to kiss you."

Deo swung around and drove her thigh between Nita's legs at the same time as she plunged her tongue into Nita's mouth. Nita gripped Deo's hair in both hands and arched to meet her thrusts. She sucked on Deo's tongue as Deo pounded between her legs. The pressure of Deo's leg hammering into her clitoris was too much.

"Oh, I can't hold it any more!" Nita felt herself shattering and jerked Deo's head back, frantically searching her face until she found her eyes. "I'm coming. Come with me. Please, oh please."

"Yes, fuck, yes," Deo cried.

Nita's breath fled as Deo kissed her and her body erupted. Then there was nothing, nothing except pleasure and Deo.

❖

Nita stroked Deo's hair as Deo slept on top of her, her face in the curve of Nita's neck and her thigh still cradled against Nita's center. The weight of her body was far from uncomfortable. Nita marveled at the strange sensation of contentment that came from holding a woman who had just orgasmed in her arms so thoroughly, so completely, that she had drifted off in the aftermath. She felt powerful, she felt protective, she felt humbled. Deo's trust frightened her, but the intimacy terrified her even more. She had learned to do without this kind of connection. She had learned not to hope for it. She had almost succeeded in learning not to want…anything. With Deo, she had surrendered to the wanting, but that was all she was willing to risk.

"Deo," Nita murmured. "Deo, hey. We have to get up."

"Sure?" Deo kissed Nita's neck and rolled her thigh suggestively between Nita's legs. "You're still wet."

"And you're insatiable." Nita played her hands up and down Deo's back, then squeezed the hard muscles in her ass. She wanted to wrap her legs around Deo's thighs and pump her still engorged sex into Deo until she came again. She couldn't, precisely because she wanted to so much. She had to get some distance before she was incapable of saying no. "We both need to go to work."

"I hear rain."

Nita watched rivulets of water stream across the skylight above their heads. The sky beyond was the color of ash, thick and foreboding. "You won't be going up on any roofs today."

"No chance you can go in late?" Deo nudged her crotch into Nita's leg. "I'm getting another hard on."

"When aren't you?" Nita laughed shakily. She wanted her. She wanted her in ways she hadn't imagined possible. Wanting her inside her body was the easy part. That she understood. That she could even control, if she wasn't touching her. The part she couldn't, wouldn't embrace, was the comfort, the peace she felt when they talked and Deo listened. When Deo understood. When Deo accepted. "Come on, rise and shine before you get too worked up."

"Too late," Deo muttered, pushing up on her arms. "Why do I feel like you're running away?"

"I'm not," Nita said flatly, carefully keeping her voice level. She had to set the limits, and quickly, before the pull of Deo's desire undid her. "There's nothing to run away from. We agreed, remember? One night. One night to let the pressure out of the steam cooker we seem to have fallen into."

"Did it work for you?"

"You know it did."

"And that's it?" Deo grated. "You get off a few times, then you walk out and forget it?"

"Don't make it more than it was," Nita said softly. She touched Deo's face. "Or less."

"I want to see you again."

"Deo, get up." Nita pushed lightly against Deo's shoulder. She couldn't have this conversation with their bodies tangled together, with the slick slide of Deo's skin making her so hot inside. Not when Deo was hard and wet against her leg. "Please."

Deo pushed up and off until she was sitting by Nita's side. "I'm not Sylvia. I'm not going to force you to have sex with me."

"She didn't force me," Nita said coldly, refusing to ascribe her guilt to someone else. "I wanted her to fuck me."

"You think I buy that?"

Nita threw the covers aside and got out of bed. She unhurriedly began gathering her clothes from the floor. "What you think about it doesn't matter."

"Don't do this, Nita," Deo said, swinging from bed and standing naked beside her. "Don't pretend last night wasn't good."

"Last night wasn't good, it was excellent." Nita pulled on her blouse. "Your reputation doesn't do you justice."

"You know that's not what I'm talking about."

"What do you want?"

"I already told you. I want to see you again."

"For sex." Nita slid into her slacks.

"No."

Nita snorted.

"Yes," Deo exclaimed, clearly frustrated, "but not just—"

"What kind of arrangements do you usually make with women who you want to have sex with more than once?"

Deo frowned. "What you do mean, arrangements?"

"What do you say to them?"

"Jesus," Deo muttered, grabbing a pair of jeans from a nearby chair and yanking them on. "I don't sign a contract."

"All right. Terms then." Nita found her purse, fished out a clip, and pulled her hair back. "No expectations. No strings. Nonexclusive. Right?"

A muscle bunched along the edge of Deo's jaw. "More or less."

"That could work," Nita mused. "It might be good to blow off steam again, so to speak."

"What?" Deo snapped. "You'll call me for a fuck?"

"Actually I was thinking of something a little more civilized—along the lines of dinner and sex." Nita found her shoes and gathered the rest of her things. "Would you drive me home, please?"

Deo shrugged into a work shirt, her hands trembling. "I want more than sex."

"Since when?"

Deo grabbed Nita's shoulders, then immediately loosened her grip when she saw Nita wince. "Since you."

Nita's resolve wavered. Deo was angry, but her eyes were soft.

Soft and gentle, and wounded. Nita wanted to believe that Deo wanted more than her body. She wanted to give in to the longing to confess her fears and uncertainty, but she didn't trust her own needs. She'd lost herself once, and Deo unhinged her in much the same way Sylvia had. She couldn't deny her physical urges, or even control them when Deo was around, but she could keep from risking her sanity again. She eased out of Deo's grip. "I'm sorry. I'm not interested in anything more than last night."

"Last night was already more than just sex." Deo kicked into Docksiders and headed toward the hall. "You can pretend anything you want."

Silently, Nita followed her retreating back. It might work. If she could somehow just keep her affair with Deo in the bedroom. And keep Deo out of her mind.

❖

An hour later Deo slammed into the real estate office, dripping water in streams onto the floor.

Elana Torres broke off talking with Pia, who sat on the corner of her desk, and regarded Deo with surprise. "Something on fire? Hard to believe with the weather."

"Joey around?" Deo said, stomping over to her desk to collect her messages.

"He's got an appointment with me in an hour for therapy," Pia said. "Considering the weather, he probably just figured he'd show up at the job—"

"We work whether it rains or shines. He knows that." Deo grabbed her mail and shuffled through it, scarcely able to read the addresses through her fury. When she had dropped Nita off, Nita had kissed her on the cheek and thanked her for a great time before sliding out of the truck and disappearing without a backward glance. Thanked her! Jesus Christ. What was she now, a fucking gigolo?

Pia appeared at her elbow and asked in a low voice, "*What* is wrong with you?"

"Nothing."

"Oh, crap, Deo. Don't pull that with me."

Deo tossed aside her mail and stabbed the button on her answering machine. Nita's voice hit her like a hammer. *Deo, it's Nita—*

"Fuck," Deo seethed, punching the stop button.

"Ah ha." Pia tugged Deo's sleeve. "Let's go have coffee."

"I've got to get out to the site."

"It's pouring, Deo. There's not much work going to happen today."

With a sigh, Deo surrendered and let Pia drag her to a coffee shop around the corner.

"So, what gives?" Pia asked.

"I don't know. I wish I did." Deo pushed her coffee aside. Her stomach was queasy.

"Let me guess. Nita."

Deo nodded.

"You slept with her."

"Yeah."

Pia sighed. "Deo, sweetie. Nita is not like your usual…girlfriends. I mean, some of them I've really liked, but… they were goodtime girls. Party girls. Nita is, I don't know, *deeper* than that."

"What's your point," Deo grumbled.

"I love you, you know that, right?" Pia gently stroked Deo's hand. "Right?"

"Just say it, Pia." Deo was tired, and her head hurt, and—worse—her heart hurt.

"I just mean, she probably expected something besides goodbye in the morning."

Deo laughed bitterly. "Wrong. What she expected was I'd be available next time she wanted a dependable fuck. Other than that, she's not interested in my company."

Pia's jaw dropped. After a second, her eyes narrowed. "She said that? She said that to my cousin! Why that—"

"Whoa. Whoa. Easy." Deo laughed in spite of herself. "Even you just said that's about all I'm good for."

"That's different. I can say it about you if I want to." She closed her fingers over Deo's hand. "What am I not understanding here?"

"Nita and I…we've got this thing, this energy between us," Deo said, feeling helpless. "More than physical. But she doesn't want it to be about anything except sex."

"Because she thinks you're a player and won't ever change?"

"I don't know. I think…I think she's okay having sex with me, because she can control that."

"She can? That doesn't sound like you."

Deo remembered the way it felt when Nita teased her right up to the edge of coming while refusing to let Deo touch her. It was maddening and frustrating and made her come harder than she'd ever come in her life. And if she didn't stop thinking about it now, she was going to have to drive out to the beach for a little solo action in the truck before she went to work. "It's different with her."

"Uh-huh." Pia rested her chin in her hand. "So her reluctance isn't necessarily about you and your fucked up ways."

"Thanks, Cuz." Deo couldn't very well say that Nita had been abused by some woman and acted like Deo would treat her the same way. She rubbed her eyes, wishing she was still in bed and Nita was holding her the way she had this morning when she was still half asleep, stroking her and making her feel like she belonged somewhere. "There's some other stuff going on. I don't think it's all about me."

"Good," Pia said briskly, sitting back in her seat. "Because if it was just that she didn't like you for anything other than your talented hands and your hot mou—"

"Jesus, Pia. Cut it out." Deo blushed. "You're my cousin. You're not supposed to say stuff like that."

"Oh, please. I've been listening to girls swoon over your skills for years." Pia smiled as Deo squirmed. "Does she really mean something to you? It's not just your ego acting up because you've finally run into a woman who doesn't want any more from you than you're usually willing to give?"

"No. She makes me…" Deo's throat tightened and she looked away until the tension in her throat eased. "She makes me feel like I matter."

"Oh, sweetie," Pia whispered. "You do."

"Yeah, well. You've always made me feel that way. But this is different."

"I know." Pia stroked Deo's clenched fist where it rested on the table. "If Nita doesn't trust you or what she's feeling for you, then prove to her that she can."

"How," Deo whispered.

"Don't give up."

Chapter Twenty-Two

Nita stared at the lab report, but she didn't register the values. Her mind was completely consumed with Deo. Exactly what she feared would happen was happening. She craved her. The way her skin slid under her fingertips, the way her breath wafted over her breast as she slept, the way her eyes gleamed when she was pleased or being pleasured. She ached to hear Deo murmur her name and to feel the tender touch of her fingertips against the small of her back. She longed to share her thoughts, knowing she could tell her anything because she had already confessed her worst secret and her greatest shame, and Deo had not rejected her. She'd only to recall the soft brush of Deo's hot mouth on her tense and waiting flesh and she was ready to explode.

"God, not again," she whispered.

"Nita?"

"Oh, sorry," Nita blurted, feeling herself color when she realized Tory was standing in front of her desk. She hadn't even heard her come in. "I was just…" She lifted the paperwork in explanation.

"I hate to bother you but Reese is here, and there's a problem."

Immediately, Nita stood, her first thought of Deo up on a roof in this gale. Her stomach lurched. "Is someone hurt?"

"Oh," Tory said quickly. "No. I'm sorry. It's something else. She's next door in my office. Come over when you can."

"I'll come right now," Nita said, hurrying to join Tory.

Reese turned from the photographs she had been perusing on the wall and nodded to Nita, her expression grim. "How are you this morning, Nita?"

"I'm fine, Reese," Nita said, grateful for how much practice she had in allowing her professional performance to hide her emotional chaos. She wondered what people would think if they knew she was so desperate to see and touch another woman she was practically coming apart. Knowing that her urgency stemmed from her long relationship with Sylvia and the uncertain, often frantic nature of their interludes, didn't make the desperate longing any easier to tolerate. But she'd had a lot of practice living with unrequited need too. "Is there some problem with the post on the victim from last night?"

"Not that I'm aware of." Reese gestured to the chairs in front of Tory's desk and waited until Nita sat beside Tory, then said, "We received a bulletin about an hour ago that seriously bad weather is headed our way. In fact, there's better than an eighty percent chance we're going to see hurricane force winds up and down the Cape in about seventy-two hours."

Nita started. "Here? I've never heard of a hurricane this far north."

"Apparently, it happens every twenty or thirty years or so." Reese lifted her shoulder. "Depending upon wind patterns and ocean temperatures, hurricanes have tracked up the coast this far or even farther."

"I'm on the disaster response committee," Tory explained to Nita, "and all of the emergency personnel—EMTs, fire rescue, the Sheriff's Department—will be on twenty-four hour alert until this is over. If you're planning to stay—"

"Why wouldn't I?" Nita interrupted.

"The Cape is only a mile or so wide at this point," Reese pointed out. "We're going to get flooding and the roads will probably go out. We'll definitely lose power."

"In other words, things are going to get nasty," Nita said, "and we're going to be cut off from the rest of the Cape and the mainland."

"Very possibly," Reese replied.

Nita looked at Tory. "There are going to be injuries, not to mention the usual medical emergencies."

"Yes," Tory said. "And if it really gets bad, we're not going to be able to transport people out, possibly for days."

"I'm staying." Nita turned to Reese. "I know you've already got a plan in place, but can you just run it down for me."

"You and Tory will oversee all emergency medical management. Make sure the clinic is well stocked, and if you can identify patients who could get into trouble without immediate access to hospital facilities, get a list to me so we can evacuate them now."

"We've got a handful of patients who drive to Hyannis for dialysis or have home units," Tory informed her lover. "They would be better off on the mainland just in case we're looking at four or five days without power. Even generator backup might not be enough."

"I'm following two children with sleep apnea using positive pressure ventilators at night," Nita pointed out. "We should advise those families."

"Yes." Tory grabbed a notepad and started taking notes. "Reese, when you make the general announcement, remind everyone that they should be certain to have enough medication to last ten days along with all the other necessities. Bottled water, batteries, lanterns, packaged foods—the usual disaster items."

"I'll call the hardware stores as soon as we're done to let them know there's going to be a run." Reese dropped her hand to Tory's shoulder as she wrote and caressed her softly. "Gladys and the Chief are working on an announcement right now and we'll get it out on the radio within the hour."

"Nelson? Don't tell me he's in the office," Tory said with a frown.

"He's at home for the time being. He threatened to come in, so I sent Gladys over there to keep him in the loop. That's as quiet as we're going to be able to keep him."

"What about the extended care facility?" Nita glanced at Tory. Between the two of them they did site visits once or twice a week to the elderly residents of Beech Forest Manor. She could think of at least a dozen patients who were bedridden or who required intensive care around the clock.

"Reese?" Tory asked.

"Several of the officers are on their way there now to talk to the facilities director," Reese informed them. "We're hoping that most can stay with family members off Cape. As for those who can't be relocated within the next twenty-four hours or who have nowhere to go, we'll move them to a more central location if we have to."

"Town Hall?" Tory asked.

Reese nodded. "That's what I was thinking, or the church, or both depending on how many people we have without power or whose houses sustain structural damage."

"Should we evacuate the whole town?" Nita questioned.

"Currently, we're recommending that people leave voluntarily," Reese answered. "But even if the state orders an evacuation, you know not everyone is willing or able to leave."

Tory sighed. "I know." She covered Reese's hand with hers as she continued to make notes with the other. "Neither one of us is going to get home much until this is over. Will you call Jean and Kate and ask them to take the baby and the dog." Tory met Reese's gaze. "And leave today."

Reese leaned down and kissed the top of her head. "Already done. They'll stop by here so you can say goodbye to Reggie, and then they're going to drive to your sister's."

"That sounds great. It will make keeping in touch with everyone easier." Tory rubbed her cheek absently against Reese's arm. "Thank you, darling."

Nita averted her gaze, feeling as if she were intruding on a private moment, even though there was nothing inappropriate about anything Reese and Tory said or did. Still, every gesture, every intonation, every unspoken word was so intimate, it left her aching. Totally without volition, she thought of Deo and was struck by an overwhelming urge to call her. She just wanted to connect with her before the world went crazy.

"What should we do about regular patient hours?" Nita asked, trying to maintain her focus. She couldn't think about Deo now, even though part of her wanted nothing else.

"For today, we'll keep them as they are," Tory said. "I'll have Randy call everyone who's scheduled for the following week and bring the urgent ones in tomorrow. The rest we can reschedule if we need to."

"Sounds like we have a plan." Reese cupped the back of Tory's neck and kissed her cheek. "I'll call you. Don't work too late."

Tory gripped Reese's arm and kissed her mouth. "Be careful."

"Always," Reese murmured. She straightened, nodded to Nita, and strode out.

Nita watched her go, appreciating why men and women would follow her into battle. She radiated not just confidence and competence, but that supreme certainty that defined command presence. Nita recognized it because her father had it. So did Sylvia, except Sylvia's confidence was laced with cruelty. Unlike Reese, Sylvia was motivated by power, and sex was her weapon. Nita had been as enthralled by Sylvia's power as she had been subjugated by it. Now she wondered why.

"Please let me know what I can do," Nita said, rising. "I'm going to get back to seeing patients."

"Thanks." Tory caught Nita's hand. "And thanks for staying. If this gets as bad as Reese thinks, we're really going to need you."

"This is my home now. I'm not leaving."

"I almost forgot—your house! You'd better call Deo and make sure she knows what's coming."

"If we get a break, I'll run down there and talk to her," Nita said quickly before she could think about what she was doing and change her mind.

"Go now. We can handle things here. And who knows when you may get another chance."

"I won't be long," Nita said, already starting for the door. Her heart speeded up with anticipation, and she didn't even try to pretend it wasn't because she would soon see Deo.

❖

"Deo!" Joey yelled up the stairwell. "You got company."

"In a minute," Deo called back, bracing the plywood against the new French doors with her shoulder as she rapidly drilled in four screws to hold the wood in place. She scanned Nita's bedroom. It was as secure as they were going to get it. Putting the drill aside, she dusted off her hands on her pants and started down the stairs. She slowed as she reached the bottom. Nita was waiting for her.

"Sorry, I know you're busy," Nita said uneasily.

"That's okay." Seeing Joey's avid stare, Deo took Nita's arm and led her into the dining room out of earshot of her cousin and the other guys. "I thought you were at the clinic?"

"I am. I was—I..." she swept her arm to take in the rest of the house. The ground floor windows were already covered with plywood to protect the new glass from the expected winds. "I guess you know about the storm?"

"Contractors live and die by weather bulletins—just like fishermen." Deo shrugged. "Don't worry about this place. We'll get it buttoned up tight."

"I'm not worried about the house." Nita realized she had no good reason for running across town and Deo must know that. Oddly, she didn't care that her motives were transparent. "I just wanted to make sure you weren't going to be standing up on the roof when things got bad."

"Once we finish here, I'm going into town. There's a disaster response team—"

"I know about it. Reese was just out to the clinic."

"I volunteer. Helping the merchants board up their storefronts, getting boats into dry dock, whatever heavy lifting needs to be done," Deo admitted almost shyly.

"That sounds critical—and difficult. It's already raining harder, and the wind is coming up." Nita touched Deo's hand briefly and just the fleeting contact calmed the wild churning in her stomach. "Don't worry about this place. Go do what you have to do so you won't be out there when this gets worse."

"Worried about me?" Deo grinned, but her eyes held no hint of laughter.

Deo's searching look was so intense that Nita couldn't help but lean toward her. The ache of emptiness she had been carrying since they'd parted suddenly filled with heat. She gasped.

"What?" Deo's voice was low, husky. She caressed the outside of Nita's arm from her elbow to her shoulder and down again. "What?"

"You will be careful, won't you?"

Deo moved a step closer. "Is that what you drove over here to say?"

Nita's thighs trembled and she backed up a step until her back touched the wall. "I just…the house…I just wanted to—" She shivered as Deo braced both arms against the wall by her shoulders and snugged her pelvis into Nita's. "Oh, don't."

"You say no to me a lot," Deo murmured, drawing her lips along the edge of Nita's jaw. "Why is that?"

"Because, because…" Nita turned her head and covered Deo's mouth with hers. She slicked her tongue over Deo's lips and just as quickly pulled away. "Because I usually want to say yes."

"You know," Deo rasped, flexing her thighs and rubbing her crotch over Nita's, "that doesn't make any sense."

Nita stroked Deo's cheek. "I know. I'm sorry."

Deo rested her forehead against Nita's and slowly shook her head.

"Don't be sorry. Just don't run away from me."

"I'm afraid," Nita whispered.

"I know." Deo kissed her, gently. "So am I."

"Can't we just keep it simple?" Nita implored, digging her fingers into Deo's shoulders. She loved her muscles, how strong she was, and how tender despite it.

"Simple." Deo pressed closer, fusing her belly and breasts to Nita's. Her mouth was against Nita's ear, her lips hot and silky. "You mean simple like...just sex."

Nita leaned her head back and closed her eyes, hoping if she couldn't see Deo she might be able to think clearly. In the next instant, she realized how foolish that was, because with her eyes closed all she could do was *feel*, and Deo was pressed against her, her body hot and hard and demanding. "I don't know what I mean anymore."

Deo let out a long sigh. "Good. That's good. That's a place to start from."

Nita laughed shakily and opened her eyes. "Now who isn't making sense?"

"Why did you tell me this morning that you didn't want anything from me except a fuck now and then?"

Deo's words sounded as if they were forced out through ground glass, and Nita knew that she had hurt her. Her fingers shook as she pushed them through Deo's hair. "I'm sorry. I didn't mean to use you." Nita imagined how it must seem to Deo, because she knew how diminished she had felt when Sylvia had come to her for sex but wouldn't allow her anything else. "God, Deo, I'm so sorry."

"Answer the question," Deo whispered. "What are you so afraid of?"

Nita turned her face away. She couldn't answer that question, because if she did, she'd have to face what it meant, and she wasn't ready. "I can't."

"I'm not going to sleep with you again until you tell me. It might drive me crazy, but I mean it." Deo gently turned Nita's face back to hers and kissed her, a deep slow possessive kiss. "I think about you all the time. I want you right now. Inside me. I want to fuck you and come inside you."

Nita groaned. "Stop."

"Sorry. I can't." Deo tilted her head, listening to the rain drum against the wood-covered windows. "I've got to get back to work. Something big is coming."

Before Deo could disappear, Nita gripped her shirt. "I don't know when I'll see you again. Will you call me? I can't…I can't think, I can't work if I don't hear from you." She bunched Deo's work shirt in her fists and pressed her forehead to Deo's shoulder. "God, I hate this."

"Hey, hey, it's okay." Deo lifted Nita's face with her fingers beneath her chin. "Nita, I'm not going anywhere. You can talk to me anytime you want. Just call me."

"Could it be that easy?"

"We'll have to see, won't we?" Deo kissed her again, gently, and backed away. "Drive carefully."

Nita let her get all the way across the room before she called after her. "I lied this morning. I want to see you. Just…see you."

Deo looked over her shoulder. "Then I'll find you."

Chapter Twenty-Three

Nita sat with Tory and the disaster response coordinators in a small stuffy room in Town Hall. Someone had closed the tall narrow windows against the heavy rain that now fell in unbroken sheets, and with only fans to move the heavy air around, she felt like she was breathing wet cotton wool. She could barely remember everyone's names. It was after eleven, she'd seen patients for over twelve hours on not much sleep the night before, and she was worried. Worried about the impending storm and what it meant for the community, worried that she and Tory might not be able to handle a full scale natural catastrophe even with the help of the highly skilled local EMTs and paramedics, and worried about Deo. Deo hadn't called, and when Nita had finally broken down and tried her office number around nine p.m., her call had been forwarded, but she hadn't reached Deo.

"Camara Construction."

"Hello, this is Nita Burgoyne. Is Deo around?"

"Oh, hey Nita…I mean, Dr. Burgoyne…it's Joey. Last I heard from her she was still out on the harbor, tendering people in from their boats. The sea's already too rough for people to ride this out on board."

"How long will she be out?"

"Dunno. Quite a while yet, I figure, and then tomorrow she's got a list of places that need their windows shuttered. Going to be a crazy few days."

"Yes," Nita said absently, wondering when Deo would sleep. She worried that Deo was doing difficult work in dangerous weather when she had to be exhausted. Would she be careful on the water, the water that held such pain for her?

"She'll be checking in soon. You want her to call you?"

"No. No…just tell her I called."

"Sure. Hey…you want her cell phone number? She doesn't always get the calls out there, so you might get relayed right back to me—"

"That's not necessary, thanks. Sorry to bother you, I know you must be busy."

"No problem. Uh, hey, Nita. I was wondering…"

"Problem with your hand?"

"No. Pia said I'm doing great. I was just wondering if you'd like to have dinner some night. You know…with me."

It took Nita a minute to decipher what he'd said, because she didn't register his meaning at first. Then, she struggled for the right thing to say. "Joey, that's really nice of you, but I don't think so. Thank you, though."

"Yeah, that's okay. Deo said you wouldn't go for it."

"Did she." Nita wondered just when and what Deo and Joey had discussed about her.

"But what the heck, if you don't try you'll never know what you might be missing, right?"

"Right," Nita said slowly. "You're absolutely right."

Now, more than two hours later, Nita still hadn't heard from Deo. She hoped Deo wasn't still ferrying people back and forth in the harbor. Growing more desperate by the minute just to hear Deo's voice, she nevertheless made mental notes on the plans being discussed. Deo was doing her job, and Nita needed to do hers.

"Reports from the head of the business bureau indicate that most of the tourists have already left or will be leaving in the morning," Reese said to the group. "If the forecast hasn't changed by midday tomorrow, we'll order a mandatory evacuation of all nonresidents. That should give everyone time to get off the Cape even though we anticipate travel times could be close to twelve hours. That still gives us a twenty-four-hour window before the big winds and surf get here."

Someone who Nita thought might be the head of the town council gathered up a pile of papers and said, "Then I think we've done everything we can for the moment. Let's reconvene tomorrow morning at eleven for an update."

Tory turned to Nita as the other members in the room began to leave. "I've had Randy block out tomorrow afternoon for urgent patients. I can come to this meeting if you want to run out to Beech Forest in the morning and see how many residents are staying."

"That's fine. I'm available if you need me sooner."

"Great, thanks. You should try to get some sleep while you can."

"Yes," Nita said, even though sleep was not what she wanted. She bid Tory and the others good night and fortified herself for the short walk to her car.

Outside, the night was moonless, and shards of rain slanted beneath the inadequate cover of her umbrella and battered her face. Giving up on the hope of remaining dry, Nita slammed her umbrella closed and made a run for it. Once inside the car, she looked toward the harbor, wondering where Deo was. The visibility was so poor she couldn't see anything at all. Frustrated, she started her car, but instead of heading toward home, she drove in the opposite direction toward Deo's condo. The parking space in front of Deo's unit was empty and Nita pulled into the adjoining spot.

"Five minutes," Nita whispered. "I'll just wait for five minutes, and if she doesn't come home, I'll call her again in the morning."

When she realized she was staring at her watch, Nita tilted her head back and closed her eyes, trying not to silently count the seconds.

❖

As Deo jumped from her truck and made a dash for her condo, she heard a car door open and close nearby. Surprised that anyone was out in the middle of the night in the worst weather she could ever remember, she slowed and peered through the rain. A second later, she recognized Nita. Her swift surge of pleasure was almost immediately replaced by concern.

"Jesus, Nita," Deo yelled, grabbing Nita's arm and pulling her under the shelter of the short roof that protected her front door. "What the hell are you doing out here? It's four in the morning!"

"I just stopped by to see if you were all right. I guess I fell asleep." Chilled from her sudden soaking, she cuddled closer to Deo as Deo fumbled with the lock. "I should go so you can get some sleep."

Deo pushed the door open and tugged Nita inside. She kicked the door closed with her foot, grasped Nita's shoulders, and kissed her hard. "Don't be crazy. You're not going anywhere."

Nita automatically wrapped her arms around Deo's shoulders and kissed her back. "You've got to be beyond exhausted. Everything has just gotten so crazy so fast, I wasn't sure when I would be able to see you again." She hugged Deo closer. "Now I have. That's enough."

"Maybe it is for you," Deo murmured, kissing Nita's neck. "But it isn't for me. I need a shower to get warm, and then I want to crawl into bed with you."

Nita leaned back and smiled fleetingly. "What happened to your mandate about no sex?"

"I didn't say anything about sex."

"Good, because you're going to sleep." Nita grasped Deo's hand, guided by instinct and too tired to think of all the reasons she shouldn't be doing what she was about to do. She wasn't just tired—she was frightened, she was cold, and she was lonely. Life had turned upside down in twenty-four hours, and the one solid point in her universe was Deo. "Would you mind very much if I shared your shower?"

Deo shot her a glance. "Do I look dead to you?"

"No," Nita replied throatily, "you look…delicious."

"Cut it out," Deo said unconvincingly.

Nita laughed. "Say that like you mean it."

"I can't."

"Good."

When they reached the bathroom and Deo began shedding her clothes, Nita realized she'd made a mistake. What Deo needed was a hot shower and as much sleep as she could get. And Nita couldn't even look at her without wanting to touch her. She backed toward the door.

"On second thought, I'll skip the shower for now."

Naked, Deo reached around her and held the door closed with her hand. Her body pressed against Nita's. "Take your clothes off."

"Deo—"

"Do it, Nita," Deo whispered and moved in for a kiss.

"You said you weren't going to have sex with me." Trembling, Nita turned her head away so that Deo's kiss only caught the corner of her mouth. "This is cruel."

"You don't like the way you feel right now?"

Drawing a shaky breath, Nita shook her head back and forth. "I don't like wanting you so badly it hurts and knowing I can't have you." She turned her head back, struggling not to cup Deo's breasts in her hands. "I'm trying to give you what you want. You said you didn't want it to be just about sex."

"What do *you* want, Nita?" Deo held still even though she wanted to rub herself over Nita's body. "Forget about me and what I want or what you think I want you to be. Just say what it is you want."

The silence grew until the air felt so heavy Nita didn't think she could pull it into her lungs. Her heart raced and her chest ached. She couldn't remember the last time she thought about what she wanted instead of what she couldn't have and shouldn't desire and didn't dare dream of.

"Tell me," Deo said, her eyes boring into Nita's, her mouth just a breath away from closing over Nita's.

"I want…" Nita shuddered and gripped Deo's arms. Deo's skin was so hot she felt feverish. "I want to make love with you and not be afraid you'll be gone as soon as you come. I want to see you on the street and not have you pretend you don't know me. I want…god, I want…"

"Go ahead," Deo whispered. "You can say it."

"I want not to hate how much I want you."

"Do you?" Deo inched away until their bodies didn't touch, but she cradled Nita's cheek in her hand, still watching her eyes. "Do you hate wanting to make me come?"

"No," Nita said breathlessly.

"Do you hate wanting me inside of you, making you come?"

Beyond words, Nita shook her head.

"Are you afraid of me?"

Nita closed her eyes. The intensity in Deo's face made it impossible for her to think. She was turning liquid inside, her bones were melting. She felt so exposed it was as if she had no skin. She almost expected to look down and see rivulets of blood collecting around her feet.

"Nita," Deo murmured. "Nita, are you afraid of me?"

"No, God, no."

Wordlessly, Deo unbuttoned Nita's blouse. Then she reached around her and released her bra, gently baring her breasts. She kissed her as she opened her slacks and pushed them down along with her panties. "Let's shower."

While Deo turned on the water and the room filled with steam, Nita removed her shoes and the rest of her clothes. The shower was small and when she stepped inside she couldn't help but touch Deo. "I suggest we make this fast, or I can't be responsible for what happens."

Deo grinned as she lathered her body with a bar of soap. "What happened to that great self-control?"

"I lost it somewhere after the second time you rubbed your breasts over me." Nita refused to look down, because if she saw any more of Deo than her face, she was going to drop to her knees and take her right there. "Give me the soap."

"I have to be back out there in about three hours." Deo swirled soapy circles over her breasts and belly with both hands. "I've been keyed up all night, because of everything that's going on and because when I wasn't too busy to see straight, I thought about making love with you."

Nita turned her back so she couldn't touch her. "The shower will relax you and you'll be able to sleep."

"I need to come first. If you weren't here, I'd fantasize about you and masturbate."

"God," Nita moaned. "Stop it."

Deo pressed against Nita's back. "You can watch me or you can let me fuck you."

Nita leaned forward and braced her arms against the shower wall, the tension in the pit of her stomach so profound she wasn't sure she could keep standing. "If I let you come inside me, will you go to sleep then?"

"Yes," Deo grated, thrusting against Nita's ass.

"Well, seeing as how it's therapeutic." Nita pivoted, but immediately pushed Deo away with both hands on Deo's shoulders. "Go get ready. I'll be there in a minute."

"It's what you want?"

Nita kissed her softly and ran her fingers through her hair. "Yes. It's exactly what I want."

Deo stepped out of the shower and grabbed a towel on her way out of the bathroom. Nita took her time drying off, enjoying the novel feeling of not needing to hurry, of not fearing that if she didn't grab every ounce of pleasure just as quickly as possible, it would all disappear like mist at sunrise. She was excited, her skin so sensitive it was almost painful to touch. She was wet and swollen, and she throbbed with the persistent ache of desire. Her arousal felt wonderful, and it was beyond wonderful to set it free.

Nita wrapped a towel around her breasts and joined Deo in the bedroom. A single light burned on the far side of the bed, illuminating Deo as she lay on her side, a sheet pulled up to her waist, her head propped in her hand as she watched the door. She smiled as Nita approached.

"I thought you might fall asleep," Nita said, letting the towel fall.

"Not likely," Deo said, lifting up the sheet.

Nita slid beneath it and reclined on her side, facing Deo. She traced the circles beneath Deo's eyes. "Sweetheart, you're so tired."

"I need you," Deo whispered. "More than anything."

When Deo inched closer to kiss her, Nita felt a firm weight settle against her thigh and caught her breath. As she drew Deo's tongue into her mouth, she caressed Deo's side and the curve of her hip until she reached her knee. Then she skimmed her fingers up the inside of Deo's leg until she closed her fingers around the cock nestled between Deo's legs. She pushed her tongue deeper into Deo's mouth and slowly rotated her wrist.

Deo groaned and pushed her hips forward.

"Don't be in a hurry," Nita whispered, kissing Deo's throat. She kept up the motion of her hand, a steady, rhythmic push and pull. Deo's breath shivered in and out and Nita clenched inside. "I love to excite you."

"You're making me a lot more than excited. I'm so pumped." Deo jerked and thrust into Nita's fist.

"Be good." Nita licked Deo's nipple. "You're not allowed to come in my hand. Not this way."

"Then stop what you're doing," Deo gasped.

Nita laughed and pushed Deo onto her back, then straddled her. She hissed in a breath as Deo's cock bumped against her sex. "Oh, I'm going to like having you inside me."

"Jesus," Deo whispered, sliding one hand down between them to steady herself. "I need to be inside you. Are you ready?"

Nita leaned forward and kissed her. "Mmm. Very. Hold still now."

Watching Deo's face, Nita slowly settled down, taking her inside one slow inch at a time. Briefly, Deo's knuckles brushed against her clitoris and Nita bit her lip to distract herself from the jolt of pleasure that threatened to trigger her orgasm before she was ready. Finally, when Deo was completely buried, she let out her breath.

"Feel good?" Nita whispered.

"Great." Deo's thighs quivered with the effort not to move. "Will you do something for me?"

"If I can." Nita's lids drooped as the pressure grew inside her.

"Will you let me make you come first this time?" Deo tilted her hips ever so slightly, pressing into Nita's clitoris. "I want to watch you come while I fuck you."

"Yes," Nita gasped. "I'll do anything you say."

Deo cupped Nita's breasts in her hands and rubbed her thumbs over her nipples. "Just don't fight it. I don't care if you come in thirty seconds. Just trust me and let go."

Nita covered Deo's hands with hers and rocked back, forcing Deo even deeper. Then she slid forward, and back again. Once, twice, faster, and then faster until her hips were a blur and her breath rushed out in broken sobs. Her fingers linked with Deo's as white heat filled her belly, then her breasts, and finally exploded deep inside her. Her head fell back and she screamed wordlessly.

Feeling as if her chest might implode, Deo jerked upright and wrapped Nita in her arms, half sitting as Nita whimpered and trembled in her lap. Before Nita stopped coming, Deo carefully guided her sideways and onto her back, following her until she was between her legs and still inside her. Burying her face against Nita's neck, she struggled to hold still until Nita caught her breath.

"Nita," Deo groaned, "Nita, I have to fuck you. Please, please can I?"

Nita fisted Deo's hair in both hands and weakly wrapped her legs around the backs of Deo's thighs. "Come inside me. I want you to come inside me."

Deo bit down on Nita's neck as she eased out an inch, then sank into her again, out an inch, in again, then two, then three, then more until she was pulling all the way out and driving back in with every stroke. Nita raked her nails down Deo's back as Deo's thrusts grew erratic and her breathing frantic.

"Come, baby," Nita murmured, stroking Deo's sweat soaked back. "Come inside me. Come hard."

Deo pushed up on both arms as she pumped down with her hips. Then she threw her head back and cried out, her eyes wide and blind with pleasure.

Nita stopped breathing, paralyzed with wonder. She'd never seen anything as beautiful in her life. When she tightened her legs and pulled Deo into her as far as she could, the sudden unexpected pressure forced her into another orgasm.

"Don't you move," Nita gasped as Deo collapsed on top of her. "Don't you dare move. I'm still coming."

"Can't," Deo mumbled, her head pillowed on Nita shoulder. "I'm wasted."

"That's good. That's just really good." Nita laughed and stroked Deo's hair. "You sleep now baby."

Nita lay very still, listening to the angry world outside and the steady, comforting sound of Deo's even breathing. When her muscles finally relaxed, she let Deo slip out of her and eased Deo onto her side. Deo muttered a faint protest but didn't move as Nita carefully untangled her so she could sleep comfortably. Then she curled up in Deo's arms and closed her eyes, satisfied and unafraid.

Chapter Twenty-Four

Tory sat up on the sofa, alert to the sound of quiet footsteps on the deck. A shadow moved across the glass doors, and she heard the quiet snick of a lock sliding open. The restless unease that was always with her when Reese was away disappeared instantly.

"I'm here, darling," Tory called softly. There was enough light from the almost-dawn that she didn't bother to turn on the nearby lamp.

"Why aren't you upstairs in bed?" Reese asked, her voice sounding hoarse as she settled onto the couch next to Tory. She pulled off her tie and tossed it onto the end table, then loosened her gun belt and laid it carefully by her side.

"Because you're not there." Tory leaned her cheek against Reese's shoulder and wrapped an arm around her waist. "Have you been out all night?"

"Most of it." Reese sighed and leaned her head back. "We're going to get hit, Tor. With high winds and storm surge at the very least."

"When?"

"Late tomorrow and on into the night, probably." Reese stroked Tory's arm. "Did you hear from Kate?"

"They made it to Cath's about midnight. Traffic was backed up everywhere. The baby was asleep."

"Mmm."

Realizing that Reese was nearly asleep, too, Tory lifted Reese's legs and guided her down until she was stretched out on her back. After retrieving Reese's holster and placing it on the nearby table, she unlaced her shoes and dropped them on the floor.

"Can't sleep now," Reese muttered.

"Yes you can." Tory curled up beside her, draping her body over Reese's, and closed her eyes. Reese was rumpled and tired and barely present, but she was warm and her body was solid and her heartbeat steady. She was everything Tory needed to anchor her in the coming storm.

❖

Nita heard the shower running and checked the clock. Just after six a.m. She stretched and the muscles in her inner thighs protested. Smiling, she thought about why she was sore, and the memory of straddling Deo's tight, narrow hips while she rode the thick length of her made her clench inside. Tossing the covers aside, she rose quickly and hurried into the bathroom.

"Morning," Nita said, slipping into the shower next to Deo. She wrapped both arms around Deo's waist and kissed her.

"Sorry," Deo murmured after a minute. "I was trying not to wake you."

"That's all right." Nita smoothed her hands over Deo's shoulders and down her arms. "I need to call Tory. I have a feeling we're going to be running the clinic twenty-four hours a day from now until this is over."

"How are you feeling?" Deo soaped her hands and caressed Nita's breasts, giving a low growl of approval as Nita's nipples hardened into dark pebbles against her palms.

Nita caught her breath sharply. "I woke up thinking about you inside me."

"I woke up wanting to come inside you again."

"Handy," Nita whispered, her eyelids flickering as Deo played with her breasts.

"Are you going to let me?" Deo skimmed one hand down Nita's belly until her fingertips touched the soft triangle with the diamond-hard center nestled between her legs. Then she circled slowly and pressed.

Nita whimpered and let her head fall back against the shower wall. "Oh, baby, that feels so good."

"To me too." Deo's breathing kicked up a notch. "You didn't answer."

"What was the question?"

Deo slid a finger inside her. "Whether you were going to let me come inside you again."

"Oh yes. Yes. As often as you like."

"I'm going to make you come now."

"I know."

"You know why?" Deo murmured, kissing Nita slowly.

Nita shook her head, her eyes closed, pelvis lifting to take Deo deeper.

"Because I love to make you come, and you know it."

Nita forced her eyes open. Deo was very close, her dark eyes black, all pupil. She was staring so intently Nita could feel the heat on the backs of her eyelids. Deep inside her orgasm unfurled and spread, powerful wings beating against the heavy air of her desire. "Is it really so simple?"

"No." Deo added another finger, then another, and another. She barely managed to get her arm around Nita's waist as Nita's legs gave out. Still, she held her gaze as Nita trembled on the brink of orgasm. "It's not simple at all."

"Don't let me fall."

"No, no I won't." Deo slipped her tongue deep into Nita's mouth and Nita came.

❖

"You and my dad should leave this morning," Bri said, yanking on her uniform pants. She shoved in her shirt and hastily threaded her belt through the loops. Carre sat on the edge of the bed watching her, and Bri could feel her bristling from across the room. Without meeting her eyes, she repeated what she'd been saying since the night before. "It's not safe here, babe, and I'm going to be out on patrol pretty much all the time from now on."

"I can take care of myself, Bri," Carre said. "You don't have to worry."

"But I will." Bri leaned her shoulders back against the wall and stuffed her hands in her pockets. "My dad just got out of the hospital."

"I know, baby, and that's one reason I'm staying. You know he's not going to leave." Caroline crossed the room and wrapped her arms around Bri's shoulders. "When you go in today, I'll head over to Nelson's. We'll be fine."

"If you'd just go inland, I wouldn't have to worry," Bri said, afraid she sounded like she was whining. In fact, she was pretty sure she *was* whining.

"What are you scared about, baby," Carre said gently.

Bri shook her head.

Carre bumped her pelvis into Bri's and bit her lightly on the tip of her chin. "Say."

"Cut it out," Bri said grumpily.

"Nuh-uh." Carre nibbled on Bri's lower lip. When Bri cupped her butt, she smiled. "Better. But you still have to talk."

Bri growled and skimmed her hand under the back of Caroline's T-shirt.

"We're not having sex," Carre whispered, kissing the corner of Bri's mouth. "We're just having a moment."

"Thirty seconds will do it."

"Yeah," Carre said breathily, "maybe. But you're not getting thirty seconds. Not unless you tell me what you're scared of."

"A couple weeks ago, I thought my dad was going to die," Bri said so quietly Carre could barely hear her.

Carre grew very still, holding Bri. Waiting.

Bri took a shaky breath. "That was really scary."

"I know, baby."

"No, you don't know what I mean." Bri cupped Carre's face. "I love my dad, I do. But you…with you it's different. I won't be able to come take care of you if things get bad. If something happens to you because I'm not there, I'm going to lose it for good."

"Oh, baby, no," Carre whispered. She threaded her fingers into Bri's hair and caressed her neck. "I'm going to be fine, and you are going to do what you need to do, because people are depending on you. And because it's your responsibility and that's who you are." She kissed her softly. "Don't you think I'm afraid for you?"

"I'll be okay."

Carre smiled. "You expect me to trust you, but you have to trust me, too."

"Just be okay. Okay? Please."

"Promise. I love you."

Bri rested her forehead against Carre's and closed her eyes. "Me too. So bad."

"Got thirty seconds?"

"I just got dressed." Bri said, sounding unconvincing.

"Okay. A minute and thirty seconds, then." Carre grabbed Bri's hand and pulled her toward the bed. "Get over here and give me something to think about until I see you again."

"Two minutes," Bri muttered, fumbling with her belt. "I've got at least two minutes."

❖

At the sound of a gunshot, Reese grabbed the marine next to her and dove for cover, scrambling with one hand for her weapon while shielding the body beneath her with her own. She swept the ground in front of her, and her right hand closed over the grip of her revolver.

"Keep your head down," Reese grunted, yanking her weapon free from its holster.

Tory clamped both hands around Reese's wrist. "Reese! Reese, we're safe. You're home. Reese!"

Forms took shape in the murky light. The desert, cold and black as death at midnight, blindingly bright and scorching in the light of day, faded from her mind's eye and Reese saw her living room, her kitchen, and beneath her, her wife. "Tory. God, Tory. Did I hurt you?"

"Darling, no, of course you didn't." Tory smiled shakily. "Put your gun away, darling."

Reese stared at the weapon gripped in her hand and Tory's fingers clenched around her wrist so tightly they were white. "I'm sorry. God. What was that?"

"I don't know. Maybe a tree coming down." Tory released her hold on Reese's arm. "It doesn't matter. Everything is all right."

"No it isn't." Reese pushed away, re-holstered her weapon, and slumped back against the sofa, not looking at Tory. "Did I hurt you? I'm sorry."

Tory sat up in the narrow space between the sofa and the coffee table, which had been pushed aside when Reese had pulled them off the sofa and onto the floor. Her hip ached from landing on it, but that wasn't what hurt her. Reese looked haunted, tortured, and she simply couldn't stand it anymore. She got to her knees and straddled Reese's lap. She held her lover's face in both hands and forced Reese to look at her. "You are not to say that to me anymore. You have never hurt me.

You never will. You have nothing to be sorry for. You're exhausted. That was instinct. Your instinct to protect me. To protect those you love and are responsible for. I love you for that."

Reese's eyes were bruised with uncertainty, and Tory slid her hands higher, into Reese's hair. She leaned down and kissed her. "You did your duty. You served when called. You have nothing to be ashamed of just because part of you questioned why you were there." She stroked Reese's face. "I let you go, because I knew that you had to, but I'm not ashamed that I didn't want you to go. I won't apologize for that, and I won't apologize for saying that I don't want you to go again."

"Tory," Reese whispered, circling her waist. She laid her cheek between Tory's breasts. "If I didn't have you I'd be lost."

"No you wouldn't," Tory murmured, brushing her lips over Reese's forehead. "But you don't have to worry about it, ever. I promise."

"I have to go to work soon."

"I know. So do I."

"I wish you weren't going to be here for this." Reese kissed the base of Tory's throat, then lower between her breasts.

"I can't be anywhere else. You're here, and I won't leave you. And I have a responsibility too." Tory reached between them and opened the buttons on her blouse, then cradled Reese's cheek against her breast. "Listen to my heart. It beats for you. You and only you, for all my life."

Reese shuddered and Tory felt tears on her skin.

"I know you'll be careful," Tory said, "and so will I. And when this is over, we'll make love and I'll make sure you know just exactly where you belong."

"As if I could forget," Reese whispered, tilting her head back and grinning weakly.

Tory smiled. "Well, I'll enjoy reminding you just the same."

❖

Nita curled up in the big chair in Deo's bedroom and watched Deo dress. She loved to see her move, especially naked. When she stretched to pull pants off a hanger in her closet, the muscles in her back and shoulders bunched and rippled. Her ass tightened, and Nita had a quick memory of running her hands over those muscles and digging her fingers into them as Deo thrust between her legs. She must have made a small sound because Deo turned in her direction.

"What?"

"Nothing."

Deo narrowed her eyes and studied Nita in the soft light from the bedside lamp. Nita's skin held a hint of heat beneath the smooth tan surface. "You're thinking about sex."

"No I'm not."

"Uh-huh." Deo stepped into her briefs, then pulled on her pants. Naked from the waist up, she walked toward the dresser on the wall behind Nita. She stopped by the chair, leaned down and kissed Nita soundly, then kept going. "Yes you are. Why don't you want me to know?"

Nita was about to make a flip reply about preferring to take her by surprise, and then the entire building shook, rattling the windows in their casements. The room dimmed as the scant light from the cloudy gray sky disappeared. Rain hammered against the skylight. A small TV on Deo's dresser was turned down so low the sound of the weatherman's words were barely audible, but the map behind him with its large red arrows and heavy black circles centered over the New England coast told the story with dramatic effectiveness. Nita appreciated, as she hadn't until that moment, that before the day was out they were all likely to be in deadly danger. "I can't look at you or think of you without wanting you, and that makes me uncomfortable."

Deo jerked a white T-shirt over her head, then grabbed a clean khaki work shirt from a pile in her dresser drawer. Leaving both untucked, she settled onto the arm of Nita's chair and regarded her contemplatively. "Desiring me doesn't feel good."

"Actually," Nita said softly, "it feels wonderful."

"But."

"If I forget it's just sex, I feel vulnerable. I don't like that feeling."

"Just sex." Deo nodded, then lifted Nita's hand and pushed it under the bottom of her T-shirt, against her bare belly. Nita gasped and Deo's muscles quivered. "That's sex. Your skin, my skin, our bodies. It feels good."

Nita said nothing, but inside she was burning.

Deo drew Nita's hand away from her stomach and clasped her fingers. "Sylvia hurt you with sex. I won't."

"I know."

"My cousins are all volunteer firemen, and so are half of my construction crew. I'll probably be lending them a hand if they need heavy equipment, and then if it's even half as bad as the predictions, it'll take us weeks to clean up." Deo kissed the back of Nita's hand, then released it and stood up to finish buttoning her shirt. "I'm going to be thinking about you while I'm out there."

"I'm afraid I'll be busy too," Nita said softly, sensing more behind this almost ordinary conversation because Deo's eyes were so intense they seemed to be on fire.

"Thinking about you, wondering where you are, worrying if you're all right—that's not sex."

"Don't, Deo," Nita said, rising quickly, her heart beating so hard in her chest she almost couldn't breathe. The door to the hallway was just behind her, and she had a frantic desire to flee. "Don't. Don't make it any more than it is."

"Why not?"

Nita shook her head. "I'm just getting used to trusting my body around you."

"You gave Sylvia your body, but you wanted her to want more." Deo picked up her keys. "Why don't you want me to?"

Because, Nita thought, *because I've already given you more than I gave her, and she almost killed me.* When Nita said nothing, Deo just shrugged and smiled wryly. She pushed open the bedroom door and held it for Nita to walk past her into the hall.

"I said I wanted to come inside you," Deo said when Nita drew alongside her. "I love the way it feels when I start to come and you wrap your arms and legs around me so tight. Then I'm coming and I feel myself pouring into you."

"God, Deo, don't do this now." A pulse thundered between her thighs, and she shimmered inside, silver-hot like molten steel. "We can't."

"I know," Deo rasped, "but I have to say this. When I said I wanted to come inside you, I thought I just meant I wanted you to hold me inside your *body*." She rested the tips of her fingers over Nita's heart and kissed her very gently on the mouth. "I think I was wrong."

Nita covered Deo's hand and pressed it harder against her breast, leaning into her, shamelessly drawing on her strength. She couldn't give her what she asked and she feared the coming storm. It wasn't the angry rain and brutal winds that threatened to take Deo away, but the bitter clouds that shrouded her own damaged heart.

"Please be careful," Nita whispered.

"I'll call you." Deo smiled a little sadly and pushed a folded piece of paper into Nita's front pocket. "Or you call me. This time, Nita, it has to work both ways."

When Deo turned and walked away, Nita followed, afraid that she had no idea how to give what Deo needed or take what Deo offered. Maybe that was the reason she had never said no to Sylvia. Maybe she'd been a coward and taken the easy way out. Deo deserved more. Much more.

Nita raced through rain that beat against her skin like a thousand needles and wrestled open her car door. Before diving inside she turned and saw Deo standing beside her truck, staring at her with the wind and rain lashing her hair. Waiting.

"I don't want to lose you," Nita shouted into the wind. The words flew back into her face, and as the sky howled, she heard Sylvia's voice, felt her pounding inside her. *You're mine, I'm not going to lose you. You're mine. You're mine. You're mine.* Frantically, she gripped the top edge of the door as it threatened to blow off the car or slam her back into the metal frame. She wasn't Sylvia. She wouldn't be her. Taking, taking, never giving. "Deo! I don't know how to let you inside!"

Deo grabbed the door handle, her body shuddering. "I'll be back!"

As Deo yanked open her door and threw herself into her truck, Nita surrendered to the onslaught and almost fell into her front seat. Even with the windshield wipers on, she could barely see. Drenched, shivering from more than the icy rain, she was aware of Deo's truck backing out and disappearing. Then she was alone in the raging storm.

CHAPTER TWENTY-FIVE

Hello? Hello?" Tory strained to hear through the static. "Hello?"

"Tor…it's me," Reese said. "Time for…close…clinic. We've… wash outs…all up and dow—"

"I know. No one can get here anyhow. We're on our way in to town."

"… careful."

"You too. I love you. Reese?" Tory shook the phone as if that would bring Reese back, and pressed it to her ear so hard it hurt. "Reese? Darling?" She slammed the phone down. "God damn it."

"Anything I can do?" Nita said breathlessly, brushing water off her face with both hands. Her lab coat was soaked from the shoulders to thighs.

"You're doing it. Did you and Randy get the emergency supplies into the Jeep?"

"Yes. Everything we can reasonably move."

"Sally will come into town with you and me. I think we should send Randy home."

Nita nodded. "Where are we setting up?"

"Emergency aid center will be at Town Hall. Between the two of us and Sally, the paramedics, EMTs, and some of the locals who have medical training, we should be okay in the short term."

"I just heard on the radio that we're three hours from maximum winds, but even after that it's going to blow pretty hard for another twelve. Who knows how much flooding we'll get." Nita draped her dripping lab coat over the hook on Tory's office door.

Tory scooped up her keys. "We can pretty much plan on being at Town Hall until tomorrow night. Did you bring a change of clothes and things?"

"Another set of these." Nita gestured to her jeans and T-shirt, far more casual than her ordinary work attire. "When I got home this morning, I had a feeling I wouldn't be getting back there anytime soon. I came prepared."

"This morning? Meaning you were out all night?" Tory asked as they hurried down the hall.

"Uh-huh." Nita held the door open for Tory, who gripped the handrail to steady herself on the slick stone landing as the wind threatened to upend her.

"Must have been something special to get you driving around in this last night," Tory shouted as they linked arms and dashed towards the Jeep where Sally and Randy huddled in the back seat, waiting.

"I didn't plan on it," Nita shouted back. "But she *is* special."

Tory spared Nita a quick glance as she pulled open her door. "Deo?"

"Yes." Nita bolted for the other side of the car and clambered into the passenger seat.

"Everybody all set?" Tory called, glancing briefly over her shoulder to Sally and Randy. At the chorus of yeses, she put the Jeep into four-wheel-drive and sluiced her way out of the parking lot that now resembled a small pond. She wanted to get Randy safely home, and she wanted to get into town. She'd be needed there, and she'd be closer to Reese.

With too much water sheeting over the windshield for her to see anything at all, she gripped the wheel and drove the road from memory, praying she wouldn't hit a downed tree or electric wire. The tension inside the Jeep was hot and thick, but her people—her friends—were good in a crisis, and she trusted them to handle whatever might come. She spared a second look in Nita's direction and grinned.

"Deo, huh," she muttered under her breath. "Good for you."

"Yes," Nita whispered. "Yes, I really think she is."

❖

The lobby of Town Hall with its wide, curving staircases flanking each wall was bustling when Tory, Nita, and Sally arrived. Tory immediately dispatched Sally to set up a triage area in a shallow alcove just inside the front doors, and she went in search of the medical staging area. From the cacophony of voices growing louder with each step she took, Tory surmised that a fair number of the townspeople had already decided to take shelter there rather than ride out the wind and water at home. She slowed at the foot of the stairs as she spied someone she hadn't expected to see.

"Nelson! What are you doing here?"

Nelson Parker, fifteen pounds lighter than his usual weight, still looked imposing in his sheriff's uniform. He grinned sheepishly. "I'm not doing anything here I wouldn't be doing at home. Just minding the phones." He pointed to a short wave radio and an array of receivers lined up on a nearby table. Caroline sat at one end of the table with a stack of files in front of her. "Someone's got to coordinate the various response teams, and I told Gladys to stay home with George and mind their house. Talking doesn't take much energy. Besides, Caroline won't even let me lift the report folders."

Tory frowned. "As long as all you do is talk. And you don't leave this building. I mean it."

"I understand."

"Have you seen Reese?"

"Just a little while ago. There's some folks cut off way down at the West End where the roads are flooded out. She took one of the big trucks down to get them."

Tory bit her lip. She wanted to call Reese just to be sure she was all right, but she probably had patients waiting. "Will you let me know when she gets back…or if you hear from her?"

"Sure thing."

"Thanks." Tory headed up to the auditorium on the second floor. A large banner with a red cross made it pretty hard to miss the emergency medical station. So did the tall dark-haired woman in a white T-shirt and black jeans who sat on a stool suturing the forearm of an elderly woman.

"KT!" Tory exclaimed. "What are you doing here?"

"Didn't want to miss the party," KT said, shooting Tory a grin.

"I already told her she was foolish," the sprightly octogenarian said, giving KT a fond look. "Coming in this direction when everyone else is going the other way. Of course, the girls are prettier out here."

KT laughed and eyed Pia, who stood nearby with a clipboard. "Some of them sure are."

Tory clasped KT's shoulder briefly. "We can use the help. Thanks."

"No problem." KT caught Tory's gaze. "It's a good time to be with family."

"Yes," Tory murmured, accepting an intake sheet from Pia for someone with a sprained knee. "It is."

❖

Two hours after she arrived, Nita finally took a break. Glancing around the room, she was satisfied that all the urgent patients had been dealt with. While she, KT, and Tory had screened or treated everyone in need of medical care—chiefly for problems stemming from attempts to secure or evacuate homes—volunteers saw to the townspeople who had come seeking shelter. Now, everyone had a cot, a small bag of snacks, and sundries. From the weather reports and the din of driving rain against the windows, the worst of the tempest was nearly upon them.

Nita wasn't frightened for herself. The 100-year-old building had undoubtedly weathered nature's wrath many times, and she had no doubt it would again. But in the rare free minutes she'd had between tending the sprains, lacerations, and occasional broken bone of some of those emergency workers and storm victims, she feared for Deo.

Hundreds of residents and tourists had refused to evacuate in the hopes of riding out the hurricane in their homes and hotels. Already some areas of town were flooded, and the real people in danger were those stranded and the rescue personnel who attempted to reach them and their animals in trucks and small outboard boats. Deo was one of those rescuers. She was out in the storm somewhere, assisting with her trucks and generators and other emergency equipment.

Nita hadn't seen her for over twelve hours, and she wondered if Deo had stopped long enough to get warm and catch a meal. She worried that she'd take chances, risking herself in atonement for the one life she hadn't been able to save.

"How are you doing?" Pia asked, sinking onto the bench against the wall where Nita huddled to get out of the fray.

"Oh," Nita said, her heart tripping crazily for just a second, Pia's coloring, her dark beauty, was so like Deo's. "I'm all right. A little tired." She laughed self-consciously, glad Pia couldn't read her mind.

"I can't actually remember the last time I slept a full night."

"Me neither." Pia rested her head against the wall. "I told KT I didn't want her to come, but I'm glad she's here. Have you heard from your family?"

"No, but I'm not too worried about them, because…you know, a cop's family. They'll be looked after."

"That's good." Pia tracked KT on the far side of the room as KT and Tory wended their way between cots, checking on patients. "It's funny how things work out. KT and Tory used to be lovers."

"Really."

"Mmm. A long time ago. They were separated for a lot of years, but I don't think they ever stopped loving each other. And now," Pia said softly, "KT is mine and somehow we're all family." Pia shifted her gaze to Nita. "Family isn't always what we expect it to be, is it?"

Nita laughed bitterly. "No, it certainly isn't."

"Joey's out on a cleanup crew with Deo," Pia said. "I didn't want him to go, but he wouldn't let her have all the fun." She shook her head. "He worships her. I think he wants to grow up to be just like her because he thinks she gets all the girls."

"He might be right," Nita said, strangely unbothered by the allusion to Deo's reputation with women. Deo had awakened in *her* arms that morning. Deo had come for *her*, unguarded and vulnerable, the night before. That was truth. The rest didn't matter.

"All my brothers love her, but it doesn't make up for Gabriel. Deo said she told you about Gabe."

"Yes."

"That's a big deal, that she told you, you know."

"Yes, I know. I know how much she's suffered." Nita sighed. "I hope she isn't out there taking chances…trying to prove something."

"My uncle is the only one who hasn't forgiven her. It was an accident, for God's sake. She was just a kid, and we all did dumb things when we were kids. Jesus, it was just as much Gabe's fault for going out with her as it was hers for taking a boat out when she was drunk."

"What?" Nita frowned. "What did you say?"

Pia looked confused. "About what?"

"Deo wasn't driving that boat. Her brother was."

"No. That's not what the sheriff said. That's not what Deo told us either."

"Who do you think told the sheriff what happened?" Nita stood abruptly. "Of course she wouldn't blame her brother. He was dead."

"She told you *Gabe* was driving?" Pia jumped up. "God damn her. I can't believe she did that—let us all believe all this time that *she* got Gabe out there when no sane person would be on the water."

"Why can't you believe it?" Nita said, her attention drawn to a noisy group of men in yellow slickers and heavy black rain boots coming through the door. In the midst of them, she recognized Deo. "She'd rather hurt than hurt someone else. Excuse me."

Nita caught up to Deo in the coffee line.

"I bet you could use a sandwich to go along with that coffee."

Deo's look of surprise turned to one of pleasure. "I was hoping you'd be here."

"Were you now." Nita knew there were people all around them, but she couldn't see anyone except Deo. She couldn't hear a single voice except hers.

"Yeah."

After Deo got her coffee, Nita took her hand and led her to a quiet spot beneath the broad sweeping staircase. "Is this your first break all day?"

"More or less." Deo sipped her coffee, then brushed her thumb over Nita's cheek. "You okay? You look a little tired."

"Someone has been keeping me up nights."

Deo grinned. "Really."

"Really." Nita parted Deo's rain slicker and slid her hand inside, settling her palm on the crest of Deo's hip. "And when she's not keeping me awake making love to me the way no one ever has, *I'm* awake thinking about it."

"That's funny." Deo leaned closer and brushed her mouth over Nita's. "I've been thinking about the same thing all day. Keeps me warm out there."

A wolf whistle sounded from somewhere nearby and Deo scowled, sliding her arm around Nita's waist as she scanned the nearby faces. Then she grinned. "Joey, take your eyes someplace else."

"What, and miss all the action?" Joey skidded to a halt next to them, the coffee in the cup he held in his uninjured hand sloshing over the rim. "Hi Nita."

"Hi Joey," Nita said. "Are you taking care of that hand out there?"

Joey glanced down at the splint on his forearm as if he had forgotten it was there. "Oh yeah. I can do most anything with it now."

"If you re-injure it," Nita warned, trying to sound stern but finding it hard to raise any temper with the charming young man, "it will just take months longer to heal."

"Forget that," Deo grumbled. "He's been freeloading long enough."

"Listen," Joey said eagerly, "I just heard there's a bunch of power lines down and a few buildings caught fire. Fire crews are out already, but they're probably gonna need some of our equipment. We should go, Deo."

"Okay," Deo said, never taking her eyes from Nita's face. "Send Marco and his crew out with the other truck. Then grab us some sandwiches and I'll meet you outside in a minute."

"Got it. See you, Nita."

"Bye, Joey." Nita leaned into Deo and the icy water from Deo's soaked jeans seeped into hers. "You're cold. You should rest awhile before you go out again."

"I'm okay."

"If you work like this you'll get hurt."

"I'm okay. Better than okay now." Deo kissed her again and tossed her cup into a trash can. "I gotta go."

Struck by sudden disquiet, Nita pulled her closer, wrapping both arms around her waist beneath the heavy slicker. "Don't try to be a hero."

"Me?" Deo laughed. "You know that's not my style."

"Don't pull that attitude with me," Nita said gently. "I know how brave and caring you are—even if you try to hide it."

"What?" Deo's voice caught. "I'm not—"

"Yes, you are. I see you looking after Joey. I see you out there in this miserable, dangerous weather, hour after hour, helping everywhere you can." Nita could still feel Deo's pain when she'd told her about Gabe, and that other storm, and all she'd lost. "I *know* how much you care—you never told your family what really happened that night with Gabe. You took all the blame."

Deo jerked. "Who told you that?"

"Pia." Nita tightened her grip when Deo tried to pull away. "Don't be angry with her. It just came up." She laid her cheek against Deo's, her mouth close to her ear. "I think you're wonderful."

"Yeah?" Deo relaxed in Nita's arms. "It matters, what you think. It matters a lot."

Leaning back so she could see Deo's face, Nita read the questions in Deo's eyes. Questions Nita knew the answers to but feared to say. A loud crash sounded somewhere outside. The floor vibrated and shutters clattered. Deo was about to go back out into that angry night, and Nita couldn't let her take all the chances. "*You* matter to me, Deo. You matter a lot."

"That's good," Deo whispered. "Because I'm falling in love with you."

Nita didn't know how to believe her, wasn't sure she dared. She had never been enough for anyone—not enough for Sylvia to choose *her* over the privilege of a life that was a lie, not enough for her family to stand by her against the brotherhood of blue. Why should Deo change her free-wheeling ways for her? Nita's voice shook. "I didn't think that was your style."

"Neither did I." Deo smiled a lopsided smile. "But I think you hooked me the first time I saw you at the clinic. You were cool and beautiful and a little pissed, and I fell a little bit in love—"

Nita pressed her fingertips to Deo's mouth. "I should tell you not to say that. Hell, I should probably run." She moved her fingers and kissed her. "But I'm not going to. Call me when you get a chance. I need…I need to hear your voice."

"You won't change your mind, will you?" Deo eased free of Nita's grip and backed up a step. "You'll be here?"

When their bodies separated completely, Nita ached. She wanted to reach out and grab her, hold her there. Keep her inside, out of the storm. Inside with her. Nita shivered. She wanted her inside *her*.

"I won't go, Deo," Nita said just as Deo started to turn away. Deo looked back, the questions still in her eyes. "I'll be here waiting for you."

"Then like I said before, I'll be back."

Nita watched her until she disappeared with another group of excited men and women. She recalled the suffocating loneliness she used to feel watching Sylvia drive away. She didn't feel that way now. She missed Deo immediately, but unlike with Sylvia, the ache came from something she had found, instead of lost.

CHAPTER TWENTY-SIX

Pull up onto the sidewalk over there," Deo told Joey, pointing to a ring of emergency vehicles parked haphazardly around the mouth of a wide access alley that led to one of the huge wooden piers in the far West End. A commercial fishing building on the end of the pier was burning, and the flames and the reflections from the light bars on top of the police cruisers, rescue rigs, and fire engines shimmered eerily through the inky rain.

"They've got a lot of boats up in dry dock," Joey yelled, yanking on the emergency brake. "If the pier collapses and takes them too, it'll be a hell of a loss."

"Raise the other guys on the walkie-talkie," Deo said, already out of the truck, hard hat in hand and a Maglite under her arm. Frigid rain lashed the back of her neck. "Tell them to get out here with hydraulic winches and joists. We'll shore it up if we have to."

"I'm on it."

Deo ran down the pathway, struggling for balance as her boots sank into the saturated sand. Closing in on the conflagration, she skirted thick coils of fire hose and mounds of equipment that suddenly loomed up out of the darkness like predatory beasts. Even fifty yards away, the heat from the burning building caused sweat to stream down her face. Squinting through the billowing smoke, she spied Reese.

"Reese!" she shouted above the roar of the inferno. "How bad is it?"

"Might save the building," Reese yelled back. "If the pier doesn't collapse. Incident Commander's down there now checking it out."

"Let me go see what he needs."

Reese lifted the restraining tape that Bri and Allie had used to cordon off the area, although there were no gawkers to discourage. "Got a radio?"

"Yeah."

Deo didn't see anything at first except the burning building, and then she caught the wink of a flashlight under the pier and followed the blinking pinpoint of light. Soon she came upon three men standing ankle deep in water underneath the 200-year-old pier. The tide was out or they would have been up to their thighs in sea water. The creosote soaked pilings supporting the pier would not burn easily, but they *would* burn. Unfortunately, time and weather and ocean salt had weakened some of them already. Above their heads, the fire raged.

Recognizing Alan Peterson, the fire marshal, Deo sloshed over to him. "How does it look?"

Peterson spared her a glance as he hammered a metal temperature probe into one of the horizontal joists. "We're okay for now, but if we don't contain the spread mighty fast, we're going to lose this pier. Some of these beams are going to go up like kindling."

"We can probably jack it up in enough places to buy you some time," Deo said. She'd only worked this close to a fire once before, and that had been nothing near the scale of this one. The sound of air being sucked into the building to feed the fiery furnace was like an enormous dragon breathing in huge rasping gusts.

"If we don't do something fast, it won't make any difference," Peterson yelled back. "I'll have to pull my team out of there and let it burn."

"I've got a crew on the way. Five minutes."

"Okay, you've got fifteen."

"I hear you!"

Deo ran toward the street and met Joey coming down.

"They're here!" Joey exclaimed breathlessly. "They're offloading gear onto the Jeep and will have it down here in just a couple minutes."

"Let me show you what we've got," Deo said, grabbing his arm. She guided him back down the circuitous path, tugging him along when he slowed to gape at the fire.

"Holy cripes," Joey shouted. "They'll never save that building."

"Let's worry about the pier." Deo shone her light over the ancient timbers. The sky overhead was now a rosy grey. The fire above them was closer. "We need to get supports under here to shore up the joists, every twenty feet or so."

"Man," Joey said, gazing upward. "It's almost right on top of us."

"We've got a little time," Deo assured him. "Come on, let's get our crew down here."

Deo turned and sprinted, slowing when she realized Joey wasn't with her. She looked over her shoulder and saw that he had stopped to stare at the burning building again. "Joey, move it!"

He turned, his back to the pier and the pyre above, a look of innocent amazement on his face. He didn't see the section of roof above him break free and start to fall. Deo didn't even have time to scream. She launched herself at him and struck his chest with her shoulder mid-dive just as the world erupted in flame and fury.

❖

"Tory," Chief Nelson Parker said in a low urgent voice. "I just got a call from Bri. She says casualties from a fire on one of the piers are coming our way. ETA two minutes."

"Did she give you anything else?" Tory swallowed back a wave of fear. Why had Bri called? Why not Reese? "God, Nelson, we're not set up for major trauma here."

"At least one serious. The others didn't sound too bad—a few burns, couple lacerations."

"All right." Tory motioned to KT and Nita to join them as she continued thinking aloud. "We'll stabilize here and transport anyone who needs it. Nelson, I need a vehicle standing by that's capable of getting out of here, no matter what the roads look like."

Nelson grimaced. "I'm not sure we can do that. Route 6 is pretty much underwater."

Tory shook her head. "I don't care if you have to pull a boat out of the harbor. If I have injured that need transport, I want them transported."

"Trouble?" KT asked, her demeanor nonchalant but her eyes sharp and intent.

"What's going on?" Nita looked from Tory to KT, her expression turning to alarm.

"We have incoming," Tory said, hurrying towards the treatment area. "Nelson, get some people to clear a path through the lobby up to here. And ask Sally to come up."

"I'm on it," he said.

"KT," Tory said, automatically assuming the role of team leader. It was her town, her clinic, her call. "You're the trauma surgeon. You'll get the most serious. Sally, Nita, and I will take the others. If you need help, call me."

"Pia can give me a hand," KT pointed out. "She's an excellent assistant."

"All right, fine." Tory surveyed the corner of the room where they had piled their emergency medical supplies and instruments. "Hell, we don't even have treatment tables. Keep the patients on the gurneys they come in on and treat them there."

"This reminds me of operating in Southeast Asia when I was a resident and I did that charity tour," KT said, her eyes bright with adrenaline and anticipation. "Remember, Vic? I told you we had to work with flashlights when the generators went out."

"Hopefully we're a little better off than that," Tory muttered, but she wasn't entirely certain that was true. Her worst fear was that they'd have serious injuries they wouldn't be able to handle with their limited resources. She met KT's gaze. "We could be in trouble here."

KT swept a hand down Tory's arm and squeezed her fingers. "Don't worry. I've got your back."

"Thanks."

"I'd better get Pia and set up."

Tory watched KT amble away as if she had all the time in the world. She knew that blasé manner was a practiced disguise perpetrated to instill calm in others. KT was already mentally planning, organizing, and executing any number of potential emergency scenarios in her head, and as soon as she saw her patient, every action would be choreographed with deliberation and certainty. Tory trusted Nita's competence, but she depended on KT in a far more personal way.

"Nita," Tory said, refocusing. "You triage—your ER training's more recent than mine."

"Got it," Nita said, grabbing several packs of sterile gloves and tucking them into the waistband of her jeans.

"Let's hope we don't need blood," Tory said. "We'll have to make do with—"

"Here they come," Nita announced as the loud thud of the heavy front doors banging open followed by a rising jumble of voices signaled the arrival of the paramedics with their casualties.

Nita leaned over the balcony and tracked the progression of the emergency teams across the lobby and up the stairs. Three grimy firefighters and a paramedic maneuvered a stretcher up the stairs with surprising speed. Behind them, paramedics and police officers guided several more walking wounded. At the top of the stairs, Tory directed the stretcher bearers toward KT. Nita focused on the other injured still slowly making their way up. Her stomach sank when she recognized Joey Torres leaning on Bri Parker for support. His face was streaked with soot and blood, and his clothes were soaked. Then she picked out the brunette officer, Allie, with another injured fireman.

Why wasn't Deo with Joey? Anxiously, Nita scanned the crowd again. Deo wasn't there. Deo wasn't anywhere she searched.

Fighting a wave of dizziness, Nita pushed her way to the stretcher.

"Oh no," she whispered.

Blood seeped down Deo's forehead and angry red blisters covered the left side of her neck. Burns. Sandbags cushioned Deo's head. Head injury?

"What happened?" Nita demanded, struggling for calm. She wanted to shove everyone out of the way so she could touch Deo, just touch her. "Where else is she hurt?"

"Put her over here, guys," KT directed. "Let's have a look."

"Deo," Nita said, as if expecting Deo to answer. "Deo, sweetheart?"

Pia pushed into the crowd. "Deo? Oh my God."

"Baby," KT said to Pia, blocking her view of her cousin on the stretcher, "let me take care of her. You go help the others."

Nita tried to edge around KT to get to Deo, but a hand on her arm held her back.

"Let KT work, Nita," Tory said. "She'll take care of her."

Nita spun away. "I won't get in the way. I just need to—"

Pia caught Nita's arm. "Tory's right, honey. Come on. Joey's over here. He needs your help."

"Joey." Nita took a breath and the part of her that functioned despite her own anguish and fear clicked on. Her mind cleared. "Yes.

Of course." She looked to Tory. "You'll let me know as soon as I can see her?"

"I'll make sure you're notified as soon as KT gives the word," Tory said.

Squaring her shoulders, Nita forced herself to turn her back on the scene of KT working on Deo's still form. It was the hardest thing she'd ever done in her life. She fisted her hands, hoping to stop the trembling before she reached Joey. Pia was already with him, kneeling in front of the chair where he slumped, a bloody gauze pressed to his cheek.

"What happened?" Nita asked as she pulled on gloves. She glanced at the clipboard by his feet. His blood pressure was a little bit low, but Sally hadn't noted anything urgent.

Joey shivered and his eyes glistened with tears. "Oh man, I fucked up. How's Deo? Is she hurt bad?"

"KT is looking after her right now," Nita replied, her voice sounding strangely flat to her own ears. Funny, her whole body was numb, but she knew exactly what she had to do for Joey. "Let's take care of you. Tell me how you got hurt."

"The building…part of the roof…it was on fire and it fell."

Nita placed her index finger on the radial side of his wrist. His pulse was thready and fast. If he wasn't young and healthy, he'd probably be in shock. "Pia, would you get him a blanket. He's wet and cold."

"I'll be right back, Joey, sweetie," Pia said, rising quickly.

"Deo pushed me out of the way," Joey continued miserably. "I didn't see it falling, and she pushed me out of the way." Tears ran down his face. "Something hit her and she fell and I…oh, fuck, it's all my fault."

"It's okay. Let me see your face," Nita requested abruptly. She couldn't hear any more about Deo if she hoped to be able to work.

The laceration on his cheek was long, but not too deep.

"Are you hurt anywhere else? What about your hand? Did you re-injure it?"

Joey stared down into his lap. His splint was wet and sandy but intact.

"It's okay. I didn't fall on it." He turned anguished eyes to Nita. "Can I see her? Can I please see her?"

"In a little while." Nita straightened and her vision dimmed. For a second, she thought she might faint, and then she felt a steadying hand on her elbow.

"Hey," Reese said gently. "Nita, are you all right?"

"Yes. Yes, thanks." Nita took in the white bandage wrapped around Reese's left hand. "You'd better let me look at that."

Reese followed her gaze, then shrugged. "It's nothing much. A few burns."

"She pulled Deo out from under the stuff that was on fire," Joey announced. "She saved her."

"Then I owe you thanks," Nita said. "More than I can say."

"No you don't," Reese said. She scanned the area, her gaze landing on the activity around the stretcher. "How is she?"

"I don't know yet." Nita couldn't think about what was happening behind her. She couldn't think about Deo lying so still, blood on her face. She couldn't. "Is there anyone else injured?"

Reese shook her head. "Just bumps and bruises. Nothing major."

"You need that hand looked at," Nita repeated.

"I'll have Tory do it," Reese said. "I want to let her know I'm okay."

"Yes. Yes, you should do that. Go find her."

"Nita, you okay?" Reese peered at her with concern.

"Yes. Fine. Go ahead. Tory needs to see you."

Reese hesitated, then stepped away as Pia returned with a blanket and wrapped it around Joey's shoulders.

"Can you irrigate out that laceration on his cheek," Nita asked, "and steri-strip it closed. I don't think he'll need sutures."

"Sure. I'll change that splint too." Pia gripped Nita's arm. "Why don't you go see what's happening with Deo. Maybe KT can give you an update now."

"Thank you. I'll do that."

Nita didn't recognize herself. She'd been in the midst of more medical emergencies than she could count. She'd taken care of the young and the old, victims of horrifying car crashes and brutal assaults and senseless accidents. She'd handled it all, calmly, even remotely. And now, she was terrified. The very thought of Deo being hurt left her disoriented, as if she were cast out to sea, far from land with no idea which direction led to safety.

She had to get to her.

The chaos around Deo had settled down to a controlled flurry of activity, and Nita was able to get close enough to see her. She wasn't awake, but her eyes moved restlessly beneath closed lids. A white sterile cloth with a hole in the middle covered her stomach, and just as Nita looked down, KT made a two-inch vertical incision below Deo's belly button.

"Is she bleeding internally?" Nita felt an icy hand grip her heart.

"Don't know," KT responded without looking away from what she was doing. "Her blood pressure's been a little bit up and down, and I want to make sure nothing is going on inside. We can't rely on X-rays or CT, since we don't have any." She tossed Nita a grin. "So we'll have to do it the old-fashioned way and look."

"What about her head?" Nita asked.

"She's got a good bump on her temple."

As KT talked, she slid a clear plastic IV tube into Deo's abdomen through the incision she'd made, and Sally hooked up an IV bag to the other end. The clear fluid ran into Deo's abdomen. Nita knew that in a few minutes, they would lower the IV bag and let the fluid run out. If it was clear, there was a good chance there was no internal injury. If Deo was bleeding inside, it would be pink or red. If that happened, Deo might very well die there, because as good as KT was, she couldn't operate in the middle of Town Hall.

"The scalp laceration's no big deal," KT went on. "Her pupils look fine. With luck, it's just a concussion. Reflexes are normal, so I think her neck's okay, too."

"Thank God."

"You want to assist here?" KT asked.

"I'll get Tory if you need help," Nita said, her legs suddenly weak. "I can't. I…she's…we're lovers."

"Hell, Nita, why didn't you say something." KT shook her head. "I'm okay here. You should go sit down until I can fill you in the right way."

"I'd rather stay."

"Okay, then pull up a chair and hold her hand."

"What?"

"Hold her hand. It will be good for her, and it'll be good for you."

"I might be needed if we have more injured."

"If Tory needs you, she'll let you know." KT deftly inserted a series of sutures closing the incision in Deo's abdomen. "Right now, just be her lover."

"Yes." Nita reached for an unoccupied chair and pulled it close. She sat down and took Deo's hand. It was cool and still. She held it to her cheek. "That's just exactly what I want to do."

Chapter Twenty-Seven

Tory assured herself that KT had things under control with Deo and that none of the firefighters or paramedics were suffering from smoke inhalation or other life-threatening problems. Then she went in search of her lover.

"Nelson," Tory said sharply, coming upon Reese and Nelson in a huddle at the perimeter of the activity. "You're supposed to be sitting down monitoring communications. Not briefing with your officers."

"I was just—" Nelson began.

"And you," Tory said, grasping Reese's sleeve, "require medical attention. Now. I don't have time to go through our usual song and dance about this."

Reese took one look at Tory and said, "Chief, I'll check in with you later."

Nelson's eyebrows rose, but he merely nodded and hastily made himself scarce.

"Sit down right here, darling," Tory said more quietly, guiding Reese to a wooden folding chair. Her initial relief at having seen Reese walking in under her own power had given way to alarm when she'd seen the smudged bandage carelessly wrapped around her hand and forearm.

"How are you doing?" Reese asked, obediently sitting.

"I'm not the one who's injured." Tory pulled on gloves and carefully removed the gauze. "How did this happen?"

When Reese hesitated, Tory pulled off her gloves, squatted down in front of her, and braced her hands on Reese's thighs. Looking up into her face, she said gently, "I already know that you're all right. I won't be frightened by hearing how you got hurt. It's important for me to know. I'm your lover."

Reese brushed her fingers over Tory's cheek. "I keep wanting to protect you, but I can't, can I?"

"You do protect me." Tory smiled wearily. "But not the way you think. I don't want to be protected from the truth, especially not when it's your truth. But you shelter my heart, and that makes me strong. That's the gift you give me."

"Thank you," Reese murmured. She looked at her hand. "Deo got hit with burning debris. I pulled her away from it and got a bit singed."

Tory waited.

"The wind came up faster than anybody expected," Reese said, covering Tory's hand where it rested on her thigh. "The fire really took off, and a section of the roof broke loose. It was a flaming torch, and it came down so fast there was no time to do anything. There was no time. No time to warn anyone. No time to find cover."

"God, that sounds terrifying."

"I had people on the ground and no way to warn them."

Reese's gaze turned inward and Tory realized she wasn't recalling the events of an hour ago, she was back in Iraq with the night on fire and her marines dying. Tory's first instinct was to bring Reese back, out of that place, away from that horror, but she didn't. Instead, she held Reese's uninjured hand more tightly, biting her lip to hold back the words of comfort Reese didn't need.

"I couldn't get to them in time. Some went down. I lost them." Reese focused on Tory's face, her eyes filled with torment. "I lost them, Tor."

"Not tonight, you didn't," Tory whispered, praying she was saying the right thing. She wouldn't insult Reese by denying what Reese had gone through out there in the desert. If Reese felt responsible, nothing she could say would change that. But she didn't have to stand by and let Reese suffer for the rest of her life for something Reese couldn't change. "Casualties of war, isn't that what you're taught? That people die, no matter what you do. I know in my heart if you hadn't been there, more would have died. I know that with everything I am. And if you won't believe me, believe this—Deo's alive tonight because you were here, doing your job."

"I do believe you." Reese tugged on Tory's hand and pulled her up and against her body, then rested her cheek against Tory's breast. "Tory, you are the truth in my world."

Tory stroked Reese's hair. "Then trust you did your best, and trust it was enough."

Silently, Reese nodded.

Catching movement out of the corner of her eye, Tory saw Bri halt hesitantly a few feet away, her worried gaze fixed on Reese. She smiled and motioned her over. Then she gently drew away from Reese and found another pair of sterile gloves. "Let's see that hand, Sheriff."

Reese held out her arm as Bri joined them.

"Got a report for me, Officer?" Reese asked, her voice strong and steady.

"Yes ma'am," Bri said smartly. "The fire chief just radioed in. Both fires are under control. The rest of Deo's crew is still working on the pier, but it looks good."

"Good. What about civilians?"

Bri glanced down at a paper in her hand. "The chief got calls from a dozen families who are without power or are flooded out. They'll need to be evacuated to here."

"Who's on that?"

"I told Smith and Allie to grab something to eat, and then start with those families with elderly or kids. Is that okay?"

"Sounds good." Reese winced as Tory trimmed torn skin from around a blister on the back of her hand.

"Sorry," Tory murmured. "These aren't too bad, but they'll do better if I get rid of some of this debris." She sighed. "I really wish you could manage not to use your body as the first line of defense."

Bri laughed and Tory glared at her.

"Uh," Bri said, backing up a step. "So that's it, then. I'm just going to grab a coffee and say hi to Carre, and I'll be ready to head out."

"I'll be with you in five," Reese said. "Don't forget to restock the cruiser with emergency supplies."

"Roger," Bri said, hurrying away.

"How's she doing," Tory asked, applying burn ointment to Reese's hand.

"Solid. She's got a natural instinct for command."

"That's good, isn't it?"

Reese chuckled. "Better than good. Someday, she'll take Nelson's place."

"Not you?" Tory taped the gauze she'd wrapped around Reese's wrist and got unsteadily to her feet. She wore her ankle brace, but after eighteen hours on her feet, nothing could prevent her leg from stiffening. Reese rose quickly and slid an arm around her waist.

"These few weeks as acting chief have been more than enough for me," Reese said. "Now it's about time *you* took a break."

"I'm all right."

"No you're not. Come on."

Tory tried to protest, but Reese just ignored her.

"Sit here," Reese commanded, indicating a bench along the wall. "I'll be right back."

Bowing to the inevitable, Tory slumped down, leaned her head back, and closed her eyes. The sound of Reese calling her name and gentle shaking brought her awake. She rubbed her face.

"Oh my God, I fell asleep."

Reese handed her a cup of coffee and a hastily assembled ham and cheese sandwich. "For about five minutes. Here. Refuel, Dr. King."

Tory took a bite because she was too tired to argue and suddenly realized she was hungry. She finished the hasty meal and washed it down with a gulp of coffee. "Thanks."

"Just doing my job," Reese said as she leaned down and kissed her.

Reese's eyes were clear and sparkling. The pain that so often rode through them was gone. Tory brushed Reese's hair back with her fingertips. "Welcome home, darling."

"It feels really good to be here. I love you."

"I love you." Tory listened to the rain and the wind. The storm was not over, but perhaps the worst had passed. "You've got people to see to, don't you?"

"I do."

"You will be careful out there, won't you?"

"I will."

"Then go, Sheriff. I'll see you when you come home."

Reese kissed her one last time. "I'll be home just as soon as I can."

Tory watched her go, content in knowing that Reese would always do whatever it took to come home to her.

❖

Deo awoke with a start and immediately tried to sit up. Something was holding her down, and for a second, she thought she was underwater again. Gasping, she struggled to get to the surface.

"Deo, baby," Nita said urgently. "Deo, it's all right. Lie still."

"Gabe!" Deo gripped Nita's arm so tightly Nita cried out. "Where's Gabe?"

Nita leaned over so Deo could see her face and stroked Deo's forehead. "There's been an accident, sweetheart. You've been hurt, but you're going to be all right."

"Nita?" Deo whispered, growing still.

"Yes, baby. I'm here."

"Gabe's dead, isn't he?"

Nita thought her heart might break at the forlorn sound of Deo's voice and the terrible naked pain in her eyes. "Yes, baby, he is. It was a long time ago. It was an accident."

Deo closed her eyes and Nita kissed her forehead.

"It wasn't your fault," Nita murmured. "Do you hear me? It wasn't your fault."

"What happened?" Deo asked, finally opening her eyes.

"What do you remember?"

Deo frowned. "Storm. Back then, when Gabe died." She shivered. "And tonight. Another storm."

"Yes. There's a hurricane."

"Joey!" Deo jerked almost upright, then fell back with a grimace, clutching her abdomen. "Oh. Jesus. That hurts."

"You have to lie still," Nita snapped. Even though the abdominal pericentesis fluid had come back clear and KT had pulled the tube out, pronouncing Deo stable, Nita was frantic that something serious could be going on and they'd missed it. "You've been hurt. Joey is fine."

"He's not dead?"

"No. No, baby, he isn't. He might have been hurt, but you made sure he wasn't." Nita wasn't certain how well Deo was able to distinguish the past from the present, and she didn't want her to suffer through the pain of losing Gabe again. "Joey is here somewhere. In a minute, I'll find him so you can talk to him. How do you feel?"

"My head hurts. So does my belly." Deo smiled fleetingly. "It's good to see you though."

"It is so good to see you, too." Nita kissed her on the mouth. "You've got some burns, nothing serious, and a good bump on your head. KT had to make a small incision in your stomach to check for bleeding, but you're okay."

"I remember now. Sort of. A big fire." Deo frowned. "We needed to work on the pier. Joey. Joey was behind me and the building was burning. Burning. God, Nita, the flames were right on top of him!"

"Easy, sweetheart," Nita soothed. "Joey might have been hurt, but you took care of him. Do you understand me? You took care of him. He's all right."

"Why are you crying?" Deo asked.

"What?" Nita touched her cheeks and was stunned to find they were wet. "I…I guess I'm happy. You make me happy."

"Yeah?"

"Yeah," Nita said softly. "Now, close your eyes and try to rest."

"Okay," Deo said wearily, struggling to keep her eyes open. "Will you stay with me?"

"I might have to leave for a few minutes, if I have patients, but I'll be back. If you need me, I'll be here. I promise."

"That's good. I love you," Deo whispered, and closed her eyes.

Nita caught her lip, feeling the tears she couldn't seem to stop on her cheeks again. She'd never understood what it meant to cry from happiness. Sylvia told her countless times that she loved her, but her love had been a weapon. Deo's was a gift.

"You need something?" Allie asked quietly. "Coffee or soda or something?"

"No," Nita said, brushing at her face as she looked up at the young officer beside her. Like every other member of the emergency response teams, Allie's face was streaked with sweat and grime, and shadows marred her flawless skin. She was, nevertheless, strikingly beautiful. "I'm holding up. How are you?"

"Fine." Allie glanced down at Deo. "Is she going to be all right?"

"I think so. We just need to watch her carefully for another twelve hours or so." Nita wondered how much Deo's sometime-girlfriend had heard. The look on her face as her eyes skimmed over Deo said there might be more than a casual fling fueling her concern. "I should check with Tory and make sure everyone's taken care of. Would you mind sitting with her for just a few minutes in case she wakes up again?"

"Sure," Allie said, her voice registering both surprise and gratitude. "I've got about five minutes. What should I tell her if she asks for you?"

"Tell her I left her in good hands and that I'll be right back."

Allie grinned. "Smooth."

"Thank you."

"I'm Allie, by the way, a…friend of Deo's." Allie held out her hand.

"Nita Burgoyne. I'm Deo's lover."

"There goes my summer," Allie proclaimed.

Laughing, Nita nodded. "Looks like it." She squeezed Allie's shoulder. "I won't be long."

"I'll tell her."

Nita hurried in search of Tory. She didn't want to leave Deo for long, not until she was certain she was completely out of danger. She wondered fleetingly why she wasn't jealous, and then she realized that Deo could have had Allie or likely any number of other women. But Deo wanted her. Her.

It felt good to be wanted for who she was. And it felt even better to tell the world that Deo Camara, the sexiest, bravest, and most compassionate woman she'd ever known, was her lover.

CHAPTER TWENTY-EIGHT

"Sit your ass down and stop being a pain in mine," KT growled.

"But—"

"But nothing, Deo. You've got a hole in your belly that needs to heal and a lump on your hard head that's going to have a neighbor if you make me tell you again to stay in bed."

"Is she giving you a hard time?" Nita asked, skirting around the makeshift screen that shielded the cot where Deo lay from the rest of the room.

"No," Deo said quickly.

"Yes." KT motioned Deo down. "Pull up your shirt."

Deo lay back and complied.

Nita held Deo's hand as KT removed the neat square bandage covering the incision below Deo's navel. She peered over KT's shoulder to get a look at the incision.

"It looks good, don't you think?" Nita asked.

"It's fine." KT straightened and skewered Deo with a frown. "But you're still not ready to go back out there."

"When—"

"The storm's wearing itself out," Nita said. "The real cleanup will start in a day or two. Don't worry, there will still be plenty left for you to do."

"Listen to the lady," KT said. "Then I won't have to hurt you."

Deo grinned as KT disappeared. Carefully, she shifted on the narrow cot and patted the space next to her, indicating Nita should sit. "Are you on a break?"

Nita settled beside her with a sigh. "For a few minutes. I just finished suturing a Labrador Retriever's front paw."

"Stretch out beside me."

"I don't want to hurt you."

"You won't." Deo rubbed her back. "I've missed you."

"I've missed you." Kicking off her shoes, Nita curled against Deo's side. "You scared me."

Deo cradled Nita's head against her chest. "I'm sorry. I didn't mean to."

"I know," Nita murmured. "Don't do it again."

"I won't." Deo kissed Nita's forehead and felt her relax.

"I don't want to lose you," Nita whispered.

"You won't." Deo listened to Nita's breathing deepen and realized she was asleep. She stroked her shoulder protectively, savoring her closeness and her trust.

Pia poked her head around the screen. "Deo—"

Deo held a finger to her lips and gestured to Nita.

"We have to talk," Pia mouthed, giving her a glare that was part fondness, part ire.

Figuring it was about Gabe, Deo nodded with a sigh. Pia disappeared, and Deo drew Nita closer. For now all she wanted was the peace that holding Nita brought to her. As she drifted off, she let herself hope that what was growing between them would not disappear when the winds blew the storm out to sea.

❖

Nita turned the corner behind her new house just in time to see Deo ratchet down an enormous extension ladder that had been braced against the rear roofline.

"You're not supposed to be doing that kind of work," Nita called out, striding forward rapidly.

Deo glanced in Nita's direction, the steel ladder braced between both outstretched arms. Her sweat-soaked hair was tied back with a red bandanna, and she wore baggy khaki shorts and a faded, sleeveless blue T-shirt cut off somewhere in the vicinity of her navel. The row of black sutures that KT had placed just one short week before stood out starkly against her smooth, bronze stomach. Faint red blotches were the only remnants of the burns on her jaw and neck.

"Hi there," Deo said, her grin gleaming against the tan that had deepened under the relentless sunshine that had followed in the wake of the storm.

Nita tried to project a stern expression, but it was difficult when faced with such stunning beauty. She wondered if the initial shock at seeing Deo would ever lessen and doubted somehow that it would. Some small part of her, she suspected, would probably never believe that Deo might actually be hers.

"Believe it or not," Nita said, stopping by Deo's side, "those stitches in your abdomen are there for a reason. That incision goes all the way through, and I prefer keeping everything that's inside exactly where it belongs."

Deo slung one arm over a rung of the ladder and leaned it against her hip. Then she kissed Nita. "It's only five o'clock. You're early."

"You're ignoring me."

"Impossible." Deo checked the yard. It was empty. Then she wrapped an arm around Nita's waist and pulled her close. This kiss lasted longer, a lot longer. "Missed you."

Nita rested her cheek on Deo's shoulder. She smelled good—like hard work and promises. She felt strong. Her heart beat rhythmically against Nita's breast, steady and sure.

"I missed you too. Things were quiet so I decided to sneak out. The service has me on beeper call."

"Does that mean you're mine for the night?"

Deo's voice was low and husky, and the weight of it settled in the pit of Nita's stomach and spread like warm whiskey. They hadn't spent the night together since the hurricane.

Once KT had cleared her to do light labor, Deo and her crews had worked from well before sun-up until far after sundown clearing debris from the streets, making temporary repairs on roofs that needed to be replaced, boarding up broken windows, and pumping out flooded basements. Fortunately, Nita's house had sustained little more than cosmetic damage, and Nita had insisted that Deo leave it until others with more urgent needs were taken care of.

When Deo had called to say she was at the house and invited Nita to meet her for dinner, Nita couldn't wait to see her. She replayed Deo's question. *"Does that mean you're mine for the night?"*

Nita turned the concept around in her mind. *Mine.* It could mean so many things. She had been Sylvia's—heart, body, and soul for almost a decade—and in all that time, she realized now, she'd been little more than the object of Sylvia's lust. Deo had offered her more, given her more, in the time they'd been together than she'd ever thought to dream of. With Deo, she felt cherished and desired and…loved.

"Do we need to carry this somewhere?" Nita asked, reaching for the ladder.

"Just help me lean it against the fence. Joey or one of the other guys will get it later."

When they'd stowed it away, Deo took Nita's hand. "Come on, I want to show you something."

Still thinking about how different—how right—she felt with Deo, Nita followed her through the house to the second floor and finally up the narrow winding staircase to the widow's walk.

"Oh," Nita exclaimed. "The new railing looks great. When did you do this?"

"This afternoon."

Nita frowned. "You weren't supposed to work."

"I only supervised." Deo smiled. "You like it?"

"I love it." Nita crossed the narrow walkway, braced her hands on the railing, and lifted her face to the breeze. The air smelled crisp and clean, and she breathed deeply. When Deo came to stand beside her, Nita slid her arm around her waist and leaned against her. Watching a fishing boat round the bend at Long Point and churn into the harbor, Nita thought about the generations of women who had stood in this place before her.

"I read somewhere that the wife of the original sea captain who built this house used to light a lantern up here when she saw his ship come home, and all the women in town would know that their husbands were returning."

"Must have been lonely, watching and waiting and wondering if they'd come back," Deo remarked.

"Yes." Nita shifted and wrapped both arms around Deo's waist, drawing her closer. She kissed her and tasted salt on her lips. "Is your family still planning the barbecue that got rained out?"

"Yes. Are you still going to be my date?"

"I'd like that." Nita hesitated, then asked gently, "Are you ever going to tell them what really happened with Gabe that night?"

"Pia's been after me to." Deo looked out to sea. "But I don't think so."

Nita wasn't sure she could keep the secret in the face of Deo's pain, but she would try if she had to. But first, she would try something else. "I think he might want you to. If the situations were reversed, wouldn't you?"

"Yes," Deo said softly, still turned away.

"Why did you tell me?"

Deo faced her. "I knew from the beginning the one thing we had to have was trust. I would never lie to you."

"Thank you." Nita threaded her fingers through Deo's. "Whatever you decide is all right with me. I just hate to see you hurting."

"You changed all that," Deo confessed. "You make me happy."

"A few minutes ago, out in the yard, you asked me if I'd be yours for the night."

Deo's eyes grew questioning. "Do you have other plans?"

"No," Nita said softly. "But I realized there's something I needed to tell you."

"Look, if you think we're moving too fast, I..."

Nita shook her head. "Wait."

"I don't want you to feel pressured," Deo went on hurriedly, "just because I...I said I love you."

"Did you mean it?"

"Yes," Deo said immediately. She caressed Nita's cheek. "But I know you might not believe me, because of things you might have heard about me or—"

"Deo," Nita said firmly, "the only thing I'm listening to is you. And my heart."

"And what does your heart tell you?"

Deo's need was so plain that Nita ached. "That's what I've been trying to tell you." Nita kissed her. "I don't want to be yours tonight."

Deo stiffened.

"Not *just* tonight. I think...no, I *know*, that I want to be yours for a lot longer than that." Nita looked into Deo's eyes. "I love you."

Deo sighed, a heavy rush of air that sounded as if she'd been holding her breath for a very long time. "That sounds so good to hear."

"It feels so good to *say*," Nita said in wonderment. "In fact, it feels great."

Nita pulled off Deo's red bandanna and combed her fingers through Deo's hair. The wind promptly ruffled it into maddeningly sexy disarray again. "God, I love the way you look."

Deo grinned and bumped her pelvis into Nita's. "Just the way I *look*?"

"Stop that," Nita chastised. "Now that I know what it's like to make love with you, I want you all the time. And it's been a week since you've touched me, and I'm about going out of my mind. Don't tease."

"I'm not teasing." Deo kissed a path down the center of Nita's throat and Nita moaned. "Let's go to my place. I want to make love to you."

Nita caressed Deo stomach, skimming her fingertips next to the row of sutures. "We should probably wait a few more days."

"I can't wait," Deo muttered, brushing her mouth over Nita's breast and making her nipple harden beneath the silk of her bra and blouse. "I've waited all my life. I need you in my mouth."

"Oh God, Deo. Don't do that. Don't say that." Nita gripped Deo's hair and pulled her head away from her breast. "I can't stand it."

"I need to be inside you again, Nita." Deo's hand shook as she touched Nita's cheek. "I can't tell you how right it feels to be that close to you."

"You don't have to tell me," Nita whispered. "I can feel it."

"Then let me make love to you. Now. Please."

"I'm afraid I'll hurt you," Nita protested. "I want you too much."

"You can never want me too much." Deo cupped Nita's face. "You can never love me too much."

"Well," Nita whispered, "I'm going to spend a very, very long time trying."

"Then let's get started."

The wind picked up and Deo's hair whipped around her face. Her eyes shone with unrestrained joy. As Deo tugged Nita down the stairs from the widow's walk, Nita whispered thanks to whatever fates or fortune had brought this love to her.

About the Author

Radclyffe is a retired surgeon and full time author-publisher with over twenty-five lesbian novels and anthologies in print, including the Lambda Literary and Golden Crown Award winners *Erotic Interludes 2: Stolen Moments* ed. with Stacia Seaman; *Distant Shores, Silent Thunder; Justice Served;* and *Promising Hearts*. She has selections in multiple anthologies including *Wild Nights*, *Fantasy, Best Lesbian Erotica 2006* and *2007*, *After Midnight, Caught Looking: Erotic Tales of Voyeurs and Exhibitionists*, *First-Timers, Ultimate Undies: Erotic Stories About Lingerie and Underwear*, *A is for Amour*, and *H is for Hardcore*. She is the recipient of the 2003 and 2004 Alice B. Readers' award for her body of work and is also the president of Bold Strokes Books, one of the world's largest independent LGBT publishing companies.

Her forthcoming works include *In Deep Waters: 1* written with Karin Kallmaker (October 2007) and the romance *The Lonely Hearts Club* (February 2008).

Books Available From Bold Strokes Books

House of Clouds by KI Thompson. A sweeping saga of an impassioned romance between a Northern spy and a Southern sympathizer, set amidst the upheaval of a nation under siege. (978-1-933110-94-3)

Winds of Fortune by Radclyffe. Provincetown local Deo Camara agrees to rehab Dr. Nita Burgoyne's historic home, but she never said anything about mending her heart. (978-1-933110-93-6)

Focus of Desire by Kim Baldwin. Isabel Sterling is surprised when she wins a photography contest, but no more than photographer Natasha Kashnikova. Their promo tour becomes a ticket to romance. (978-1-933110-92-9)

Blind Leap by Diane and Jacob Anderson-Minshall. A Golden Gate Bridge suicide becomes suspect when a filmmaker's camera shows a different story. Yoshi Yakamota and the Blind Eye Detective Agency uncover evidence that could be worth killing for. (978-1-933110-91-2)

Wall of Silence, 2nd ed. by Gabrielle Goldsby. Life takes a dangerous turn when jaded police detective Foster Everett meets Riley Medeiros, a woman who isn't afraid to discover the truth no matter the cost. (978-1-933110-90-5)

Mistress of the Runes by Andrews & Austin. Passion ignites between two women with ties to ancient secrets, contemporary mysteries, and a shared quest for the meaning of life. (978-1-933110-89-9)

Sheridan's Fate by Gun Brooke. A dynamic, erotic romance between physical therapist Lark Mitchell and businesswoman Sheridan Ward set in the scorching hot days and humid, steamy nights of San Antonio. (978-1-933110-88-2)

Vulture's Kiss by Justine Saracen. Archeologist Valerie Foret, heir to a terrifying task, returns in a powerful desert adventure set in Egypt and Jerusalem. (978-1-933110-87-5)

Rising Storm by JLee Meyer. The sequel to *First Instinct* takes our heroines on a dangerous journey instead of the honeymoon they'd planned. (978-1-933110-86-8)

Not Single Enough by Grace Lennox. A funny, sexy modern romance about two lonely women who bond over the unexpected and fall in love along the way. (978-1-933110-85-1)

Such a Pretty Face by Gabrielle Goldsby. A sexy, sometimes humorous, sometimes biting contemporary romance that gently exposes the damage to heart and soul when we fail to look beneath the surface for what truly matters. (978-1-933110-84-4)

Second Season by Ali Vali. A romance set in New Orleans amidst betrayal, Hurricane Katrina, and the new beginnings hardship and heartbreak sometimes make possible. (978-1-933110-83-7)

Hearts Aflame by Ronica Black. A poignant, erotic romance between a hard-driving businesswoman and a solitary vet. Packed with adventure and set in the harsh beauty of the Arizona countryside. (978-1-933110-82-0)

Red Light by JD Glass. Tori forges her path as an EMT in the New York City 911 system while discovering what matters most to herself and the woman she loves. (978-1-933110-81-3)

Honor Under Siege by Radclyffe. Secret Service agent Cameron Roberts struggles to protect her lover while searching for a traitor who just may be another woman with a claim on her heart. (978-1-933110-80-6)

Dark Valentine by Jennifer Fulton. Danger and desire fuel a high stakes cat-and-mouse game when an attorney and an endangered witness team up to thwart a killer. (978-1-933110-79-0)

Sequestered Hearts by Erin Dutton. A popular artist suddenly goes into seclusion; a reluctant reporter wants to know why; and a heart locked away yearns to be set free. (978-1-933110-78-3)

Erotic Interludes 5: *Road Games* eds. Radclyffe and Stacia Seaman. Adventure, "sport," and sex on the road—hot stories of travel adventures and games of seduction. (978-1-933110-77-6)

The Spanish Pearl by Catherine Friend. On a trip to Spain, Kate Vincent is accidentally transported back in time...an epic saga spiced with humor, lust, and danger. (978-1-933110-76-9)

Lady Knight by L-J Baker. Loyalty and honour clash with love and ambition in a medieval world of magic when female knight Riannon meets Lady Eleanor. (978-1-933110-75-2)

Dark Dreamer by Jennifer Fulton. Best-selling horror author, Rowe Devlin falls under the spell of psychic Phoebe Temple. A Dark Vista romance. (978-1-933110-74-5)

Come and Get Me by Julie Cannon. Elliott Foster isn't used to pursuing women, but alluring attorney Lauren Collier makes her change her mind. (978-1-933110-73-8)

Blind Curves by Diane and Jacob Anderson-Minshall. Private eye Yoshi Yakamota comes to the aid of her ex-lover Velvet Erickson in the first Blind Eye mystery. (978-1-933110-72-1)

Dynasty of Rogues by Jane Fletcher. It's hate at first sight for Ranger Riki Sadiq and her new patrol corporal, Tanya Coppelli—except for their undeniable attraction. (978-1-933110-71-4)

Running With the Wind by Nell Stark. Sailing instructor Corrie Marsten has signed off on love until she meets Quinn Davies—one woman she can't ignore. (978-1-933110-70-7)

More than Paradise by Jennifer Fulton. Two women battle danger, risk all, and find in one another an unexpected ally and an unforgettable love. (978-1-933110-69-1)

Flight Risk by Kim Baldwin. For Blayne Keller, being in the wrong place at the wrong time just might turn out to be the best thing that ever happened to her. (978-1-933110-68-4)

Rebel's Quest, Supreme Constellations Book Two by Gun Brooke. On a world torn by war, two women discover a love that defies all boundaries. (978-1-933110-67-7)

Punk and Zen by JD Glass. Angst, sex, love, rock. Trace, Candace, Francesca...Samantha. Losing control—and finding the truth within. BSB Victory Editions. (1-933110-66-X)

Stellium in Scorpio by Andrews & Austin. The passionate reuniting of two powerful women on the glitzy Las Vegas Strip where everything is an illusion and love is a gamble. (1-933110-65-1)

When Dreams Tremble by Radclyffe. Two women whose lives turned out far differently than they'd once imagined discover that sometimes the shape of the future can only be found in the past. (1-933110-64-3)

The Devil Unleashed by Ali Vali. As the heat of violence rises, so does the passion. A Casey Family crime saga. (1-933110-61-9)

Burning Dreams by Susan Smith. The chronicle of the challenges faced by a young drag king and an older woman who share a love "outside the bounds." (1-933110-62-7)

Fresh Tracks by Georgia Beers. Seven women, seven days. A lot can happen when old friends, lovers, and a new girl in town get together in the mountains. (1-933110-63-5)

The Empress and the Acolyte by Jane Fletcher. Jemeryl and Tevi fight to protect the very fabric of their world: time. Lyremouth Chronicles Book Three. (1-933110-60-0)

First Instinct by JLee Meyer. When high-stakes security fraud leads to murder, one woman flees for her life while another risks her heart to protect her. (1-933110-59-7)

Erotic Interludes 4: *Extreme Passions* ed. by Radclyffe and Stacia Seaman. Thirty of today's hottest erotica writers set the pages aflame with love, lust, and steamy liaisons. (1-933110-58-9)

Storms of Change by Radclyffe. In the continuing saga of the Provincetown Tales, duty and love are at odds as Reese and Tory face their greatest challenge. (1-933110-57-0)

Unexpected Ties by Gina L. Dartt. With death before dessert, Kate Shannon and Nikki Harris are swept up in another tale of danger and romance. (1-933110-56-2)

Sleep of Reason by Rose Beecham. While Detective Jude Devine searches for a lost boy, her rocky relationship with Dr. Mercy Westmoreland gets a lot harder. (1-933110-53-8)

Passion's Bright Fury by Radclyffe. Passion strikes without warning when a trauma surgeon and a filmmaker become reluctant allies. (1-933110-54-6)

Broken Wings by L-J Baker. When Rye Woods meets beautiful dryad Flora Withe, her libido, as hidden as her wings, reawakens along with her heart. (1-933110-55-4)

Combust the Sun by Andrews & Austin. A Richfield and Rivers mystery set in L.A. Murder among the stars. (1-933110-52-X)

Of Drag Kings and the Wheel of Fate by Susan Smith. A blind date in a drag club leads to an unlikely romance. (1-933110-51-1)

Tristaine Rises by Cate Culpepper. Brenna, Jesstin, and the Amazons of Tristaine face their greatest challenge for survival. (1-933110-50-3)

Too Close to Touch by Georgia Beers. Kylie O'Brien believes in true love and is willing to wait for it, even though Gretchen, her new boss, is off-limits. (1-933110-47-3)

100th Generation by Justine Saracen. Ancient curses, modern-day villains, and an intriguing woman lead archeologist Valerie Foret on the adventure of her life. (1-933110-48-1)

Battle for Tristaine by Cate Culpepper. While Brenna struggles to find her place in the clan, Tristaine is threatened with destruction. Second in the Tristaine series. (1-933110-49-X)

The Traitor and the Chalice by Jane Fletcher. Tevi and Jemeryl risk all in the race to uncover a traitor. The Lyremouth Chronicles Book Two. (1-933110-43-0)

Promising Hearts by Radclyffe. Dr. Vance Phelps arrives in New Hope, Montana, with no hope of happiness—until she meets Mae. (1-933110-44-9)

Carly's Sound by Ali Vali. Poppy Valente and Julia Johnson form a bond of friendship that becomes something far more. A poignant romance about love and renewal. (1-933110-45-7)

Unexpected Sparks by Gina L. Dartt. Kate Shannon's attraction to much younger Nikki Harris is complication enough without a fatal fire that Kate can't ignore. (1-933110-46-5)

Whitewater Rendezvous by Kim Baldwin. Two women on a wilderness kayak adventure discover that true love may be nothing at all like they imagined. (1-933110-38-4)

Erotic Interludes 3: *Lessons in Love* ed. by Radclyffe and Stacia Seaman. Sign on for a class in love...the best lesbian erotica writers take us to "school." (1-9331100-39-2)

Punk Like Me by JD Glass. Twenty-one-year-old Nina has a way with the girls, and she doesn't always play by the rules. (1-933110-40-6)

Coffee Sonata by Gun Brooke. Four women whose lives unexpectedly intersect in a small town by the sea share one thing in common—they all have secrets. (1-933110-41-4)

The Clinic: Tristaine Book One by Cate Culpepper. Brenna, a prison medic, finds herself drawn to Jesstin, a warrior reputed to be descended from ancient Amazons. (1-933110-42-2)

Forever Found by JLee Meyer. Can time, tragedy, and shattered trust destroy a love that seemed destined? Chance reunites childhood friends separated by tragedy. (1-933110-37-6)

Sword of the Guardian by Merry Shannon. Princess Shasta's bold new bodyguard has a secret that could change both of their lives. *He* is actually a *she*. (1-933110-36-8)

Wild Abandon by Ronica Black. Dr. Chandler Brogan and Officer Sarah Monroe are drawn together by their common obsessions—sex, speed, and danger. (1-933110-35-X)

Turn Back Time by Radclyffe. Pearce Rifkin and Wynter Thompson have nothing in common but a shared passion for surgery—and unexpected attraction. (1-933110-34-1)

Chance by Grace Lennox. A sexy, funny, touching story of two women who, in finding themselves, also find one another. (1-933110-31-7)

The Exile and the Sorcerer by Jane Fletcher. First in the Lyremouth Chronicles. Tevi and a shy young sorcerer face monsters, magic, and the challenge of loving. (1-933110-32-5)

A Matter of Trust by Radclyffe. When what should be just business turns into much more, two women struggle to trust the unexpected. (1-933110-33-3)

Sweet Creek by Lee Lynch. A celebration of the enduring nature of love, friendship, and community in the heart-warming lesbian community of Waterfall Falls. (1-933110-29-5)

The Devil Inside by Ali Vali. The head of a New Orleans crime organization falls for a woman who turns her world upside down. (1-933110-30-9)

Grave Silence by Rose Beecham. Detective Jude Devine's investigation of ritual murders is complicated by her torrid affair with pathologist Dr. Mercy Westmoreland. (1-933110-25-2)

Honor Reclaimed by Radclyffe. Secret Service Agent Cameron Roberts and Blair Powell close ranks to find the would-be assassins who nearly claimed Blair's life. (1-933110-18-X)

Honor Bound by Radclyffe. Secret Service Agent Cameron Roberts and Blair Powell face political intrigue, a clandestine threat to Blair's safety, and the seemingly irreconcilable differences that force them ever farther apart. (1-933110-20-1)

Innocent Hearts by Radclyffe. In a wild and unforgiving land, two women learn about love, passion, and the wonders of the heart. (1-933110-21-X)

The Temple at Landfall by Jane Fletcher. An imprinter, one of Celaeno's most revered servants of the Goddess, is also a prisoner to the faith—until a Ranger frees her by claiming her heart. The Celaeno series. (1-933110-27-9)

Protector of the Realm, Supreme Constellations Book One by Gun Brooke. A space adventure filled with suspense and a daring intergalactic romance. (1-933110-26-0)

Force of Nature by Kim Baldwin. From tornados to forest fires, the forces of nature conspire to bring Gable McCoy and Erin Richards close to danger, and closer to each other. (1-933110-23-6)

In Too Deep by Ronica Black. Undercover homicide cop Erin McKenzie tracks a femme fatale who just might be a real killer...with love and danger hot on her heels. (1-933110-17-1)

Erotic Interludes 2: *Stolen Moments* ed. by Radclyffe and Stacia Seaman. Love on the run, in the office, in the shadows...Fast, furious, and almost too hot to handle. (1-933110-16-3)

Course of Action by Gun Brooke. Actress Carolyn Black desperately wants the starring role in an upcoming film produced by Annelie Peterson. Just how far will she go for the dream part of a lifetime? (1-933110-22-8)

Rangers at Roadsend by Jane Fletcher. Sergeant Chip Coppelli has learned to spot trouble coming, and that is exactly what she sees in her new recruit, Katryn Nagata. The Celaeno series. (1-933110-28-7)

Justice Served by Radclyffe. Lieutenant Rebecca Frye and her lover, Dr. Catherine Rawlings, embark on a deadly game of hide-and-seek with an underworld kingpin who traffics in human souls. (1-933110-15-5)

Distant Shores, Silent Thunder by Radclyffe. Dr. Tory King—along with the women who love her—is forced to examine the boundaries of love, friendship, and the ties that transcend time. (1-933110-08-2)

Hunter's Pursuit by Kim Baldwin. A raging blizzard, a mountain hideaway, and a killer-for-hire set a scene for disaster—or desire—when Katarzyna Demetrious rescues a beautiful stranger. (1-933110-09-0)

The Walls of Westernfort by Jane Fletcher. All Temple Guard Natasha Ionadis wants is to serve the Goddess—until she falls in love with one of the rebels she is sworn to destroy. The Celaeno series. (1-933110-24-4)

Erotic Interludes: *Change Of Pace* by Radclyffe. Twenty-five hot-wired encounters guaranteed to spark more than just your imagination. Erotica as you've always dreamed of it. (1-933110-07-4)

Honor Guards by Radclyffe. In a wild flight for their lives, the president's daughter and those who are sworn to protect her wage a desperate struggle for survival. (1-933110-01-5)

Fated Love by Radclyffe. Amidst the chaos and drama of a busy emergency room, two women must contend not only with the fragile nature of life, but also with the irresistible forces of fate. (1-933110-05-8)

Justice in the Shadows by Radclyffe. In a shadow world of secrets and lies, Detective Sergeant Rebecca Frye and her lover, Dr. Catherine Rawlings, join forces in the elusive search for justice. (1-933110-03-1)